L [illegible] e

The Immortal Elements

BOOK ONE

To: Georgie ♡

Even from afar you've been a source of inspiration & fire ♡

Always know that within you lives a burning & vibrant soul ... even on the dark days. The world needs You ♡

MELANIE FROME

with Gratitude,
Always

Melanie Frome

ISBN: 978-1-9992492-0-5

DEDICATION

For my family who raised me.
For my family who embraced me.
For the ancestors who are my past.
and…
For my son and our future.

ACKNOWLEDGMENTS

I would like to thank far too many people, places and experiences to list on a single page, and I hope that those not mentioned by name will always know how much I appreciate them.

Janna Hockenjos, Editor Extraordinaire, whose excitement for this story brought me back to life & reignited my desire to bring the dreams onto these pages.

Alf W., who did not think me crazy when I walked through the gates of Eilean Donan and asked to see the family tree hidden inside the walls. And for his faithful support these past years and willingness to be my first reader, editor-of-sorts and for never losing hope.

For Karen P., Louise C., Breana A., Maja K., AJW Photography, Moon Sister, Soul Sister, GFYW Tribe, SMF Community, Ignite Evolution Fitness Tribe, Acroyoga Family…and basically everyone who has supported and encouraged me to keep going…

And, finally to all those who wanted to dim my light, who asked me to fade away…F*ck You! All you did was fuel my *Fire*!

PROLOGUE

Standing at the gates of castle Eilean Donan, my ancestral home, in the west highlands of Scotland, I cannot help but wonder if I shall ever return. I must look to the future, yet my thoughts are drawn to the past and the events that brought me here and are the very reasons I must leave.

The ever changing moon, the master of tides and time, shines bright tonight. The moon has been my silent companion since that fateful night. It was the night my father told me I would be married to a man I had never met and ignited the beginning of my rebellion. It was also the night that I became the prey of a lethal predator.

My name is Moireach Siofre MacRae, and the hunt for my life began in London and took me to the west highlands of Scotland in the year of our Lord 1666.

I was born with a power that others want to control. I am one of the Immortal Elements.

CHAPTER 1

As the cool winds tug on my hair, blowing it softly around my face, I cannot help but feel like an eternity has passed since that night in London which changed my life forever. Had it really only been one whole cycle of the moon? So much had happened, yet I still found myself missing the bustling streets of London and the people. But most of all, I missed the dancing.

The Minuet and the Allemande were the fashionable dances at court, and I had learned from a very young age all the choreography for any events that took place in the aristocratic society of London. The dances left little room for innovation, individuality or freedom. Only those who were born among the lower class had such a privilege. No respectable lady of the nobility would be caught in a common tavern or coach-house alongside the bawdy women of the night. All ladies that is, but me.

My whole life had been spent learning philosophy, etiquette, languages, theology, writing, music, and the latest dances from the royal court—only to become the wife of an honourable gentleman of the nobility and provide offspring to continue the family lineage. As a dutiful daughter I played my role, living by the rules and expectations beset upon me by society and family. Yet from a young age, I held a seed of rebellion inside of me and struggled against the norm, feeling constrained. And in truth, I had hoped that one day the wildness I felt beneath the surface of my skin would lessen.

As a young child, I would escape the confines of the manor and with it the mundane expectations placed upon me as a young lady of noble birth, in order to spend time outside in nature. Upon discovering my hiding spots in the bushes or trees, my keepers would often find me covered in all manner of greenery. I would be admonished and reminded that it was not acceptable for a girl to behave in such a way. The older I got, the harder it became to find opportunities to indulge what was viewed as frivolous behaviour. So, I buried my head in books, and stoked my curiosities through new people and situations. I have never been shy or demure, much to my father's chagrin. Fearless from the young age of two, or so I was told.

My father would often tell me that my boldness would get me into trouble one day, making comments under his breath about my mother's blood running strong within me. Not only had I inherited her raven-red hair—a unique deep auburn shade closer to the colours of dark cherries than any natural hair I had ever seen—but apparently her unwavering spirit, as well.

My mother died bringing me into this world nearly twenty years ago. On a night when a thousand lightning bolts cut across a full moon sky and the sound of thunder was heard for miles, she bled to death before she could hold me. I had been told that my mother's dying words were that I should be named Moireach, which means Lady in Gaelic. In his grief my father refused to hold me in his arms and exclaimed that he would not name the child that had killed his wife.

Nanny Gwenyver, who had been in the service of my family long before I was born, was the first woman to cradle me in her arms, and she would become the closest thing I would have to a mother. She had given birth to three sons, and

I suppose had always wanted a daughter, so raised me as if I were her own. She had often hugged me fiercely and reminded me that there was fire in my blood, and each night brushed my long curls before putting me into bed.

"Locks so dark red that at night it looks like the black feathers o' a raven," she would say, casting a far-off look. "And when light shines upon it becomes so fiery that it creates a crimson halo around your face. Locks just like yer mother's."

Nanny would tuck me in under the covers, telling me tales about my mother as if they were bedtime stories, always reminding me that my wild spirit was not something to be tamed, but something to be nurtured. Then she would leave me sleeping soundly to dream of angels, and men who could change into animals. All of the stories were meant to entertain the imagination of a young child who had lost her mother, or so I had thought. Little did I know how much truth was weaved into those tales.

"Your mother was a fire angel," she would tell me. And that she had met my father and fallen in love with him—something which was always absurd to me, for the notion of any woman finding my father charming was absurd. My whole life my father had been reserved towards me, as though he preferred to treat me as a business associate more than a daughter. I had assumed he would have preferred to have a son. It was not until years later, that he shared his pain of losing his beloved wife that caused him to keep his distance.

From a young age, the two eldest sons of Gwenyver, Roderick and Kenneth, had become my keepers and in an unusual way, taken on the roles of elder brothers and sometimes even that of fathers. And as I got older, they would affectionally call me Lady M. Meanwhile the youngest, Colin, who was only two years older than me had been my childhood companion.

When I was nine-years-old, my curiosity led me to a poverty-stricken part of London where Kenneth, Nanny's middle son and our horseman, found me arguing with a rather large brute who I found beating a young woman. I was insisting that he could not treat anyone in such a rough manner and he should be ashamed of himself. It was unfathomable to me that anyone would deserve such cruel ordeal.

My life up until that point had been very privileged and sheltered, and although my father was strict, he was never unkind. And never was physical violence present in my life, not even amongst our servants. It was unfathomable to me that anyone would be treated so inhumanely. Kenneth, ten years my senior, had arrived just in time and presented enough of an intimidating figure to stop the man in his tracks. No harm came to me that day and through some unspoken agreement, I was given permission to explore my wildness, within reason, and as long as Kenneth was my companion. Like a big brother, he had a part in raising me. Meanwhile, Lord John Alexander MacRae focused on conducting his business in the shipping trade that allowed us to continue our life of luxury in the district of Westminster.

At first I thought that Kenneth resented his role as childminder. Then, as time went on, I saw that he too enjoyed the escape from the confining space and expectations of the household. Together, we would venture into the city and sometimes into the outlying countryside, so that I could learn more about the world. I was insatiable, and Kenneth would delight in showing me something new that I would never have learned in the carefully chosen lessons my father had set out. Over the years, he and I formed a very close bond and somehow I never questioned the nature of our companionship. As I got older, there was less and less time for excursions, the lessons increased and household responsibilities required my presence more often. With each passing year, father placed more restrictions and limitations on the friendship I held with Colin. Reminding me that it was inappropriate for a lady of my standing to tumble about in the grass or other childish behaviour with someone of the opposite sex. In my early teens, after I first experienced my moon blood, father decided that my time with Kenneth, alone, should be limited, but my young mind did not understand until years later why. So, to keep me occupied, father started educating me in the ways of the shipping industry. Evenings sitting by the fireside, talking about the ledgers, shipment and upcoming negotiations became treasured moments that allowed me to feel close to the man who kept me at arms length. And they kept me distracted from feeling the loss of Nanny and her son Colin, when they were sent away shortly after my thirteenth birthday.

And then came the night, almost five years ago during my fifteenth year, Kenneth and I had been on our way home, rather late from the markets, when the carriage wheel broke off at the axel. While he worked to repair it, I was drawn inside by the music coming from within the carriage inn by the side of the road. With my cloak wrapped comfortingly around my shoulders to keep away the chill and mist of the night, and the hood drawn up around my head not only for warmth but to hide my distinct hair, I stood quietly outside the window. I saw men and women dancing with such spirit, in a style I had never heard about or seen. Kenneth found me standing awestruck, and it took but a moment for him to know that nothing would deter me from going out on my own to find places to dance like *that.*

From then on, he took it upon himself to ensure that my secret escapes would never amount to any trouble, and I was able to satiate my desire to move, to feel free and more alive. In the years since that first night of visiting the forbidden pubs, taverns, and carriage inns of the common class, no unpleasant incidences had ever occurred. Not even in the places where ladies of the night offered their bodies for lewd activities. Kenneth's presence, standing six-feet-six inches tall, was more than assurance enough that no man would approach me. Over time the taverns, and the people who gathered there, became used to my sporadic visits, and I was left alone to enjoy the rare and treasured moments of freedom unknown to most ladies of my status.

When I let the melodies take over with full abandon, my heart soared. My whole body felt on fire and free. Oh and how I relished the change of attire. A chance to rid myself of the long-waisted corsets worn by the upper class. I had procured some simple linen skirts and blouses from our laundress, paying her more than they were worth in order to secure her confidentiality. I wore sturdy black timber-heeled boots, perfect for the jigs and reels played in the less respectable establishments. And when my petticoats would get too warm, I was grateful that the fashion allowed women to pin up the overskirt, a cooling relief from the many layers. But mostly, I enjoyed the excuse to kick higher and raise my skirts to a discreet height so as to let my legs breathe and move. There was something liberating about the lightness in my feet, moving my body to the rhythms; simply allowing the music to move me. My soul craved it, and with all my learning I could not provide a logical explanation. Those moments brought me to life, awakened something within me that normally I had to suppress. The relief I felt was indescribable.

Then one night in London nearly a month ago, my life started spiralling in a direction I could never have imagined. Earlier that day my father had announced that he had finalized a marriage proposal with a man I had never met. I could not hold my tongue and do as I was bid. Instead, I spoke my mind, argued with him, and demanded I be given a choice. He slapped me across the face and told me that I would do as I was told. When father sent me to my room that night, I paced in circles and I felt the sparks of rage for the first time in my life. Feeling like a caged animal, I dressed in my dancing clothes, and for the first time I used the tree climbing skills of my childhood and ventured onto my balcony. Looking down across our grounds, I knew exactly where to step my feet and where my hands would have a hold. Landing quietly on the grass, I snuck to the stables and found Kenneth. Startled, but not truly surprised, he too had been just as shocked and dismayed by my fathers' declaration as I had been. Over the years we had become close, as brother and sister. Once again, he knew my mind—and my heart. He readied the horses, and we left the manor discreetly, after everyone had gone to sleep.

At the tavern, I lost myself in the music within the crowd, and, as always, I was somewhere near the centre of the room willing my legs to kick higher and higher. Each jump and spin whirled my skirts around in a wonderful cooling breeze around my calves. There was a man playing the bagpipes, standing on the bar tables with the two men playing the fiddles. In front of a window sat a giant of a man, with a girth to match his instrument, who banged away on the sizeable round drum, the likes of which I had never seen before. This tavern was a favourite of mine, as they always had the most wonderful musicians who would improvise on the latest court songs, and tonight was no exception as they played a bawdry rendition of "The Butcher and the Tailor's wife"—a song about a tailor who suffers indignities at the hands of his rather promiscuous wife. Men were prancing around trying to woo the women of the night with their kicks, spins and jumps. These men knew me and knew that I was not a woman to be propositioned. Women kept their distance from me, dancing coyly around the men, using their handkerchiefs as a lure. Frankly, I did not understand the mechanics of such flirtations. My own remained tucked inside my right sleeve, only to be drawn out when my skin was desperate for relief—the only thing I had that belonged to my mother. A dark crimson cotton, trimmed in black satin, with her initials sewn onto one of the corners in thick black velvet.

IM, for *Isabella MacRae*

Just as the song was reaching its peak, I was getting ready to soar with it to the sky. This was the part I yearned for every day when I had to sit through monotonous etiquette lessons, sewing, cooking and learning how to be a good respectable wife. The moment I could abandon everything I was raised to become and simply be free. But instead I felt a coldness sweep across the room, stopping me in my tracks. My feet stood still on the earth, and I looked around the room. No one else appeared to have felt it, the chill that ran up my ankles, higher along my legs, and wrapped itself around my inner thighs. It nearly brought me to my knees from shock. Meanwhile my eyes were drawn toward the far right corner near the bar. Among all the drunks who used the bar to help keep themselves upright, I saw *him* for the first time, standing so still it was as if he was not a part of this time or place.

I took a few breaths to steady myself and let my mind discover what my gut had already felt. Standing close to six-feet-tall, with a dark grey waistcoat hugging his shoulders, he did not blend in with the rest of the crowd. While most men leaned sloppily against the bar, he stood with his feet firmly planted, as if nothing would sway or move him from the space he occupied. He exuded a glaring confidence that somehow kept other men from infringing on his space. Strong, the figure of a man who had known physical work in his past. Yet the quality of his waistcoat indicated he was in a position that no longer required him to perform such labour. He appeared to be on alert, observing, searching for someone. Very few men were wearing their hats, but he was, making a statement, with the brim angled down over his eyes. I caught only a glimpse of thick wavy blonde hair, peeking out from underneath the dark blue leather material, which was longer than the current style and well past his shoulders. I wanted to see his face.

I advanced towards him, slowly, so as not to be obvious. I was thankful for my uncanny ability to get lost in a crowd, mostly due to my height of precisely five feet. "I only want to see his face," I told myself. "*Nothing more.*"

I am not sure who was more startled out of us two when he looked up and our gaze met across the room. It seemed as if everyone else had stopped moving, and for a brief period of time he and I were alone together. That one moment would be forever etched into my memory. His eyes a piercing green, and me standing at the edge of the dance floor, still swaying my hips to the music and holding the edges of my skirt. My hands felt warm and I feared I might start to fidget, so simply having something to grip helped keep me grounded and focused. His eyes held my gaze for what seemed like an eternity. The chill I had felt turned to a burning sensation as he started walking towards me, each step slow and methodical with the predatory grace of a stalking lion. My instincts screamed at me to move, *to run.* I did not. I could not. I would not.

Just a few feet away from me, he stopped and tilted his head slightly to the left. He lifted his chin up, took a deep breath in through his nose, and his nostrils flared. With all these people around us, had he found my fragrance? My blend of soft vanilla, warm coconut flower, and just a hint of Scottish rose oil. It seemed as if his eyes had taken on a deeper shade of green. I looked down bashfully for a split second, for reasons unknown to me at the time, before my boldness took over and I glared right back at him. I placed both of my hands on my hips in defiance, still holding onto my skirts. As a result, allowing far more than a hint of skin to be revealed.

This only made him smile, a little lopsided sneer. It was enough to excite and frighten me in a single breath. I caught a glimpse of what looked to be a shimmer of silver down the right side of his face, a jagged scar ran along his cheek, from ear to jaw. He stepped forward, ready to accompany me on the dance floor. This was something unexpected, since I had always ensured that no man would ever dance with me.

I took two steps back and collided promptly with Kenneth's midriff, who reached his large hands around my shoulders and turned me around.

"Lady M," He whispered just loudly enough for me to hear. "We best leave before the night watch alerts yer father that his carriage is outside this establishment."

Holding my wrist firmly, he pulled me away from the man with the mesmerizing green eyes. Glancing over my shoulder, I saw irritation on his face, before he turned towards the other set of doors that lead outside.

Inside the carriage, I positioned my feet on the seat across from me and slid the layers of skirts up to my knees to feel the breeze on my skin. Leaning back against the headrest, which was always too high for my head, I slouched in my seat to rest more comfortable against the cushions. Travelling through the dirty streets of London after a night of dancing felt oppressive, so I looked up to the skies. The weight of the conversation with father felt just as distressing. He was forcing me to marry a man I had never met without discussion. All the way home I gazed at the full moon casting its shimmering light across the rooftops and through the clouds. When I reached for the comfort of my mother's kerchief inside my sleeve, my fingers produced nothing but air. Panic set in. This was the only treasured belonging from my mother that my father had ever given me. I took several deep breaths trying to recollect every step of the evening and was about to signal Kenneth to turn the carriage around. *Was it on the dance floor? Or had it fallen when I had stepped into the carriage?* I would have to come back on the morrow, when I was supposed to be on errands.

The gentle rocking of the carriage was a hypnotic rhythm, and I was reminded of what my father always said about Kenneth. "He is the only man in the entire kingdom that could guide the horses in such a way that the carriage ride is smooth, soft, and gentle." My father had been suffering from migraines for nearly two years, so this made Kenneth even more invaluable to him. My hand rested on the edge of the carriage windowsill, my fingers still feeling the cool breeze. As the streets widened, and the quality of the air changed, I knew we had arrived in Westminster and were only a few minutes away from home. The manors were sprawled out farther apart, and the buildings were not so cluttered which allowed for the air to move freely between the grounds.

"What in heavens…?" I cried out in surprise.

I had felt a touch on my hand. It was like ice, yet soft and almost comforting. As if someone had placed their hand directly on top of mine, while the carriage was still moving. That was not possible. Leaning out the window, I looked back and saw empty streets. The lanterns looked hazy, a mist was rolling in from the river again. But there was no sign of any person, not even a night watchman.

At our gates, Kenneth brought the horses to a stop, and exchanged a few words with his older brother. Roderick acted as our guard, protector and made for a rather intimidating butler.

Roderick, the oldest of the three sons of Clan MacKenzie, born of George and Gwenyver, was also larger by a few inches in both height and girth than Kenneth. His barrel chest and expansive shoulders could fill most doorways. With his ebony hair always tied back with a black ribbon, the natural dark ruddiness to his complexion, and eyes of mahogany brown, one is immediately aware of the intensity surrounding this giant. I liken his size and strength to that of a bear, with big hands as large as paws. I once watched him lift an entire carriage that had fallen on its side, trapping the passengers within, and then put it back into its rightful place without so much as a single grunt of effort. Yet, despite his gruff appearance and size, he was always the gentle giant in my life.

Kenneth, the middle son of Gwenyver, nearly as tall as his elder brother, although leaner, with wide shoulders. His strength, complimented by his tenderness and a gentle nature, made him the ideal man to handle the horses, even the wild untamed ones. It also meant, he would rather spend his time outdoors and away from the crowds of people. His chestnut eyes have gold flecks, and his skin has a warm rich golden glow, from being outside so much. Unlike his brother, his matching chestnut brown locks fall just past his shoulder, always tied loosely with a strip of leather and often tangled with bits of straw giving him a very youthful and sometimes mischievous appearance at times.

Roderick walked up to the carriage door, and reached inside, offering assistance down the steps that always seemed to be built for larger people. Accepting his hand, I gingerly took my first step out of the carriage., still distracted by the events of the evening. My eyes were drawn to the skies, the full moon capturing my attention with the intensity of its silver light which gave the clouds an iridescent glow.

"Lady M, I trust yer adventure satisfied this evening, aye?" Roderick always asked after a night of adventure, and that night had been no different. He would then raise an eyebrow and give me his endearing, quirky smile. And I would always acknowledge his smile with my own mischievous smirk and innocent shrug. Not that night.

"Welcome back home then." he said, with some hesitation.

As I craned my neck to look up in his direction, I caught movement just beyond on one of the church's steeples which was on the other side of our manor's grounds. Nanny always said I had the eyes of a cat in the dark. Standing on the rooftop, amongst the stone angels that decorated the corners of the place of worship, was a man. His hat tucked low enough to ensure his face remained unseen. The long coat draped across his shoulders was not moving despite the wind blowing from the north. It could not possibly be, and yet somehow I knew it was the man from the tavern. The solid and steady stance gave him away, both feet planted firmly, as if he knew nothing could bend or break him, and so still he could have been one of the stone angels that decorated the corners of the church steeples.

I felt the same chill travel up my calves and past my knees, only this time it continued sliding up my arms, across my corset and up my neck, determined to bring a shiver to my spine.

"Roderick!" I whispered. "Do you see that man up there?"

And promptly fell into a faint.

That night heralded the beginning of such a strange series of events, I still have moments where I doubt my sanity.

CHAPTER 2

The morning after I had so curiously fainted into Roderick's startled arms, I awoke in my bed still dressed in last night's adventure attire. My shoes had been placed by the door, and cloak hung on the hook by the door. Kenneth would have been busy with the horses and the carriage, so it must have been the elder brother who had brought me to the sanctuary of my room.

"Daughter, it is past rising time." The knock on the door, accompanied by my father's booming voice woke me from a strange dream. "Please join me for breakfast immediately, as we have much to discuss."

For a moment, I feared that he might have been told about last night's desperate escape and its unusual ending. That morning I felt tired, sluggish, and my head was filled with a dull ache and fog—as if I had drunk an entire jug of wine, instead of the one cup of the watered-down wine, having a dislike of the ales served in the taverns. So disoriented, I nearly tripped out of my bed to open the window to get some fresh air. When I looked down, my breath drew in sharply, and I covered my mouth with my hands to stifle the sound. There on the ledge was a dark raven-red feather, the same colour as my hair. Nearly the length of my forearm, it was larger than any bird feather I had ever seen.

"Daughter!" His voice thundered through the door again. "I expect an answer when I speak to you. I am still your father, despite our quarrel from yesterday."

If I didn't answer promptly, he might have marched right into my room and seen I was still dressed in my attire from the previous night.

"Father, I shall be with you presently."

It was the proper and polite response he would expect from an obedient daughter.

"Please make haste, as we have much to discuss this morning."

Still feeling bewildered from the night before, I was immediately nervous about what awaited me below. Not waiting for the heated water normally brought up by my maid, instead dousing myself with cold from the wash basin by my vanity. My skin crawled from the shock, but it helped wash away any remaining fog that threatened to cloud my mind. I rushed through my normal morning bathing ritual. Nanny had established a daily bathing routine using clean cloths and special herbs, which I continued even after she left. Having become accustomed to a less stale body smell, I found it intolerable when I was in close proximity with others who had forgone their monthly or weekly wash, as was the fashion at the courts due to the expensive and time consuming labour involving a full body immersion bath in a copper tub.

Looking through my wardrobe, I chose a myrtle green dress that brought out the emerald flecks in my eyes, with a rich violet satin ribbon to tie around my waist. As I stood by my vanity, waiting for my maid to arrive in order to help lace up the outer corset, an unfamiliar feeling prompted me to place the feather between the fabric of my corset and the dress. I stole one last glance towards the window and prepared myself to face my father at the breakfast table.

I wondered if he was suffering from another of his headaches, but found him already engrossed with the morning papers, sipping on one of the teas I prepared for him daily—to ease the pain of the migraines

"I don't believe I have seen you wear that dress before," he said, glancing up to acknowledge my presence, briefly assess the outfit, and provided his usual nod of approval. "It suits you and will make an appropriate impression later today when you meet your future husband."

And with that he continued to eat his porridge, a ghastly concoction which I have hated since I was a child. The warmth of the indignation I had felt the day prior started in my belly, and my breath tightened underneath my corset. I recalled the previous night—the mysterious man I saw, losing my mother's hand kerchief, fainting in Roderick's arms, and I decided that my energy would best be saved for other things. Besides, the sting of my father's hand against my cheek from the day before was enough to make me hesitate. I would endeavour not to sound agitated, sarcastic, or sullen.

"May I know the time and place of the meeting?"

"Kenneth has been instructed to bring you to The George Inn Dining room promptly at 5 o'clock. After you have finished breakfast, you may go about your morning errands as usual, ensuring that the household shopping is completed." He looked up at me questioningly. "In addition, I have provided a list for this coming weekend when we will publicly announce the engagement at a special gathering held here."

Normally, I am quite ravenous in the mornings and have a rather un-ladylike appetite, but that day I could barely finish my tea. My thoughts were whirling about chaotically, as I desperately wanted to say more on the matter.

"Father, may I have your leave?"

He had noticed nothing of the food on my plate, too focused on the documents in his hands. They appeared to be new shipping manifests that had been delivered, and he was eager to reconcile the recent investments.

"Of course. I shall expect you to arrive on time."

He did not even look up.

Returning to my room, I found the window open when I could have sworn I had closed it. A gentle breeze blew through as I turned to grab my matching myrtle green overcoat and bonnet. I did not want my hair to attract any attention that day. I sat down on my armchair for a moment to collect my thoughts. Looking at my face in the vanity mirror, I tried to see myself as others might. I had been born with a full head of the same raven-red coloured hair as my mother, but curly, and with amber coloured eyes flecked with emerald green. Most babies come into this world with healthy pink skin, yet I had been so pale that the blue veins were visible. Nanny, who had given birth to three strong sons, often remarked how fragile I was and fretted that I might not see my first birthday. She was of an older faith, and likened me unto that of a changeling child. *Siofre,* and that is how I came to have such an unusual middle name. Nigh on twenty-years-old, and I was considered to be a spinster by many. In the aristocratic circles, most ladies were wed anywhere between the age of thirteen and seventeen.

Even so, not once had Father ever mentioned to me before yesterday that there had been any thought of marriage. He had signed a contract with William Cameron, a widower a little more than twice my age. The shock was very real, but it seemed that I would lose this fight, as my one act of rebellion had not changed my circumstances. My father and I never shared a close relationship that was filled with affection, but we did retain an intellectual companionship not often found between father and daughter. He raised me as a he might have a son, providing me with tutors and learning of such quality that few noblemen could boast, let alone other women.

I met Roderick in the kitchen on my way to review the obligatory shopping with our housekeeper Mary.

"Lady M, ye look well this morning." Roderick said. Though it was a question, not an observation.

Looking around, I realized Mary was already hard at work preparing various foods for later that evening. That would explain Roderick's hesitant tone.

"Why yes, thank you Roderick. I appreciate your concern over my health."

Neither of us really liked Mary, who in these past few years had become more unreliable thanks to her frequent consumption of the wine kept in the kitchens. In typical fashion, she was barking orders at the maids, and the scullery boys. Roderick offered his arm out to me and reached for the shopping basket I always carried for these outings.

"May I walk ye to the stables?"

Trying to rest my hand inside the crook of his elbow always felt awkward, given his height. My hand would end up resting near my own shoulder, but I appreciated his steady arm that day with some relief. His strength, his presence, and his calming nature helped to sooth the rage I felt growing at being forced to meet Mr. Cameron later that day.

Looking up at Roderick, I was reminded that he was nearly the same age as my father, both in their fourth decade. Though he had never married, nor did he have children, his face was hardly marked by his years. Indeed, he had the visage of a much younger man. I realized then with a sadness that my father had seemed to have aged quickly in the last two years, looking more like he was sixty-years-old, instead of his forty-five.

"Lady M, what happened last night?' Roderick's voice remained quiet until we were out of earshot of the kitchen.

"I ha' watched ye since birth and in all these years ye have no been the delicate faintin' type despite yer wee fragile outward appearance." His Scottish brogue became more prominent when he knew we were out of earshot of the other servants.

"Roderick, tell me you saw him? Did you look to the roof of the church?"

"Ye mean, I was supposed to look up into the dark and catch ye all at the same time? He laughed. "Now, my eye sight is better than most men, especially in the dark—"

"—You didn't see anything?"

"Ever since ye were a wee lass playing hide and seek, ye ken that yer eyes are stronger and sharper than my own."

Perhaps I had imagined it after all.

"What I do ken is that ye saw somethin' that caused ye to fall into a faint. You are no weak-minded woman who flutters about nervously at the slightest thing like those empty headed ladies at court. We have known that since ye were a wee lass. Do ye no remember the year that Colin and ye snuck away during country outing? Just before my ma and he returned to the highlands, near yer thirteenth birthday? Ye convinced wee Colin to go join ye on a merry chase away from our watchful eye…"

"Yes, but—"

"—and that boar came crashing through the undergrowth so fast the poor lad didna get oot o' the way fast enough. It was you who tore off the bottom of yer petticoat skirts, to help wrap the open wound on his leg. The amount of blood, bones, and flesh exposed that day were enough to make even me a little queasy, yet you showed no fear. And might I add it was yer quick actions that kept the lad from bleedin' oot."

He looked down at me with affection crinkling up the corners of his eyes.

"Yes, I do remember." I replied, remembering the shock of father when I returned with bloody petticoats.

"Kenneth told me what happened last night. He saw ye leave the dance floor to walk toward a man, as if ye had full intention of talking to him. Or worse, dancing wi' him. Is this true?"

So, Kenneth had noticed my sudden halt on the dance floor, and that had prompted his appearance behind me.

Before I could answer, the carriage pulled up beside us.

"Little brother, here is our Lady M," Roderick said handing me off to Kenneth. "Please do ensure that she doesna wander too far from ye today, otherwise I will ha' to beat yer hide into next week."

Listening to the large giants joke about beating each other up always brought a smile to my face. They would never lay a hand on each other, in anything but affection and care. Despite the ten years age difference between the two, they were as close as any brothers could be. There would have been hell to pay if any other man should choose to fight either of the MacKenzie's. Even so, though it was a seldom occurrence, there would be some drunken fool who would see their size and decide he had to prove his manhood and strength against one of them. Those moments never ended well for the man picking the fight. The brothers never chose altercations, but they never walked away from one without leaving the aggressor regretting their advance.

"Big brother, ye ken what John has asked o' me today?" Kenneth only ever referred to my father as John, instead of Lord MacRae, when something was amiss. Both the MacKenzie's shared a closeness, a friendship even, with my father that meant in private they simply referred to him by his given name.

"He has asked me to bring her to The George Inn to meet her betrothed, that bloody Mr. William Cameron, who insisted on meeting there. And our Lady M still recovering from that slap across the face for fighting him on not being able to choose her own husband."

Roderick stood still for a moment, closed his eyes and took a deep breath before replying.

"Aye, I could barely believe my own eyes when John raised his hand to her."

"MacKenzie's, I am standing right here, could you kindly not refer to me in the third person as if I wasn't?"

"Sorry lass, this marriage shall not take place, if ye dinna wish it so. We promised yer mother on the day of yer birth that ye would marry for love, and nothing else. Dinna fret, I will send a letter to our mother, explaining that John is forcing yer hand in marriage. She will ken what to do."

"The engagement announcement is this Saturday and I believe the intention is to finalize the wedding date later today." Kenneth responded, nervously chewing on a piece of straw. "Send cousin Michael wi' the letter. We can trust him. And he can take Sage, as there is no faster horse in all of England."

Once Roderick agreed to immediately pen the letter, Kenneth and I left through the gates of our estates in

Westminster and travelled towards the busy streets of central London. I could tell when we got closer to our first destination, the bakery, when the quality of the roads changed and the smell of fresh baked goods wafted through the windows. The streets with the most traffic were also the streets with the deepest carriage wheel grooves which made for a bumpier ride.

Bringing the horses to a stop just outside the entry way, I had a moment to pause and prepare for the whirlwind of tasks ahead before that dreaded meeting later today. When Kenneth opened the door he held out his hand to help me down the wobbly carriage steps, I put my hand in his and brought the other up to shield my eyes. So bright was the sun that shone through the clouds, I was momentarily blinded, and my last step down was more of a stumble. As I tried to right myself, I felt a shadow spread across my face, certain that a cloud had found its way to hide the warmth coming down from the sky.

"Bloody hell, Moireach!" Kenneth never cursed like that in public. "Is that what ye saw last night?"

I pulled my hand down to see, standing on top of the bakery, the tall figure of a man wearing a long cloak and a hat that shadowed his face. My heart started to race, but before we could speak further, Mrs. Forsythe had came out of the bakery to greet us.

"My dear Lady MacRae," Mrs Forsythe cooed. "I was so pleased to receive your father's letter about your upcoming nuptials."

"Tha—ank you, Mrs…—-" I stammered.

Kenneth, seeing that I was struggling with my emotions, took me by the elbow and guided me inside. My attention was not with Mrs. Forsythe, the bakery, nor the list of the many delicacies my father had requested for the upcoming event. Still, she proved to be wondrous for organizing that day's baked goods and those needed for Saturday. As we left, I nibbled half-heartedly on a small sweet loaf, a treat she made sure I took. I could not stop thinking about the man I had seen, those green eyes and the mysterious coldness that came from nowhere and yet seemed to emanate directly from him. I wanted to see him again. It was so strange to think that I had only seen him once, but I could not keep my thoughts from returning to him. It was then I remembered what I had lost the night before.

"Kenneth, I need your help." I said, peaking my head through the carriage window as he was closing the door. "I lost mother's hand-kerchief last night. I don't know where, but I need to find it. Please, may we go back to look?"

"Why, ye wee troublemaker!" he said with a huff. "Alright, we shall go back to the Tavern, but ye must stay inside the carriage and speak to no one, understood? And dinna think me daft either, I can see ye are hoping to see that man again—the one across the dance floor last night. It's as plain as the freckles sprinkled across yer nose."

I stared down with some embarrassment that my feelings were so obvious.

When we arrived at the tavern, it was closed and would not open again until the evening. Looking around for anyone who might be employed and might be able to help us, Kenneth ventured to the back. Walking past the front doors, around the corner of the building towards the alleyway which led to the delivery entrance for the tavern, I was left alone in the carriage. While I honoured my promise of staying in the carriage, I nervously fidgeted with my fingers, trying to resist the urge to bite my nails—an old childish habit I had long ago forgotten. My neck began to strain from looking out the window so often. It had been my hope that returning here might result in another glimpse of the man who occupied my thoughts, but after what seemed like hours Kenneth returned empty handed.

"Lady M, no one has seen it," he whispered, as he climbed inside the carriage where he could speak to me without prying ears chancing upon our conversation. "I even offered a bribe, a considerable one at that. Is it possible ye dropped it outside?"

"I honestly don't remember dropping it or losing it. I keep it inside my sleeve, where it is safe—always. Kenneth, I don't know what happened." My eyes started to glass over as the tears threatened to fall down my face.

"Ach dinna do that! Those silver tears coming down yer face is one thing on this earth I canna bear. It's the only reason I brought ye oot last night. After John slapped ye, and ye refused to shed a single tear then—I kent ye had to dance—it was the only way to help ye calm that fire of yers."

He winked as he stepped outside of the carriage.

"Thank the old ones that my mother never had any daughters to curse me wi' sisters, just one o' ye is bad enough!"

Leaning through the window, he kissed the palm of his hand and placed it on my head. He had not done that in many years. It was such a simple and affectionate gesture, it surprised me. It also made me wonder what else was happening that he would return to that habit, one stopped long ago when my father had indicated it was inappropriate.

We were on to our next stop at the butcher shop, not too far from where we were now. I grew more disheartened with each destination, as it brought me closer to the dreaded meeting. I could not bring myself to think of Mr. Cameron, instead I allowed my thoughts to wander back to the stranger. A slow smile grew on my face, and heat warmed my cheeks as I felt my heartbeat pulse just a little faster.

The final stop before the dreaded meeting, would be at Mrs. Abernathy's flower shop near the Covent Gardens fruit and vegetable market. I had been visiting the small corner store since I was a child. Father was very fond of flowers, and being very particular about them—insisting on only blooms of the highest quality. Once I became of age to help him manage some of the household tasks, he realized that I too shared the fondness for plants and all things botanical. I was tasked with arranging all the greenery for our home. Every room was filled with ornate ceramic pots of planted lilies and fresh cut orchids of many colours. Our estates had lush rose bushes surrounding the exterior of the walls and even some wild ones growing along the stone walls on the edge of the property. Roses were not permitted inside. They were a painful reminder of my mother who held a deep love for the lush red petals. For the upcoming betrothal festivities, my father had left specific instructions that our largest room, always intended for entertaining and gatherings, be decorated in opaline white Easter lilies.

The shopkeeper, Mrs Abernathy, would always show me every selection in the shop, sharing with me her exceptional knowledge of each flower and plant, even sharing some of her techniques of pressing certain plants to obtain healing oils that could influence health and mood. As I waited for her, I browsed the blooms in season. Eventually, she emerged from the cold room, where the most delicate of flowers were kept, holding a small wooden box for me. I could not help my anticipation to see what she had created. She was renowned for her talent, and some whispered that she must be part fairy. Or at the very least have a wood nymph secreted away somewhere to do her bidding. Mrs Abernathy's cuts always lasted five times longer than any other shop in town and the blooms always the richest and vibrant of colours.

"Lady MacRae, I am so honoured that your father has chosen me to provide the flowers for your betrothal celebration." she said, accompanied by a curtsey. "I will of course ensure the very best, as your father requested. But I also made something for you when you meet your husband-to-be—if I may…"

Inside the wooden box were three beautiful blooms gathered together by a white ribbon—a corsage to wear against my breast. A deep crimson Scottish rose in full bloom, a white five-petaled flower that I did not recognize until I leaned in and caught the scent of Vanilla, and a flower the same shade of purple as the violet ribbon tied around my waist that looked like a rose had made love to a lily. I smelled coconut.

"Why, Mrs Abernathy, this is enchanting, and so thoughtful." I stood still, while she pinned it to the edge of my corset just above my heart, and held back the tears that sprung to my eyes.

Even though I abhorred the event it symbolized, it was the fragrance my mother used to wear. The very same which I had learned how to craft over the years, with the aid of

Nanny and Mrs Abernathy, who provided the raw oils pressed from the flowers. The very same I chose to wear every day… paying homage to the woman I would never meet.

"Lady MacRae, your father asked me to never mention this in your presence. This last flower, it was your mother who brought me the very first one and showed me how to grow it. It only blooms once a year, and is very rare. She never told me from which exotic lands she found it, but I promised your mother I would always keep one for you. That the time would come that the flower would be part of your betrothal."

My mother had been here…I had not known that she had spent any time in London.

"May I ask when she first brought you this flower?" I dared to inquire, hoping that she would not become too suspicious with my interest.

"Why it must have been a little over nine years before you were born, before she met your father. Now, if you will excuse me, I have one more order to finish before I close up."

With that, she turned around, leaving me to stand in stunned silence. My mother had been in London nine years before I was born. *Why would my father not want me to know of this?* I promised myself that the next opportunity I was given to speak with Mrs Abernathy again, I would find out more about her, given the chance. After all, the people in my life who had known her, rarely spoke of her. My father had commanded that her name never be spoken in his presence.

When I stepped outside, Kenneth was reaching for the other boxes but nearly dropped them when he saw the corsage pinned just above my heart.

"Kenneth, are you quite alright?"

"Ach Lady M, if only yer mother could see ye today. She woulda been at yer side every step o' the way. Only she wouldna ha' wanted ye to marry William Cameron. It was always in her mind that ye would marry a man o' yer own choosing, not being contracted like so many other women o' high birth. She wanted ye to find love, as she did."

As he turned around, I could have sworn I heard a little sniffle, making me wonder if *he* was holding back tears. I knew if I gave myself permission, my tears would flow freely and they would not stop. Nanny had taught me long ago to present a refined, composed lady while in public. Those lessons would help me keep my composure today, as I grappled with the choice of the duty of a daughter to her father and my own free will.

As I climbed into the carriage, I sensed someone watching. As Kenneth closed the door, I leaned out the window and my eyes were immediately drawn upwards. There he was standing on the rooftops again with a hat that covered most of his face, the cape hiding the shape of his body. He was clenching both of his hands into fists, as if he was agitated. Fear crawled across my skin, sending shivers down my spine and a cold pain in my belly. I had sensed something different about him from the moment I had lain eyes on him. Yet if I was honest with myself, it also excited me. My heart raced to think of the possibilities. *Could he be stalking me?* Even without knowing his purpose, nor intentions, I would rather be whisked away by the stranger, than stay and watch the contract between my father and Mr. Cameron be signed.

"Lady MacRae, by yer leave?"

Kenneth called from the front of the carriage. We rode farther away from the flower shop and the stranger, and too soon my thoughts were pulled away from him. I would have to meet the man my father was forcing upon me, and as Kenneth navigated the rough streets of London, across the bridge, and down the road to the George Inn, I felt more nauseous to my stomach the closer we got.

The carriage slowed to a stop, and I heard Kenneth speaking softly to the horses. They trusted him. I, too, trusted in him, and wished with every breath that he would take me away from this place. But he and I both knew better. He opened the carriage door for me. Looking up into his eyes, I wanted to find escape. Something. Anything to let me know he would not let this happen. He avoided my gaze.

At the front steps, we were greeted by the liveried servant who guided guests to their seats. Kenneth had promised he would stay just inside the dining room and would watch over me, just in case I needed support. I was shaking on the inside, but my outward appearance was always that of a composed lady. It took no time at all to find my father, Lord MacRae seated inside, and already sipping his favourite Scotch. Threading my way through the path created by the other tables and their guests, I headed towards him, but was stopped short by a man who grabbed my arm from behind. A red-faced man, with stocky round shoulders, and rather large, rotund abdomen dressed in a muted brown frock and beige coloured trousers. He had wispy brown strands coming from his balding head. With an awkward motion, he forced my hand to his lips. He did not bow, as is customary, but instead brought his body closer to mine. The smell of rotten meat doused in cheap ale overcame my senses.

"As expected, your father did not mislead." He looked me up and down as if I were no more than cattle for appraisal. "Your beauty is beyond compare, and with such a figure that I am sure you will give birth to plenty of strong and healthy sons."

I loathed him instantly, vowed never to let him touch me.

"Daughter…" my father said, with hesitation in his voice. "Please greet your husband to be… William Cameron."

"Mr. Cameron." I nodded my head slightly.

For the next hour, I sat in a fog, listening to the two men talk about the upcoming betrothal festivities. They would invite every aristocratic family in London to be present at the formal announcement. They discussed what day would be best for the wedding and how many children I was expected to bear and concerns about my age. Eventually, they agreed how much the wedding contract would be worth. I barely noticed when the talk switched from wedding planning to their mutual business interests and the plans they had to invest together in more shipping ventures to the Americas. I might as well not have been in the room.

A proper lady, of respectable and aristocratic lineage, simply nods her head when spoken to and does not offer her opinion on such important matters as her own engagement and the marriage contract. This expectation had never bothered me before, but I found that it did not sit well with me that day. My cheeks were warm, and my body fought the urge to tremble as a deep churning began in the pit of my stomach.

"Lady MacRae, may I call you Moireach?" William Cameron said, finally, addressing me. "Ha, of course I may. I must ask what is that fragrance that you are wearing?"

His face was splotched, as if he indulged too much drinking alcohol or perhaps in the sun. His eyes were a dim brown and rather bloodshot, like that of a sleep deprived traveller. The lines around his eyes and forehead, not only told of his age, but of his character, giving him a sullen appearance. His smile revealed yellow, rotten teeth and released a foul odour from his lips.

"Mr. Cameron…" I could not bring myself to call him William. "I didn't know you had an interest in such trivial things as a woman's perfume. As a matter of fact, I blend my own from vanilla, rose, and a rare exotic coconut flower using the same recipe my mother used to wear. And Mrs. Abernathy made this special arrangement to suit for the occasion of meeting my future husband."

I was barely able to get those last few words out of my mouth without feeling like bile was moving up my throat. He moved closer to me, inhaled my fragrance, and scowled. Leaning towards me, he started to pluck a few petals from each of the flowers on the arrangement. His gesture, far too familiar to be respectable and he was destroying the carefully prepared gift from Mrs Abernathy. He was spoiling something of beauty for no reason at all. How I yearned instead for the rooftop stranger and his shadow.

"Well, as lovely as it is for a young unmarried woman, I will have to insist that you cease to wear that fragrance as soon as we are married!" He was glaring at me. "I find it too sweet, and somewhat distasteful. Far too much like the harlots on the docks. My wife will wear respectable lavender or lilac. John, can you please see to it that she has a new fragrance prepared in time for the wedding? In fact, I would like to insist that she wear it for the upcoming announcement."

He leaned back, lit his pipe, and the smell of oil filled my nose. This man just told my father that my mother smelled like a whore, and father had said nothing to Mr. Cameron about the insult.

"Of course, William, I will ensure that my daughter is exactly as you have requested," he said, taking a hasty sip of scotch.

"Now, the betrothal will be made official this Saturday," Mr. Cameron said. "I am very eager to place that ring on her finger. I have also decided to bestow upon her the honour of a family heirloom, a marriage brooch which I will pin to her bosom in front of all the guests. John, I requested we live together for a year, before the marriage, as is customary in many circles, yet you have insisted that not happen. Respecting your wishes on this account, I insist the wedding take place sooner rather than later. Shall we set the date now?"

"William, this contract was only agreed upon yesterday." father admonished him. "As for living together before the marriage, we have seen too often where a woman is left alone when the man decides to abandon his promise. My daughter will not be shamed such. And for the wedding date, I believe we should set it sometime in the spring. This will give us all ample time to prepare and finalize the details of the contract."

Father leaned back and waited.

"To be honest, I was intending for sooner. I am impatient to start a family. As you know, my previous wives had the misfortune of dying before they could give me offspring. However, I understand the need for time and would be agreeable to exchanging the nuptials this winter."

My thoughts spun wildly. Christmas was only a few months away and he was married before? More than once? Why had father not seen fit to share that with me?

From that moment, my quiet rebellion turned towards a fury fuelled by self-preservation. I was enraged at being used as a negotiation device for future shipping ventures. My father had involved me since I was sixteen years of age in any decisions that would impact our family and the business, and respected my intellect. But not this time. He had not been acting at all like himself for a nearly two years now, ever since the migraines began.

William's presence created an instinctual fear in my whole body that defied logic. I would have to find a way to elude this outcome before the dreaded wedding day. I might be able to return to Eilean Donan without anyone being the wiser as to my whereabouts. Nanny would keep me safe.

Over the years, she had taken on many roles in my life —mother, sister, cook, caretaker, confidante, and when my health required it, nursemaid with her expansive knowledge of herbs. Nanny's family was known for being able to heal with plants and were often sought out by many for cures. My thoughts flashed back to my thirteenth year, when my monthly courses started, my moon cycles, and how that had triggered events that led to the argument between father and Nanny which led to her returning to Eilean Donan.

I still remember that afternoon, we had sat for a few hours together while she taught me about the moon cycles of a woman. In her wisdom, she explained to me in much more detail what this new stage in my development meant. My small stature and beauty, in her opinion, would always be an allure to men. It was her fear that one day I might experience violence, and a man would overpower me in order to claim my maidenhead. She had told me of a concoction that could be brewed into a tea that would prevent me from getting with child.

"Given her age, I must insist that she submit to a test of purity." I was startled out of my thoughts by Mr. Cameron. "To ensure that she is not only of proper child bearing condition, but also to confirm that she is indeed a maid, untouched."

"William, would you truly put your future bride through such a harrowing experience?" my father replied with some consternation. "We both know that most physicians out there do more harm than good. Do you not recall what happened to the daughter of Lord MacDonald?"

My father's discomposure prompted Mr Cameron's servant to move closer to his master. His suit of clothes of such poor quality, he could have been mistaken for a beggar, let alone the stench emanating from him.

Neither of the two men discussing my honour and virtue had noticed that Kenneth had appeared behind them, silently. He too had noticed the menacing stance of Mr. Cameron's servant. Only I had become aware of my keeper's presence and gave him a slight nod of my head to indicate my gratitude. It was clear that he had heard the words spoken at the table, and even though his face remained calm, I could see that his fists were clenched so tight that the knuckles were turning all shades of white.

"John, I must be assured of heirs." Mr Cameron leaned back in his chair and pulled strongly on his pipe. "And I certainly cannot allow myself to become the laughing stock of London, if I were to wed her under a false guise of innocence. Why, that would make me a cuckold and that would be completely unacceptable."

"William, the young woman died of a blood infection only a few weeks after the test because the instrument used was contaminated." My father spoke more firmly. "You would subject your future wife, my daughter, to such a risk with a procedure like that?"

I saw a small glimmer of hope, a chance to stop this insanity and escape the dreaded fate I had been assigned.

"Father, if Mr. Cameron insists on humiliating me in such a manner, questioning my reputation and respectability, perhaps the wedding contract should not proceed?"

I held my breath, and waited. Looking at both men, seeing father hesitate in order to gauge William's response to my outburst and he waiting to see if my father would admonish his daughter. But it was my keeper, Kenneth, who broke the standstill between the two men.

"I beg your pardon, Lord MacRae. Our family is familiar with the Abbess at Denny Abbey. She has an excellent reputation of being honest with considerable knowledge in the ways of medicine. I do believe that she performed this very function for the Earl of Devonshire and many others. No one has spoken ill of her procedure and every lady has returned intact and in proper health."

"Why, Kenneth, I do believe you are correct. I have also heard of the Abbess and I believe that she would be well suited. William, are you in agreement?"

Father's voice rung with a confidence I had not heard all afternoon.

"Frankly, John, who performs the test and provides the proper verification is of no concern to me, as long as they are qualified and confirm what you have promised."

He kept staring at me with those murky, threatening eyes. When he started to chew on his lower lip, it gave me the impression he would rather have been gnawing on a part of me. I could not bring myself to look back at him. I looked up at Kenneth whose eyes went wide at the sight of something outside the window.

I turned to look. Unmoving and solid, the wind pulling at his coat and his hat low over his face. Standing on the other side of the road, on the side walk, he was staring straight at me, despite the glare from the windows and obstructions the other guests presented. Then he brought his right hand to his heart and lowered his chin, bowing to me. Noticing my distracted look, Mr. Cameron twisted to see what had caught my attention. *Nothing.* He returned his scrutiny back to my father.

"John, I believe we have come to an agreement," Mr. Cameron said holding up his glass. "Please arrange to have Moireach visit the Abbess as soon as possible after the betrothal announcement."

Discreetly, I turned toward the window again, in hopes of glimpsing the stranger, while the two men who had decided what would happen in my life without my input toasted each other. I felt a searing heat coming from the depths of my belly, and if I did not get some fresh air I would burst into flames.

CHAPTER 3

My father and Mary, our housekeeper, spent the remainder of the evening planning the details for the upcoming celebration. On the following Saturday, I would be presented as the future Mrs. William Cameron at one of the largest gatherings London would see for some time. My betrothal would be officially announced and a brooch would be placed upon my breast by the man I would be forced to call husband, a public and binding token of our contract. Meanwhile, I was in a complete state of shock, walking around the house in a stunned daze. After supper, Kenneth found me heading towards the stairs, leading towards the attic, without the faintest idea of why I was there.

"Lady M, come wi' me to the stables," Kenneth whispered, so only I could hear him—just in case one of the servants was in the vicinity. "Roderick and I wish to converse wi' ye without prying ears hearing us."

Guiding me across the hallway, thereby avoiding the kitchens, and back towards the imperial staircase that lead us to the main floor. We managed to avoid crossing paths with the other servants, and most importantly, Mary, who might question my state.

Through the large hand-carved wooden doors that led out into the courtyard, we walked around the dark grey stone walls of my home. Once outside, my senses flared with the life around me. The smell of the air, and the rose bushes just outside the walls, the horses and the hay; the breeze moving across the trees and with the fading sun still offering a gentle warmth—all brought me out of my stupor. Together, we made our way towards the barn which housed the hay for all of our livestock, and where our carriages were housed. Roderick was waiting for us.

"Now listen, Moireach." Roderick spoke first. "If ye can just make it through the rest o' this week. Use that damn fire-born stubbornness o' yours, I trust we will receive news from Mother in time to help us prevent this farce o' a contract."

He hesitated, glancing at his brother before bringing his compassionate gaze towards me.

"We willna allow this to happen. To be honest, Kenneth and I canna quite understand why John is behaving in such a manner. He has ne'er talked about marriage for ye in all these years."

Roderick sat down on of one the bales of hay, and I found myself at eye level with him. To my annoyance Kenneth kept pacing, until I pulled on his sleeve and made him sit down beside his brother, so I could look them both in the eyes.

"What do you know of his previous wives, the ones Mr. Cameron spoke of today?"

"Lass, dinna fasch yersel' over that." Kenneth said.

Though he was not able to look at me directly, and his speech had reverted to the west highland Scots dialect, which only came out when he was worried, and ironically, when he was telling me to not worry.

"Nae brother, she deserves the truth and complete honesty." Roderick punched his brother hard enough in the shoulder to knock him off the hay, but still in a playful manner.

"After all, who else will tell her? John has lost himself, but we swore an oath, remember?"

Kenneth righted himself on the ground and pulled some hay from his hair, and leaned against the side of the bale his brother was still sitting on.

"Alright, fine. As soon as I heard about the contract, I made some discreet inquiries. Dinna ask me who or where, but the news I received wasna encouraging. William Cameron has had four previous wives, none o' them lived past the first year o' marriage, and not one bore him any children. You, Lady M, are intended to be his fifth."

"Do you at least know what happened to them?" My heart fluttered with an anxious rhythm.

"What I was able to find oot in such a short time is no promising, as the servants in the households were verra reluctant. The deaths o' the wives ha' all been attributed to failing health, the plague mostly. Mr. Cameron received large dowries for each o' them. What is most perplexing is that all the fathers o' those wives died within a year as well. And for some reason, no one seems to be concerned about that."

"How could no one be concerned about the deaths of four women and their fathers?" I nearly squeaked out my question.

"The physician we were able to find, who treated the fathers, was able to confirm that they had all been experiencing ailing health anywhere from one to three years prior to the weddings." Roderick was well acquainted with many doctors in London, due to his role in our house as caretaker of the staff.

"And what makes all o' this more frustrating is that twenty years ago no one had ever heard o' any William Cameron. It's as if this man has appeared from nowhere. A grown man in his thirties wi' no known family connections who had spent the last twenty years building an empire o' riches and power. All o' which was multiplied by his widows' dowries."

"Roderick, father has been struggling with migraines for over a year now!" I gasped with fear.

"Now Lady M, we ha' no proof o' any connection but we will find out all we can." he sighed, and stood up slowly—as if he was carrying the weight of the world on his shoulders.

"Ye best get yersel' back into the house, before Mary has something to gossip about." Kenneth also ducked low.

I returned to my room and sat in the windowsill. Staring up at the moon and stars, I gathered my feet beneath me, and sitting in a manner of a child, I tucked my dress around my toes to provide a little warmth. The breeze through the casement brought the crispness of autumn and the looming threat of winter, and along with it a wedding I could not bear to think about. Tomorrow the dressmaker would come before breakfast to take my measurements for a brand-new dress that would have to be made in record time. Father and William had chosen powder blue satin with cream coloured lace trimming. I had never liked that shade of blue, and always thought it made my already pale skin have a sickly blue tinge. Once again, my opinion was not taken into consideration.

I had become accustomed these past few years to being treated like an equal, although not like a daughter, at least a respected business partner—which did not require my father to exhibit much emotions. It appeared that my voice would no longer be heard in matters of business, politics, theology—or my own life.

As I walked over to my bed, and started to unlace my corset, I realized I had forgotten about the feather near my heart, the one that had stayed tucked away inside my corset all day. Running my fingertips along the soft edges, I thought about the rooftop stranger again. Some inner voice told me to place it under my pillow. Lying under my covers of cotton and wool, I realized I feared the man who would be my husband more than I feared the man from the tavern, the stranger who had mysteriously appeared and vanished on more than one occasion.

I dreamt about the stranger that night.

Standing in an unknown room with rough stonewalls and a large hearth with a blazing fire. An expansive white fur covered the floor, and my bare toes could feel the tickling of the hairs underneath. The stranger stood before me with his back to the fire, the light cast a shadow over his face so that I could still not glimpse his true nature, his hair a golden halo casting a shadow across his face. Reaching down he took my right hand in his, and carefully brought it up to his lips and kissed my pulse-point ever so gently. My lips parted, and my breath quickened. I feared that if I made a single sound, the moment would be lost. He brought up my other hand to his softly parted mouth and pressed the inside of my wrist to his lips.

Raising both of my hands up to his face, I revelled in the feel of my fingertips grazing his cheeks as he inhaled the scent coming from my skin. Something in his eyes changed. Not heeding the tingles of danger my spine was experiencing, I stepped closer to him. Everything felt right, excitement sending shivers across my skin. His name did not matter, his touch did. He leaned down and placed an affectionate kiss on my forehead, then slowly feather light kisses down the tip of my nose, over to my cheeks and on top of my eyelids… Grazing my jaw line and nibbling on my chin… I thought he would never reach my lips which were parted in anticipation.

Finally! I opened my eyes and he took my face between his hands and brought his lips down on mine. The heat was scorching; all dread left my body and was replaced by a vibrating excitement. He too seemed surprised by the fire between us and pulled away too soon, leaving me dizzy.

Refusing to let the heat triumph, he wrapped his arms around my waist to pull me in closer. Each movement so slow and careful, as if he was afraid he might break me. Feeling the heat of his skin through my nightshift did nothing to dampen the way my body was starting to react. His lips moved down my neck, his mouth creating more fire along my sensitive skin.... Drowning my neck, my collarbone, and all the way down to the ends of my shoulders with soft, yet urgent, kisses… driving me to insanity. My legs began shivering, not from the cold that I felt coming from somewhere, but from the pleasurable delights that his flicking tongue promised. When I thought I could bear no more, wanting to feel his lips on mine again, he brought his mouth to my left ear. He was breathing heavily, making me realize that he too was struggling with desire. He flicked his tongue along my earlobe and then placed another enticing kiss along the top of my ear.

I grasped his sleeves and tried to pull him away in order to find his mouth, the need to taste his mouth again drove me beyond the point of boldness.

He chuckled, then whispered gruffly into my ear.

"Not yet my sweet love. But know this now and always... you are mine."

His low, husky voice startled me awake. My body was still shivering with the excitement and there was a warm and hollow sensation in my belly, one that I had not felt before. My breasts felt heavy and tight and my nipples were painfully erect. I was aching with desire. In all my years, I had never once thought about a man in such a way, nor had I ever experienced such dreams. I had listened to some of my friends snicker in the card room over a glass of sherry about things that happened in their marriage beds. They had never mentioned that a woman could also feel such heat, such need…such *fire.*

I felt the warmth of the morning sun through my covers and looked past the edges of my bed towards the window to discover that I had forgotten to close the curtains. With my body still feeling a warm tingling sensation all over, and my skin sprinkled with goosebumps, I paused. It was only Tuesday morning, and *he* had filled my thoughts more often than not since I first glimpsed him. I no longer wondered if I would see him again.

I climbed out of my bed and looked to the windowsill. Another feather. Nearly the same size, and, of course, the same colour as my hair. Taking it gingerly between my hands, cradling it softly as if it might disintegrate, I retrieved the feather from beneath my pillow. Holding one in each hand, I concluded they must be from the same mysterious bird.

I placed them inside the hidden drawer, alongside my journals, for which only I had the key. The drawer was a secret that Nanny had shown me, promising me that no one else knew of its existence. I looked at the two feathers lying side by side and wondered what kind of bird they might be from. I made a point to remember to ask Kenneth later that day. After all, he was our resident animal expert, and a large bird with those colours should be easy for him to recall.

By the time I was dressed in my shift, the dressmaker, who had made all my dresses since we moved to London, was already in the hallway waiting for permission to enter my chambers. Mrs. Driscoll was nothing if not efficient.

"Fair morning to you, Lady MacRae," she said, once I opened the door. "Let's see if your measurements have altered any. Although I highly doubt it, as you are the only client of mine who has not changed since the day she came to womanhood. I wish the other ladies of the court would understand that the more they indulge in those sweet tables at all of those functions, the more I have to let out their dresses to make room!"

I couldn't help but chuckle along with her at that comment, having witnessed many a time when other ladies complained bitterly about the tightness of their garments. She whirled her measuring tape around me in a rather chaotic manner. Only those who knew her understood that there was a method to her madness, and frankness.

"And would you know why your father has chosen such unflattering colours for the dress he wants me to make in less than four days?"

"I am afraid I was not part of the discussion nor given input into the final decision," I said, finally able to voice my frustration to another person. "So, I'm afraid you will have to ask him directly."

"Hmmm," she said mischievously, curling a finger to her chin. "I had always hoped to make you a rather daring dress in shimmering silver and black with dark ruby accents. Also, to alter the corsetry that would be more suitable for a woman of your stature, yes? Out of all my clients, you are the only one who could possibly wear those colours and the new pattern of corset I have been experimenting with."

I smiled.

"My father does want this to be the most talked about event of the year. I do believe that he and my future husband would want everyone to be gossiping about the beautiful bride-to-be for months, don't you?"

Mrs. Driscoll winked.

"Yes, I would be honoured to wear something you designed especially for me."

It was hard to concentrate at breakfast. Not only did my thoughts of the dress bring a grin I had to suppress, but the delicious memory of my dream flooded my mind. The heat rushed to my face when I allowed my mind to linger on each sensual moment, and I could not allow Father to notice.

"Father, may I have your leave?"

I spoke the words hoping my nerves would not betray my unease. He looked up from his papers.

"Daughter, I am relieved to see you behaving as a proper lady should again. I will be leaving for Dover with Mr Cameron to finalize a land transfer this afternoon and shall not return until Friday evening. Mary has all the instructions for the festivities. Kenneth and Roderick have also been given their roles."

He glanced at me, when he sensed that I wasn't leaving yet.

"Father, before your departure, I would like to make a trip to the apothecary, while out on errands today," I said. "If that pleases you?"

I curtsied to get his attention, not once forgetting about my thoughts of rebellion.

"For what purpose?" he asked, cocking his head to the side.

"I want to replenish the willow bark and feverfew for the teas that ease your headaches. I would not want you to suffer while you are away or miss the celebration of my betrothal. Also, I will need freshly dried lavender and lilac to prepare Mr. Cameron's desired fragrance. If you remember, he insisted I no longer wear the same perfume of my mother—of your wife."

I stood up straighter, somehow taller.

"That is very thoughtful of you, dear daughter. I will be glad of fresh teas to help with these plaguing headaches. And I do appreciate your efforts of compliance in regards to these sudden events. I am sure *William,* as you should call him, will be most pleased that you have taken such care to abide by his wishes so quickly. Very well then, I will instruct Roderick with the purse and Kenneth to take you."

I returned to my bedroom and sat very still on the edge of my bed. After several deep breaths, I looked down at my dangling feet. I could never touch the floor, so high was the bed, and I loved to wiggle my toes off the side. It brought memories of being pushed on a swing as a child, always by Nanny or Roderick. I closed my eyes and allowed myself the pleasure of that childhood memory. Until it vanished. *He* was there. I sensed his presence, standing somewhere outside of my window, or on some rooftop close by. My skin prickled with goose bumps, which brought the moist sweat beading down my back to a cold shiver of ice. I slid off the bed, tip-toed towards the window, all the while wondering if he could see me through the soft white gauze curtains. Just as I reached the front of the windowsill, the sun was bright again.

"Oy, move yer wee arse!" Kenneth called up to me, so we could be on our way. He never spoke with such familiarity with others around. With servants out of hearing, and father having retired to his private study and was not to be disturbed for hours, he felt comfortable in allowing his brogue to slip out.

I slipped on my small, black velvet boots, thinking about dancing. I wondered if Kenneth would accommodate another night so soon. Father would not be home, and Mary drank herself to sleep to the point where nothing but the fire brigade could wake her.

It was not the dancing I was craving. I wanted to gaze into those green eyes again. How my thoughts had become so obsessed with a man I had never met, defied all logic.

Kenneth and I arrived at the apothecary shop in Fish Street Hill district early that afternoon. The building was made almost entirely of wood, with only some stone around the doorway, which was rather unusual given this borough's predilection for fires. In fact, in the last twenty years, the apothecary shop had escaped nearly half a dozen fires—untouched. Townsfolk always gossiped about possible witchcraft, as if needing an explanation as to why the building survived unscathed.

Looking at the shop from the street, you could see that the building looked different from the surrounding structures. It was covered in a dark brown patina, almost black. The secret was the wood, or rather how the wood had been treated, Mr. Bernd Reitberg, the apothecary, who had owned the shop for thirty years, had shared with me. When it rained, water would form beads on the surface of the wood that would cascade right down to the earth. After many a storm, one could see an oil-like gloss on the wood, and this treatment acted as a deterrent for flames as well.

Aside from its mysterious resilience, it was quite unusual to have an apothecary shop as open to the public as this one. After all, the Worshipful Society of Apothecaries was founded only fifty years ago, and certain people still remained distrustful, which meant most of the apothecaries had their establishments in less savoury parts of town. No one in my social circles had ever spoken of visiting, and we rarely saw other women inside. It was clear that Mr. Reitberg had respected Nanny and her wealth of knowledge, because when she and I would visit, he would always bring us into the back of the shop—where all the real treasures were tucked away. Mr. Reitberg's walls were lined with shelves upon shelves filled with glass jars of all sizes and shapes, none of which had labels. On one particular visit, I asked, out loud to my surprise:

"How do you possibly remember what is in each jar?"

"A man who has a passion for his work will always know," he had said.

Since Nanny's departure, my visits became less frequent—only when an urgent need called for special herbs and tonics. But that all changed in the last year, when my father's increasing affliction with headaches had been bringing me back here every month.

As I made my way up to the stone entrance, I turned around to see Kenneth patiently standing, waiting with his horses. He had always grumbled when I made him come inside, complaining the scent of dried flowers made his eyes itchy, so I had grown accustomed to entering the shop alone.

"Good day to you Mr Reitberg," I said, swinging the heavy, painted door open. "I am here to purchase dried lavender and lilac for a new perfume."

He looked up from his books, removed his spectacles from the bridge of his nose and placed them in his front breast pocket.

"My dear *Fraulein* MacRae, I am so pleased to see you again."

As luck would grant it, we were alone in the shop, and he stepped out from behind the wooden counter to embrace me in a tight hug. A gesture, a man unwed would never have dared in public, given my unmarried status. It would have been deemed inappropriate. He was nearly the same height as me, only being few inches taller, but with shoulders twice as wide and a body shaped almost like a square. The silver hair only made his light blue eyes shine brighter, nestled in a face with deep wrinkles and lines that spoke of an impossible age to guess.

"Bernd, I need your assistance with some additional tonics. Perhaps we could find them on the back shelves?"

"One request at a time, please *ja*? Why in *Gottes willen* would you want dried Lavender and Lilac? I cannot think of a more confusing fragrance for one such as lovely as you. Like your mother, the vanilla and rose blend is much more suitable for your constitution. The one you are wearing right now."

He stood within less than a foot from me. A strange habit of standing within a person's close perimeter, would often cause others some anxiety. For me, it brought a sense of comfort.

"And why are you addressing me by my first name? Are you in some kind of trouble?"

"My father has signed a contract with a Mr. William Cameron for my hand in marriage. The betrothal will be announced this Saturday, in a rather grand affair at the manor."

Disgust came over his face, his mouth turned down into a grimace, and his eyes narrowed to a scowl. He walked to the front of the shop, turned the sign over to read CLOSED, and let out a dismissive grunt. He motioned me to follow him back to the room filled with treasures.

Among the bones of dozens of animals arranged along the far back wall, were glass jars filled with smoky liquid that housed further oddities. My limited knowledge was able to identify some of the various specimens, mostly reptilians, floating in alcohol tinctures, and what appeared to be a collection of eye balls. I daren't guess from what creatures. And some of them, looked like they were still moving. Eery.

"Now, *Fraulein*, I must insist you tell me everything," Bernd said, safe in the privacy of his treasures. "Our dear Gwenyver MacKenzie warned me that one day you might come to me for help. She made me swear on things holy only to me that I would help you—no matter the cost. She has a second sight, that woman. She has saved my life more than once. Oh, but I say too much, stories best saved for another time, *ja*?"

It took nearly an hour to tell him everything. I reached a point when I could not stop the tears from falling down my cheeks. To my surprise, he used one of his small glass vials to collect them, while whispering words in a language I did not understand.

"Have no fear, *meine kleine*!" he said, once I had shared everything. "Would I be safe to assume that you have no interest in bearing this man's offspring?"

I nodded.

As the afternoon wore on, we worked together over pestle and mortar. He, instructing me precisely on how to mix the right herbs and administer the right dosage every night, me watching his every move. Starting a month before the wedding, each night, I would have to boil a quart of water, and slowly stir in the blended mixture we had prepared—dried thistles, dried smartweed leaves, ground ginger, mugwort, and Queen Anne's lace—a concoction that would prevent conception as long as I was taking it daily.

"Bernd, there is yet another favour I would ask of you…" Too soon the herbs were sufficiently powdered and I still had not yet worked up the courage to ask for the item I desired most. "Nanny had spoken of a preparation that would end a man's life—."

"—*Fraulein* MacRae, you must explain to me for what purpose you wish this tincture." He shifted nervously from one foot to the other. "I cannot in good conscious, provide you with anything that would harm your own person… you must understand."

"The thought of ending my life on the night of the wedding has crossed my mind, ever since I met the brute of a man, but it would go against every fibre of my being," I voiced. "Knowing only a little of what befell his previous wives, I want to be sure I have something with which I can protect myself, should the worst happen. There will be no succumbing to hopelessness. I will not be forced into a marriage with a man whose past is littered with the dead bodies of previous wives, whose very presence makes my skin crawl."

The words I had just spoken left me full of fire and a strength that warmed the very depths of my belly.

"Then we will surely need to use those tears of yours," Bernd said. "It will be your revulsion, your fear, and your rage that will give this concoction its bite."

"How?"

"A woman's tears can be used for many purposes, whereas a man's tears do not have the same power. It is not just legends of mermaid tears of which I speak, but that of ordinary women who all have powers within them—if only they would awaken to the possibilities."

I never questioned why he was willing to help, after all he had said Nanny had saved his life. However, I did make a mental note to ask him in the future for more details. When I stepped out of the shop, I noticed that the sun had begun to drop in the sky, and the colours of the clouds were changing from their gentle white to radiant oranges, reds and violets as the sun made its journey into the sunset. I could stare at the horizon for hours on some days, so much did I enjoy the luminous colours that the sky displayed. Under my arm, I carried the paper bag filled with dried lavender and lilac of the highest quality, along with the willow bark and fever-few for father's headache pains. Inside my purse was the herbal tincture that I would begin a full moon cycle before the wedding, to ensure that no child would be born under any circumstances. And within the folds of my corset rested another purchase, a small glass vial, filled with my tears and other elements which Bernd had not revealed to me, that promised a quick death to the one who might consume it.

"Lady M, we are running late for our next appointment." Kenneth was looking around rather nervously. "Please let me help ye up."

"Kenneth, what is the matter with you?"

"Lass," he whispered. "I could swear I ha' now seen William Cameron's carriage pass by three times."

And without further comment, he jumped to the front and we were on our way to the next appointment—with the butcher my father had chosen for the event. Kenneth remained on edge, looking about so much that I feared he would strain his neck. When I noticed the shabby carriage, not only at our next destination but then again when we stopped to water the horses, I too felt the prickly sense of being watched. The occupant never exited, nor did anyone else visit that carriage at these stops. I was curious to know why my movements would be monitored, meanwhile Kenneth remained fixated on the state of the horses pulling the dilapidated carriage.

"Bloody hell, I am fighting every urge to go over there and whip whoever is inside so they can look like the lashing those poor darlings have on their backs." Kenneth whispered under his breath, appalled at the horrendous plight of the horses of the mysterious carriage.

A carriage with horses in such a ghastly state could not possibly belong to Mr Cameron, a man of status and wealth. Yet when the man directing the horses turned in our direction, I recognized the same shabbily dressed man who had accompanied Mr Cameron to the George Inn the day before.

By the time we arrived home that evening, the feelings of dread had started to creep into my bones. Roderick was there to greet us at the gates, and he leaned into the doorway of the carriage to offer me his hand, raising an eyebrow as if to ask what I was thinking. I offered him a smile, hoping to appear innocent in order to avoid questions.

"Brother, when ye've put the horses away, I must speak wi' ye."

He hollered over at Kenneth who had already started to lead the animals towards the stables.

"Aye, nae bother! Just give me a moment."

I rushed to my room, took off my shoes and stockings, and tip-toed out onto my balcony, climbing over the ledge and shimmying around the corner. The shelf of stone wrapped around the whole side of the house, and gave me a foothold that I could grasp the wall and perch, albeit somewhat precariously, on the edge. This vantage point gave me full view of the barn and allowed me to eavesdrop on Roderick and Kenneth's conversation.

"Kenneth, we ha' had a visitor today. It seems word o' our Moireach and Mr. Cameron is spreading rather quickly. The first wife's sister, Elizabeth, came to our gates earlier today in the hopes o' speaking wi' our Lady. But Mary, that devil-some woman, turned her away before I could find words wi' her in private."

Roderick's words nearly knocked me from my perch. Readjusting my grip, and my toes to have a better hold, I was able to focus again. I had to cling for nearly an hour to hear to all that Roderick would tell Kenneth.

"Mr Cameron's first wife had been seventeen, wi' hair a lighter shade of red than our lass, and wi' golden skin, she was considered quite a beauty. After the wedding, no one saw her for nearly three months, and her first public appearance was at church, where her sister saw a horrific change that had overcome her. Using a cane, she had hobbled to the front o' the church to receive the bishop's blessings. Her hair, a sickly pale orange and falling out in clumps. She had lost so much weight that her face had become a hollow shell and her cheekbones protruded like those o' a skeleton. The golden skin that had glowed was now a deathly pale shade of grey wi' dark bruises under her eyes."

"Did no one think to confront Mr Cameron?" Kenneth interrupted the tragic tale.

"No brother, being inside the church meant all in attendance were there for worship. Meanwhile, her husband, Mr Cameron, was by her side, and made verra sure that no one could speak to his wife, including her own family. Only when he himself went to the bishop, did Elizabeth manage to exchange a few words, albeit briefly. The new wife tried to convince her sister that all the changes she saw were due to the pregnancy wi' their first child. Stunned, the sister was left so aggrieved she tried to speak more on the matter, when William returned."

"Fair guess that he refused to allow anyone else to speak with his bride?" Kenneth rumbled.

"Aye, and months passed, and no reports reached the family and no one was given access to the young bride and mother-to-be—until a few short weeks of The Camerons' wedding anniversary, around the same time that the bairn was to have been born, Elizabeth finally received news. Only it was not glad tidings o' a birth. It was a note from the stationery o' Mr. Cameron which read:

She is dead.

From there, Roderick's stories did not become more pleasant. Each of his wives died within a year of the wedding date, each one expecting a child, and each woman's ashes were sent to their families in the cheapest of urns. Patiently listening from my perch, I had hoped they would speak of the dead women's fathers. An uneasy feeling grew in my belly as I thought of my own father and his recent bout of migraines. But the stable doors closed, and their voices were no longer audible.

I climbed back over onto my balcony and stood looking up to the moon for reassurance. The air was still. The horses were silent. There was nothing left to do but to wait for Saturday to arrive and prepare myself to be announced as the future Mrs. Cameron—the fifth woman to hold that title. Carefully tucking away the vial of poison next to the mysterious feathers, I withdrew them from the secret drawer and padded over to sit on the edge of my bed. Running my fingertips along their edges, I found that the soft sensation eased my worries and for some strange reason gave me a sense of assurance. The satchel with the herbs to prevent a child were also placed in hiding. Other than the MacKenzie's, I had no one else I could trust in this house. The maids had honoured my request for privacy that night, and I began the laborious task of removing the layers of dress, skirts and corset. It was a distraction. So was brushing my hair while I sat in front of the mirror of my vanity. Turning towards my bed, I saw the feathers I had forgotten to place back in the drawer. I placed them underneath my pillow instead, hoping to dream of the stranger again.

I did not.

Something had bounced off my bedroom window pane, and I nearly fell out of bed. I tripped over my nightgown, scrambling to get to the window. Maybe a bird had flown against the glass again. During the summer months, I had found more than one bird disoriented on the sill. I looked down only to find another raven-red feather, this time tied to a small magenta velvet sachet with a black ribbon.

Holding my breath as I untied the ribbon and opened the delicate package, I let out a gasp of amazement upon seeing the small treasure tucked inside. A beautiful and delicate pendant lay in my hands—a heart-shaped gemstone of a rare crimson red amber, encased by two silver wings. Less than two inches around it fit into the palm of my hand. Holding it against my bosom, I walked back toward my vanity. Sitting down, mystified, I wondered who might have presented me with such a unique gift. The same person who had given me those feathers, now numbering three. A mystery.

I chose to keep the gemstone with me that day, tucked inside my corset and out of sight. Once it settled between my breasts I felt a warmth against my skin that took me by surprise, not shock, but in a strangely reassuring way.

The day was spent reviewing the house charter books, reconciling expenses with revenues. Sitting in father's office, surrounded by the smell of leather, paper and ink, it was a relief to be away from the chaos in the manor. And for once, I was grateful for my upbringing and my ability to focus on the details, and for the first time, I noticed a pattern emerging.

Our household accounts were closely linked to my father's business dealings, as we often transferred funds and sometimes goods between the two holdings. I went to the shelves and pulled down record books, dating back two years. The recent transactions presented some unusual spikes in funds, specifically the payments my father made to Mr. Cameron. It was enough to make me speculate on some other abnormalities I remembered. My father and Mr Cameron had started doing business together in the early spring of the year of our Lord 1664, but this past month's ledger was showing the largest payments to date. Yet, searching through the mountain of receipts and ledgers from the corresponding two years, I could not find an equal amount coming back in nor did the receipts match the figures recorded in the charter books.

As I pulled out book after book of records, I stumbled upon a smaller brown leather notebook, which had been secreted away behind the many catalogues. It was clear that it was written in my father's hand, but in a manner that was very erratic, sometimes not making any sense at all. I sat down to read, and it appeared that some sentences had been written in reverse—along with other mysteries.

According to the notebook, my father believed that William Cameron had brought the great plague with him. His scribbles mentioned several incidences that led him to this deeply held suspicion. I questioned the validity of his theory, but recognized the timing was right. The plague did come to London in the winter of 1664, which was not long after Mr. Cameron's entry into the shipping industry. Notes told of business dealings with unsavoury people and a shipment from Amsterdam, and the shipping manifest indicated cotton; however, my father had crossed out the word *cotton* and written above *RATS*.

I found that many of his notes were often crossed out and replaced with other words. As if he wrote, then changed his mind, then wrote again. Over and over. By comparing this notebook to the dates and timelines of the ledgers, I concluded that every shipment instigated by Mr. Cameron was soon followed by a public calamity. The plague, being the primary one, but also the growing tension between England and Denmark received many mentions. And there was an unusual transaction that showed that Mr. Cameron had coordinated a shipment of various food items to the Dutch prisoners held just outside of London, but for what purpose was too vague and unknown.

More disturbing to me, were the notes in which he wrote of Mr. Cameron's constant questioning about my mother, of her origins and those concerning me. With each page, it was clear that the questions were more pressing and intimate. His last entry was over six months ago and was the most confusing of them all.

"*My Cameron remedies headaches relief. Teas of Moireach none. Cameron remedies need daily. Knowing Moireach none. Cameron remedies must have. Isabella knows this pain. Why she tell not why? W needs M. Must try. Strong not. W wants M. Stop. Isabella come back.*"

With no more pages to read, and feeling quite unsettled with the confusing words, I looked up from all the papers, books and notes only to find that the sun had gone down and it was well past time that I should take to bed. Trusting that this small notebook would not be missed, given how long ago the last entry was, I brought it with me and placed it with my feathers under lock and key. Smirking as I realized my secret drawer had never held anything until just recently and was now nearly full, I tucked the gemstone alongside the rest of my treasures, mysterious as they were.

There were no dreams that night, again. My slumber deep, despite the nervous thoughts of my mind before I fell asleep.

CHAPTER 4

The morning skies were grey, and so was my mood. There was nothing on the balcony ledge for me that morning. As I dressed for the day, I hid my father's notebook in the layered pockets of my skirt. The weight feeling heavier than it should —perhaps it was only my mind playing tricks on me.

Whereas the day before was occupied with accounting, taxes, and transactions, today would be filled with my lessons. My father strongly believed that knowledge was power and insisted that I be learned in many subjects not commonly encouraged with ladies of status. So that day, as with every Thursday, I would begin with my Theology instruction, followed by philosophy, and then Latin. After the midday meal, I was instructed in the latest dances at the court, which I felt particularly eager for, hoping that the physical movement would ease the tension that had been building. Kenneth would be, yet again, my reluctant dance partner. I had hoped to find a moment in the full day schedule to ask Kenneth to take me out for another night of escape, of dancing, of freedom.

The morning lessons began with Robert Boyle, a well-known scholar with the Royal Society of London for

Improving Natural Knowledge. Normally, I was eager to meet with him, but I could no longer recall what we discussed that day, having my mind on other matters that I dared not share with my teacher.

First, there was the contract. For many years, father had refused marriage proposals for my hand after discussing the suitors with me, always strategic in asking for my input and valuing my opinion. I never thought I would have to choose between my own happiness or the path my father laid out for me. I had taken for granted that I would be given a choice in my future. Never been given cause to rebel against my family, society and all the expectations placed upon women of my status, here I was ready to start a revolution because of the inexplicable revulsion I felt towards Mr Cameron.

"Mr. Boyle, I wonder if we might halt our lesson for today." I asked. "I find myself very distracted with another problem that has recently been presented to me?"

"Lady MacRae, you haven't been focused on this lesson since we began, but I have graciously continued since you are still one of my most esteemed students. I would be delighted to discuss whatever has your mind so occupied—if you so choose."

"I'm not quite sure where to begin, but it involves shipping methods, ledgers, and certain events that have occurred in the last year or two. There seems to be a pattern, but I cannot find the missing pieces that would help reveal the final puzzle, as it were."

I stood up with the intention of getting the books from father's study.

"Oh, this sounds intriguing." he exclaimed enthusiastically. "Mind you, I do not have much experience with the shipping industry, but my knowledge in relation to patterns and numerical data is very sound. Let's see what our investigation reveals, shall we?"

Perhaps with a fresh pair of eyes, and unbiased at that, we could delve further into the ledgers. Meanwhile, the question of how to share the information contained in my father's notebook—without actually presenting it—was answered by the unexpected and most unwelcome arrival of Mary.

"Lady MacRae, I believe it's time for your next lesson!" she said, bursting through the door. "Mr. Boyle, if you would kindly see yourself to the door immediately."

The time had come for my next lesson, Philosophy, which normally held my interested and created so many opportunities for dialogue. Yet that day, I can barely remember what words were spoken or the topic discussed.

And then, the arrival of my Latin instructor, Mr. James Stansfield, heralded yet another hour passing.

Father thought he was forcing me to take these lessons in the effort of becoming more refined. In truth I enjoyed not only the intricacies of the language but also the presence of the instructor. He was rather handsome with a kind face, gentle brown eyes and a charming smile. Close to my own age, he was considered a prodigy linguist with over twelve languages spoken fluently.

As we sat in the main hall study, Mary found ways to keep interrupting us, which was unusual and had me wonder as to her motives. Mr Stansfield appeared nervous, wiping sweat from his brow and which could not be attributed to the heat, not today.

"Lady MacRae, I apologize if my behaviour appears unseemly." He swallowed nervously, and tugged at his shirt sleeves rather distractedly. "It is not often I find myself in this position."

"Mr Stansfield, whatever is wrong?"

"Lady MacRae, I was informed by letter earlier this week that today would be our last lesson. That your future husband did not look kindly upon a wife with more learning than himself." He looked down towards his shoes, avoiding meeting my eyes. "I find myself feeling already bereft at the loss of your company."

I did not understand. Father had never told to me that our instruction would come to an end. None of the other tutors had mentioned that lessons would no longer continue.

"Mr Stansfield, I am sure you are mistaken. None of my education will change, and will continue until the wedding day. It is my expectation beyond that as I am keen to keep learning."

"My Lady, I am certain of it. I was even given a rather large sum for my final payment. And now that I find myself before you for what feels like the last time, I have come to realize that our time together has been most precious to me." He blushed. "I must confess that during our lessons I have developed an admiration for your intelligence, character and if I may be so bold, your beauty. I imagined that over the last few years that perhaps you had developed a fondness for me." He looked towards the windows, embarrassed.

His confession took me by surprise, as did my feelings in this matter. I had grown fond of him, although I had never thought of him as a future husband. Though, somehow I always envisioned him in my life, perhaps not as a suitor but at the very least a companion of sorts, a friend. Now my mind was occupied by the stranger on the rooftops and the sordid past of Mr Cameron, and what wits I had were needed to navigate through the next several weeks. I could not allow another distraction in my life. Nor could I risk James, Mr. Stansfield, getting involved in any of these events. Just the little information I had learned about the man I was to marry, I knew there was danger.

"Mr Stansfield, I have always respected you and our teacher-student relationship. And of course, I have enjoyed our time together. I have had Latin tutors in the past who made the subject very boring and dull, but you have brought a dead language to life and for that I am ever grateful. I am sorry if I have been too open or forward with you in our discussions."

I was now most curious as to why he was the only tutor selected for termination of services, and resolved to speak with father when he returned.

"Of course Lady MacRae, I apologize if I overstepped my bounds." he mumbled underneath cheeks flushed, and I knew I had hurt his feelings. Somehow, I had been oblivious all this time and I couldn't help but reach out a hand and gently touch his shoulder.

Just as he looked up at me, with hope and more affection than I had expected, Mary made a boisterous entrance and demanded we leave the study. Grabbing the young man by his jacket sleeve, she ushered him out the front door before I could say farewell.

I stood there, dumbfounded. Mr Stansfield wanted to woo me. I realized I could have been happy with someone as intellectual, kind and patient as he, even if my life would have meant living within much smaller means. The very idea was so appealing that for a moment, I thought about running after him.

Mary's return blocked the path.

"Child, you best not be playing with fire. That young man could have a bright future but not if you put him in harm's way." Mary snarled those words at me.

With each passing day, her mood had kept souring and I wondered what could be the reason behind it. Somehow, there was a connection with Mr Cameron. Was she was spying for him or my father, but not enjoying her role?

She shoved me forward, and guided me towards the kitchen. A bit too stunned to protest, I could only look over my shoulder as I was whisked away.

In the small breakfast nook near the kitchen, a simple meal of freshly baked bread, cheese, boiled chicken, and tomatoes had been prepared. Instead of confronting Mary about her aggressive behaviour, I thought it best to play the role of the quiet and accommodating lady-of-the-house. My appetite had all but disappeared since meeting Mr. Cameron, but my sense of self-preservation reminded me that I needed to eat if I was to have the fortitude to face the events to come. The nook afforded me an advantageous view of both the courtyard, located at the back of our estate, and also a line of sight into the kitchens themselves. I caught glimpses of Mary moving about with her various tasks, and just as I was beginning to enjoy my meal, I nearly choked on the piece of bread I was eating when I realized whose carriage had just arrived. I broke out in a cold sweat. *Mr. Cameron… arriving unannounced.* I watched for the man who had exited the carriage and breathed a huge sigh of relief, when it turned out not to the man who triggered such revulsion in my body, but his hired help.

I tiptoed closer to the kitchen doors, in the hopes that I could hear the dialogue between Mary, who had gone to the back door, and this man. Their hushed whispers that did not inject a feeling of comfort. I was unable to discern the gist of the conversation, save hearing "the MacKenzie's."

I acted quickly and without much forethought.

"Mary, I would like some more butter for my meal?" I called out from my place by the kitchen door.

"Oh heavens Lady MacRae," she yelped, and hurriedly closed the back door on the conversation. "You should not be sneaking around the house like that! You startled me right out of my skin."

I stepped into the kitchen and watched the man return into Mr. Cameron's carriage. The poor horses were shocked into movement, and I felt a kinship with their predicament in that moment. The warmth in my belly, the frustration, and the desire to feel free made itself known once again.

"Where are the MacKenzie's, Mary?"

I had looked forward to sharing food together with them while discussing the matters of the ledgers and possibly my father's notebook as well.

"Why, they have gone to collect the new curtains that your father ordered."

She stumbled over her words, and the few steps she took were clumsy. On the counter behind her was an open bottle of wine. She had been taking advantage of my father's absence, indulging far too early in the day. I felt this state could come in handy in the future, how I did not yet know. Though, I could have sworn the curtains had only been ordered only last week, to be ready by Friday, I had decided earlier that day that I would do nothing to incite suspicion from Father or Mary. As long as they thought I was acting as a proper lady, obeying the expectations set out for me, neither would suspect the deeper rebellion that was brewing within me. Returning to the remainder of my meal, I sat in quiet contemplation for awhile. Pondering over the startling events of this morning, eating slowly to give myself more time to digest not only the food but the information. I heard Roderick burst through the back kitchen doors.

"Why on this bloody earth would ye send us on a wild goose chase like that?"

"Why, Mis—ter," Mary belched. "Mr. MacKenzie. Whatever do you mean by that?"

"The curtains werena ready, and the master was surprised that we had come so early. He remembers specifically advising you and Lord MacRae that the curtains would be available next Friday morning."

"Mr. MacKenzie, what exactly are you accusing me of? It is not my fault that the receipt said today was the appointed time for the pick up!"

"Show me the receipt!"

Roderick crossed his arms over his chest and stood in front of her barring the kitchen door, while she looked around rather nervously. Finally, after rummaging through her apron pockets, she produced a slip of paper covered in wine stains. She gingerly handed it over to Roderick, and then took several steps back, visibly holding her breath.

"This is completely useless," Roderick sputtered. "Nothing is legible. And why was this not placed with the other receipts to keep in order?"

Seeing that this might be my opportunity to show grace, and again forestall any suspicions about my inner thoughts, I walked over and placed my hand on his forearm.

"I'm sure that it was a simple error, forgotten in all the chaos happening in this house for our upcoming celebration," I said, hoping that she would not question my overly sweet tone. "Mary, I appreciate your diligence in following up with the orders for our house."

Looking up at my guardian, I gave him a slight wink followed by a meaningful nod of my head. Roderick said nothing more and followed me into the main living area, leaving Mary to sort herself out. How, I did not yet know, but it was certain I would find a way to solve this puzzle that she played a part in.

"Lass, what is going on? Why are ye being so nice to Mary?"

"Roderick, there is much we need to discuss. Mr. Cameron's carriage was here earlier, and his man servant spoke with Mary for several minutes in whispers. I was not close enough to hear much, other than *MacKenzie's.*"

"Are ye sure, lass?" He sat down on the stairs, which allowed us to have an eye-level conversation.

"Absolutely positive!"

"So, it appears that our suspicions about Mr. Cameron keeping a fairly close eye on ye has merit. How has Mary gotten involved wi' all o' this, I wonder? It seems to me that she sent us away on purpose, keeping us elsewhere from the estate to prevent us from witnessing this visitor as ye have."

"Precisely why I am choosing to appear agreeable and try to allay any suspicion, so that I may move as freely as possible. Do not think that for one moment I will accept this fate without a fight."

Having said those words, I found myself standing just a little taller.

"Alright, let's endeavour to speak wi' Kenneth tonight at dinner time, so we can discuss this more at length. Now, I do believe it is the hour o' yer dance lessons, and ye ken how much Kenneth looks forward to those."

He beamed at me with sarcasm.

When my dance lessons had first begun, Roderick with his role in our household, was the obvious choice for my suitable dance partner. That is, until we learned that he possessed two left feet and absolutely no rhythm. It took only one lesson of bruised, almost broken toes of mine to make that decision for us. Kenneth, the more coordinated and graceful of the two, was soon assigned the role—despite his preference for being with the horses. He often joked they were easier to understand than people. As I headed off to my dance lesson, I realized that I was now beginning to agree with him.

Mr Fleming, the dance master was waiting, and Kenneth arrived moments later. Even Mary made her presence known at the beginning, so I made sure to muster some extra enthusiasm for her benefit.

"Kenneth, I have been assured that today's lesson is from the latest court dances in France! Imagine that?" I forced a giggle to accompany my words. "It is called Lavolta."

"Lady MacRae, I am happy for ye but would be far happier wi' my horses." he grumbled.

He, too, had a role to play. I could see that Mary was satisfied and had returned to the kitchens. For the next two hours we learned the new dance and repeated the steps until we could perform them with our eyes closed. All the variations of the Lavolta, as they were being introduced at the English courts, required a fair amount of strength from the man. Every few steps, Kenneth would put his big hands around my waist and lift me off the floor while I had to raise my arms above me. Although our roles meant we had to move our bodies, and pay attention to the dance master, our minds were not at all present. One unfortunate and somewhat spirited lift brought my head so high, it met with the chandelier above us, bringing genuine and spontaneous squeals of laughter from me and grunts of disapproval from Master Fleming. The time did not pass quickly enough. I was eager to read through my father's notebook again. I felt certain I would be able to discover more hidden in the jumble of words.

"Thank you for a most delightful lesson Master Fleming, I look forward to next week's dance." I curtsied a farewell while Kenneth escaped to the stables without a word, which was his custom.

In our gardens, I found my favourite reading spot—the stone bench, underneath an ancient oak tree in the middle of the garden. On either side of the Oak, were two large, and just as ancient, trees—one Ash and one Hawthorne. No other gardens in London could boast that unusual combination of trees, nor the little flowers and mosses that grew around the base of each. Barely three pages into trying to decipher the confusing sentences, when I heard a noise from the rear of the gardens. I put the notebook back into my pocket and walked over to investigate the cause of the disturbance.

I found a woman, covered in dirt, falling over the garden wall. She appeared to be in her late thirties. Dressed in a simple cotton dress with a thick petticoat underneath, yet it was made from fine quality material and stitching. When she stood up, brushing her skirts and fussing with her hair, I saw the ginger-haired curls peeking out from underneath her hood. She was pleasant to look upon, but no great beauty. Her features were plain, save for her eyes. Although more deep-set, their colour was so close to mine I could not help but wonder if she might be some distant relation.

She carried herself with poise as she walked in my direction, but before either of us could say a word, she began to cry.

"Lady MacRae! It is you! I hadn't dared to hope to find you so quickly." she fell to her knees. "I beg you to please allow me to speak."

I nodded my approval and took the few steps needed to kneel beside her.

"Lady MacRae, my name is Elizabeth Moore, and my sister Kathryn was Mr. William Cameron's first wife."

Here was my first chance to find out more information about Mr. Cameron first hand, but all I could think about now was this courageous woman who had risked so much by coming here.

"May I call you Elizabeth?" I asked, sitting down beside her on the soft grass.

"Why of course Lady MacRae, and thank you for being so gracious."

I took one of her hands into my own, and looked into her eyes. I needed to hear what she had to say, but also recognized that she needed someone to listen to her story. I wanted her to feel safe, and to know I was not taking her risks for granted.

"Please, think nothing of it. You have clearly travelled a long way and I feel what you have to share with me is important. So much so that you trespassed and risked injury to yourself by climbing our walls."

"Of course… yes...." she said, tears welling up again. "Now that I'm here, I don't even know where to begin."

"Elizabeth, please take a deep breath. Slow down. Take your time." I hoped I could assure her enough to learn as much as possible.

"It was nigh ten years ago when Mr. Cameron sought out our father for a joint venture in the cotton business. My family is well known in the industry, and he sought to carve a piece out for himself. After several months, marked by most profitable business, Father informed us that William would be coming for supper."

I remained silent, giving her the space to recollect her memories and continue sharing the details of that first meeting.

"My sister, Kathryn, was the focus of his attention. And for once I was grateful I had not inherited our mother's looks. I knew something was not right with Mr. Cameron, not right at all. Yet I was the dutiful daughter, so I said nothing." She looked to her hands folded in her lap. "The courtship lasted only seven days before the betrothal was announced, and only a few weeks later the wedding took place. Kathryn was sixteen and found herself married to man that she did not know."

"Elizabeth, this may seem an odd question, your father…"I wondered out loud. "…his health. How was it during this time?"

She took in a shaky breath through her nose, as if the memory made it difficult for her to breathe.

"He had always been strong and possessed a very agile mind. Yet, I do not know, none of us knew, what was happening to him. He became ill, around the same time he promised my sister's hand to Mr. Cameron. His mind, his faculties, and well, everything failed, so much so that he was unable to manage the business. We could not get a physician to confirm what malady had beset our father and no remedies that we tried did any good."

She began to sob. I reached in my pocket for a kerchief, my fingers brushing against my father's notebook, and handed her the linen.

"Please, go on," I said as encouragingly as I could.

Elizabeth nodded, and dabbed her eyes with the cloth.

"Mr. Cameron, he offered to assist with the business ventures. Despite my older brother James having been groomed his whole life to take it over. He, my father, my—."

Her voice broke away in a torrid of emotion. I brushed away some of the hair that spilled from her cowl. Sorrow shook Elizabeth's breast, and she raised her eyes to the darkening sky. As if whoever resided up there was at fault for every tragedy she had experienced.

"He was dead within two months of Kathryn's wedding. And in going through the estate, the papers, legal counsel informed us he had bequeathed the entire business to Mr. Cameron. Not James, his son, my brother—Mr. Cameron."

"Oh, by the Lord," I whispered.

"And still, we had not seen my sister. The day of my father's funeral came and went, and nothing. We attributed illness to Kathryn's absence. Every day I tried see her, to visit her. And each day I was turned away at the door. I finally managed to sneak into the back gardens of Mr. Cameron's estate, much as I've done yours, tonight." She let out the saddest laugh imaginable. "As a child, I was often chided by our mother for always climbing into trees and was scolded for being as curious as a cat. So, I crept into the house, a mad, little mouse was I, and by the grace of God, I found her, in the master bedroom. It had been locked from the outside. What I saw, good Lady McRae, snatched the air from my lungs."

Elizabeth had wrung the kerchief to a pulp by now.

"Was she…?" I asked, not wanting to know.

Elizabeth shook her head.

"She had wasted away, her frame shrunk by the loss of nearly thirty pounds, and her hair…what strands she had left hung limply around her skull. Her skin was pale, grey, and at first I suspected the plague to be the culprit but her body showed no markings of the pocks. Kathryn was nothing more than a wisp of what she once was." Here she paused, uncertain how to continue.

I sensed her discomfort as she shared intimate details about a man I was to wed, and thereby what might be in my future as well.

"Please do not soften the details for my sake, I must know what happened."

"She admitted Mr Cameron, that beast, had taken her nightly, if you understand my meaning. At times, thrice in a single night. Every violation was quick, forceful. After each, she believed herself to drain away a little more, her energy and will, you see, was weakening. I had mere minutes with her before we both heard the carriage return and with it Mr. Cameron himself. I snuck out again, and by the grace of God remained unnoticed leaving the property. We would not see her for another month, at her first public appearance since the wedding, where she announced she was pregnant with their first child. She had deteriorated further, but was so elated about the arrival of the baby—and that Mr .Cameron had stopped forcing himself on her—I could not persuade her to leave him."

The rest of her story mirrored what Roderick and Kenneth had discovered, but it still brought a shudder down my spine and hearing her words affirm what I had already been told, still triggered a sinking feeling. She must have noticed the darkening look on my face.

"Lady MacRae, after her death we could not find a single physician who was willing to confirm that they had dealt with Mr. Cameron or my sister. There is no proof of her pregnancy, no certificate of death. It was as if she simply disappeared into thin air. The ashes that were sent to our home, now sit on our mother's mantle, but I do not believe a word that monster said about the demise of my sister. I have spent the last ten years since Kathryn's death watching Mr. Cameron from afar. He has since taken three other young women, all who bore a striking resemblance to her, all who died within a year of the marriage."

"Elizabeth, you took a great risk by coming here. Mr. Cameron's man has been to this house already once today, and I fear he may be watching over my movements. Please know that I am grateful for all you have shared and risked by coming —."

"—Yes, I saw him earlier. I've been watching the comings and goings all morning in the hopes I would find a window of opportunity to make my way inside." Elizabeth suddenly grabbed my hands and her eyes narrowed to slits as she hissed, her grip tightening like noose. "Lady MacRae, you must find a way to dissuade your father. The upcoming betrothal cannot happen.I fear your very life depends on it."

"Elizabeth, I must insist you—"

"—Tell me, can you trust those big men who serve your father? Are they loyal to you? What about the man on the rooftops who I see hovering wherever you go?"

"What? How did you know—?"

"Intruder! Trespasser!"

Mary shrieked as she came running towards us, from past the herb gardens. She pushed me to the side, away from Elizabeth's desperate clutches.

"Away from here at once, before I call the constables to have you forcibly removed and locked up!"

Elizabeth scrambled to her feet, stumbling as Mary shoved her through the gates leading to the carriageway behind the estates. Mary slammed the door shut behind her, but not before I saw a carriage speeding past and heard a scream. Fearing for the woman who had risked so much by seeking me out, I started to run towards the sound, but Mary got a hold of my arm and dragged me back inside the house, barring the way and locking the door behind us. I was pushed like a disobedient dog all the way up to my room, where she left me behind a locked door. I heard her footsteps down the hall, all the while muttering and cursing echoing after her.

Even at her worst, Mary's inebriation had never elicited such violent behaviour. Something had frightened her —something about Elizabeth. Or, perhaps I was succumbing to paranoia. I raised my hands to my head, tugging at my hair, trying to sort out the frightful events falling upon me like an avalanche. I debated climbing out my window to find the brothers, but rain began coming down in sleets. As nimble as I was, I knew that attempting the ledge with slipper stones underfoot was a recipe for disaster.

I prepared myself for bed and all the while digesting what had occurred in the gardens prior to Mary's appalling behaviour. What about the stranger on the rooftops? Elizabeth had noticed him. Was it possible that he worked for Mr. Cameron? I had hoped one of the MacKenzie's would have realized my absence and come to find me, but the night was too far gone and I knew they too were keeping up the appearance of obedience.

I thought I might never fall asleep, but the events of the day had exhausted me. That night I dreamt again—of the man on the rooftops, the one from the tavern

I found myself standing in front of the same fireplace as before. He sensed my tension, as if my worries of the day had followed me into this dreamscape. He slid a smooth hand underneath my jaw and up towards my ear. I pressed my hands against his muscled chest and breathed in his scent—a musky fragrance mixed with the saltiness of an ocean wind. Pulling me in closer, he inhaled my inner most perfume that turned sweeter by the moment as my aroused body responded to his presence. His hands slid up my back and firmly caressed the small dip in my lower back, and all the way back up to the nape of my neck. His warmth, his nearness, radiated against me.

I had never known the embrace of a man, but my body felt desire—hunger. It wanted him, and in a most desperate manner. Gooseflesh rippled along my arms as his fingers drew soft circles from my bare shoulders all the way down to my wrists. He leaned down towards me, and I held my breath with anticipation. Hesitating, breathing slowly and deeply with our lips only a few inches apart he paused. I wanted his kiss. I craved his lips, his mouth on mine. My upbringing was at war with my desire. He pressed himself firmly against my body. The inner warmth turned into fire as my body quivered with his seduction. My nipples hardened and I felt the leather of his over-coat through the cotton of my shift. I had never kissed a man, and all I wanted was for him to take control. To show me all that I had yet to experience.

He remained still, both of us enveloped in the heat that our bodies were generating. My hand travelled up his chest, my fingertips against his breastbone. I wanted to feel his heart beat. I wanted to know if it was beating as strong and fast as mine. I felt nothing. No heart, no rhythm. Yet he was so alive—a man of flesh and fire. My mind screamed at me to stop, to run, to get away from him. I begged my mind to be silent, to allow me a moment to revel in the warmth, the fire between my body and his. He placed his hand over my heart, so near my breast that I ached for him to cup its fullness in his palm. His fingers brushed along my jaw and beneath my chin to raise it. Leaning closer, his lips softly grazing mine.

Desire and passion threatened to undo me, shattering all possible control I might have. He suddenly drew away, and my body turned ice-cold. I stumbled back, but he caught me. I wanted nothing more than to stay in this dream, in his arms when his grip began to tighten… His voice was husky, deepened with lust.

"Now and always, you are mine."

I woke to the sound of thunder and rain.

CHAPTER 5

Waking up that morning to a body aroused in a way I had never experienced, and confused that I would have such dreams about a man I had never met, I stumbled through my morning washing. Discovering that my bedroom door had been unlocked during the night, I was able to call for my maid to come help me get dressed properly, as I was so distracted I chose two mismatched articles of clothing and tied the laces of the inner corset completely wrong.

Grateful for the solitude of the breakfast table, so that I was able to collect myself and decide on a plan of action for the day, I half heartedly made my way through the hard boiled eggs, the freshly baked sourdough roll and the pieces of smoked bacon.

By the time I finished my morning meal I had resolved to find Kenneth and Roderick. There was no sense in withholding pertinent information from them. I would tell them about poor Elizabeth, and show them my father's journal. Together we would find some answers.

I pulled out the pendant and the feathers from the locked drawer, perhaps it was time to share these with my keepers as well. My tutors would have suggested that I think logically—examine their appearance and analyze the time of their arrival. I placed the objects upon my bed and began a more thorough inspection of each item.

The pendant was warm to the touch, as were the feathers. Similar to a raven's feathers, but larger with shafts thicker and more sturdy than that of any bird I knew of. I lifted one to my nose and took a tentative inhale. A hint of wood smoke overpowered the scent of the sea. The feather could not have been from nearby, since London was far from any ocean. And there was was the underlying fragrance I could not place. I closed my eyes. *Nothing*. Next, I took the delicate gemstone in the palm of my hand. The craftsmanship of the silver wings was impeccable and detailed, and I marvelled at its beauteous and rare red amber. The pendant carried a different aroma—the air during a lightening storm. And whomever was leaving these gifts on my windowsill must be nimble and strong enough to climb to the balcony of my room. Like the stranger, who was quite at home on rooftops.

There was no proof of any connection between him and these gifts, nothing but my intuition, or perhaps wishful thinking. It was not yet time to share the existence of the feathers or the pendant with my protectors, at least not until I was more certain as to their origins and intent. Placing the items back out of sight for safekeeping, it was time to face the day.

On the main floor of our house, Mary was occupied preparing the food with the servants and cooks. She shouted at incoming deliveries, barking orders at the maids, far too busy to notice me as I snuck past her in the hallway towards the back kitchen door leading to the stables.

I was halted in my escape, when I heard Kenneth's voice coming from the opposite direction by the front foyer. He stood in the open doorway, both doors swung wide open with his frame nearly filling the entire space. As I approached, I only heard his voice, no one else. His speech was neither English nor the Gaelic I had heard over the years. It was guttural but beautifully soft - like the Scottish brogue which I had always adored. I wanted to hear more, and crept closer.

"Aye, ye wee nuisance," he said spinning around and poking his finger at my forehead. "Thought I couldna hear ye sneak up on me?"

"I'm only enjoying you speak the tongue of your youth, Kenneth. And mildly curious as to why you are speaking it to nothing but the air."

"Lass, this weather holds no kindness." he said, avoiding my question and looking outside towards the dark clouds starting to loom across the horizon. "Something is coming our way. I can smell it on the rain but dinna ken what it is."

He took a long look at me.

"Are ye a'right lass? Ye look awfully pale."

"I am always pale. 'Tis my heritage."

My hands wrapped tightly around the journal I held behind my back, and I took a quick breath.

"Kenneth, I need to speak with you and Roderick. In private if you please. Would you be so kind as to ask him to come to father's study?"

As soon as those words were spoken, I felt relieved. Knowing that in moments they would be able to share their insights and thoughts on the discovery of father's journal, easing the burden I had been carrying alone.

"Aye, no bother, lass." Kenneth words had barely left his mouth, when the rain started to pour down.

Waiting in my father's study for the MacKenzie's to arrive, I ran my fingers over the bindings of the journal. I wondered how he was faring in Dover, when the door opened to reveal Roderick and Kenneth. Soaked to the skin and in a most gloomy demeanour.

"Lady M, what is so important that ye pulled us away from our duties?" Roderick looked so perturbed, I was not sure if he was serious or if his sense of humour was as dour as the weather that day.

"Please Roderick, if you both will just bear with me. Yesterday, when I was in the gardens reading, a woman climbed over the back stone walls. Her name, Elizabeth Moore, and she had snuck in to speak with me—privately. Her sister was Kathryn Moore, who was Mr Cameron's first wife."

I paused to watch their reaction. They both looked at each other, exchanging a silent communication between them. Then they took the few steps towards to the desk and sank into the wooden leather covered chairs, which were not used to carrying the weight of such giants and creaked threateningly.

After I had finished recounting the events of the last twenty-four hours before Mary had locked me in my room, I leaned against father's large mahogany desk for support. *I could still hear Elizabeth's scream.* I waited, and watched as the brothers looked from the floor, to each other, and back to the floor again.

"Did ye see who the carriage might ha' belonged to?" Roderick was the first to speak.

"Did ye actually witness her being run over?" Kenneth asked before I could answer the first question.

"My dearest brothers of the heart, I do not know anything other than what I have already shared with you. And no, I did not see her body struck by the carriage—only that she was thrust roughly into the alleyway where I caught sight of a carriage rushing by, which was followed by a piercing shriek."

"Alright then. Lady M, we will keep a watch out for Elizabeth, o' that ye can be certain. We would ha' heard o' a dead body found behind our estate by now, so hopefully she wasna seriously injured. And should we ha' the opportunity to ensure her welfare, ye can also rest easy on that account."

Roderick stood up, took off his sodden jacket, and hung it on the rack near the door.

"And now, ye must tell us what ye've been hiding behind yer back."

Producing my father's secret journal from behind my back with shaking hands, I offered it to Roderick.

"I was going through the ledgers, to finalize last month's entries when I noticed something strange, like a nagging pattern. This led me to look at the last two year's worth of account books, and behind one of them I found this little notebook. Secreted away. It bears father's hand."

Roderick took the small book from my hands, turning one page at a time all the while nodding his head. Occasionally cocking his head to the side, flipping back to a previous page and then forward, it was clear he too was befuddled by this finding.

"Aye, this is John's handwriting o' that I am sure. What is strange isna his penmanship, but how he writes, especially in the last few entries." He worked closely with my father over the years, and was knowledgeable of his handwriting. "Not only the script, but the sentences start to lose their structure, and the grammar makes no sense."

"Precisely, now look here when you compare some of the ledgers against the dates in the notebook." I produced the household account ledgers and showed them the dates that aligned with my father's sporadic sentences. The three of us concluded we could not make any judgment without speaking with my father. What was clear however, was that Mr. William Cameron was involved in sinister matters, given how all the dates aligned with calamities befalling England.

"We should ha' word from mother, by Sunday I hope." Roderick said. "And, Kenneth, with all that has happened, I think it's best we bring in two more men to watch the grounds, ones we can trust. I will reach out to cousins, Connor and Duncan, and ha' them come immediately. They are already in town on some other business and willna mind seeing Lady M again."

Roderick rose out of his chair with a great sigh of relief on the chair's part.

"Aye, I believe that asking our cousins to help us watch over the grounds and keep both John and Moireach safe is very wise." Kenneth had kept silent for most of the conversation. "Ask them if they would bring their dogs as well —."

"—Why dogs?" I questioned.

"I sense that we will be in need o' their aid in the comin' days." Kenneth gave Roderick a quiet glare. "Can ye not smell it on the rain?"

"True, and speaking of smells, it's time we watched out for Mary. By the smell of her, she is in the drink before lunchtime and given her interactions with Mr. Cameron's man servant, we need to be watchful."

Roderick returned to supervise incoming deliveries, while Kenneth went back to the stables. And I returned to duties assigned throughout the manor and assisted with the incoming deliveries of flowers. I was distracted. I was confused. And time lost its meaning that afternoon.

A commotion outside brought me from my misery and the monotony, and I ran to see what it was. Standing in the rain were two roughly dressed men, dressed in dark brown cloaks, hunting kilts, and riding gear, although no horses accompanied them. They were at the front gates being yelled at by Mary. By their statures, it was obvious that they were Clan MacKenzie, not only by their tartan kilts but also their incredible size which towered over the servants. Their caps barely contained the long dark copper hair that had been tied back respectably, but perhaps hastily.

Roderick, who had been helping his brother with the latest hay delivery, came running out from the stables and placed his hands on Mary's shoulders, turning her about. He stooped down, eye level with her, what words he spoke I shall never know, but her brusque walk back towards the kitchen indicated she had lost whatever fight she was trying to win.

The cousins had arrived so soon.

He then walked over to the men and greeted them in the fashion of the MacKenzie's. Ever since I could remember, I had witnessed the comings and goings of MacKenzie men in my life. When I was just four years old, I remembered asking Kenneth to show me how, and also explain to me what it meant. He had explained that this gesture that dated back to one of their oldest ancestors and had been passed down to each generation, their way of showing respect and trust. Each man's right hand gripped the other's forearm while each left hand was placed over the heart standing opposite. They walked together towards the stables, where I knew Kenneth was taking care of the horses.

Making my way to the front foyer, to help organize the maids for their role in cleaning, dusting and mopping the floors, I was able to distract myself and absorb myself in the task for a short while.

"Lady MacRae!" Mary shrieked from the doorway. "Your presence has been requested in the stables by that boorish Roderick who presumes to give me orders!"

"Straight away, Mary," I said, making my way past her.

She snatched my arm and hissed, "You will tell me precisely what is said in that barn with those filthy men, so that I may tell your father exactly what they are up to!"

"Mary, I believe I can communicate quite well enough with my own father and will ensure that he is informed of any 'filthy' activities." I couldn't help but get my own little jab in. "Besides, I am sure you are far too busy to be playing messenger—for anyone."

She clenched her teeth, then turned heel toward the kitchens. I grabbed a hardy cloak hanging by the back doors and slid my feet into the sturdy galoshes made for weather just such as this, and headed towards the stables.

When I arrived, with mud soaked boots and shaking the excess rain from the cloak, I heard the low voices of men further back, near the horses. By some miracle, I had managed to sneak up on not only one MacKenzie but four of them.

My jaw dropped to the floor.

Logic told me that they had removed their shirts to work more freely, moving the bales of hay around the stables, and to avoid getting their shirts dirty. Still, watching four half-naked Scottish highlanders working up a sweat would bring any women to a swoon—especially given my recent dreams that had awoken something inside of me. Even Kenneth and Roderick, who were like brothers, drew my eyes. But it was something else, something more than the bare sculpted muscle. All four men showed evidence of violence, faded scars turned silver with time, along their tanned backs and shoulders.

"*Oy*, Roddie, Kenny where is that strange smell coming from?" One of the copper haired cousins asked. "It's like *she* is near, but that isna possible, is it?"

Kenneth turned, and nearly jumped out of his skin at the sight of me.

"Bloody lightning bolts in the skies! Lady M, what the devil are ye doin' here?"

All four men quickly reached for their shirts, but were not fast enough to hide what I had seen. Despite their magnificently formed bodies, it was those curious streaks of silver that had my attention.

"Lass, why have ye come?" Roderick jumped down from his vantage point, and slowly walked toward me.

"Well, I. Mary. I. She. And then…"

My porcelain skin must have taken on a deep shade of red, given how warm my cheeks felt. And the men of Clan MacKenzie shared a quiet, if not completely polite, chuckle at my expense.

"Lady M, I told Mary to send ye oot to the stables after supper. Clearly she is up to either mischief, or she's thrown back a few, aye?" Roderick cupped an invisible glass and chugged it down. "Allow me to present Connor and Duncan, our cousins."

It was not until then that I noticed that they were twins, who possessed the most unusual eyes. Connor's right eye was blue and his left was green. And there was Duncan, whose right eye was green and his left was blue. They were both shorter than my keepers, but still towered over most men standing nearly six feet four. Their skin was a rich brown, proof of their life on the roads, and with copper blonde hair loosely tied back, showing a lack of worry about society expectations. Their frame was not as wide as Roderick, but they presented a most formidable figure that would intimidate most men.

"Lady MacRae, Duncan and I are honoured to be given the chance to help protect ye and yer father. We can scarce believe how ye've grown, the last we see ye but as a bairn. Of course, we ha' heard stories of ye from Gwenyver over the years, but to see for our own eyes is another."

"Do you mean to say we have met before?"

"Och aye, the day ye were born lass but I highly doubt ye would remember that." He said somewhat cheekily. "Roderick has called upon us at this time of need and we willna fail ye. Oh, and dinna fasch yersel', our own mother canna tell us apart either."

Connor bowed and took my hand gently and kissed the top of my knuckles, in a gentlemanly fashion. He took a deep breath, before gently passing my hand over to his brother, who bowed in return and also repeated the same gesture.

"Can I ask ye to please describe Mr. Cameron's coachman and Kathryn's sister?"

Duncan was clearly the more direct of the two brothers.

Thus began my detailed narrative of events, up until the point of my encounter with Kathryn's sister.

"So, you see, I still don't really know what happened to Elizabeth, but I wonder if we …" I had just been interrupted by a strange growl which startled me into a little jump.

"Are those the dogs? I asked, looking around.

"Lady M, ye need nae worry. That was just the sound of a MacKenzie stomach when it hasna eaten in a few hours!" Duncan did have a sense of humour after all.

"And our dogs will be arriving after all the hustling about is completed for this evening." Connor was quick to comment on the absence of the animal guardians. "We want to take care in showing them the grounds without any confusion."

We agreed to have our supper in the stables with the horses and continue our conversation. Roderick ran to the kitchens and fetched two baskets filled with morsels of smoked meats, cheese and fresh loaves of bread with butter. I kept my feet tucked underneath my skirts and felt mercifully safe in the company of these MacKenzie men. They told childhood stories and tried to find ways to embarrass each other. Some tales were of boyish attempts at strength and prowess, and others were about their childish attempts to woo a girl of their age.

"So, that's when Duncan tried to convince our father that it was really the kitchen boy who had—"

Connor paused. Duncan put his hands on his twins forearms, and they exchanged a silent look. The same I had so often seen my guardians exchange.

"Aye lads, I can smell it too." Roderick stood up, and within seconds all four of the men were standing and had taken a protective stance around me, like soldiers, ready to fight an intruder, or perhaps worse.

"Daughter, what are you doing in the stables with these four men?" My father came bursting through the doors. "Why is there no other woman present? Mary should be here to chaperone!"

"Father!" I said, standing up to curtsey. "These are trusted MacKenzie's! There should be no question as to their honour…or mine!"

So shocked to see him, I hadn't given any thought as to how to greet his angry outburst but with a candid response.

"Roderick, after I take her to her room, I expect a full report," he said, his cheeks flushed and sweat dripping down from his brow. "I cannot stress how important it is that there are no more incidences that could cause a shadow of a doubt over her innocence!"

He grabbed me by my arm and dragged me out of the stables. He did not even give me a moment to grab the cloak to shield myself from the drenching rain. Pulling me across the grounds, and through the kitchens, not even allowing me to remove the boots which were covered in the mud and muck from the stables and the dirt outside. Making our way up the stairs, dragging me by my arm, my short legs kept stumbling as he forced a stride I was simply not capable of, and he kept shouting incoherently.

"Why are there four MacKenzie's? Am I losing track of them? Why did you go there? This isn't Dover? Moireach, stop struggling and just do as you're told!"

Once in my room, he flung me onto my bed.

"Father what has happened? This is not like you." I pleaded, through tears of confusion and pain. "Why are you so angry?"

"You have no right to question your father! I pray you will not be so insolent with your husband! I—" He crumpled to his knees and held his head in his hands, deep sobs racked his body. "By the Lord… will this bloody headache never leave me?"

And then he folded over into an unconscious heap on the carpet by my bedside.

Stunned by the whirlwind of the last few minutes, and witnessing my father who had never even had a cold or the flu in all my life, succumb to a fainting spell, spurned me to action. I ran down to the kitchens and prepared the special herbal tea —a concoction I knew by heart, one that I hoped would offer him comfort. Roderick found me as I was racing back up the stairs.

"Lass, are ye alright?

"Yes, I'm fine. But father has collapsed, just after complaining of another headache."

He followed me to my room, and we found Father still unconscious. Roderick moved swiftly and helped to lift him onto my bed with the pillows stacked up behind his head.

"Father, please wake up. I've made some tea to help ease your pain."

He looked aged, in just those few moments, I could have sworn there was more grey in his hair and the lines in his face were deeper. Roderick, gently tapped the side of my father's cheek, encouraging him to rouse.

"Daughter, what happened? Why am I in your room? Is supper ready?"

He awoke, visibly confused, having not been able to remember the last few minutes.

"Father, it's alright, your headache seemed to overwhelm you. Please drink some of the tea, and have two more cups before you retire for bed."

"Why are you wearing mud covered boots inside the house?" Shaking his head, as if to shake off the fog of a deep slumber.

"I brought the MacKenzie's some supper in the stables. All is well here, you were just checking on me, having heard I was turning into bed early." If he did not remember his violent outburst and rough handling of his daughter, then I didn't want to remind him. After a few minutes, quietly sipping his tea, he stood up gingerly and wished me a good night, returning to his chambers. Roderick walked him out, and as he closed the door, he gazed back at me with a reassuring nod.

Taking care of my father meant I had missed the rest of my supper, but in truth I had no appetite any more. Asking my maid to help me with the laces of the corset so that I could prepare myself for bed, my thoughts kept returning to the odd events of the past few days. After asking her leave to go, I removed the rest of the clothing myself, and choosing a night gown was only a momentary distraction.

When I laid myself to bed, all I could do was toss and turn. Tired of fighting my insomnia, I went to my little vanity to remove the feathers. I returned to bed and placed them under my pillow, and promptly fell asleep. Gratefully.

That night I dreamed.

…of the highlands, of storms sending lightning bolts across the sky, and the sound of fighting men. Yet, I saw no men in my dreams, only large four-legged animals in a foggy mist, where the shadows made it impossible to identify them… until the calamity calmed and two walked out of the mist, toward me. Bodies the size of large dogs but with features that resembled both the thick body of a bear but with the length and tail of a fox. Both creatures with same copper fur as a fox, and when they were close enough for me to see their eyes, I felt a scream trapped in my throat.

I sat bolt upright in my bed, my body trembling and drenched in sweat.

The eyes! One was blue and the other green.

CHAPTER 6

I had not been able to fall back asleep after that strange dream, and spent the hours of the early morning sitting at my windowsill wrapped in my blankets. A part of me hoped to catch whoever had been dropping these unusual gifts, but somehow I knew that today would hold no promise of escape.

Wanting to delay the inevitable, I took as much time with my bathing as was possible. Looking out the window often, I knew I was nimble enough to climb all the way down. But then what? There were simply too many people around, and I would surely be noticed. Laying all my trust with my keepers, I set out to face the rest of the day with fortitude.

Spending the earlier part of the morning signing off on receipts for various deliveries for the upcoming event, there was no opportunity to think further on my dream or discuss with the MacKenzie's, who also were occupied fulfilling their duties for the day. My time was not my own.

Kenneth was busy preparing the grounds and the stables to receive the influx of guests—and their horses. Each stall was cleaned and filled with fresh hay and water, and the back lanes had been cleared and swept for the carriages. Connor and Duncan were patrolling the grounds, well out of the sight of any incoming guests, guarding discreetly. Roderick was busy managing the event's various deliveries from all the different shops around town. He was my best chance to talk to a MacKenzie, but anytime I got near him, a sour Mary hampered all my attempts, even with all the work to be done in the kitchens. She pulled me away to oversee some menial tasks or ask my opinion on some random thing. The chaos was organized, and it seemed hopeless that I would be able to find a way to escape for even a moment. I did not know what I craved more…stillness or to find the MacKenzie's to share my odd dream with them.

As luck would have it, I was finally able to sneak out, while Mary slinked off to the cellar for more wine. I made my way along the side of the house by the rose bushes which provided some cover, and then along the hedges towards the front gate. I would go find the cousins.

"Lady MacRae, what are ye doing oot and about, if I may be so bold?" asked Duncan, not one to mince words, securing the back gates to the garden alongside his twin.

"If you can answer me why Mary is trying to keep me away from any man of the Clan MacKenzie, then I will gladly answer why I am out and about!"

I had not realized how frustrated I had been all morning.

"I apologize for my brother, Lady MacRae." Connor said, bowing graciously. "How may we be o' service?"

"I don't know where to start," I bowed my head. "And…I'm sorry for my outburst, today is a very trying day."

"May I ask how ye are faring after last night's rough treatment by yer father?" asked Connor. "I do hope that any misunderstanding on our part played no role in his behaviour. Ye are such a wee thing, and I feared ye might be injured when he grabbed yer arm so roughly."

"Connor, I may be a 'wee thing' but I am perfectly fine, thank you."

I felt resentment at being treated like a fragile doll, while at the same time rubbing my arm where my father's grip had muddied my skin with a green and blue bruise.

"I apologize Lady MacRae, it wasna my intent to insult ye." He bowed graciously—again.

"Thank you kindly for your concern—"

Duncan stepped forward, and took my hand without permission. He pushed up the sleeve of my dress to reveal the mark Father had left behind.

"Aye, I thought as much! It's too late to use leeches, but did our Aunt show ye how to make the concoction w' arnica to help bruises?"

"No, I am afraid she did not. It was never really a necessity in my younger years."

"Dinna fasch yersel'! Let us help in this matter. I will send up the mixture o' herbs for the healing o' yer bruises in a short while." Duncan kissed the palm of his hand and placed it on the crown of my head. The same gesture that Kenneth showed me just a few days earlier.

"Was there anything else, Lady MacRae?" asked Connor who spoke.

"It's silly… but I had a rather odd dream last night." My cheeks went warm, and I feared that a blush would take over my face. "In my dream, I was…"

"Tell us, lass. We shallna judge."

I looked down at my shoes, then straightened my posture. The time for downward glances was over.

"In my dream, I was in the highlands in the middle of a storm, lightning flashes every few seconds. I heard the sound of men and swords clashing and shouting. Then shapes came out of the mist. Not men, but animals. It was not until they were nearly upon me that I saw their eyes. They were identical to yours."

Connor and Duncan exchanged a single, silent glance, a nod. Just as Kenneth and Roderick did, all the time. Did all the MacKenzie's have this unspoken language?

"Ach well, that sounds like a rather disturbing dream lass, but it was still just a dream. No need to fuss yersel' over it, for it's nothing to—"

"—There you are!" Mary had snuck up behind us. "Mrs. Driscoll has arrived with your dress, and I am certain that you have not bothered to bathe!"

"As a matter of fact Mary," I retorted. "I have."

"Well then, come along now." she sneered. "Best not be seen conversing with these louts."

Duncan and Connor simply bowed, as I was dragged off yet again, towards the dreaded moment. Arriving at my rooms, I barely had a breath to myself before the dressmaker, Mrs Driscoll, had arrived with my new gown. The dress with dark colours that would be a quiet but most obvious rebellion to my betrothed's request. It had been hidden inside a linen wrapping to ensure that no one would see it before the party. No one else was permitted to see me wearing her masterpiece before the grand entrance, including me. Mrs. Driscoll insisted that I wear a blindfold while dressing and had covered the large gilded mirror in my room with a bedsheet. As she tightened my corset, I felt her adjust my sleeves, I tried to envision her creation.

"Oh my!" I could hear her skirts ruffle, as she took a few steps around me admiring her work. "Absolute perfection!

Father and Mr. Cameron had specifically requested something very different than what she had designed for me, but the fire in my belly kept me quiet, as she crooned over her work.

"Your skin is shimmering against the silver black, not pale but a beautiful porcelain, and your lips like dark cherries that the reds of the fabric have brought out. And the colour of your hair! Stunning! It it the crowning jewel for all the fabrics and the colours. Oh Lady MacRae, thank you for allowing me to create this masterpiece."

She sighed. Silence. And then she whisked off everything. The day left little time for some of the minor alternations that had to be made, and in a matter of hours, I would wear the completed ensemble.

As I sat patiently for the hairdresser to arrive at any moment, I noticed my father's pocket watch on the floor in my room. It must have fallen the night before. There had been no opportunity to speak with him after he had awoken from his faint, not just due to the late hour but his fragile mental state. I wished to tell him of Elizabeth. Surely what I had learned would sway his commitment to the betrothal. Yet, after the events of the previous night, when I saw my father, a man normally calm and composed, in a frenzied inexplicable state of rage and pain, I was no longer certain of anything. A life sealed to a man I did not know, twice my age, with a sordid past filled with four dead and buried wives?

Had fate really decided this future for me?

I made a point to remember to give the watch to Roderick to return to my father before the grand affair. There had been no feather left on the sill. I could not help but feel alone. The mystery man, from the tavern and the rooftops, had not visited me in my dreams last night. Every time I had seen him previously, I was able to feel him before I could see him. I wondered if I my imagination had run wild and he did not actually exist. After all, I only had the three feathers and the beautiful pendant. But even those were not definitive proof, as I never saw the person who left them for me, yet there was something so familiar about the gifts.

"Lady MacRae, may I come in?"

The polite knocking startled me from my day dream.

"Ah, yes! Come in, Miss Pennington."

She was an accomplished hairdresser at the royal court and known for her ability to tame any coiffeur—and also for her rather large appetite with the sweets, should they be on hand.

"Lady MacRae, one of those dashing MacKenzie men sent up this hot tea for you? Oh and I have just had the most delightful discussion with Mrs Driscoll." She curtsied, and her basket of scissors and various implements I could not identify swung from her wide hips. "We both agreed that today you will inspire a new trend with the nobility. The ladies at court will be vying for hair such as yours from here on after."

Most women were wearing powdered wigs, or their hair under elegantly embroidered caps allowing only a few loose, curly wisps of hair to escape. I did not know what Miss Pennington was planning, but I was certain Father and Mr. Cameron would not approve. Would they interpret my dress and my newly styled locks as rebellion? And I toyed with the hope that this would be enough to make Mr. Cameron change his mind about the wedding and call it off. I was both nervous and excited. But how much defiance would my father allow?

Sitting in front of my vanity, in the thin shift to be worn under the dress I had yet to see, with the mirror still covered, I closed my eyes and freed my mind to wander while sipping the surprisingly sweet tasting tea from Duncan, the one to help with the bruising on my arm. As so often before, I wished for my mother's presence, despite never having felt it before. She would not have allowed this to happen and would have opposed her husband, my father. The little I had been told about her, along with Kenneth's recent confession that she wanted me to marry for love confirmed this belief. Nanny would have always voiced her objection to my father but he did not treat her with the same respect as he would a wife. And what of the man on the rooftops? He had been woefully absent. Another childish romantic fantasy saw him rescuing me from the horrid man I was to marry and whisking me away to another life. I could feel myself tensing with the strain of playing the role of submissive and agreeable daughter, and knew it was just a matter of time before something would push me over the edge. I prayed I would be able to keep my wits about me tonight.

"Lady MacRae, if you would kindly open your eyes."

I gasped when I saw my reflection. She had transformed my wavy hair into tight curls. A large gathering of hair had been pinned to the crown of my head in a high Greek knot, creating a cascading effect of curls along the back. Throughout the tresses of my curls she had woven silver beads and bright crimson gemstones strung on a long, thin silver chain to keep them secure. They reflected with the light and created sparking red highlights throughout my dark hair.

"Now," Mrs. Pennington said, rifling through her wares. "We just need to find a lovely accent piece to pin to the side of these beautiful curls,"

"If you would excuse me for just a moment." I said, rising. "I may have just the thing. I will just need one moment alone."

I ushered a confused Mrs. Pennington out and closed the door. I retrieved the three feathers and pendant, brought each to my lips, and I kissed them softly. Whatever connection they had to the owner who chose to give them to me, I had faith that they had gifted these items with good intentions. Perhaps having them with me would help keep me safe, or simply provide me with a comforting thought as I faced the man who would wait for me at the bottom of those stairs—the man who instilled such a revulsion that I felt nauseous.

"Please do come back in." I called, smoothing my shift, as if I had not just done something odd at all.

Miss Pennington shut the door quietly behind her and clasped her hands together with delight when she saw what I held in my hands.

"Why, Lady MacRae, this is such a lovely idea! The royals will want to wear such feathers in their hair by the morrow!"

She took a dainty silver chain circlet from her box and looped the pendant through it. She placed it atop my head and centred the amber gemstone to the middle of my forehead along the hairline. Then, she clipped the feathers together with a silver wing-shaped pin and secured them to the locks that were swept up from the right side of my face. Angled upwards, just above my hair, the feathers looked as though they were a part of me.

Standing there in my simple white shift and bare feet, with my hair cascading down my back, I felt like a creature from another world. I had always hoped that Nanny would have been here for my betrothal, and for my wedding day. To tell me what to expect and share in my joy. This was not a joyous occasion. The small girl within me had hoped someone would help me escape from this nightmare, like the knights in shining armour from the fabled courts of King Arthur. Even my beloved MacKenzie's had warned me that today's events could not be prevented. Today would hold no rescue for me.

Looking down at the newly created lilac and lavender perfume which Mr Cameron had requested, nay demanded, I realized I could not wear it. Not only because it caused me to sneeze far too often, but without my signature fragrance, I felt disconnected from the mother I wished was by my side today. The scent was my own, my signature, and I realized that if I changed it, I would not be true to myself. Another act of defiance.

It was now Mrs. Driscoll's turn to complete the transformation. She and her assistant traded places with Mrs. Pennington whose work was done. The mirrors remained draped in sheets and the blindfold was carefully placed back over my eyes while protecting my newly coiffed hair. It would be nearly an hour—fixing layers upon layers of petticoats around my waist, fitting and lacing the corset that had been fashioned for just this occasion, fastening the dress and its bustles, sleeves, skirts to my frame—until the ensemble was complete. All the while, taking much care to not interfere with my delicate coiffure.

"Well, Lady MacRae, I must say the final result is more dazzling than I thought," Mrs. Driscoll exclaimed.

Roderick was knocking at my door, ready to escort me to the top of the grand staircase for my grand entrance. He halted his entry into my room, his mouth opening and closing, but no sound coming out.

"Thank you Mrs. Driscoll," he finally said. "Please make your way to the gathering along with Miss Pennington, and we will be at the stairs presently."

She left with a quick curtsey for him, and a smile for me.

"Oh lass," he began, speaking in his thick Scottish brogue. "I dinna ken what to say. If only my mother could ha' been here to see ye right now. There are no words to describe the beauty which stands before me. I'm sorry that today, which should be yer happy day, is instead a day of dread. Kenneth and I wouldna ha' allowed this to happen if John had chosen to consult wi' us first."

He placed a gentle kiss on top my head, then pulled back abruptly. As if something had stung him.

"Where did you get that?" He pointed to the pendant nestled along the crown of my head. "I dinna recall having seen ye wear that before."

He leaned down and inhaled deeply, just above the feathers.

"Oh, it was tucked away in one of the jewelry boxes." I hoped he wouldn't recognize this for the lie that it was. "I cannot recall from where."

"Do ye not?" he paused for a moment.

It was not until we reached the top of the stairs that I was greeted by the hallway mirror. In it stood a stranger wearing a dress that reached to the floor in a cascading waterfall of black satin and deep ruby silk. Tasteful bustles alongside each of my thighs revealed the black petticoats underneath. Along the edges of the rich material of the dress, black velvet and silver roses had been embroidered, and in the centre of the corset was a delicately placed rose made out of sparkling crystals. Bursting from it were lines of more crystals that looked like shooting stars. The corset reached higher along the bosom than the current fashion, which afforded me some modesty. The sleeves did not begin at the edges of my shoulders, as was the style, but instead were held secure just next to my collarbones. This created an elegant square neckline which was in contrast to the rounded designs being worn at court, and rather than billowing sleeves that drowned my petite frame, the narrow lines extended into beautiful tear drops that gave the illusion of long willowy arms.

Tonight, with my hair pulled regally away from my face, creating a halo of vibrant red around my face, my skin had a porcelain glow which was only enhanced by the candlelight. I had insisted on no powders or rouges for my face. I could not bear the feel of the harsh creams and powders that always felt like someone was trying to melt the skin from my bones. Wearing red lip stain was also another fashion I did not have to follow, as my own lips had a natural deep red hue to them. I leaned my head to the right and tried a smile. I turned to the side to discover that the dress moved as if it had a life of its own. Even when I stopped moving, the fabric with all its exquisite embroidery kept shimmering.

Hearing Roderick clear his throat, I knew it was time. He took my arm and led me to the top of the stairs. He would stand out of sight, and I was to walk down the steps alone and be announced by my father to those gathered below. I was to be presented like a valuable painting. Or livestock. A prize won in some dastardly contest.

"May I present my daughter…" My father's voice boomed over the crowd. "…the future Mrs. William Cameron!"

I froze.

He had not even used my name! I was a MacRae, yet he had not even acknowledged my heritage in front of everyone in attendance.

Roderick took a step towards me, still out of sight, but his assuring presence helped give my pause comfort.

"Lady M, I now recall where I saw a pendant like before." he whispered, as I stood just out of sight of the crowd gathered below at top of the staircase. "—The same was worn around your mother's neck the night she gave birth to you."

How was that even possible? My mind raced and I nearly panicked.

"My daughter…" hearing my father's voice above the murmurs of the crowd, caught me short.

I took a slow breath, gathering all my wits about me, and prepared to make my descent. My shoes had only just arrived that day and were a higher heel than I was accustomed. As I lifted the edges of my dress to avoid any potential mishaps where I might trip on the length, I saw that the black velvet material was accented by the same silver bursts of crystals and created a marvellous display of shimmer as I walked. As the guests applauded my grand entrance, my eyes found my father and Mr Cameron.

Father clenched his jaw, his face turning beet red. I knew he was furious. Next to him was William Cameron; wearing the very pale shade of the blue he had demanded for my dress. With a cream vest, stockings and matching blue shoes. He had chosen my colours to suit him and allow him to present a matched pair to the public—and there I stood in direct contrast to his pale colours. Rich, dark and vivid tones.

Fighting the urge to turn around and run up the stairs into Roderick's arms, I found myself counting each step I descended. Half way to the bottom I paused to allow the guests to view the bride-to-be and for me to feel a brief moment of respite. I was delaying the inevitable touch of Mr. Cameron as he would take my hand to lead me onto the main floor. Searching through the crowd, somewhere in the sea of the guests, I hoped to find a friendly face—Kenneth perhaps.

Nothing could have prepared me for the man in the crowd that caught my glance. In an ocean of pastels, corals and blues, he was unmistakable. There—standing at the back, near the front door. It was *him*. The man from the rooftops. The man from my dreams. Here, standing in my father's house. He was dressed in the same shades of black and red as my own. His crimson vest embroidered with black roses. We were a matched pair. The hat with a rich red satin ribbon around the base in the same shade of crimson red as my dress, and—as always—the brim pulled low to keep his face in the shadows. He lifted his face.

Our eyes met, and the fear I once felt dissolved into something I could not have anticipated. Hope. The stranger tipped his hat and he smirked while holding my gaze, just as he had in my dreams.

Time held its breath, or was it me?

CHAPTER 7

Among the rippling whispers of my appearance floating through the crowd, was Mr. Cameron—waiting for me at the bottom of the stairs. The last few steps were agonizing, and all too soon, he grabbed my hand and trapped it in the crook of his elbow as he led me to the centre of the room, clenching my fingers in a grip so tight I had to blink back tears.

"Distinguished guests, Lords and Ladies, I am honoured that you have chosen to attend this joyous event and share in our happiness!" Mr Cameron declared boisterously to the room. "My future bride and I stand before you humbled and grateful. We are pleased to announce that our nuptials will take place this coming Christmas. May I present, my betrothed, my beautiful Mrs William Cameron!"

No one had said my name yet!

He pulled me forward. I curtsied and tried to catch another glimpse of the stranger. Alas, height was not either of my parent's gifts, so my eyes searched the crowd in vain. Then, Mr Cameron forced me into his embrace. His lips collided with mine, the sour stench of rotting meat, stale whiskey and ale overwhelming. I pressed my lips closed, denying the invasion of his tongue, despite his repeated attempts to force my mouth open. The crowd began to murmur at this most improper gesture, but he did not cease his attempts.

The moment was disrupted by a loud clattering heard from the entrance, startling everyone present and snapped Mr Cameron back to his senses. Father looked concerned for a moment, but that too passed far too quickly. Then I saw Mary with a broom, silently admonishing one of the maids which explained the welcome disruption. Yet, just beyond Mary, in the shadows of one of the balcony window archways, stood the stranger. He met my glance and winked at me.

"We would be honoured if you would join us for our celebratory feast…" I heard father announcing to the crowd. "…and, of course, what you have all been waiting for. The dancing!"

"Alas, I must beg your indulgence everyone." Mr Cameron bellowed. "I would like to present my betrothed with the gift of a family heirloom."

Our guests paused, puzzled at the disruption of protocol, and turned towards my father to gauge his reaction. Normally, these gestures were saved for after the final course of the meal and before the dancing. Lord John MacRae, stood silently, neither approving nor disapproving.

Leering over me, he held up a brooch. Cream coloured pearls, and a pale blue stone at the centre. And clearly not matching my outfit.

"You are now my property." He muttered under his breath, threateningly.

As he maneuvered the pin to my bosom, he pushed the needle deep into my corset…and through to my skin, causing me to wince in pain.

I did not give him the satisfaction of hearing me cry out. The dark colours of my dress helping to conceal the pin prick. But it did not go unnoticed by those standing close to us —he had drawn blood.

Mr Cameron then led me to the dining hall like a dog on a leash. It was all I could do to look around with a frozen smile. Our grand hall had been transformed. The opulent royal blue curtains had been drawn back to reveal the glow of the metal lanterns outside, and windows had been opened to ensure air flow would not become an issue with such a large gathering. Our family boasted one of the most ornately carved dark oak wood dining tables in London, and the sheer size of it had required all four of the MacKenzie's to bring it out of storage from one of the other barns. I was seated between my father, on my left, and Mr. Cameron, to my right. Looking up and down the length of the large table, I could not see the stranger. Turning every which possible way, to look around at the other tables, which had been arranged around the room in a large horseshoe shape for the other guests, I could not catch sight of him anywhere. My imagination must have been playing tricks on me, or perhaps it was wishful thinking. I glanced up from my plate to see Kenneth and Roderick at the opposite end of the hall which led back to the front foyer. Even from this distance I could tell they were arguing, and the only word I could discern was *neapaigear*. Handkerchief.

I barely managed to eat a single bite. The venison stew was too salty, the main course of roasted pig was too cold, and even the sweet shortbread tasted sour to my palate. The guests close enough for me to hear were only uttering words of praise for the wonderful flavours and delicacies. Meanwhile my betrothed continued to devour every morsel put in front of him as if he were starving. Frothing at the mouth, like a rabid badger. And I was expected to share the same bed with this man in just a few short months. Nothing could have made me shrink further into myself, or so I thought.

"Well, my little bride to be," he growled into my ear. "I cannot wait to burn that dress. Rest assured not a piece of that dress stays intact. And on our wedding night, I promise you I shall not be gentle."

My fork clattered loudly onto my plate, and I looked straight ahead. Roderick and Kenneth, who were now standing on the other side of the table near the door, saw my shocked face. They returned my glance, as if they knew, as if they too had heard. They nodded towards me, offering acknowledgement, and my heart lifted ever so slightly. Taking a deep breath, I chose not to allow Mr. Cameron to see any weakness. I picked my fork back up, as if nothing had happened, and forced a few morsels of the roasted potatoes into my mouth. Praying that my stomach would not betray me by returning the food back onto my plate. I did this again and again. Finally, Father wiped his mouth, stood up from his seat.

"What a most delicious evening, each course better than the last! My compliments to the chef." He bowed towards the large man standing at the doorway, and the guest joined him by clapping to show their appreciation. "It is now time to leave the dining area, and to mingle for a short while, while the tables and chairs are removed and we allow the musicians to set up for a night of dancing."

As we exited the hall, Mr. Cameron had not once let go of his iron grip on my arm and it was starting to pain me. I was overwhelmed with all the women who approached me to congratulate me on my betrothal and make cooing noises at my heirloom brooch. No one commented on the blood which had dried on the edges of my corset. All I could do was say thank you and nod. I had to keep my wits about me. He kept turning me away from any conversation I might have, so that I had to focus on my balance and prepare for the onslaught of toasts from the men who were in his vicinity.

Tradition dictated that the Lady and Lord of the house lead the guests in the first dance. Since I was mercifully still considered a MacRae, father gently freed my hand from Mr. Cameron's arm and guided us onto the dance floor. We waited for the musicians to begin. To all those watching us, nothing seemed amiss—simply a father and daughter opening the evening for dance. He and I had often danced together, at court and at our own gatherings here in the manor. Since he had never taken another wife, I held the role of Lady of the house. The musicians began the melody, and my father took me into his arms as he had done a thousand times before.

"Daughter, what possessed you to disregard your future husband 's requests tonight?" he asked as we began to dance, in perfect, practiced tandem. "You must recognize that such defiance is not an attractive trait in a wife. This is not how I raised you. I expected better."

"Father, if you are referring to my dress, the idea was the dressmaker's and the intent was ensure that my ensemble would be the most talked about of the season, and create a stir with the ladies of the courts." I said, tension gripping my spine with the strength of a lion. "And, if you insist on bringing up who raised me, I will in turn remind you that in that you had no hand. Nanny assumed that responsibility. Right up until you sent her back to the highlands. And even then, it was the MacKenzie's who spent the most time with me."

He had nothing to say in rebuttal. Several moments passed without further exchange. His silence was enough to tell me that he had not expected those words. And then the song finished, and he handed me over to Mr. Cameron who squeezed me so tightly, painfully, that I could not catch my breath. As we danced, it was clear he had no rhythm nor the knowledge of the dance steps, and so we stumbled and his heeled shoes often stepping onto my toes, purposefully. The rest of the guests surrounded us, everyone moved in time, a cruel paradox. The lovely pastels, roses, pinks, blues, and soft lavenders of their gowns and tails encircling my solitary black and red rose.

"You, devious little hussy!" He hissed into my ear. "Once we are married there will be no allowance for such tenacity. You will be my wife, my property and I will treat you as such."

His fingers plucked away at some of the crystals along the sleeve near my shoulder, all the while smiling at the guests. I kept my thoughts on the music. If I could last until the end of the song, I would then be partnered with the highest-ranking gentleman in attendance, as was custom. Lord Calvert, a grandfatherly man of nearly seventy, whom I had plenty of occasion to dance with in the past and much admired. Just then, a man tapped Mr. Cameron on the shoulder and in a deep, raspy voice said, "Excuse me. I will have the next dance with this exquisite beauty in your arms."

Mr Cameron's shocked expression, showed an ugliness and a rage that frightened me. But he was smart enough not to cause a scene with so many guests around.

"Soon enough, she won't be so exquisite anymore!" Mr. Cameron said, as he sneered and stormed off to fetch what I could only assume would be another glass of whiskey.

It was him. The tavern. The rooftops. It was him.

His strong hands held me, comfortingly. Against his vest of red and black rested a silver chain with a medallion, which was directly at my eye level and I could not help but notice the unusual style. The antiqued, rectangular pendant was engraved with the infinity sign and a snake winding through, and what appeared to be a staff underneath. My heart felt as if it would burst. He was not a figment of my imagination, nor a dream. He was touching me, holding me, and dancing with me, as if we had been dancing together for a lifetime.

I looked up to see his green eyes sparkle with mischief, matched by a smile that reminded me of a little boy who had just pilfered some cookies from a kitchen cabinet. I did not know his name or where he came from, but from the moment he held me in his arms I felt safer than I had in Mr Cameron's. Any fear that my mind tried to hold onto, was pushed away by my heart…and my body. But the danger of that moment, dancing with him while Mr Cameron watched, could not be understated.

When I tried to speak, he placed a finger on his lips. He reached into his vest pocket and pulled out my mother's handkerchief. "What? Who? How…did you get—." I stammered. He placed it in my hand discreetly, and closed my fingers around it, while continuing our dance. I could smell the ocean, the freedom of the seas, and the salty air all around him. I knew that scent.

"The feathers…those were you?" I was finding my words. "And the pendant… Roderick said he remembered my mother wearing it. Where did you get it? Who are you?"

He pulled me in closer.

"My Lady, I have lived a thousand lives, and I have hunted across time to find you." He murmured softly into my ear. "Now that I have caught your scent, I shall never lose you. Our bond has existed since the beginning of time. Always and forever. You are my heart, and I am yours eternally. You may call me Damian."

For a few precious moments, time stood still. I did not notice that he had not responded to my other questions, and his words of adoration had an unexplainable soothing effect on me. The musicians continued to play, but silence surrounded us. No one else existed. The coldness I felt when we first met returned, and it brought a chill down my spine. Yet, there was no malice in his eyes, nor was anger on his breath. I was drawn to him by some magnetizing, invisible force, and I was afraid if I closed my eyes, even for a tiny moment, he would be gone. *Was it possible to never blink?* He licked his lips and pulled me in just a bit closer. Both of us now breathing deeply, filled with desire I had never known, heat I could not justify, and something…unknown. I closed my eyes and imagined what those lips would taste like.

Suddenly, I became dizzy, as if I had spun in a thousand circles. I heard him sigh and our dance was immediately brought to a halt.

"Excuse me," my father said, standing behind us accompanied by Roderick. "I don't believe you are on the guest list. Mr. MacKenzie is here to escort you out."

Damian took a slow, deep breath, and a fierce expression darkened his visage, a response which surprised me and caused Roderick to square his shoulders. He would fight, if needed.

"My Lady, only with your permission will I take my leave." He bowed towards me, while still holding my hands, gently but firmly. Waiting for my approval to let go.

Father looked at me confused.

"I give you leave."

I uttered the words as neutrally possible, not daring to let anyone else know the range of emotions this man had stirred within me in such a short period of time. Damian released me and stepped away. The sense of loss was so overwhelming I nearly stumbled to my knees.

"Roderick, you are to ensure that this intruder leaves the premises immediately," Father said through gritted teeth.

"Lord John Alexander MacRae, you have been known to me for some time, through your wife, may the heavens accept her return," Damian said, turning to address my father. "A word of caution. If you choose to continue to have business dealing with Cameron, you will come to regret it. As for the absurd notion that your daughter will marry him, I would heed the counsel of your two brothers by bond. For if you do not, I will be the one to assure her safety."

"How dare you Sir—" my father flustered.

Damian bowed towards me and gave me a playful wink that my father could not see, and spun on his heels to head towards the front doors, with Roderick close on his heels.

Father took my hands and led me into the next dance, forcing us around the dance floor too fast, not at all in time with the music. There was no sign of Mr. Cameron.

"Who was that man?" he asked, agitated, angry. "How is he known to you? Was it your desire to have him kiss you? *Was it?* Answer me!"

Damian, I wanted to say, feeling utterly bereft. *Damian is his name, and yes, I would have kissed him.* When the music ended, my father pushed me unceremoniously toward the refreshment table. I was so very, very thirsty. Gulping down the water faster than was lady-like, I realized nothing on the table would quench my thirst. My body felt warm, from the inside out, and nothing was cooling me down. I caught sight of Mr. Cameron, standing silent across the hall. As if he were no more than a statue skulking in the shadows.

I was whisked onto the dance floor a few more times by several men of the gentry, before Roderick returned. Catching sight of me, he gave me his reassuring nod. Father mingled amongst the other Lords, and my betrothed kept his distance for the rest of the night, for which I was incredibly relieved.

After the party was over, and the guests were seen to their carriages, father bid me to his study before I could even change my attire. Mr. Cameron was looming behind the hefty oak desk wearing an expression so smug that I wanted to run from fear.

"Daughter, you will answer for your actions!" Father was yelling. "From this moment on, you are housebound until your wedding day! The only exception shall be the Abbey where you are to be examined for your virtue. You should be grateful that William has forgiven your actions and will still honour the betrothal."

I said nothing, as Father continued his rant of unintelligible disappointment of my actions and future punishments should I disobey again. If I had any hope of seeing Damian again, I would not speak. Eventually, Roderick came to escort me to my bedroom. His face was filled with sadness as he closed the door.

"Dinna worra lass, we will protect ye." he whispered reassuringly.

As I sat down preparing to disrobe from the elegant and heavy ensemble, I had a perilous thought, perhaps it was my intuition. I lifted my hand to touch the pendant that had been tucked into my hair. I felt it pulsating, as if there was life inside of it, with its very own little heartbeat. Warm. No sooner did I have it locked in my secret drawer when father burst through the door.

"I have spoken with Mr. Cameron and we have decided that those feathers and that pendant will be removed immediately from your possession."

My father was now a man possessed, tearing the feathers from my hair, having no concern that he tore hair from my very scalp as well. When he realized the pendant was not there, he grabbed my shoulders.

"Moireach MacRae, where is that pendant?" shoving me against the bed post. "Hand it over this instant!"

"Father… it must have fallen out during the dancing," I said, in between sobs. "It wasn't really meant to be worn in the hair."

He saw my mother's handkerchief on my vanity and walked over to it. He picked it up. He brought it up to his nose.

"That damn vanilla rose your mother wore," he muttered under his breath. "She was nothing but fire and rebellion. I should have known you would be just like her."

He turned his back to me and stood in front of the fireplace. I couldn't move fast enough to stop him before he threw the embroidered cloth, and the feathers, into the fire.

"No!" I screamed and ran to the hearth

I was too late. My mother's handkerchief was incinerated by the flames, its ashes had floated up the chimney and into the night sky. Father stormed out, and I heard the door lock behind me. I fell to my knees, blinded by the tears that were falling uncontrollably and the pain in my chest that threatened to split me in two. Just when I could no longer stand the anguish, I looked through my blurred vision to the fire once more.

The three feathers were still fully intact, not burnt to ash, instead glowing a vibrant orange, as if they were metal upon a blacksmith's anvil. I stood up, retrieved the tongs from beside the hearth, and pulled each feather from the flames. I laid them on the cold marble stone around the fire place and watched the orange glow darken as the feathers cooled down, slowly turning them into a dark silver sheen. Tears rolled off my cheeks and fell onto the feathers, creating a hissing sound with each drop, as the metal hardened. I stood up awestruck.

In shock, I began to undress. Struggling with the many laces and ties of the skirts, and then the layers of the sleeves., I started to cry again. As I pulled off the top garment around the corset, the damned brooch from Mr Cameron fell to the floor.

I came to a halt.

In revulsion and without further thoughts towards any consequences, I picked it up and walked to my balcony window. Opening the latch, my feet stepped onto the cold stone outside, I hurled it as far as I possibly could.

Left in nothing but the linen shift and the corset I could not wrestle out of without help, I gave up, crawled under the covers, and cried myself to sleep.

CHAPTER 8

The morning after the betrothal, no one came to take me to Sunday church and the manor was silent. The bedsheets were cold to the touch, and yet the air in my room was oppressive. I sat up slowly, giving myself a few moments to savour the warmth and safety of my bed, only to have that feeling fade away with each heartbeat. An icy draft blew in from the fireplace. Then another. It was then that I remembered the feathers, still sitting on the grey marble from the night before.

I crossed the room, my bare feet padding across the warm slivers of sun, to pick them up. A quiet gasp escaped my lips. No longer were they raven red, but now had turned to pewter. The feathers were heavy, dense, and to my surprise, sharp. One of the seemingly forged edges cut into my left palm, and I watched it draw blood. Despite the pain I did not cry out. The dull ache in my heart and the confusion that had settled into my soul created a numbness that even the physical pain did not penetrate. I stared at the ashes.

If only my mother's kerchief had survived.

I picked up the transformed feathers, placing them safely back into my secret drawer, and found an old cloth handkerchief to wrap around my hand to stop the flow of blood. The wound had start to sting, burn even, as I pulled on a simple gown over last nights corset and shift, not wanting to wait for the maid to come help me. I recalled the events of the night before, and the burning sensation got worse. Just then, I remembered the pendant. *Was it safe?* I tried to come up with a reason as to why my father would have wanted it so much. *Could he have remembered it from when my mother had worn it?* I wondered as I removed it from its hidden place. This morning its rich ruby colour had grown darker yet. Much darker. Any light that I may have thought it had was no longer there. No pulse. No heartbeat. Tenderly caressing the silver wings wrapped around the amber pendant with my fingertips, I remembered Damian.

Blood seeped from the wrapping around my hand and smeared onto the gemstone. I felt a vibration emanate from within the pendant and my wounded hand felt as if it were on fire. I put it back in the drawer, and removed the kerchief to tend to the painful incision. The balcony doors blew open, bursting forth with such force that I thought a freak storm must have appeared over London. I rushed across the room to close them, to prevent an onslaught of incoming rain, but instead, stopped short when I saw nothing but the sun shining. Shimmering and bright, as if mocking my sanity.

On the neighbouring rooftop of the church, stood Damian, his intense gaze fixed on my window. The wind blew against him, as if it wanted to pull him from the roof. His shirt was unbuttoned well below the collar bone revealing his pale skin, a stark contrast to the black shirt and coat he wore, and black markings along his skin. More elegant than the tattoos the sailors from the docks sported, but still deeply masculine. The blush in my cheeks burned with heat as I thought of what his skin might taste like along that delicate part of his chest. I wanted to run my fingertips across his flesh, to feel him, the outline of the muscles on his torso, his shoulders, just as I had in my dreams. A quiet inferno spread from my face slowly down my neck, as my eyes finally found his. Those captivating green eyes held a puzzling look of concern with a hint of… anger, which I didn't understand.

I stood at the edge of my balcony, forgetting the pain in my hand, trying to get a better look at his face, hoping to memorize every line, every nuance. He was upset, that much I could see. He took a step forward, and I watched his coat pulled by the current of air. As he tilted his head inquisitively, the wind abruptly changed direction and was returning back to me and with it came his voice, soft and gentle, but still heavy with that deep rasp that brought a chill of delight to my spine.

"What has happened, my sweet love?"

Dizziness enveloped me. I clutched the balcony railing to steady myself and winced as my bloodied, bandaged hand grabbed the iron bar. I could not keep coherent thoughts in my head when he was around. I had the best education available and demonstrated a knack for higher intelligence. I was no dimwitted woman. I was capable and logical. Yet, I couldn't find a clear thought in my head with a magnifying glass, and it was not just the lack of cogitation that bothered me, but the constant rush of heat to my face and throughout my body when I thought of him—or when he was near.

"You are hurt! Who has done this?"

His voice growled across with the wind.

"Answer me, Moireach! Who has harmed you?"

I couldn't think, I couldn't speak. I yearned to have his arms around me once more. Each day my desire had became stronger and more powerful. *What if the fire kept growing and didn't stop?*

I opened my mouth to speak, but no sound came out. I was on the verge of tears. My hurt hand pressed against the side of my head in distress and brought fresh fire to the wound. Pain brought fresh blood as I covered my face, while I sobbed. I felt a fool, and turned my back to the window and the wind. Tears of anguish, confusion and frustration swam with the blood upon my skin.

"Words of protection be dammed, if you will not answer me, I will come to you!" his roaring voice carried by the wind. *"You better move your stubborn arse out of the way!"*

I turned just as he leapt across the precipitous pitch of the steeple and jumped. Surely, to his death. Yet, the wind caught underneath his long coat and carried him across its currents, as if he was weightless. I saw a flash of raven-red feathers as he liberated a wingspan that stretched beyond twelve feet from beneath his coat. Gliding toward me with such precision that I knew he would land on the balcony in the very same spot in which I stood.

Without a moment to spare, my feet obeyed my instincts and I stepped back inside my room just as he landed on the edge of my window sill followed by a wind that was as cold and biting as winter.

"Now, will you tell me what has happened?" Damian growled, his wings hanging over my balcony. "Why is there blood everywhere? Who has done this?"

I looked up at him. He reached out for me, but stopped, as if he was hurt.

"Moireach, I cannot come any further," he said, trying to hide a grimace. "The words of protection have been placed all around. My medallion only offers so much safeguarding before I weaken."

"Words of what?" I said finding my voice somewhere inside.

"Please, I beg of all that is in the skies, tell me what has happened!"

My whole body began to tremble.

"I cut myself…on the feathers." I stammered. "The feathers… and last night the fire. Feathers like, like… yours? Why have they burned into metal? And what old words… placed where?"

I stepped further back into my bedroom, feeling my senses starting calibrate, and to register his raven-red *wings.*

"And… what *are* you?"

Damian let out a soft low chuckle, and I watched a smile turn up the corner of his lips. He beckoned me to step closer, which made me forget my wound and ache for his touch. My body burned, hot. I took timid steps towards him, the stone of the balcony colder than ever against my bare feet and the fiery pain in my hand now creeping past my elbow. My hand was now bleeding heavily through the cloth. He reached into his shirt pocket and pulled out a black velvet cloth. He lifted it to my face and began to wipe the blood from my cheeks and forehead. All the while, his eyes remained locked on mine. A deep sob ripped through my chest, and I hated myself for succumbing to an emotion so prevalent with my gender.

"Shhh, my sweet love, I am here now." He pulled me into his arms and closer to the edge of my balcony, as if I weighed nothing. "I have found you at last, and I will not lose you now. Take a deep breath and let me hold you."

A strange warmth wrapped itself around my shoulders and down my back. Not the embrace of his arms, like our dance, but now in the embrace of his wings. He had told me to breathe deep, but I couldn't breathe. With both of my hands firmly against his chest, I pushed him away. Though my lungs felt replenished by the space between us, the action brought a fresh sizzling pain to my wound, like that of searing meat.

He took my left hand from his shirt, turned it palm up and unwrapped the blood-soaked bandage, and we both looked down to my hand. The long cut across my palm was now the same jagged line as the scar on his cheek. And it would not stop bleeding.

"Moireach, may I hazard a guess that your father threw the feathers into the fire, along with your mother's handkerchief? You must answer me clearly now. Did you cut your hand with one of the feathers?"

"Yes, he did. He threw them into the flames, but I saved them… with the tongs. I left them on the hearth stones around the fireplace overnight, and this morning when I went to hide them… I… I had to hide them so Father would not find them."

Damian brought my palm up to his lips and kissed it. I did not understand what he was trying to do. With each kiss, a stabbing coldness penetrated my hand and reached all the way up my arm. When he finished, he looked up at me. There were traces of my blood around his lips.

"You are your mother's daughter," he said, as he wiped the traces of red liquid from his mouth with the edge of his sleeve.

There was an iciness that grew from the centre of my palm—so cold it burned. The blaze beneath my flesh became too much to bear.

"By the lightening that brought you into this world, Moireach, I have not hungered for anything more in my entire existence."

I started to cry out in pain. Without warning he placed his lips over mine. Stifling the sound, soothing the fire, the potency of his kiss blocked out all other sensations. My hand no longer hurt. Only a jagged silver line across my palm remained as evidence of what had happened.

"Damian, how did you know I was hurt?"

Free from his lips, my logical mind had finally found its footing.

"My sweet love, there is so much I want to tell you, but now is not the time. What I will tell you is that the pendant you wore last night belonged to your mother, and came into my possession after her death. It was made by someone we both called family. When your blood came into contact with the pendant, it sent out a ripple across the wind and found me. I will always find you."

And with those words, illogically, my world was whole again.

"Lady M? Moireach?"

Roderick was rapping on my door.

"We need to speak with you urgently. Kenneth and I."

I rushed towards the door for fear they would discover my winged saviour in my bedchambers. But then, unsure of what to do, I hesitated, and spun back around to Damian. I found nothing but at an empty balcony. The blood soaked handkerchief was also gone.

"What is it?"

I opened the door to let Roderick and Kenneth inside my room.

"Why was I not called to church?" I said, as I peered down the hallway to make sure that none of the servants witnessed their entry. They were trusted friends—as close as blood family—but I knew that recent events would put everything into question. Having two men in my room would be more than frowned upon.

"Roderick?"

He offered no explanation and headed straight to my balcony window.

"The man who was escorted out last night…" Kenneth spoke.

"Yes?"

"He has a name?" His voice was stern, insistent.

"Damian." I whispered.

There were some secrets I would certainly keep, but his name was something I could share.

"I followed him, Damian, last night, after Roderick escorted him to the front gates. He had gone nearly three streets away from the house before turning down the alley that leads to the park." Kenneth, leaned against the chaise by the window. "Now ye ken I've never lost a quarry in all my life, but when he turned the corner there was no one in sight. The only way I coulda lost him was if this Damian ran wi's the speed o' a greyhound. Even so I woulda heard his fleeing on the cobblestones."

He paused, and waited for me to process.

"Then I heard soft footsteps on the roof—above me! I looked up to see the man I had been following."

"What happened then?" I asked, almost giddy. "Did you climb the roof?"

"Nae, Damian stepped off the edge o' the roof and vanished. Like a cat. I sprinted from the park and back to the alleyway, but there was no sign o' him. No sound, no footfalls from the rooftops, no clues. As I stood there, wondering what to do next, a short, round man appeared from around the corner o' the same building. He had sweat on his brow and was panting heavily. I took a step back against the ivy-covered walls and effectively disappeared into the foliage. The panting man ran past me, thankfully oblivious to my presence."

He then rose to feet.

"It was Mr Pimms! Mr. Cameron's personal assistant, the same man whom ye've seen conspiring with Mary."

I took a few steps back and sat on the edge of my bed, giving my full attention to what Kenneth was revealing.

"He, too, was looking this way and that, surveying the rooftops, uttering words not fit to repeat around a lady. Then, he just walked away."

I pulled the blanket from my bed around my body, still wearing nothing but the shift and corset from the night before. The chill had crept back into the room. Kenneth went to my bedroom door to look down the hallway. He was on guard. Something dangerous was coming our way, he had said yesterday. They could both sense it. Even so I could not stop my thoughts of the man who had already called me his love. Damian was now being tracked by two men—Mr. Pimms and Kenneth.

"Lady M, yer father was called away to Dover on urgent business last night." Roderick said, as he remained surveying the grounds and the rooftops through the open window. "Mr. Pimms arrived at an ungodly hour to relay a letter that John was to accompany Mr. Cameron without delay. I was not woken to join them, and Connor and Duncan, posted at the gates last night, were told not to question their Lord's will in this matter. And, Lady M, he didna ha' his proper Sunday breakfast, nor did he leave Mary with any instructions."

"Most unlike him." The idea that my father was travelling alone with a man that I already reviled, along with his concerning history, terrified me. Everything, lately, was contrary to him. "He's never not shared his travel plans with you, Roderick. What is happening?"

Roderick and Kenneth exchanged a look. Kenneth stepped away from the door, the coast being clear, walked over to me and crossed his arms over his massive chest.

"Lass, last night… the man, Damian, ye came to dance wi' approached me outside beforehand, in the polite way o' the gentry, and showed me yer mother's handkerchief. He asked for a chance to return it to its owner directly."

This last revelation surprised me, and I looked candidly at him.

"Kenneth, I have known you all my life. I trust you would not have granted access to anyone that you felt would be a threat toward my person."

"I allowed him entry. He didna feel like a threat, nor did he smell like a threat. And believe me, my nose has a talent for sniffing oot the threats. In fact, there was a familiarity about him… one I still canna place."

Learning that Damian had known to bring my mother's kerchief to them, not Father caused me pause.

"Speaking o' sniffing out threats, why do I smell blood?" Roderick questioned me, walking over closer to the balcony.

"Oh, I accidentally cut my hand on the windowsill ledge while leaning out." I hoped he would not hear the unease in my voice.

Turning towards me, his shoulders sagged, it was as if he was carrying a heavy burden. His role as our protector is one in which he had never failed, but I could see that last night had cast a shadow of doubt over him. Somehow he felt that he had failed.

"Well, MacKenzie's, there is nothing we can do right now." I said. "But do not think for one moment that I intend to be agreeable to this entire affair of events. Shall we attempt to keep a sense of normalcy around the house, so that we can leverage any knowledge gleaned from our household?"

"Aye, ye have our word."

They went downstairs to check with Mary on the preparations for the midday meal. I finished dressing for the day, with the support of my maid, deciding on a simple green gown with gold embroidery, before meeting them in the kitchens. My concern for my father weighed heavily on me.

Not long after, the three of us sat at the large dining table, well into our second helping of eggs, bread and the men with their porridge. To my relief my appetite had returned, and I was able to savour the flavours of every bite. Just when I started to feel at ease, a disturbance at the gates startled us all.

"Stay wi' the lass, brother." Roderick leapt from his chair, and his long legs took him outside faster than any of us. Kenneth and I made our way to the windows overlooking the courtyard.

"Kenneth, can you see anything?"

He had positioned himself near kitchen door with a better view, but also effectively barring any possibility of someone coming through without first having to answer to him.

"Lady M, it looks like our cousin Michael but hold just a moment more. I am waiting for Roderick to signal that it's safe to join him outside."

Coming up through the gates was a single horse with a rider practically falling off the beast. After a few anxious moments, Roderick turned towards the window and gave his brother a nod accompanied by the hand gesture that gave the all clear. Stepping into the sunshine, we were shocked to see the state of the horse and the rider. The man was near collapsing, as was his horse, both from exhaustion. Connor and Duncan, who had granted the access to our estate, jogged up behind.

"Michael! What have ye done wi' Sage?"

Kenneth's first concern was for the welfare of the horse. Sage was panting and covered in a sheen of sweat, clearly favouring one leg.

"Kenneth, I'm verra sorry but it couldna be helped…" Michael said, barely able to get the words out before he did finally fall off the horse, but thankfully into Roderick's waiting arms. "I knew… I knew I had to arrive in time to—"

"—Brother, I'll take the horse to the stable, while ye bring Michael inside and find out exactly what has happened," Kenneth said. "Connor, go wi' them, and Duncan, return to yer post. Keep a watchful eye, make sure he wasna followed."

Efficient as always, the copper haired twin spun on his heels and headed straight back to the front gates. Once inside, Roderick directed Connor to stand by the kitchen door leading into the house. There he stood and confirmed that no one was eavesdropping. I brought a jug of water to the youngest of the MacKenzie's.

"Michael, seat yourself, and here, drink, and please help yourself to as much food as you can possibly manage."

Michael rarely had the opportunity to eat in the house with the family, therefore my invitation to indulge caused him to turn a strange shade of red and trip over the side of the chair. I could not help but burst into a fit of giggles, which seemed to cause him more embarrassment. I realized I better calm down before I frightened this young man, not yet fifteen years of age. I sat down and looked encouragingly at him. He must have ridden fast and hard in order to arrive in such a state.

"Lady MacRae, I thank ye kindly for yer offer, and will gladly eat the food," Michael said, once he gained his composure. "But please dinna ask me to sit down. Exhausted as I am, I would rather lay in my bed than sit down. I ha' been on a horse more in the last week than I ha' been off a horse and if I can be frank?" He looked around at Roderick, who nodded his approval, "…me arse is likely to fall off from the numbness. So, if ye please, I will stand at kitchen counter and eat until feeling returns to ma nether regions."

The whole of us burst into laughter for a moment. We were all eager for the news he had brought, but decided to take into consideration that Michael had likely not slept nor eaten properly since he left. Kenneth, having tended to the Sage, relieved that she was already recovering, had joined us again. We waited, and after what seemed like an eternity, Michael drank the last drop of water and was ready to share.

"Roderick, Kenneth, Lady MacRae, Gwenyver is doing well and was glad to receive your letter." Michael started very formal. "She has been having strange dreams, and when I arrived, I coulda sworn she was already expecting me. She bid me give ye these letters and was verra specific that ye should each read them in privacy. Dinna share any o' the information contained therein to anyone. Not even to each other."

He reached into his saddlebag, withdrew a small leather-bound book, and handed it to me. It was a faded shade of ivory with gold and red filigree etching, tied shut with a brown leather chord. Upon the cover, was a raven-red feather with a white streak down the left side and edges made of pewter that had been melded into the leather. There was no mistaking its similarity. It was like those Damian had left with me. I slid out the small piece of parchment, sealed with a wax stamp bearing the Clan MacKenzie crest, and had been secured beneath the leather strap.

For Moireach.

My breath caught in my throat.

"Lady MacRae, Gwenyver requested ye be alone when ye read what ye now hold." Michael said, again.

Stunned. Speechless, and as if in a trance, I walked outside, alone, and to the gardens, clutching the book close to my chest. There was an aroma about it—a mustiness enveloped in rose oil, vanilla flower, and something else. Not coconut, but something else. Not too sweet, almost foreign. Unknown. I sat on the stone bench, the one carved with flowers, fairy creatures, and the silly gnome with the crooked nose. I came here often as a child, for beneath the massive canopy of the oak tree, there was refuge. My fingers shook as I opened the small piece of folded paper.

My darling Daughter of My Heart -

This journal belonged to your mother. She began writing in it on the very day she knew she carried you inside her. She made me promise to keep it safe until the day arrived that you would need to know where she came from and the world you are a part of. I had hoped to never see this day. Alas, it is time. Listen to your heart. Trust my sons. We shall see each other sooner than you may think.

Your mother of the heart,

~ Nanny Gwenyver

Oh, and would you please remind my sons that I am not getting any younger and they are past due for giving this old woman the grandchildren she is meant to have.

I almost dropped the journal, my grip weakened for a moment from the shock. Forgotten was the loss of my mother's handkerchief. She once held *this* in her hands. *Written in her own hand.* Slowly unwrapping the chord, I tucked Nanny's note inside the book. I stroked the feather with my thumb, its sharp metal edges firmly embedded into the leather of the journal. This feather was a brighter red than that of Damian's with that strange white pattern across the side. I opened the journal, to find words written in garnet ink. I began to read and before long tears slid freely down my cheeks.

To my beloved daughter,

My heart aches knowing I will not see you grow up into the powerful, courageous and beautiful lady I know you are destined to become. I ask your patience and beg forgiveness for what you will learn in these pages. Know that my love, my strength and all that I am will always be a part of you.

Your loving mother,
Seraphina

In my eagerness, and excitement, I turned the page. I would have to exercise caution. No one could see me read it, or know I had it in my possession, especially father. After the recent few days, I feared his reaction. I would have to devour the words in those rare moments when I could find privacy. I looked around the garden. For now, I would keep reading…

My darling child, today I felt you within my body and I knew that my life would change forever. I asked Gwenyver to bring me this book so that I could begin to write my story for you. So many secrets, lies and hiding in the shadows blur the visions, but I know that by bringing you into this world, I will change the balance forever.

I have always been known as Seraphina, yet when I met your father, I chose to call myself Isabella, after one of his great-grandmothers. Your father has shown me a life I never knew possible. He was just a young lad of fifteen, when he rescued me from the fires of the storm, nursed me back from the brink of death. He sheltered me from the clutches of those that would seek to end my life. The last nine years with

John have been wonderful. I had always known he wanted children but I had thought it was not possible for such a one as me.

But I am getting carried away again; I need to start at the beginning for you. But which one? When did my life begin? When John found me in the fires of the storm? When I felt you within my body? Or did my life begin in a time before time, when my kind watched the earth from the heavens?

I beg your forgiveness if my story is not in order and if I jump from time to time. There is simply so much to share. My thoughts are confused, on where to start and what to share and when. I know that the first thing you must know, if all else fails, is that one day HE will find you.

This morning when I felt your life within me, I walked along the loch with Gwenyver and told her everything. She has promised that she would ensure that her sons would know of our secret and that they would be strong enough to protect you. You will have the protection of all of Clan MacKenzie. The day I know will come, the day the search for his prey will end and the hunt will begin…

Of our kind, I will share more later but for now you must understand that we have lived longer than time itself, and as such we have knowledge and abilities you cannot yet imagine. I chose the highlands, because I knew one of my sisters had spent time there, and had found sanctuary. It was on the cliffs where your father found me during the fire storm of my devising. Having survived a battle with another, my wounds were severe. To protect myself from further discovery, I created the most powerful shield known to my kind, I lost consciousness and suffered the reopening of old wounds. I was close to death when John found me. Yet, even now nine years later, I still feel the drain and loss of my energy, and fear for your future. For now, I am comforted knowing that none of the others of my kind will know of your birth. I dread what your life may become in your twentieth year, for by then I know the strength of my blood will have waned. My kind will be able to sense your presence across the lands.

You must be watchful for him. He may appear as someone you can trust, but you must listen to your heart. He bears marks on his neck and along his collarbones.

Your birth will herald a change in the hunt, but how I do not yet know. Tonight I shall sleep with the love of a thousand suns in my heart simply knowing you are coming.

I closed the journal.

My mother had not been human!

Though she had not revealed what kind of being she was, only that her kind lived in the heavens. The feather must have been hers, a winged being like Damian. I had to pause and close my eyes, to recall the night I danced in his arms. I had been too distracted. My memory could only grasp at the moment he was with me on the balcony, healing me. Damian had a mark on the right side of his neck, black streaks that barely peaked above his collar. I had overlooked it, thinking it was possibly a tattoo, like those of the sailors on the docks. My life had changed with his arrival and despite the puzzling chill, I felt safe with him. *Could he be the Hunter?*

"Lady MacRae," Mary barked at me from behind. "Your father left quite suddenly this morning, and I am not sure what instructions have been given."

And with that my day turned into a haze of activities that did not allow me any further thought or even moments of privacy to read more of my mother's journal. Yet, throughout the day, I felt the comforting weight of the journal against my thigh. By chance I had chosen the one dress, with a simple skirt that had a pocket along the side, fairly hidden. I had secreted the pendant there as well, and now my mother's journal shared that space.

When night came, I was determined to convince Kenneth to take me out so that I could dance one more time. Father's orders of house arrest still echoed in my ears, yet I knew in my heart that I needed to move, to lift my legs and allow myself to be swept away by the music. With Father and Mr. Cameron out of town, this might be my last chance for such an escape. I felt caged, trapped…like a wild animal.

Making sure that I followed all the normal habits, routines and tasks of a Sunday, to rouse no suspicion with Mary and also to keep myself occupied and distracted. The hours passed far quicker than I had thought and I found myself sitting in my room after supper. That is when the frustration rose to the surface again. I needed to move. I needed to feel free.

I took the dress, corset and petticoat, the ones I wore for only these occasions, from the closet. I dressed quickly and stood before the mirror—very critical of my reflection. I had seen beautiful women in London and never considered myself one of them. My colour, shape, and size produced such an odd result that I had never considered myself attractive. My hair was unique in colour, but as of late I had noticed strands of pure white. Any respectable young lady would pull out the moment she saw them, but not me. My eyes, also a strange colour, not brown nor hazel but a deep amber that were framed by ebony eyebrows. My pale complexion was the canvas for the freckles sprinkled across my nose and cheeks, and my lips were full with a pronounced cupids bow, almost too big for my face. Yet now knowing that my mother was something not human was perhaps the reason behind my peculiarity. I pulled the cloak up around my shoulders.

Making my way down the stairs as quietly as possible, avoiding the hallway leading to the servants quarters, I headed towards the stables where I knew Kenneth would be spending time with the horses. One look at me, and he knew.

"Lady M, are ye sure ye want to go oot tonight?"

Kenneth stood up, wiping his hands on the cloth tied around his waist.

"May I ask you something?"

"Of course, Lady M, anything,"

"Kenneth, you have known me since birth. You knew my mother, although you never speak of her. Do I resemble her in any way?"

"Everyday I ha' watched ye grow, I see a little of her in ye. Ye ha' her hair, down to the curls that bounce beside your ears. Ye ha' her eyes, the deep sherry amber surrounding the flecks in yer eyes, only hers were green compared to your gold. If ye coulda only seen her eyes. They were the gateways to a restless soul."

"Kenneth, Nanny sent me a journal, my mother's, of which I have only read the first page." I was determined to hear truth for a change. "I know she was different. Have *you* always known that?"

"Do ye ha' to ask me such things?" he shifted uncomfortably.

"If not now, when? What other time could there possibly be?"

"Verra well," Kenneth said, in a tone of resignation. "On the night ye were born, our mother called me and my brothers outside o' her bedchambers, Seraphina's. We were just young lads then, not quite men but no longer boys, except for wee Colin, all but a bairn of two-years-old. All three o' us stood in the hallway, hearing her screams as each lightning bolt struck the castle. Mother told us that night what she was."

I walked closer to him.

"Yer mother came to us on the night of a horrible storm o' fire, with lightning that threatened to rip the skies apart, and she left us on such a night, the night ye were born. *She was an angel.*

CHAPTER 9

Leaving the barn, I walked towards the carriage, wearing my simpler clothing to dance at the tavern, and paused. I remembered seeing Damian standing so confidently at the back of the crowd the night of the party, and I smiled. He had held me as if he never wanted to let me go. Dared I hope that tonight's adventure would reunite me with him?

"Lady M, please dinna take any more risks." By the time I reached the carriage door, Roderick had appeared from the shadows. "Kenneth and I want ye home, to protect ye here, but know we canna lock ye up as yer father wishes us to do."

"Thank you, Roderick." I said. "I feel trapped, my heart is racing. I will suffocate if I do not get out, even if for only a short time."

Letting out a sigh of resignation, he kissed the top of my head, offered his elbows graciously, and guided me inside.

The carriage ride took noticeably longer than our last excursion, and when we arrived, I saw that Kenneth had brought me to a new place. This did interfere with my hope of chancing into Damian. Since reading my mother's journal, my desire to see him again grew stronger, and I wanted to see the marks on his neck up close to determine if the threat she described was him. *Please don't let it be him, the Hunter.*

The unfamiliar tavern showed promise. I heard the fiddles, foot stomping, and laughter echoing through the night as we arrived.

"Let me go in first lass, and have a wee look around, aye?" Kenneth called through the window.

So I waited, for what felt like an eternity for his return —and permission. Looking up at the hanging sign above the doorway, I read the name, *The Cock & Bull.*

"Lass, let's go in." Kenneth opened the door, and helped me out. "Only this time no strangers, aye?"

Just inside the entry way, I paused to look around. The tavern boasted rich wood furnishings, and the largest silver tankard I had ever laid eyes on. Along the walls were paintings of great castle homes—Eilean Donan among them—and the heads of animals were mounted above the length of the bar, which really was quite standard. There was a bull, a buck, a boar, and a bear, but it was the head of a black wolf which frightened me. Enormous eyes glowing green, its sharp teeth bared, eternally ready to clench around its prey's helpless throat. But those eyes… they were almost… *human.*

Upon seeing the wolf, Kenneth stopped and reached out to rest his hand on my shoulder, barring me from going forward. He faced the creature's head and put his right hand over his heart, the same gesture I had seen MacKenzie's use in greeting each other.

"*Dhullah i síochåin fratretum mo pace dheartháir,*" he whispered under his breath towards the wolf head.

"What did you say, Kenneth?"

The words sounded Gaelic, but I was beginning to understand that there was an older language the MacKenzie's used.

"Lady M, I wished peace for him."

"For a wolf? Why? Whatever for?"

"I canna explain right now, Lady M," he grunted, "Remind me later, and I shall, alright?"

The tavern was filled with dozens of patrons from various ranks in society, registering by their clothes. Men and women dancing together with such abandon that I soon lost track of all thought and joined the melodic madness of the crowd. Time was always lost to me when I danced, and the liberation of no longer feeling trapped gave my legs strength to jump and kick higher. Sweat trickled down along my spine and between my breasts. It was exhilarating. Liberating. All of which came to a grinding halt when a coldness crept up my calves towards my thighs. My heart leapt. *Damian?* I spun around, looking in every direction, but did not see him. Only Kenneth, now standing before me.

"Moireach, leave now!" he said. "Go through the back, past the men's lavatory. Go up the alley way towards the—"

"—Kenneth, why? Whatever is—"

"—To the bridge, lass! No matter what happens, keep going until ye reach the other side. Michael is waiting. Dinna look behind ye or wait for me. Just go!"

"Michael? Why is Michael there? I pray you tell—"

"—NOW!"

He squared my shoulders and pushed me toward the back, where the small hallway led towards a black wooden door with green tinted glass. I had nearly reached it, when a group of drunken men stumbled out of the men's lavatory. One of them grasped my shoulders.

"Well…oh, what's yer name ya pretty…little…" he slurred. "How much does yer cost?"

"I'm not for sale!"

I kicked the heel of my boot into the man's shin, and to both of our surprise, it was hard enough to allow me past him and his companions. Once at the door, with my hand on the doorknob, I paused. I could feel the coldness creeping up from the ground and up along my legs, trying to freeze me where I stood. Glancing over my shoulder, I saw Kenneth arguing with someone while his large body barred the hallway, preventing the other person from coming through. The commotion was starting to draw a crowd.

"She is mine." As the crowd hushed, I heard the sneering, serpentine-like voice that had instigated the confrontation. "Stand aside before you join your brother on the wall."

It's not Damian!

Knowing it was not his voice, I decided that there was no time to ponder the threats uttered. The coldness grew unbearable, and it was still trying to constrict my legs. I feared I wouldn't be able to take another step if I did not leave now. The tavern door was heavy, and it took me three attempts to push it open. Outside, the alleyway was dark and damp, its cobble stones slick with moisture. Light from the street lamps struggled to shine through the mist coming up from the river, and everything was bathed in a foggy haze. To my left, a few hundred meters away, I saw the stairs that would lead me to the top of the bridge. I hesitated. Kenneth was still inside. I heard the shouts of angry men.

"Ye shall not ha' her! Yer grimy hands will just ha' to play wi' yer own shrivelled willy for amusement!" My guardian jeered at this unknown attacker.

"You think me foolish enough to allow your childish taunts to irritate me?"

The clamour of the crowd within rose, nearly drowning out the thudding sound of something big and heavy being thrown against a wall, a noise that was immediately followed by the grunting of a man in pain. I turned back to the bridge and ran, my heels kept stumbling between the cracks of the cobblestone. I heard the back door blasted off its hinges. I stopped, frozen. The splinters of wood clattered to the stones and looking back I saw bits of green glass glistening across the cobble stone street. Just then, a hefty and rotund man wearing a long, brown leather cape staggered out. He was holding his hand to his left eye, blood running down the side of his face, matting his dark blonde hair.

I feared it was Damian, despite the different voice, but when he stepped under the street lamp, I saw the rest of his face—dirty blonde locks that came down in straggles, bypassing a large nose with a deep wine hue, and a jaw of such proportions to have almost been comical were it not for the raging anger that distorted his features. There were dark black caverns where his eyes should have been, and he bore an uncanny resemblance to William—a younger and more crude version. The man kicked at the steel lamp post, and to my surprise, it crashed to the ground and oil from the lamp flowed freely, lighting a blaze in its path.

It was then that he saw me, staring at him, open mouthed. And I could scarcely move from the fear that gripped my body.

"Bloody hell," he wheezed. "Your man gave me a time about wanting to take you. Good lot that did him!"

Shocked into action, I ran for the bridge. I heard his footfalls closing in on me, the force of his gait shaking the ground underneath. The bridge was only steps away, when I felt the hot stink of his breath on my neck and his calloused hand snatched my wrist with such force that he lifted me from the ground, spinning me in mid air. I felt my shin hit the side of the stairs, tearing the skin. I began to bleed.

He forced my face within an inch of his grimace.

"You smell sweeter than anything I've ever tasted before. Shame I have to—"

Somehow, even in my panic, I had the wherewithal to remember the pendant I carried with me. My free hand found the inside of my pocket, and I grasped the gemstone. I squinted my eyes shut…*Damian*!

"What did you just do?" he grunted. "What was that?"

I opened my eyes to see a large hand coming towards my face, filthy and with blood ground deep underneath his fingernails. The size of it would have surely covered my entire face. The sound of heavy footsteps came from just behind that hand.

"She is not yours!"

Damian!

He grabbed my enraged attacker's wrist, his eyes ablaze with pure rage and disgust. Startled, my attacker loosened his grip and I was free. Tumbling to my knees, where I landed harshly, distracted my rescuer for only a moment.

Within seconds, the two shrugged off their leather capes, unleashing wings. Damian had saved me from… another…

"Moireach!" he grunted. "Get up those stairs now!"

I scrambled up the steps that led to the bridge, hearing the angels brawl grow louder with each blow and each bellow behind me. I found Michael waiting for me with a horse at the top.

"Thank the heavens ye are alright Lady MacRae!" He reached around my waist and lifted me onto the saddle. "I was further down the bridge, where Kenneth had told me to wait, but I heard the commotion and when the other horse ran off from fright, I knew there was not a moment to waste."

Safely on the bridge, I looked down to see the two men, nay, angels, engaged in a fierce fight. The unknown assailant hurled Damian against the base of the bridge. His impact knocked several stones loose, and we felt the columns shake underfoot. Still, the blow did not faze him. He grabbed the attacker by the lapels, lifted him off the ground, and pushed back with the force of a hundred bulls straight towards the river. The two then growled unintelligible sounds, as they hurtled down towards the water where both spread their wings simultaneously.

Although they were both angels, they could not have looked more different. Damian at least resembled a man. Whereas the viciousness and ghastly hygiene of the creature who had first attacked, had twisted his face into less than human and the manner in which he moved was more serpentine than man. The dark wings appeared tattered and were covered in muck, as were his pants.

Locked in combat, their wings had lifted their feet from the ground and a current of air blew in from the river sent them crashing through the windows of the bakery of Thomas Farriner. Only a few moments passed, before a large explosion shook the entire block of houses, and flames shattered through all the windows of the surrounding houses and buildings.

"DAMIAN!"

The scream was torn from my throat, as Michael tightened his grip around my waist and started our gallop home. As the fire spread rapidly through the streets, Michael spurred the horse onwards down the unfamiliar roads. It took all my strength not to fall off the horse, even with young Michael holding onto me. He had been given instructions not to take the most direct route, as a precaution against possible pursuers. When we arrived at our estates, Roderick stood at the gates, accompanied by two of the largest dogs I had ever seen, and the largest horse from our stables, his own named Dartanian. He looked from Michael to me.

"Where is Kenneth?"

"I dinna keen," Michael muttered. "Lady MacRae came running up the stairs on the bridge like the devil himself was after her, but she was alone."

"He made sure I got out of the tavern." I said, jumping down from the horse. "But I do not know what happened to him, after—."

"—That's not all cousin, if it wasna for that suicidal stranger who jumped off the bridge to land right behind the ox-shaped attacker, she wouldna ha' gotten away," Michael said. "The brute had seized our Lady MacRae and was about to do her harm."

"Lady M, get yerself to yer room right away." Roderick said, motioning me inside. "I must find my brother. Michael, no one passes these gates. Use the words my mother gave ye to protect the walls. And take Duncan here wi' ye."

Roderick jumped astride his horse and galloped through the gates, with one of the two guard dogs taking chase. *Duncan?* But there was no time to ponder the strange reference.

Grateful yet again for Mary's drinking, which ensured that she would not wake, I made my way up the stairs and into my room. After I changed into my night dress, I sat down to clean the cut on my shin when I heard the horse arrive outside —but no voices. I was frozen to my seat, terrified that Roderick had only brought back a body. Within moments, he came bursting through my door carrying Kenneth in his arms. Both of them covered in soot and ash.

"Roderick, why have you brought him to my bed chambers?" I asked, running over to him. "Should you not have taken him to the hospital, or the physician's house?"

Ignoring me, he placed his brother's body gently on my bed. I gasped, horrified to see Kenneth's body so pale through the torn and bloody shirt. I pulled back the cloth, which revealed a cut, a wound that barely sliced the surface of his skin.

"But Roderick… it's just a scratch."

"Lady M, his injuries are more severe than they appear." Roderick's voice was laced with panic. "Before he fainted, he said the Hunter cut him wi' a strange knife, shaped like a very large feather."

I felt like time stopped. Roderick glared at me intently. Searching.

"The wounds this weapon inflicts dinna heal. I canna stop the bleeding. Please, dinna let my brother die!"

There was nothing and no one who could help him. *Except Damian.* I reached into my secret pocket and pulled out the pendant.

"Please Damian," I said, looking out my window. "If you are still alive, I need you now!"

Roderick gave me a questioning look, and I showed him the pendant.

"Damian is the only one who can save Kenneth now." I looked directly at the man I had trusted all my life. "He is an angel if you haven't figured that out by now, like my mother, and like the attacker…and don't think for a moment I believe that you did not know. Assuming he is still alive to hear my call, I know he can save him."

Roderick nodded in understanding, and held Kenneth closer, while I kept my eyes towards the windows. Hoping that Damian was alive, not only to save my beloved MacKenzie… but for my own heart that could not deny the feelings he awoke within me.

* * *

We had been able to slow the flow of blood, but Kenneth had already lost so much on the journey from the tavern to our manor. At my insistence, we used the strongest brandy in the house to clean the wound, while he mumbled in that strange Gaelic dialect. When his brother shrugged his shoulder, as if he didn't understand the words, I knew better than to force the issue. Now was not the time.

"Lass, could ye manage a few moments on yer own wi' Kenneth?" Roderick asked. "I want to make sure Michael has said the old words o' protection properly, and check in wi' Connor and Duncan."

"Of course, I won't leave his side."

I paced around the bedside, dread filling my thoughts when even those were interrupted by Roderick's return. He was nearly as grey in colour as Kenneth. Both brothers with beads of moisture running from their brow down the side of their face. One was physically dying, and the other suffering from watching his brother's pain. I feared the worst. I could not bear the thought of Kenneth dying, yet, even in this moment my heart hoped for Damian.

"Roderick, it is possible that the man, I mean, the angel who answers to this pendant is dead." I stated flatly. "That the monster that attacked Kenneth also killed him."

"I canna guess if yer angel is alive or dead." Roderick's shoulders slumped. "What I do ken is that if he is alive and arrives here…well, Kenneth is my brother and I will sacrifice *anything* to help him but I willna break my oath."

We took turns offering Kenneth small sips of cold water and wiping his brow with a cool cloth to try and relieve his fever. Kenneth's skin had turned a lifeless porcelain, and despite our best efforts to slow down the flow of blood, it had not stopped. We would soon run out of linens to soak up the blood, and the small wash basin was overflowing. The sun had begun to rise, and with it, our hope was waning. The weight of the pendant in my skirt folds became heavier, and started to pulse. At first I thought it my imagination, but before long, it was an intense throbbing. Startled, I jumped from the bed, and pulled it out of the pocket and held it in my hand. Roderick looked up.

"Lass, what is it?"

I ran to the balcony to open the doors. When I looked out, I could see no one. My heart faltered.

"My sweet love." His voice carried across the wind, same as before. "Would you be so kind as to ask your giant to release the bindings around your bedroom, if he wants me to enter to help his brother?"

Roderick came to stand behind me, and placed his hands on both of my shoulders. This time I was not the only one who heard.

"Fallen One." Roderick looked straight at Damian, across the way, standing next to the stone angels on the steeple. "Before I release the bindings, I must ha' yer word that ye willna harm or take Moireach. I canna hand her over to one o' yer kind, despite my desperate need for ye to heal my brother."

"You have my word. Now, please let me save him before he bleeds out."

Roderick stepped around me, shielding me from the window. He used his hands to draw a large crescent moon in the empty space in front of the balcony, and started speaking in that same strange Gaelic language that Kenneth had been mumbling in his weakened state.

"Ishnael kleem fortidana malkiel solvo."

As the words left his lips, glowing embers of silver and blue light appeared in the places his hands had been drawing those curious symbols. When he finished, he took a step back and there was a small flash of silver blue light before Damian landed just inside my bedroom window. He curled his wings underneath him and with a small cold brush of air they disappeared. I had no time to process what had just happened.

"We are not even close to the New Moon that would help him regain his strength." he said, walking towards the bed, getting close enough to examine the thin red line across the ribs and the greyness of the flesh around it. "I will do what I can but will need your help. You must hold him completely still, no matter what happens."

He turned towards Roderick.

"Are you strong enough?"

"Aye, I will hold him, but if this is going to be as painful as I suspect, I will fetch Connor who is just outside the door."

"Are you strong enough—MacKenzie?" he asked, again.

"Damian!" I yelped. "What in heavens does the New Moon have to do with Kenneth regaining his strength? And…"

I wanted answers, but was so bewildered from all the events that I sat down on my vanity stool in stunned silence. I had enough wits about me to know that time was of the essence if we were to save Kenneth. My answers would have to wait.

"My sweet love, there are things you do not yet know about your protectors. Now is not the time or place, but I promise you that I shall tell you everything."

Roderick had returned with Connor.

"Good, with both of your strength, we can keep him still," Damian stated, bringing his attention back towards Kenneth. "Roderick, you sit up behind him with his shoulders against your chest. Hold his shoulders and arms steady. Connor was it? Stay at the bottom of the bed and hold those legs down."

Damian wasted no further time. He peeled off the remnants of Kenneth's shirt and now reached for the same cloth that we had used to wipe the wound clean. He sniffed it.

"Moireach, what is on this cloth? I smell more than blood. Is it—?"

"—It's Brandy, and it might seem unorthodox, but Nanny has always insisted on cleaning wounds with the strongest alcohol in the house to prevent inflammation."

"She has taught you well then. This might have been the reason he has not bled out sooner."

I watched the men take their posts around Kenneth. Damian was smaller than both of the MacKenzie's, yet that morning he seemed as if he was the giant in the room. My bed creaked loudly from the weight of these men. Damian leaned forward, and placed his lips carefully on the wound, and then moved along the gash, ensuring that no spot was missed. Each kiss, as it were, sent waves of pain through Kenneth who threatened to break free of Roderick's grasp. The wound began to seal, and Kenneth was shaking so badly that it took both men to hold him down. I sympathized, having known the burning of an angels' kiss on a cut from an angel's feather.

Without warning, Damian stood up and walked towards me with a deep growl emanating from his throat.

"Ye gave yer word! Connor, stop him!"

Roderick tried to jump out from underneath his position behind his brother's shoulders but was lodged further back than he realized. Damian, stumbled across the floor, falling at my feet as his knees buckled. He had fainted.

"I dinna think he is goin' anywhere." Connor stated matter of factly, looking down at the angel.

Roderick had finally untangled himself from out underneath Kenneth, walked over, and lifted Damian into his arms.

"Moireach, dinna tell me ma about this." he said, laying him down on my bed by Kenneth's side. "She would tan my hide if she kent I had allowed an angel in yer bed and next to my sleeping brother. Bloody Moon, I would never hear the end of it."

Roderick collapsed into the large arm chair, and I stared at the two grown men in my bed —one the size of a small horse.

"Lady MacRae…" Connor said walking over to me. "I will now take my leave. Duncan and I will watch over the grounds. Rest now, while you can."

"Thank you Connor."

I curled up on the chaise lounge alongside my balcony. I could not help feeling overcome with exhaustion. While Roderick stayed tense, eyeing the two men in the bed, I drifted to sleep. What seemed only mere moments later, I was awakened by a growling noise. It took us both several glances around the room to realize that the rumbling was coming from

Kenneth's stomach. It was loud enough to wake even the sleeping angel at his side.

"What the bloody lightening is that noise?" Damian shot up, looking confused, having obviously woken up in unaccustomed surroundings. "Are we under attack?"

Roderick and I had already begun quietly giggling, both from the hysterical relief we felt that Damian's healing had worked and the absurd sound coming from the sleeping MacKenzie on the bed. We could barely get the words out to tell Damian that no one was attacking—except possibly Kenneth's stomach.

"Would someone please tell me what is so funny that ye are ignoring the wounded invalid over here?"

Kenneth woke up to laughter, and as I raised my finger to point at his belly, it answered for me. He was so startled by the sound that he actually jumped half out of the bed and landed on his backside on the floor.

The relief I felt was indescribable and I stared in wonder at the three men, the three most unusual men.

That moment started a most unusual truce between the fallen angel who had already captured my heart in such a short period of time, and the brothers of Clan MacKenzie.

CHAPTER 10

As the sun rose, while the rest of the household was still sleep, I tip-toed down to the kitchen to scrounge some food for the three men in my bedroom and myself. There was bread, cheeses and sausages tucked away in the cold storage, along with a dozen boiled eggs. Carrying them in a wicker basket, I hoped it would be enough to curb their hunger.

I found Kenneth and Roderick huddled together, on the far edge of my bed, speaking in hushed tones. Damian was standing on my balcony, looking up into the sun, and taking deep breaths. He was the one worse for wear that morning. He had rolled up his sleeves of his navy blue shirt and his bare forearms bore a multitude of scars, small silver white lines similar to the one on his cheek. For the first time, I could see, entwined amongst the scars, black markings, tattoos that didn't make any sense. Wrapping around the curvatures of his muscles, they wound towards his neck and collarbone. Walking towards him, I put the wicker basket, on the bed, the food almost forgotten.

"Words of gratitude dinna seem enough for what ye've done for my brother." Roderick, reached Damian before I did, "But I ha' been wondering, since ye flew through the windows…how ha' ye been able to breach the words of protection we ha' placed around the manor and the grounds?"

"Ah yes, I was wondering when you would ask." he replied, faintly. "I was given a precious gift many years ago. This medallion I wear was presented to me by one George MacKenzie, your father I believe?"

Roderick stood at attention, and crossed the room to stand next to his brother again, who was still laying on the bed, leaving Damian's place on the balcony wide open for me to get closer.

"What on earth would possess our father to give ye the power to cross barriers that the words o' protection can create?"

"I fought side by side with your father against a horde of my fallen brothers—saving his life." The angel on my balcony, muttered as he leaned against the open window-frame. "Choosing to keep our alliance secret these last twenty years, has allowed us both to gain information that would help protect Moireach."

"It allows ye to cross." Kenneth murmured from the pillows. "But do ye feel anything?"

"My, you are far more observant than the others. Yes, it allows me to cross the barriers but when I do my skin feels like it is crawling with a million voracious fire ants who are determined to gnaw me to the bone." For the first time I noticed that Damian constantly shuffled about. "The further past the barrier I go, the worse it gets."

"Yet ye risk it for her?" The eldest brother, took another step towards me this time. "For Moireach?"

"MacKenzie, when it comes to my sweet love Moireach," he reached for me then, "I am afraid I don't know how much choice I actually have in the matter."

"Damian, I cannot thank you enough for saving Kenneth and my own life."

I traced a few of the lines on his arm. A searing fire passed through both of us, leaving us short of breath. Our eyes met, and we both smiled.

"My lady, my sweet love, you have no idea what has stirred inside me since I first laid eyes on you. I do not even know where to begin."

He took me into his arms, dispelling the cold of the morning air, and allowing warmth to surround us both.

"Lady MacRae!" an unwelcome voice barked from behind my closed door. "You are to leave for the Abbey this morning for your examination! Your father sent strict instructions with a messenger last night."

I let out a groan of frustration. How was Mary even awake this early? She should have been asleep for at least another hour, thanks to her nightly romance with the wine bottle.

"Thank you Mary, I shall be ready within the hour."

The subject of my purity had not been raised since the engagement party, mind you only two days ago, and *now* I was expected to leave that same day. Damian pulled me closer.

"What examination?"

"The question of virginity has come up due to my age." I said, feeling flush with heat, my hands curling up into little fists. "I am being subjected to a purity test, at the insistence of Mr Cameron."

Damian's look said a thousand words and none of them pleasant nor polite.

"Lady M, my mother's letter to me counselled trust and patience." Kenneth was the first to speak, while he shuffled himself to the edge of the bed preparing to stand. "We must appear to obey Lord MacRae. She wants us to make our way to the Abbey."

"Kenneth, how can you be so calm about what I am being forced to go through?" I asked, turning to face him with spit and fire in my breath. "Do you have any idea of how torturous an examination is? The young Duchess Camfrees spoke to me of the horrors she experienced."

"Calm yersel', lass. She said we could trust the Abbess. She didna say more but I am certain that ye willna ha' to endure the same cruel fate."

I turned back to face Damian, but found nothing but empty air.

"Bloody hell, he sure knows how to make a quiet exit!" Roderick exclaimed.

"Well then if we are to trust the Abbess, let us make ready to depart." I said, feeling the loss of the angel's presence and weighed down by defeat. "But I swear to you both, I will not be forced to submit to that indignity. I am done obeying my father in all matters."

The brothers exchanged nods, stood up and prepared to leave to allow me some privacy to wash myself and change into a clean dress. It was when I turned from the window that I heard his parting voice on the wind.

"My sweet love, always keep the pendant with you. And find a way to bring the three feathers with you to the Abbey. Keep them hidden, wrap them in velvet. You will understand why later."

"What if I don't feel like bringing the feathers?" I muttered indignantly under my breath. "Then what?"

"You feisty woman, or perhaps banshee might be more suited to your temper. Bring the damn feathers!"

So startled was I to hear him again, I stumbled back a step. How was it possible that he heard my words? I ran to the balcony. There he was standing on the rooftop, next to the stone angels. He tipped his hat in my direction and smiled, turning away and disappeared behind the steeples. *My guardian angel.* Closing the windows, I turned towards my keepers.

"Lady M, what feathers?"

"The last few days, I found strange feathers on my windowsill in the mornings. I didn't share with you because I had no idea as to their origins. Now, as we all know, they turned out to be his."

"Lass how can we do our duty in protecting ye if ye dinna share wi' us?" Struggling with his shirt, Kenneth looked at me with heartfelt sorrow in his eyes.

"I'm sorry, both of you, I had no notion of what the feathers might mean, so I honestly thought nothing of it."

Reaching for both of their hands, I looked up at each of them. "I promise that I won't keep anything from you again."

Nodding acknowledgement, they both left me to prepare for the day. Roderick supporting Kenneth's shaky wobble, but we could all see that the worst was over and his strength was returning.

I took my time getting dressed. Organizing my belongings for a few days stay, I decided to bring my mother's journal. With less fear of the purity test hanging over my head, I suddenly found myself eager for the lengthy travel time that would allow me to read at my leisure without interruption. The feathers were of similar size that I was able to place them within the leather binding of the journal, which I then wrapped in a thick velvet cloth. The pendant I hid between my breasts, just above my corset. I would use its powers to summon Damian if the need arose again. As I passed through the kitchen on my way out, the maid having already gone ahead with my packed luggage, I heard Mary talking to someone just outside the back door.

"She is being taken to the Abbey this morning. Here is the route they are taking." The sound of ruffling papers interrupted the flow of words. "But both the brutes are going with her so you must have at least ten men if you want any hope of—."

CRASH!

My elbow had knocked into a terra cotta bowl holding some apples from our orchards. I had been so focused on getting closer, so that I could hear what she was saying, I did not notice my surroundings. The clatter startled her, and she whirled about.

"Why Lady MacRae," she hissed. "Since when are you a filthy, sneaky little spy?"

"I beg your pardon, Mary?"

Standing in front of the door, barring my view, she burst out laughing.

"Oh Lady MacRae, never mind. Do you have your things ready for the journey?" She pretended as if nothing had happened, and much to my chagrin, had allowed whoever was on the other side of that door to make a hasty departure.

"Yes Mary, I have prepared all I will need and was just heading to the stables to depart."

I purposely brushed by her in the hopes of seeing who she may have been talking to, but by the time I got to the door, no one was there. Yet a peculiar smell lingered, one that reminded me of William Cameron—rotten meat that had been doused with cheap ale.

"Lady MacRae?" Roderick called out from behind me.

Turning around, I saw him leaving father's office, with a package in hand, and together we walked outside to meet Kenneth and the carriage. Two of our strongest Shire horses, known for their endurance and strict obedience to Kenneth, stood tethered to the front of the carriage. My own horse, Samson, an extremely rare Irish Hoby which Gwenyver had brought down from the northern hills on my thirteenth birthday as a present was tied to the back. He was beautiful, a rich black with deep tones of auburn. And he had a pure white blaze down from his forehead to his velvety nose. Next to him was Roderick's own horse, Dartanian—the Clydesdale-Shire bred by the Clan MacKenzie for generations, large and strong enough to carry the men of the family. *We rarely brought the extra horses on other travels.*

Kenneth would guide the carriage while Roderick would ride his own horse. The two cousins, Duncan and Connor, would stay behind to wait for my father's return.

"Kenneth, I just overheard Mary speaking with someone outside the kitchen doors." I whispered as he walked me toward the carriage. "And I am fairly certain she was telling them the route we have planned to take.

He looked down at me. Paused. Then scanning our vicinity, somewhat uneasy at first, but then without a word helped me into the carriage. *He had heard me, so why wasn't he saying anything?* I leaned out of the window and watched him walk rather casually over to his brother, pretending to adjust the harness on the monstrosity of a horse. While they spoke, walked to the carriage together, I noticed that Roderick had brought a large leather wrapped bundle from the sheds and was loading it onto the back of the carriage in the storage section next to my own luggage. I recognized it from the hunt many years ago. It was his bow, along with arrows and the quiver.

"We would hate to disappoint anyone looking for us on the road." Kenneth winked as he looked back through the carriage window. "It's too bad, because Roderick and I thought we might take ye along a more scenic route."

I felt relief knowing that were outwitting Mary and whoever she was conspiring with. I already suspected it was Mr Pimms, the lackey of Mr Cameron and it made me very nervous to think about the implications.

As soon as we left our gates, I took out my mother's journal. Turning the pages and learning more about her life, and her kind. I could not help but feel as if I was waking up for the first time in my life.

My darling daughter, for the first time in a millennia I feel satiated, fulfilled in a way that not even the love of your father has been able to accomplish. Feeling you grow inside of me, has created magical feelings I never thought possible. I can honestly say that out of all my sisters, I would have considered myself the least maternal of them all. Most of my life was spent leading battles, planning strategies and somehow always fighting. The Morningstar shone so bright that I never once questioned his motives, his methods or his tactics. I was the one who convinced my sisters to join his cause. It is because of me that we too were banished from our home in the skies, and the guilt I have carried with me has often threatened to undo me. There is so much I wish you to know and I yet I fear what you will think of me. The MacKenzie's will always be there to protect you, and my dearest friend Gwenyver will stand in my place…as your mother. And the grief I feel, knowing that I will not see your first steps, hear your first words or share your excitement when you fall in love. I have been teaching my friend words spoken in my native tongue, the language of angels, some of which possess magical abilities here on this earth. My oldest sister, discovered this generations ago when she was running away from a horde of our brothers who were determined to capture her. I have used these to protect the lands of Clan MacRae, your home, and your father. I wish I could see beyond the time of your birth, but my visions stop there. It is my dearest hope that you will find your strength, that you will fall in love and experience what is possible when you have someone to share your life who supports you, loves you and does not judge you or worse, try to change who you are. Your grandmother gave your poor father a rather hard time about his choice of wife, but to no avail. He never made me feel like I was too strong, or too much, or worse, not enough. The Hunter will come for you. I pray to the skies that what I set in motion while you are still in my womb will bear fruit.

My mind spun with questions. How had I been so ignorant to this other world? How much did my father really know about my mother? Starting to feel a bit dizzy trying to read her words in the moving carriage, I put the journal aside. The gentle rocking of the carriage combined with last night's exhausting escapade, made me quite sleepy. Thankfully, I was small enough I could lay down on the bench with the blanket wrapped around me to get some rest.

I awoke to commotion outside and a rather sudden bump which almost bounced me right off the bench. The carriage was moving at a much faster pace than we had set out with, and this was causing everything to bounce roughly—including me. Struggling to sit up, I peered out the left window to see Roderick riding with a torn harness, using only his legs to hold onto his horse. His torso was twisted to face the rear, while gripping his bow and arrow. He looked focused. Releasing the arrow—a slender, deadly missile—and a howl pierced the air. A rippling shriek of pain and agony followed.

"Get yer heed back inside!" Kenneth shouted.

I obeyed, but my curiosity got the better of me, and I moved to the other side of the carriage to see if I could get a better view. Gripping the ledge of the door, fighting for balance, struggling to see what was pursuing us.

One, two… six, seven—ten beasts! They were as big as bears but with the misshapen faces of wolves thanks to the tusks of wild boars protruding from their jaws with violently glowing red lizard eyes gleaming from their skulls. Their bodies were covered in both matted fur and reptilian skin, the tail ending in a sharp point that looked as dangerous as a scorpion's tail. Nothing in my worst nightmare could have imagined such a creature. One of them was closing in on us. I pulled away from the small window, fearing it might reach in to claw at me, but before I could reach the safety of the bench, the beast had slammed into the side of the carriage flinging me across to the other side where my head hit the corner of the bench—hard. And the world went black.

* * *

I felt warmth of the sun on the side of my face, and my body throbbed in discomfort. Silence surrounded me. I opened my eyes to look around. The carriage, tipped over on its side, supply boxes broken loose from their bindings, and contents had spilled all around me. As if struck by a typhoon.

Slowly, gathering my wits and ordering my aching body to move, I froze at the sight that lay before me. The torn and bloody limbs of the monsters who had been attacking us lay scattered all around me, the stench of sulphur filled my nose, making me gag. There was no movement amongst the remains of the battlefield, and my eyes searched desperately for the MacKenzie's. I crawled over to the splintered carriage door, pausing to wipe what I thought were tears from my face. To my surprise, my palms were now covered in blood. That bump on my head had been worse than I thought. Looking around I felt exposed, and I could not see my guardians anywhere, so I squeezed through the remains of the window frame, feeling only marginally safer inside the battered, upturned carriage.

I had fully intended to remain inside, which offered but meagre shelter from the surroundings. Alas, the fractured wood had other plans. The beam underneath me—even with my slight weight—came crashing down and me along with it onto the grass and fully exposed. Momentarily forgetting about who might hear me, I released an explicative series of words most unfit for a lady.

It was then I heard noises behind me. The shuffling of heavy feet. I held my breath and turned around. Before me stood two of the largest animals I had ever seen—a bear the colour of midnight and a wolf with chestnut fur. Both covered in blood. Their teeth bared with flesh from what I hoped were the beasts attacking us, dripping from their fangs. They walked towards me, slowly. Purposefully.

My heart stopped, and my jaw dropped. My breath came in shallow gasps. I inched my way closer to the meagre protection the broken carriage offered. Thoughts of finding a weapon, anything with which I might fight off these new animals came first and foremost to mind. I wished for Damian's presence, but in my fear and confusion, I did reach for the pendant to call to him. Tears blurred my vision. The bear and wolf kept their approach, clearly intent on reaching me. I searched the grounds around me and saw a splintered wood beam the size of my arm. There were nails sticking out along one side. Only two more steps to reach it. Looking ahead at the creatures, I moved slowly and leaned down to grasp it between my hands. Weapon in hand, I widened my stance to prepare for the onslaught—preparing to fight them. In hindsight, it seemed absurd. I had never held anything in my hands for defence, and certainly had no idea what to do.

They shifted their weight onto their hind legs and lifted their upper body. *They were walking like men.* With every step they took, their bodies started to change. *Step*…hind legs straightened and fur disappeared. *Step*…front paws shrank, morphing into human arms and hands. *Step*…the bear's thick neck narrowed and the hair on top of its the skull grew in length while the wolf's snout retracted, melting into his face. In moments they were… *men.*

My body decided to react rather unfavourably to this shock, and my legs lost all control, and I crumpled to the ground. There I was, with my legs sprawled out in front of me, still clutching my makeshift weapon. I looked up. Roderick and Kenneth stood before me, and they were as naked as the day their mother brought them into this world. My sight, directly, awkwardly, at the same height as their members. Yet again, something I had never witnessed before.

"Lass, it's us." Kenneth said, coming closer. "Ha' nae worry, everything is alright now."

"Lady M, please dinna be afraid." said Roderick. "It is us."

"Kenneth? Roderick?" Somehow, finding myself able to stand again, albeit clumsily and very uncertain of how long I would have the strength to stay upright. "I've…I've seen enough to question my sanity today, so would you mind putting some clothes so that I can at least attempt to keep my wits about me?"

"Oh, for christ sake!" Roderick swept his hands in place to cover his privy parts, as did Kenneth. "Bloody hell and shite on the dark one!"

They bolted to the back of the carriage to rummage through the chaos for something to wear, which gave me enough time to steady my feet and collect my thoughts. Moments later, Roderick returned and attempted to check me for injuries.

"Would you cease your worrying?" I swatted his hands away. "Other than the cut along my head and some scratched up palms, I am not injured. What I want is a bloody explanation, not an examination!"

Much had happened while I had been knocked unconscious. I heard Kenneth's sharp whistle, coaxing the horses to return from the safety of the trees. To my dismay, there were only three of them remaining, thankfully Samson being among them. I dared not search the grass for the missing body of the poor carriage horse.

"Lady M, we ken these creatures that attacked us today."

I listened silently to Roderick, watching Kenneth calm the horses and gather the few belongings that had survived the upending of the carriage.

"They are the slave-pets o' the dark fallen ones, the ones who keep wrecking havoc and ha' sworn to capture ye. Our father told us stories o' those who capture our kind."

"Your kind? Did I hit my head harder than I thought?" I nearly shrieked.

"Aye lass, the MacKenzie's are shape-shifters. We will catch ye up on our family tree once we get on the road. But for now, ye need to understand that the fallen ones force them to drink a concoction made wi' their own blood, causing excruciating pain as the bodies fight the poison that spreads through their body. It's the blood that connects the shape shifter mind wi' that o' their master, resulting in these horrible creatures who will obey every command until their own death releases them from a lifetime o' slavery."

"Roderick, I am at my wits end and I have never had hysterics but my heart is beating so fast that I might just start! First angels, now shape-shifting men and slave pets?"

"Aye, I ken, we kept this secret from ye for all these years because it was yer mother's wish to ha' ye live a normal life for as long as possible. She had hoped there would never be a cause for ye to ha' to ken of these dangers."

"Well, I am done living in a fairytale, and I want to know. Now. All of it."

Just as I demanded to know, Kenneth had returned from tending the horses and joined us, bringing with him two satchels of clothes.

"Ye'll ha' to wait, lass. We must move now." Kenneth looked at me in earnest. "Are ye fit to ride? We have a fair way to go yet and we must make haste."

"I cannot ride side-saddle for that distance in a dress without slowing us down. I'll need a pair of trousers."

Kenneth found a pair for me amongst the spilled luggage. I rolled up the cuffs and searched for something to make a belt. A piece of cloth torn from the carriage bench would do. I tied it around my waist, and the brothers exchanged looks of amusement. The trouser legs were far too wide and it looked like I was wearing a skirt on each leg. But it would suffice

"Aye lass, that should do until we can reach the Abbey." Kenneth chuckled.

Climbing the saddles, we started our travels towards the Abbey and during our journey, the brothers took turns revealing more to me about their life, their past and in odd way, part of my history too.

"Our kind, the shape shifting people o' the north, ha' known about the fallen ones since the beginning o' our existence. As children we are told bed time stories on how to defeat them. The only thing that can harm them is their own feathers, after they have been tempered wi' fire into smooth metal weapons." Roderick shifted uncomfortably in his make-shift saddle. "The MacKenzie clan does ha' another advantage mind you, in that our origins allow us the strength that equals that o' the angels when they remain in their human form. But it is in our chosen animal form that our teeth and claws allow us to penetrate the skin and inflict damage."

"Roderick, why were there so many of them? Is that normal? Were they all following one master's commands? Or...?"

"As we prepared to end the life o' the last remaining beast, it started to shift back into his human form. This rarely happens…" Kenneth interjected. "He remembered who he was, and shared wi' us what he knew before he took his last breath. They all answered to the same dark master. Their mission was to kill us, and to bring ye back to him alive. He wanted to ensure success and thereby sent ten of his creatures. Whoever the dark one is must be very powerful. Every time they create a slave it saps a little power from them which takes years to replenish. What is worse, he has more o' them." He clasped his hands together, as if he were remorseful.

"Kenneth, why are you so sad? This creature tried to kill you, did it not? Does it really deserve your pity?"

"We pity every one o' those monstrosities, lass." Roderick spoke so quietly, it was near a whisper. "They were once our kin before the blood poisoned them. Somewhere in his poisoned mind he remembered his life from before and used the last o' his strength to change back. He was our cousin Graham, who has been missing nearly a year, and well, he recognized me. He told me that his master had dozens more slave-hounds. When I asked if he could tell us the location, or any other information that might be o' use to us, he cried that he didna ken. The master is very cunning. Keeping packs o' beasts separate, wi' different missions, operating from various estates across Europe."

Stunned into silence, I swallowed my questions and decided it was best to absorb only so much information at any given time. We rode hard and fast. Not knowing how many more hellhounds were on our heels, Kenneth led the way while I rode just behind him, and Roderick as our rear guard. We arrived at the abbey after nearly three hours of riding, and me listening and struggling to process this new information about the world I had not known existed.

The abbey had been built in the twelfth century by Benedictine Monks and was now home to a well-respected group of nuns known for healing and helping women with childbirth.

The dark grey limestone of the outer walls were imposing, and the front gates, made of sturdy timber and covered in iron bars, seemed impassable. The grounds surrounding the outer walls was barren of trees or plants for nearly fifteen feet all around. It would have been difficult for anyone to approach without being noticed. As I looked up, I could see a nun posted at the top of each corner which had a raised partition like that of a tower. They appeared to be watching across the grounds, as if guards on duty. It was unusual to see a place of worship with such a defensive wall. *How odd for an Abbey.*

We knocked at the gates and an older nun answered us from behind the doors. Kenneth was tired, and Roderick was starving. We all wanted to get inside to safety, but she refused us entry. We had not arrived in the carriage, and we were not properly attired, a lady dressed in trousers, and filthy from the road, and the MacKenzie's' gruff attempts fell on deaf ears.

"Sister, my name is Lady Moireach MacRae, and we are expected." I said, sure that my greeting would gain us entry. "We ask that you allow us inside to meet with the Abbess."

The nun retreated inside, saying nothing. We waited, and I looked up at my two giant brothers, my protectors. Men I had known all my life and yet today, I realized there was so much I did not know.

"Why of course Sister Shelga, these are the very guests we ha' been waiting for!"

My thoughts were interrupted by the arrival of the Abbess, who had taken the briefest of peaks through the little window in the door. When the large gate door finally opened, we were allowed access. Both men had to duck in order not to hit their head. Meanwhile, I found myself looking up at a rather tall woman.

"How…do you know us?" I asked.

"Well, my heavens!" she said with a laugh. "I would recognize my brother's sons anywhere, they are the very spit of him. And you, dear petite lady, ha' yer mother's unmistakable hair. Welcome Lady MacRae, and please nephews would ye both give yer aunty a big hug?"

CHAPTER 11

"Well, lads?"

The Abbess stood with her hands on her hips, exuding a rambunctious confidence unexpected from a nun.

"Hmm, yer mother warned me ye two might be cautious."

Kenneth placed a hand on my shoulder and subtly pulled me towards him. He had also tugged the horse's leads to bring them closer.

We had all expected a small, frail old woman. Instead, this Abbess stood at least six feet tall. She was not unattractive, then again not conventionally pretty either. Her features were feminine, but her mannerisms were rough. The lines in her face made me think she might be closer to Roderick in age. Her granite grey eyes were too large for her face, her nose long, and her lips appeared doll-like on an otherwise large canvas. She wore a black cowl that hid what hair she might have.

Roderick took two steps forward to plant himself directly in front of me.

"Our apologies Lady Abbess, but we ha' never met ye before and we are well versed on our family tree," he said to her with formality in his tone. "Any aunt of ours would likely be much older than yerself. Can ye prove who ye are?"

The Abbess looked from Roderick, and then Kenneth.

"My sire was Lord Hector MacKenzie, and I am the youngest sister of yer father, George."

"Lady Abbess, that is where ye are mistaken." Roderick now took one threatening step forward and I sensed Kenneth shift his stance behind me. "Our father is the *youngest* child of Hector and Morag MacKenzie. Who are you?"

"Lads, I can appreciate the concern, and the caution." She was steadfast. "It's good to see that yer mother raised ye wi' yer wits fully intact. Verra well, if ye insist, let's first bring the horses inside so Sister Abigail can give them water and food. They look in need of some rest."

The brothers turned to look at each other, and a silent exchange took place.

"Roderick, I cannot sense anything unusual on the winds." he whispered. "We can leave the horses here without worry—"

"—Aye lads! Yer horses will be safe, and for now so shall we." The Abbess interrupted their whisperings. "Now, if ye will kindly follow me. I would rather do this in the glade just through the thicket, and not in front of the nuns."

"Roderick, Kenneth, your mother said we could trust her." I said, as the Abbess began walking away, motioning us to follow. "Can we please just get this over with? I am tired, hungry and frankly, my mind is a jumbled mess."

I did not care that I sounded like a spoiled child. The more we delayed, the higher the risk of the hellhounds finding us out in the open and exposed.

"Lady Abbess, thank you," I said following her lead away from the safety of the Abbey walls.

Roderick bowed, and Kenneth handed over the horse's leads to the nun waiting to care for them. The Abbess made her way beyond the gates and towards the small wooded area across the dirt road. We walked in silence, through thickets, past the brush and under the shade of the Oak trees.

"Kenneth, what will we do if she is not who she claims to be?" I whispered.

"Dinna fasch yersel'." He patted my shoulder reassuringly. "We will figure something out, we always do."

The Abbess brought us to a small circle of emerald green grass surrounded by large, wild mushroom —it was *a fairy circle*—where there was just enough space for all of us to stand. She turned to face us, and then paused. Collecting her thoughts, and looking to us with fervent eyes, she spoke.

"My name is Athdara, youngest daughter of Lord Hector MacKenzie, born in his final winter years. I am of the clan blood and honour our old ways until my last drop of blood be spilled and my body be returned to ash and earth."

The MacKenzie's became solemn.

A quiet sigh escaped her lips, removing her cowl, letting it slip to her shoulders. To reveal what she had been concealing—long locks of the purest white, just as the first snow of winter. Her granite grey eyes were grave. Somber.

"I am the child produced from the union of yer grand-sire, and o' a woman, named Jayne, …who did not survive my birth."

She bowed her head and lowered herself down onto one knee. Her two hands reached around to the back of her neck, and she started to unlace the binds on her tunic. Once she pulled her arms free from the sleeves, holding the cloth against her body to hide her nakedness, she slowly rose to stand. She turned her back towards us. Across from her left shoulder and all the way to her right arm, five savage scars, faded to a strange silver with crimson beneath.

The two brothers were stunned into silence, exchanging a knowing look between them, and even I could hazard a guess that those scars had been inflicted by a hellhound.

"I was born in 1626, in fact only shortly after yer own birth Roderick, and we share the same stars. I was raised in the farthest northlands above the lochs, where I stayed until my thirteenth birthday. That was when yer father, my brother, came to see what my role would be in our family. To our knowledge, I am the only female shifter o' our clan since our very first ancestor. It was decided that I would always remain hidden, as a secret weapon of sorts, for the one day I might be called upon to help protect our future—you Lady MacRae."

She lowered to her knees once again. Her transformation was slow, especially when I thought back to how swiftly the MacKenzie's had changed back to their human form. It was filled with stifled moans that indicated something deeper than discomfort was present. Once, the transformation was complete, Kenneth and Roderick knelt before her, their heads bowed. I promptly followed suit, understanding this was a gesture of respect.

I lifted my eyes and slowly rose to my feet. The animal, tall enough that even seated its eyes were level with mine, was unlike any I could have imagined. The fur was pure white. Her eyes were still the same granite grey. Her visage was that of a wolf, but with a wider and thicker neck. She had the shoulders and upper body of a bear, yet her legs and lower half were that of a thick-legged wolf, including the tail. Her form was both wolf and bear, yet neither. She stood on all fours, looming above me.

"Roderick, how is this possible? "Kenneth muttered. "Father told us that Grandfather was infected by a dark one in his last months—the winter years."

"Shhh, Kenneth…" Roderick countered under his breath. "Let me think."

The exchange of words between the brothers brought Athdara a little closer. I tentatively reached out my hand, and she brought the bridge of her nose just under it. Breathing slowly, I placed my palm on the softness of her fur. She then pawed at the ground, if only for but a moment before she began to shape-shift back into her human form. Slowly, and with that same discomfort. The brothers averted their eyes as she put her tunic back on.

"Lads, I think it best we make our way back inside the Abbey before I share that story." she said, lifting the cowl to cover her white locks. and tucking stray strands hair underneath. "Because if neither of ye can smell the dark one's hounds on the air, let me tell ye that I can. I've placed the protection words all around the Abbey walls, they will keep us safe and let ye all rest. But only if we are *inside*."

The brothers shrugged their shoulders in agreement, and as she walked past them in a direct line, straight back to the gates, they exchanged another one of the infamous silence looks between them. We followed her back through the brush and towards the safety of the walls. As we walked through the smaller gateway into the Abbey, I felt a strange vibration across my skin, like the ripples after a pebble has been dropped into a still pond.

"What ye felt is the power o' the old words protecting this place." Athdara said looking back directly at me. "Consecrated grounds never were that effective in keeping the dark ones and their hounds at bay, but the magic o' the old words strengthen holy ground and get a wee bit o' extra longevity from it, and that will keep us safe. It was your mother who gave me the words that protect this place."

Giving me no chance respond to this sudden news, she led us the courtyard, towards a large set of doors that had been inscribed with markings I did not recognize, yet they somehow felt familiar. When the doors opened, the smell of fresh oven baked bread and delicious chicken roasting over the fire welcomed us.

"Take as much food and drink as ye like, and we shall retire to my private quarters so that I can tell ye the story of how I became the first female shapeshifter o' Clan MacKenzie since our first Lady of Water."

Athdara spoke in muted tones to avoid others hearing us, but turned and gave me a mischievous wink. I took one last glance towards the gates, and watched Sister Abigail latching a rather large wooden beam across the gates and putting the final lock into place. While I took in my new surroundings and noted the quiet organized chaos of nuns moving around the grounds, I felt a small sigh of relief. For now, I could stop running. I felt safe.

"Here ye go, lass, eat as much as ye can. After today ye must be fair starved." Kenneth handed me a plate laden with roasted chicken, potatoes, carrots, turnips and bread.

We carried our abundant plates with us and followed the Abbess down the corridor and to a broad thick wooden door with imposing iron locks. Past the doors, we entered a large open space with some comfortable seating large enough to fit the MacKenzie men, surrounding a rounded hearth, already warm with fire crackling. The room had several tapestries to keep out the chill, and I noticed they all depicted scenery with animals and humans sharing space in nature. Once seated, the brothers looked to Athdara while devouring their meal.

"As ye ken, our grandsire, Lord Hector MacKenzie had been infected by a dark one in his winter years. Lady MacRae, our kind often seek the wild mountains or the harsh northland coasts in the final years o' life. We dinna ken why, but it has always been so. Our elderly seek solitude and the freedom to shift whenever they like."

She looked towards me.

"We are unsure o' how he was captured, but the dark master was powerful enough to overcome even Hector, long held to be not only the greatest and most powerful o' our clan but also the canniest. He was held captive along the far north east coast in an estate separated by cliffs and deep rivers. A young woman named Jayne, less a servant and more a slave herself, worked for the dark master in the kitchens. She was unawares o' what took place underground but she had heard o' the legends of the shape-shifters, the selkies, but she had never seen one o' us."

"Athdara, are all your transformations as uncomfortable as it appeared to be?" I interrupted with the question that had been on the corners of my mind since watching her.

"No, I'm afraid to say that I am the only one I've heard o' that experiences physical pain during the shift."

"Athdara, am I mistaken in observing that the change also drains ye a wee bit o' energy?" Roderick asked, as he, too, would not let go anything unnoticed.

"Ye are not. Over the years, I ha' become accustomed to the impact on my body every time I shift, and over the years I ha' found the fortitude to shift faster if the need arises. I am able to recover faster now, simply by eating a large meal right away."

She leaned heavily back into her chair.

"Now then, let's return to my beginnings. Jayne's role was in the kitchens preparing food and taking the meals to the various occupants o' the castle's living quarters. One day she stumbled onto the secret door that the dark master used to enter into the lower caverns o' the castle. Hearing sounds, and being a rather curious lass, she followed the stairs to the end where she saw Hector in his human form locked in a cage. She was awestruck by his size, and his gallant charm. They exchanged kind words that day, and she promised to return. Each day after she would bring him food and other comforts as often as she could. It was because of her actions that our grandsire stayed strong in body despite the torture he endured. After a few months, she developed a fondness for the aging MacKenzie and he for her. They had started to devise a plan to escape, together."

Athdara sighed.

"Those were the days before he was given the toxic potion that would change him forever. One fateful night Jayne crept down the stairs wi' more food, as was her usual, when she heard screaming. The dark master had forced the vile liquid down Hector's throat and left him to experience the brutal transformation alone and in great agony. We dinna ken how long it took, but by the time she found him, he was already turning, She tried to free him from the cage, but the poison running through his veins had already taken hold. When she managed to unlock the iron bars, he pulled her into the cage and in a blind rage o' lust and violence, he violated her." Athdara paused here, looking at me with a question in her eyes.

"Yes, I am familiar with the act," I blushed. "Although I have no knowledge of it myself."

"After he had released himself inside o' her, he had one moment of awareness—but it was enough. He remembered who he was and realized what he had done. The regret and sorrow he felt went so deep that he let her go, and just before the final turn took him, he pushed her out of the cage. He pulled the door closed, and wi' his brute strength broke the key in the lock, so that he couldna escape and she would come to no further harm. It was that moment of pause, that saved Jayne's life that day—"

"—Athdara, we had been led to believe that those monstrosities couldna create offspring." Roderick asked, his mouth full of bread, lips dripping with butter.

"Aye, and to this day, we know o' no other in existence like me," she said smoothly. "Perhaps because he had not fully transformed yet, some parts o' the humanity allowed for him to pass on his seed, successfully. Jayne escaped. Hector had told her o' a safe haven where she would be welcomed, an ancient convent that still honour the old ways far to the north, near Orkney. The nuns there took her in, being distant relatives of the MacKenzie's ye ken, and when she realized she was pregnant, news was sent to Lord George MacKenzie, yer father. He arrived only moments before my arrival, having just attended yer birth in the wee early hours o' the morning, Roderick. Ye ken it's not normal for a man to be in the same room as a woman giving birth, but the violence of the labour meant he wanted to be there to help this young woman bring me into this world. But no one expected the bairn to be born in its animal form. I was conceived in violence and that is how I entered this world. My shapeshifter form tore my mother's body apart. She did not survive." She paused her narrative, letting out a mournful sigh for the mother she never knew, and I felt an immediate kinship with her.

"George decided that I would need to be raised in secret. And so I remained in that very convent until seven years ago when my brother sent word to me that Denny Abbey would need a new Abbess. Apparently, Gwenyver had returned to Eilean Donan and had a vision. It would be important that someone trusted be here when the time should come."

The brothers and I had no words. We looked to each other and then back to the Abbess who had lived her whole life in secret. For the sole purpose of being here, without ever knowing for what reason, except she would be needed.

"Lady MacRae, I would be pleased to share stories o' yer mother if ye like?" Athdara was changing the subject. "I was visited by her often when I was growing up, before she met yer father. She is the one who taught me the words that now protect this Abbey, and showed me how to fight and control my shapeshifting powers properly."

My heart leaped with this news, just as the sound of thunder rumbled in the distance. The brothers rose from their seats, setting their plates on the wooden chairs they had just occupied.

"I would—."

"—Bloody hell, the hounds!" Kenneth exclaimed, standing up to walk to the doors, and gesturing for us to follow.

They had tracked us to this place of sanctuary, and were now determined to find a way in. We rushed out to the corridor, and the Abbess took us to the left and up through stairs to a south facing tower. Just as we reached the top, we saw one of the beasts climb a nearby tree. Walking across a few large branches, it leaped towards the walls which seemed too far away to be of any concern, but fear still gripped me. Mid-flight, and I saw a bright flash of silver light burst from the walls—like lightening. The hound yelped in pain as it fell to the ground, out of sight. *The words of protection.* Kenneth came to put his arms around my shoulder and pulled me away from the edges of the tower. We watched several other hellhounds make attempts at crossing the boundaries. Each time they were repelled by the spell, the words of my mother's ancient tongue, that Athdara had weaved around the Abbey walls.

"Now that is verra impressive." Roderick said. "Would ye consider sharing those words wi' me, dear aunt?"

"Aye, that I would. They are most effective and only need to be renewed once a year during the Winter Solstice." she replied. "Now then, the sisters within this Abbey have all been trained these past seven years to withstand a lengthy siege. They know about the hellhounds, but not the origins." She gave us another one of her mischievous grins. "I've taught them to believe it is Satan sending them to test their faith."

Assured that for now, we were safe from any threat of the hellhounds. Athdara, after assessing the surrounding areas just past the Abbey walls, and feeling satisfied we were safe, led us back down the stairs. Back into the warmth of her quarters, we continued our meal in silence.

"Enough o' this glumness! I've wanted to swap stories wi' ye lads since I kent ye would be coming!" And dropped her plate onto the table for emphasis.

And so, an evening of sharing the events of this past week, including the newly formed friendship with Damian, along with stories of shape-shifters and childhood escapades helped to keep us occupied from the dangers lurking just outside the walls. The howls were dulled by the thick walls protecting us, and the flashes when a hound leaped, became less of a distraction as time went on.

Even the brothers shared openly of their lives as children, and I was able to learn more about them for the first time in my life. Perhaps it was the exhaustion setting in, but with each story I found my gaze turning towards the fire. It was as if I could see the action in the flames. Images and voices were leaping from the heat in tandem with the words I heard from the storyteller. Confused, I looked at my companions.

"Are you seeing what I'm seeing?"

"Seeing what lass?"

Roderick looked around the room, instantly alert to possible dangers.

"The shapes in the fire." I whispered. "Can you hear the voices?"

"No lass," Athdara assured me. "Just the flames and the crackling o' the wood. You must be fair exhausted. Let's retire for the evening and get as much sleep as we can. Tomorrow, we will discuss what's to happen next, and get ye back into proper attire, aye?"

Perhaps it was the rigours of the road that had caused me to hallucinate, I thought as I was shown the way to my room. I did not even bother to change clothes, having only enough energy to take off my shoes, and dropping the oversized trousers to the floor, leaving me in my long sleeved shirt. That night my dreams came quick and vivid but also very jumbled.

Cages, blood, and swords. An older man in a cage with an iron neck collar and iron cuffs around his wrists and ankles, which had rubbed his skin raw and bloody. He was dirty, and his dark hair, the same colour as Roderick's, hung limply around his brow, a grizzled white beard hid his chin; his body bent over and tired. At first, he was sitting on the filthy dirt floor, but then someone came to the cage to throw some mouldy bread through the bars. When the old man struggled to stand, I saw how big he actually was—taller than Roderick and with shoulders nearly twice the width.

"I willna take it willingly," He gripped the bars, and glared at the person on the other side. "Whatever is done to me is o' no consequence. She is safe from the likes o' ye and yer brothers. I am but an old man in this war and ha' been ready to die for years. I ha' watched my family and bloodline grow strong. Ye will ha' to kill me."

The voice that spoke next in my dreams sent shudders of ice down my spine.

"You will swallow every last drop. The change will happen. You will forget the life that you are so at peace with. She will be found, and your life will have had no purpose. And soon there will be more hellhounds than MacKenzie's."

And then it was I, looking out from the cage. The hands holding the bars were my own. I looked up at the captor and stared into piercing green eyes that had burned themselves into my heart.

I woke up screaming.

CHAPTER 12

Still gripping the blankets tightly around me, shivering from fright, and feeling a moment of confusion as I woke up in unfamiliar surroundings. All I remembered was the vivid green eyes, but I could not recall if the face had been Damian's. The silence outside was eery. Having fallen asleep to the sounds of hellhounds outside, I had somehow expected to hear them upon waking. The soft knocking on my door startled me, it was the Abbess.

"Lady MacRae?"

"Come in, Athdara." I called out.

"I thought I heard ye cry oot? It's still before sunrise. Are ye alright?"

She sat down on the edge of my bed, and I sat up under the covers.

"Yes, I am thank you for asking. Just had a bad dream."

"It's nae wonder, look at what has befallen ye these last few days? May I call ye, Moireach? I ha' heard that name used by my sister-in-law so often I feel that it is the only name I can imagine calling ye."

"Of course, you may."

I managed a polite smile on her behalf.

"Before we meet up wi' my nephews, I wanted to ha' some time alone wi' ye. Would ye walk wi' me in the garden, Moireach? We can gather some fresh vegetables and herbs for our breakfast."

After last night's nightmare, gathering herbs and vegetables was the last thing I wanted to do. I felt as if I had been run over by a runaway carriage. Still, I needed answers, or, at the least, some sort of explanation.

"If you would be so kind as to permit me time to dress? I will be in the garden shortly."

"As soon as ye can, lass." her expression turned somber. "There is much I want to share with ye."

Once in the garden, we walked along the paths and Athdara guided our way along the rows of plants, all the while talking about the various ways to help them grow. I noticed she was gazing left and right and keeping an eye on the proximity of the other nuns who might hear us. Then she directed us towards the furthest corners of the gardens. She was methodical in choosing the right vegetables—carrots, tomatoes and peas. We could now carry on our conversation out of hearing range from the other nuns moving about the grounds carrying out their morning tasks.

"I dinna ken how much ye ha' been told about yer mother, but I saw her journal in yer hands yesterday," she said, as she uprooted a carrot. "I apologize if I am jumping ahead in the story, but it is important. I had hoped time would be in our favour, but now I am nae so sure."

Walking towards the shaded part of the garden, a boxed section filled with herbs, we slowed down. Athdara, still alert to the presence of others, pointed to the chives and the rosemary. I leaned down and started gently pulling from the stems and added them to our basket.

"How much do ye ken o' the MacKenzie history, Moireach?" she asked.

"To be honest, I didn't even know about Roderick and Kenneth until yesterday." I frowned. "So, I have no knowledge at all."

She rested her free hand against my shoulder, and with a full basket, guided me away from the herbs, walking down the path that lead to the orchard trees behind the garden. She sat me down on the stone bench, because it was isolated and nowhere near any of the buildings.

"Thousands o' years ago, the heavens cast oot beings unlike any o' those found on this earth." She placed the basket on the ground at her feet. "Immortal beings wi' wings from the losing side o' a war we know nothing about."

"Angels?" I whispered.

"In physical shape, aye, they are the angels that the bible writes about." She turned her eyes towards me with a soft smile. "But even that book only contains snippets o' the true story. Our ancestors ha' passed down the knowledge for centuries, and the story o' my family—the shape-shifters—starts many generations after the arrival o' those winged beings. This leaves a gap, hundreds o' years that we dinna ken what they did, what their lives were like or what took place in history."

"Did my mother share anything about her past with you?" I whispered.

"As a matter o' fact, she did. She had been banished, along wi' others, fallen ones as we call them, who had rebelled against their king. They had followed a charismatic but dangerous leader, who started the war which raged on for a millennia. Finally, the king overthrew the rebellion and cast them out, banishing them to the earth, and forced to live wi' humans."

"A rebellion against…a king? The being we call God in the bible?" I asked. "Do you mean to say there were other angels that returned back to…the skies?"

"Aye, it does seem that way yes. The victors returned to their kingdom I suppose you could call it, in the skies. Your mother was always a little vague on the details. Your mother never shared what actually caused the divide amongst her people. But she did speak o' the murderous acts o' her fallen brothers, and the viciousness wi' which their leader led those remaining loyal to him. After sometime, most o' the fallen ones had fallen into a state o' despair, desiring nothing but their own death."

"Why?" I interrupted.

"They had not only been banished from their home, without any way to return. Many had left families behind. But it's not just that. When they were sent here, they were stripped o' almost all o' their powers combined wi' a deep never-ending hunger, an acute and painful desire. Nothing would ever satiate them. They were cursed, and the way you mother described it —a never-ending life o' agony. She joked once that not even the bible described the kind o' hell they lived wi' everyday."

I was taken aback by this.

"My mother was faced with living an eternity…of feeling *hungry*?"

"Aye, when yer mother arrived on this earth, she too felt the gnawing hunger. Understand lass, it's not just a hunger for food or drink, its a much deeper ache in their body that drives them to seek out the extremes o' all o' life's experiences in the hopes they can feel a moment o' peace."

"Did she…" I disrupted her story.

"If she too turned violent? I'm afraid she did admit to a period o' time in which she became tangled up in the emotions, the violence and the bloodshed. But even that didna provide the relief she sought, so she walked away from her fallen brothers, and set out on her own."

"And her sisters?"

"To be honest, she didna say what her sisters were doing during her time of darkness. Her story and our legends collide somewhere around 900 years ago. They both speak of a time, when one o' these fallen angels discovered that a true death could be possible. During his travels, he was inexplicably drawn to a small coastal town in a land we now know as Italy. There he found a young woman, whose very presence triggered feelings in him—desire, and more. He became obsessed. He chased the woman to the edge o' the cliffs along the coast o' Salento. In the struggle to free herself from him, she fell to the rocks below, but he leaped after her. His wings unfurled too late, and both crashed to their death on the rocks."

"So, he died because she died?" I said, hand covering my astonishment.

"Yer mother witnessed this event, along wi' one o' the other brothers. This angel's death, triggered the Great Hunt, when fallen angels hunted humans as prey—called their soul-prey. My family's story begins almost 200 years later, when a mortal man became the soul-prey o' a fallen angel but through some chance, managed to defeat him—surviving. One o' yer mother's sisters, one o' the Elemental Twins, found the injured man."

"The Elemental Twins? Are those the sisters of which she writes about in her journal?" I was starting to connect some of the writings from my mother's journals to what Athdara was sharing with me.

"Aye, amongst the fallen ones were only eight females that had joined the rebellion. Four sets o' twins, each pair representing an Element: Earth, Water, Fire and Air. Yer mother was one o' the Fire Elementals. When joined together, they had the ability to control the element, but separated they are almost powerless. With one exception, somehow they are able to create spells using words and symbols from their native angelic language. None o' the fallen brothers, the males, ha' any ability like those of the sisters."

"So, she had a twin?" I blurted out. "Are there any other children from these… Elementals? How come I am so… normal? How come I—?"

"—Aye, yer mother has a twin named Daphine. We believe she is still alive, but we dinna ken her whereabouts. As for other children, we know o' only one other than you. Another girl, and *she* is the story o' how my kind, the shape-shifting MacKenzie's, came into existence."

Athdara leaned her head back against the tree behind the bench to gaze up at the skies, as if she needed to rest before she continued.

"Once a fallen one catches the scent o' their soul-prey, they become the Hunter. One human, a MacKenzie, showed exceptional strength and courage, by not only defeating the Hunter, but surviving. The story o' how he accomplished this remains a mystery. We do know he was found, injured and near death by Meridia, a Water Elemental. She found him on the far north coast o' Scotland beside the dead body o' one o' her winged brothers."

"She wasn't angry....at the death of one of her own kind?"

"No, actually the Elementals held a tenderness towards humans and had grown tired o' fighting and watching the horrific actions o' their brothers. So, ye see, Meridia nursed this man back to health and they fell in love. She stopped her wandering, and reminded by his side from then on. He knew full well the type o' creature she was and the danger that would always be present by choosing her as his mate. He chose her anyway. After some years, their happiness and their bond produced a child—a miracle. The first o' my ancestors, the first o' the shape-shifters. A girl child, Dylynn, that proved to ha' uncommon abilities controlling the water around her but also using the transformative powers o' the element to change her body. As a wee lass, she often chose the body o' a seal, and spent hours and days in the waters, the place where she felt most at home. She gave rise to the myths and stories o' Selkies, now renowned throughout Scotland."

"The girl had special powers at an early age..." I felt disappointed. Here I was nearly twenty years of age, and I was nothing if not ordinary.

"Lass, ye must be patient. Dylynn was raised by her mother, taught from the moment she arrived into this world but it was also her powers that made her a target, to be hunted by the fallen ones. Meridia knew that they would seek out her daughter, ever since the birth heralded a vibration that could only be felt by her kind. So, she showed her mate, the MacKenzie, how to use angelic words, as spells o' protection to keep their daughter hidden from the ones who would do her harm, or worse, use her powers. And as their daughter grew, she too was taught how to wield the words that could keep her safe. Remember, the fallen angels, the males, dinna ha' the power to create spells using their angelic language. This gave Meridia and her family a distinct advantage."

"That explains why Damian couldn't speak the words himself to break the protection!" I felt elated at being able to puzzle the pieces together, albeit slowly. "The medallion your father gifted him with…who put the spell on it, I wonder?"

"Ah yes, the one whose very name brings a blush to your face, dinna think I've not noticed. And that would have been yer mother, she worked the smith fires and poured the silver herself while weaving angelic words through it."

"She made the medallion?"

"Ach aye, she was a fabulous silversmith. This bracelet I wear was a gift from her when I was but a lass."

Lifting her wrist and drawing up the sleeve of the nuns habit, and showing a slim, curved cuff with an intricately engraved pattern of roses.

"Now, lass would ye kindly let me continue?" she smirked. "Back to my ancestors…they didna ken what the future would bring. As soon as she could walk, they trained her to fight and how to kill the fallen ones, should they come to hunt her one day. Many years later, around Dylynn's twentieth birthday, one o' the winged brothers did find her. He was drawn to her in such a way he didna ken if he wanted to possess her or kill her."

"How did this angel find her?"

"A few weeks prior, Dylynn had turned twenty years old, and both mother and daughter felt something change in her body. It was as though, she was giving off a vibration, a signal. One that mimicked the signal o' the Hunt. The fallen one was the closest o' his kind, and was pulled in by the energy."

"My twentieth birthday is not for another month." I blurted out loud. "If I were truly one of these Elemental children, that strange vibration hasn't happened yet. How did they find me? Am I Damian's soul-prey?

"I'm afraid we dinna ken that yet. Mind ye, from what I can gather someone has been watching yer family for many years. Someone has known o' your father's connection to yer mother. The one you call Damian has caught yer scent, whether it is pure coincidence that he was in the tavern that night or he has been the one watching yer family, I canna guess. Given what he has shared wi' ye, and what ye describe has happened between ye two I am fairly certain ye are his true soul-prey. Whereas the vibration that will trigger on yer twentieth birthday will call to all the fallen angels within range, bringing even more danger to you. Now, please let me finish telling ye about Dylynn."

"Of course, I apologize for the disruption, there is just so much that I am learning and trying to understand." I sat back on the bench, and focused on Athdara's words.

"She was on one o' the northern beaches wi' her father, training wi' the specially crafted swords created by her mother, when the fallen one couldna restrain himself any further. Leaping off the nearby cliff, gliding on his wings down to the sands, he attacked. Her father, the man who had once cheated death by killing his own Hunter, jumped to her defence, but time had aged him and the battle was over before it began. The fallen one knocked the older man to the ground while still in flight, and turned around only to land on her father's chest and smashing his fist through the rib cage and straight to the heart."

When Athdara paused, I could not help but think of my own father, and how my heart would break should I lose him.

"Meridia's scream of anguish was heard across the moors and over the cliffs, as she felt her soulmate die. This was enough o' a distraction for the Hunter that gave Dylynn a few precious moments to gather her wits and launch her own attack. Using the swords for the first time as true weapons, not just training tools, she wielded them wi' such a ferocity that the Hunter was taken aback. She evaded his blows wi' quick lithe movements, and was able to use her smaller stature to get in close to slash at his legs. With the arrival o' her mother, Dylynn saw an opportunity to use her connection wi' the water element to aid them in their fight. She called the waves to her, and they crashed into the Hunter over and over again from all sides, the salt water stinging his eyes and blurring his vision and stopping his forward advance on the two women. Together, mother and daughter, were able to defeat him by severing his head from his body and so, they were able to take revenge for the death o' her father and keep Dylynn safe."

"So, if she can kill a fallen one, does that mean I could too?" I asked, recalling my nightmare.

"Well, I suppose in theory ye could. Only, Meridia had trained her daughter her entire life to fight, to know hardship and to know everything about her ancestors and her strengths. You, lass, ha' twenty years o' catching up to do. Dylynn, is my ancestress, the first o' my kind. All o' the Clan MacKenzie began wi' her….and yet, we dinna ken a thing about the man who sired her first child."

"I was not raised like Dylynn, my mother died giving birth to me. I certainly do not have any powers. Why are they hunting me?"

"My sister-in-law, Gwenyver, told me years later that during yer mother's pregnancy, she would see visions in the fire. They showed her that she wouldna survive yer birth. She saw many other things, o' which she refused to speak. When the time was near for yer arrival, all o' Clan MacKenzie was called to Castle Eilean Donan and a promise was made that we would protect ye, keep ye safe and give ye a chance at leading a normal life."

"But…Athdara, you were not at my birth. Roderick and Kenneth would have remembered you."

"Ye are right. Seraphina had a vision in a fire, that one day I would play an important role in yer life, but only if our enemies didna ken about me. So I wasna there because my brother had sent word to me that I should stay hidden. It was important that the fallen ones who were hunting ye and yer mother didna ken o' my existence. I had given my oath to yer mother many years prior, she was my mentor, my guide and my friend. The closest thing I had to a sister."

"I don't even know where to begin. If my mother had a vision as you say, then she foresaw my arrival at Denny Abbey, and knew I would need your guidance, and protection." I reached out my hand to place on her long arm in a gesture of acknowledgement and appreciation. "Damian is a fallen one, but he has protected me at every turn and even saved Kenneth's life." My head was spinning with confusion. "How can I be his soul-prey? He hasn't tried to hurt me."

"This is why we had to move fast, to get ye to safety." Athdara said. "We dinna ken the master who hunts ye now wi' his hellhounds, and wi' yer twentieth birthday so close, we couldna risk the chance that yer vibration will call more o' them. At least not until we can get ye within the walls o' Eilean Donan. Gwenyver has worked very hard these past seven years to protect every stone wi' angelic words to create impenetrable barriers for the hellhounds and the fallen ones."

"Did my mother speak more of her sisters?" I asked, now leaning forward with a keen interest. "Can we reach out to them for help?"

"Aye, she told me the names o' all her sister-in-arms. Seraphina, your mother, and her sister Daphine are the Fire Elemental Twins. Meridia, who is the matriarch o' the MacKenzie's, shapeshifters, and her sister Nerimis are the Water Elementals. Demitrinia and Persephone are the Earth. And finally, Airia and Etherinia are the Air. They live scattered across the world, in all directions, so as to protect each other and themselves from their fallen brothers."

"If Dylynn is your ancestor…" I just had to ask. "What…? What will happen if I have children?"

"My people are the only known descendants o' any o' the Elementals. We ha' no knowledge what yer children may become, should ye choose to have any. We dinna even ken o' the powers ye may have inherited from Seraphina. Dylynn was born wi' her abilities fully embodied, and was raised to learn everything about them, to embrace them as part o' herself and to protect her own life from those who would seek to end it."

"Why would my mother have not wanted me to know about my heritage? Why did she deny me the benefit of learning about these powers?" I was visibly distressed as I processed all that I had just been told. "I hate feeling trapped, like a victim, like some stupid damsel in distress."

"Lass, she must ha' had her reasons." Athdara, pulled me in closer offering a comforting hug. "And now, we best be back to the kitchens before we are missed. Or worse, my nephews start eating the kitchen tables from hunger."

The tall and graceful woman stood and began the walk back to the kitchens with the herbs and vegetables we had gathered. As I followed her, my head was still spinning with the knowledge she had shared, and how my life was now changed forever. My mother had visions during her pregnancy, and had acted on them in order to protect me. The entire Clan MacKenzie had been gathered around her during the last month and all had made a vow to protect me. How much of this did my father know, I wondered.

Together we sat around the long wooden kitchen table, and enjoyed a hearty breakfast of warm roasted vegetables with fresh baked bread, eggs and a cheese wheel brought in fresh that morning. The hellhounds had renewed their attacks and the muffled sounds kept us all alert. As the MacKenzie's discussed what we should do next, I noticed one of the nuns kept finding excuses to be near our table, her body leaning towards our conversation as if she was trying to hear us. The Abbess did not appear to notice, nor the brothers. Perhaps all the craziness of the past week was making me paranoid.

Once we had finishing eating, the Abbess took her nephews on a patrol around the Abbey's grounds. With the renewed attacks, she wanted to be sure all the precautions put in place were still holding strong.

I made my way back to the room that had been assigned to me. I sat on the bed, feeling as though my head would burst into flames. My life had a meaning beyond who my husband would be, how many children I would have and what type of home I lived in. To think that I had spent nearly twenty years living a life not of my choosing, but simply following expectations of others. How trivial so much of that now felt. There was so much more to this world that I had believed, and it struck me as ridiculous at how sheltered of a life I had been living. My companions had been born with powers, inherited from their ancestor, another daughter of an Elemental Twin. But here I was, and I felt powerless.

From that moment, I decided that I would learn as much as I could, as fast as I could. My father had always said knowledge was power. I took my mother's journal from my pack. Cradling the leather-bound pages in my lap, I flipped through until I had found where I had left off.

My darling daughter, for I know you will be a girl. All the first children are destined to be girls. Today you have made your father so ridiculously happy. He placed his hands on my swollen belly and you pushed your little feet right back at him. He is convinced that you will be a boy because of the strength that he feels within my belly. Your father only knows that I am an angel. With his strong beliefs in the bible, I did not have to make up any other lies. After I showed him my wings, he never asked any other questions. He accepted me for what I am, in that moment, and never pressured me for answers about my life before I met him. I wanted him to know something about me. After all, he will be the one to care for you when I am gone.

I have had visions in the fire again. My end will come on the night of your birth. It aches my heart to know this. I will treasure every moment from now until then, and prepare this journal of my life for you to read one day.

You must know more about the Hunter. Many years ago, I travelled the continents, searching, wandering. It was in Rome that the dark one and I crossed paths. At first, he made me believe he was still pure of heart, not corrupted by the hunger we feel. He showed me the wonders of the old city of Rome and all was well.

Until one day I arrived at his estate and found the front gates unlocked. After wandering through the hallways, I heard sounds coming from behind the kitchen wall. As I stepped closer, I saw scratches upon the hearth. They were claw marks, and lead to a hidden entrance and a narrow flight of stairs. Descending, I became aware of a stench so strong that I gagged. It was rotten flesh, blood and sweat. The steps opened up inside a large ancient cavern, and at the centre was a cage with bars as thick as your fathers forearms. Inside was a large man with long black hair hanging in a matted mess down his back, with deep brown pleading eyes. His entire, beaten body shook with pain.

He watched me and slowly stepped to the back of his cage. I had kept my wings hidden, yet, he saw me for the being I really was.

"Woman, I see ye as the Angel ye are, I beg ye for mercy. Please kill me before the change happens." His words were uttered through gritted teeth as pain threatened to break him. I had no knowledge of what was taking place, and I told him so.

In short and forced breaths, he told me about his people. A tribe of Celts in the north called the MacKenzie clan, descended from the first girl child of my sister Meridia whom I had not seen in a millennia. The men in their family had the power to shift into large and powerful animals, and their mission was to protect not only the child, but other humans, from the angels who hunted them…the same ones who had hunted me and my sisters for a millennia.

He then told me of several fallen ones who had caught one of his ancestors after discovering their ability to shape-shift. They experimented on him. They discovered that if the blood of an angel was fed to a shape-shifter that it would transform him into a vicious beast. The Scotsmen called them hellhounds. These beasts, once turned are slaves and have absolutely no free will, and are undying and loyal to the master that created them. They would even destroy their own families if ordered to do so. The man they once were was lost, and never returned to human form, except for sometimes in the final throes of their death. Doomed to live out their days in slavery. The brother with whom I had spent these last few weeks was such a master who would use his own blood to mutate good men into monsters.

I asked him how I could possibly help, and would it not be better if I released him? He lowered his head and explained to me that he had been fed the concoction only that morning because he would not reveal the location of his clan in the north. The change would happen at nightfall. He did not want to spend the rest of his living days as a slave, a monster…as a hellhound.

I have killed before but his death weighed heavy on my heart. I will forgo the details, but he died with a grateful look on his face.

Knowing that I could be discovered at any moment, I ran up the steps, my wings unfurled, ready to take flight. I ran straight into him. He knew. He leaped into the air with his wings at full span. He grabbed my throat pressing me up against the wall.

We fought. It was only through a slight misstep on his part that allowed me the space to swing my still heated feather past him and shred through his throat. This brought him to his knees but not his death.

I ran to the lands of the Celts and sought protection with the descendants of my dear sister Meridia.

I laid her journal on my bed, my heart caught in my throat. I needed air. I made my way down the halls towards what I thought were the garden. Several hallways later, I had gotten myself all turned around. A nun stood at the end of the hallway, the same one I had noticed before at breakfast trying to snoop on the conversations happening with the Mackenzies. She was talking to someone in a rather conspiratorial tone.

"My dearest woman, tell me, my love," The voice distinctly male. "Have they arrived?"

"Oh my beloved David, they are here, just as you told me they would be." I saw her hands reaching towards the body hidden from my view by the door. "The abominations are proud of their lineage and think they are protectors of the weak. My love, my angel, you and I must protect this poor girl who thinks these beasts are her saviours. The Lord Almighty has sanctioned our union and his blessings will give us victory."

She sounded crazed, almost fanatic.

I snuck further down the hall to try to see who she was talking to. Standing behind the crack of the door, I saw a tall man with a slim, and lanky build and a very angular face. His thin lips made his grin look like that of a snake. His black hair had a strange sheen to it, an iridescent blue shimmer. The skin was a shallow pale, with a yellow hue about it, as if he was suffering from some malady. Wearing a simple black frock, and plain trousers, he was quite ordinary, if it hadn't been for his strange colouring.

"You are a warrior queen from heaven reborn on this earth." I heard him say. "Lead me to them, so that I can witness their abomination. And then, I will call on the soldiers of God to destroy these vile creatures and rescue the poor girl who has fallen under their spell."

He kissed the nun so intensely, it made my skin crawl. With a flushed face, she took him by the hand and led him towards the opposite wall. He glanced back. It was then that I saw his eyes. The deepest blue with irises of putrid yellow. Saying a prayer of thanks that I had not been discovered, a shiver ran up my spine, and I bolted as fast as I could and somehow found my way back up to my room, climbed out the window, and rather ungracefully fell into the rose bushes below. Picking thorns out of my hands and arms, as I sprinted to the last place I saw the Abbess and my protectors—on the high wall, near the tower bell, overlooking the lands surrounding the Abbey.

"MacKenzie's!" I shouted louder than I had ever before.

Just then, I saw the nun and the man called David on the other side of the courtyard, like me, looking towards the tower bell. When Athdara saw them, her eyes widened with alarm.

"Roderick, Kenneth!" she screamed. "Shift! Everyone else get to safety now!"

It was as if the world had slowed on its axis. I watched as iridescent black wings with shimmering blue ripped through his long waist coat, and he launched himself off the ground. The nun shrieked triumphantly. He was not attacking the MacKenzie's.

He was heading straight towards me.

CHAPTER 13

Petrified, unable to move, I watched the scene unfold. The blue-winged angel, David, hurling towards me from across the courtyard, the MacKenzie's leaping from the tower to land between me and the onslaught of the attacker. Trusting in their strength, I felt confident in their ability to fight off this new threat.

Amidst the chaos, I saw the Nun was running to the grain storage just to the right of me, and I found her actions most curious. Feeling returned to my body. It was time to take action.

I ran after her. I wanted to catch her before she did further mischief, but she snuck inside before I could reach her. I stood in the hallway just outside the open door, and caught her stepping backward, bumping into the sacks of grain.

"Oh my dear child, you don't know the wicked beasts you have been travelling with." She was beaming from ear to ear, with a rather crazed expression on her face. "Don't worry though. We will protect you and destroy them with the wrath of God. Oh my beautiful Angel David will—."

She had thrown open a hidden door behind the sacks of grain, and a dozen hellhounds burst through the door. To my astonishment, they tore her apart. I tried to block out her screams, hands over my ears, running down the hallway with no sense of direction, but somehow finding my way past the sleeping quarters and to the kitchens. I was just past the stairs, when Athdara, still in her human form, came bounding around the corner.

"Lass, we ha' to leave now," she said, grabbing my arm. "The Fallen one who is attacking us is known to me. His name is Abbadon, and he willna stop until he has killed everyone and taken ye wi' him. Come wi' me. There is a hidden door through which we can escape. The lads will join us as soon as they can."

She pulled me back in the direction the grain storage.

"Athdara! Nooo!" I shrieked. "That crazy nun has already let the hellhounds through that door. I saw. They killed her."

"Bloody hell!" she yelled.

We changed course, reaching the courtyard in time to watch the hellhounds flood the grounds. The rest of the nuns had barricaded themselves behind the thick walls of the church, behind the fortified with words of protection doors, after their Abbess had called the alarm. The air was filled with the howls and roars from the hellhounds.

He found us, looming up behind from the hallway we had just raced through.

"There you are! That stupid nun almost made me doubt her sanity."

The voice stopped us dead in our tracks.

"I can smell shifter blood on you woman," he said, his eyes devouring Athdara. "So…the rumours of a female shifter are true, after all."

Athdara stepped forward, pulling me by my hand to keep me behind her. He had blocked any further escape across the courtyard. The hellhounds were running wild in the hallways and across the grounds. We were trapped.

"I must admit you are much prettier than the rest of your brood." Abbadon spoke as if he had all the time in world. "I cannot wait to—"

A deafening roar came from behind him. The brother's had broken through the pack of hellhounds, leaving half a dozen dead in their path. The bear and the wolf were upon the angel, who spun around, surprised. Given this brief moment of distraction, Athdara and I ran towards the north east corner of the courtyard, leaving in our wake the sounds of the savage fight—growls, grunts, screams—otherworldly bodies locked in combat. Sobs caught in my throat as I thought of my protectors risking their lives, yet again.

We cut across the gardens next to the courtyard and once at the Roman Latrines, Athdara stripped her nun's habit to reveal dark brown leather pants made for travel and a grey peasant blouse, cinched with a matching leather vest. She had custom leather boots to fit the length of her legs, with heels and the toes capped with metal. She pulled me towards the farthest corner of the latrine, to the last of the long bench-like seats made of wood, and pulled the thick board covering the top off one of the seats, discarding it behind us. The stench of the excrement rose through the exposed opening. My disgust was interrupted by a howl at the entry of the latrine a mere fifteen feet from us.

A hellhound had found us. It ran towards us and leapt into the air towards me and flinching with fear, I closed my eyes, waiting for the end. The sound of cloth tearing, followed by a strangled yelp from the hellhound, and I opened my eyes just as Athdara's claws plucked the hound from mid-air and smashed him to the ground. She stood, the human half of her pinning it down with her boot to its chest, while her upper body was covered in white fur that had split through the sleeves of her blouse. The hound struggled to get to its feet, trying to gnaw through the leather of her pants, down to her flesh. With one swipe of her bear-like claws she tore his throat from his body. Nearly decapitated, it fell motionless. Athdara limped over to where I stood, took a deep shuddering breath, and transformed back to her full human form, with the blouse sleeves hanging in shredded tatters, torn from her transformation.

"Do ye trust me?" she asked, stepping up onto the ledge of the last seat.

"Why of course I do! Why do you—" I stammered in confusion.

"Because I need ye to step up on the side o' this hole, in front o' me—and trust me." Gingerly, stepping up onto the edge of the latrine next to the gaping hole, I looked down with disgust as the stench became stronger.

"Now, step forward."

Not giving me any time to respond, she grasped my wrists and pulled me towards the exact spot she intended. I landed in a vat of human waste and sludge-like water that nearly reached up to my knees and tugged heavily at my skirts.

"Turn right lass, there is a tunnel on the other side," she said, landing in the muck right next to me. "We ha' to be very quiet. For now the smell will make it near impossible for the hounds to find us, but they can still hear us."

I tried to breathe as shallow as possible, knowing what caused the foul stench. It was a small miracle I did not vomit. The bog of human waste made it hard to keep my boots on, they kept getting stuck in the muck. As she led the way through the dark pathway, holding my hand, it narrowed with each step. After what may have been minutes or hours, we both stopped. S*moke?* The Abbey, now just above us, was on fire.

"We must hurry, the entire Latrine is made of wood and will burn quickly." Athdara said, still holding my hand, guiding us ever forward. "The last thing we need is to celebrate the escape from them beasts only to succumb to smoke inhalation."

As we trudged onward, I could hear the hellhounds above us bounding across the grounds of the Abbey, accompanied by their howls. The galloping speed of the beasts shook the tunnel walls, and sometimes knocked the dirt from above us loose. Just as we saw a dim flicker of light—the end of the tunnel—scraping noise began to close in on us from behind. Athdara pushed me forwards, prepared to attack whatever was coming for us. She began the transformation of her wounded body, which would only be more painful due to the vicious gash on her leg.

"Stop!" Roderick yelled out. "Athdara, it's yer wee nephews."

Now closer to the light, I was able to see Kenneth by his side, who was limping behind his brother. Both were wearing tattered trousers, but their torsos were bare and covered in lacerations and bleeding from too many open wounds to count.

"There is nothing wee about either o' my nephews," Athdara muttered quietly, but relieved to not have to complete the transformation. "But I appreciate the sense o' humour. Ye are verra much like yer da'."

Nearing the edge of the tunnel, our way was slowed by the shrinking of the walls. I was able to continue to walk upright, but my companions had to hunch very low to avoid hitting their heads and to be able to exit safely. On the other side of the tunnel was an open field. As we clambered from the earth, far from the abbey, feeling the sun on my skin had never felt so good. Breathing in the fresh air brought us all renewed vigour, albeit brief.

"We must find a healer, and quickly." Kenneth gasped, looking at his brother. "Athdara, the hound's claws and fangs were dipped in a poison."

It was then that I saw Roderick's shoulder in the light of day. The bite was deep, and he was bleeding dark red, almost black, and tinged with malevolent purple. I looked to Athdara, who was sweating profusely and examining her leg, which had swollen to nearly double its size and was oozing the same shades of liquid as his wound. She turned her gaze towards the Abbey one last time.

"Aye lads, it appears we must make haste." She muttered through gritted teeth, as the pain of the wound got stronger. "May the powers o' heaven receive the souls who perished this day."

We were all covered in the dirt and waste that lined the tunnel walls. Roderick and Kenneth had collapsed onto the grass, and Athdara had just walked away from the Abbey and the life she had known for the last seven years. Looking at my three guardians, injured while protecting me, feelings of frustrations and anger boiled under the surface. Everyone was getting hurt around me—for me, because of me—and I could do nothing to help them. *What was the point?* This deranged notion that I could control an element was now absurd.

"Come, we only ha' a short way to go lads." Athdara leaned down to aid Kenneth in lifting Roderick back onto his feet. "See that grove o' trees? We must reach them."

The short journey cost Roderick dearly. He fainted at the foot of the large Ash tree that Athdara had guided us towards. Kenneth, helping his brother into a more secure position before he too sunk to the ground, exhausted and feverish. She leaned her right hand heavily onto the tree trunk for support, and looking up into the thick branches, made little cooing noises. She then reach up with her other hand. Curious, I treaded closer, and through the leaves a small falcon hopped onto her forearm. She whispered to it, and it flew away.

"Are ye a wee bird whisperer now, Auntie?" Kenneth groaned through his teeth, trying to keep a sense of humour in our rather grim situation.

"No lad, but that wee bird is going to bring us the help we sorely need." She sighed, sinking into the ground beside Roderick.

We stayed underneath the coverage of trees and bushes to avoid possible prying eyes from above. We were still covered in filth, the MacKenzie's were not even wearing shoes or boots, and my own were completely covered in the human waste from the tunnels, so it was unlikely the hounds would find us by scent alone—or so the shapeshifters assured me—as long as we stayed quiet. Given the condition of my companions, I did not think that noise would be an issue… they were barely breathing.

As we sat, I looked at the state of my companions, my protectors, and couldn't help but wonder what it was all for—I was almost twenty years old, and no sign of the elemental powers—was I really worth all this suffering?

Within the hour a large caravan of gypsies drove by a few hundred yards from where we were resting. By this point, all of my guardians were suffering the ill effects of the poison in their blood. Their bodies sweating from fever, and their breath barely discernible from the wind rustling through the tops of the trees.

"Moireach, ye must run to 'em. Ask for Silvanus." Athdara barely managed to whisper, before her eye lids fluttered and she too slumped against the tree trunk.

I ran as fast as my legs would allow, my heavy mud encrusted skirts threatening to trip my approach. I reached the outer edges of the caravan completely out of breath and unable to speak. One of the men jumped off the wagon, and pulled a dagger from his waist band. He walked towards me, dagger in hand.

"Please!" I cried out, putting up my hands. "I must speak to Silvanus."

I began to sob. The man paused, then took a few long strides across the grass, to stand right in front me. I wanted to warn him not to stand too close, still feeling nauseous myself from the stench of the tunnels, but his nose had already crinkled up with disgust. He started to laugh out loud.

"Silvanus, come here," he shouted. "This is not a child after all, but I believe she is the maiden we ha' been told about. And from the smell o' her, she has been in yer Athdara's tunnels. I tell ye that woman never ceases to amaze me."

The man who emerged from the wagon in the lead, was a stocky and sturdily built man of average height with curly black hair peaking out from underneath his wide-brimmed hat. His loose grey shirt, was open at the collar, revealing layers of silver and gold necklaces. As he sauntered over, I noticed that rings adorned each of his fingers and metal bracelets jangled on both of his wrists.

"Well, you are unquestionably the lady of which we have been told, Lady MacRae," he asserted, his voice was smooth and raspy all at once and his gold-flecked green eyes looked me over carefully. "And I, Silvanus, am at yer service. Now, where is Athdara? And I believe there are others? Why are ye alone?"

"Just behind me, hidden in the trees. With my… her… nephews. They are all injured."

Silvanus whistled over his shoulder, and immediately gypsies appeared, opening up the wagons.

"We are going to need bigger blankets." One of the men stated flatly. "If the rumours are true that is."

Several men pulled large thick blankets from the back of the last wagon.

"Now, tiny lady, bring us to their place among the trees."

We found them all in the same place I left them. Kenneth and Roderick, who were still unconscious, and Athdara, who had somehow held onto consciousness.

"Silvanus, I kent ye wouldna keep me waiting long."

"Oh my sweet woman, oot picking fights again?" He knelt beside her and took her into his arms, kissing her cheek softly. Tears were running down his face, as he held her.

"I dinna pick fights, but I sure as hell finish them." she chuckled. "Now, *go*! Ye must collapse the tunnel."

"Athdara, dinna ask me to leave yer side."

"Silvanus, the longer ye delay the more ye risk all o' us being found by the hounds. We didna kill them all, and Abbadon is still on the loose."

Gently laying her back against the tree, he stood up with a mischievous smirk on his face, and pulling a strange rounded bottle with ominous oily black fluids on the inside from a bag he had draped around his shoulders. He walked past us, whistled, and one of the horses broke free from the caravans and galloped in our direction. As the steed passed by Silvanus, mid-stride the gypsy hoisted himself up into the saddle, and rode off in the direction of the tunnels we had just escaped through.

We watched from afar. As he reached the entrance of the tunnels, he bound off his horse, and ran inside. I held my breath, fear for Silvanus and what might be in the tunnel, but moments later he bolted out and was galloping towards us.

"Lads, finish the harnesses, and let's get them to the caravans straight away," he called out to his men. "If I've measured the contents correctly, we ha' less than five minutes."

Sliding off the saddle with ease, he walked towards Athdara and lifted her, with care, and held her close to his chest. Neither said a word but she leaned in and their foreheads touched, while both of them took a deep breath together. It was such a sweet moment of affection, that I felt a pang of jealousy at never having experienced that in my life. With the brothers hoisted onto the make-shift stretchers, prepared and harnessed by Silvanus's men, we ran towards the caravan. We were nearly there when we heard the sound of booming thunder and felt the earth below us rumbling. The horses did not falter in their course, and we did not slow our stride. There was no time to celebrate the destruction of the tunnels.

I counted twenty wagons, some with wooden canopies, others with covers made from coloured fabric. Each led by a team of two, sometimes four horses. After the success of the explosion, some of the men who had rushed to our aid at Silvanus's command split off to find their respective wagons and families. Others saw to it that Athdara, the brothers, and I were taken to the largest wood covered wagon, where Silvanus joined us.

I stepped inside to find an old woman, sitting on the right side of the wagon. She was dressed in many colours, layers of skirts gathered about her legs, and with hands weighed down by bracelets, cuffs and rings. Her dark grey hair shimmered under the light of the lantern, and was only partially covered in an embroidered scarf tied in a knot at the nape of her neck. The deep wrinkles and tanned skin showed a woman of advanced years. She hadn't moved when I entered, and I feared for a brief moment she might have been dead… until she did move and started to mumble under her breath.

"Lady MacRae, this is my mother Kezia." The voice of Silvanus was calming and full of sincerity. "She is our healer, and I promise ye, will ensure that each o' yer guardians will survive the poison o' the hounds."

Roderick and Kenneth lay side by side, near the opening, filling the width of the wagon, while Athdara had been brought further inside and resting on a thick padding of blankets. The men, who had lifted the giants into the wagon, had stayed outside and moved to the front, leading the horses and the rest of the caravan away from the tunnels.

I let out a loud sigh. My body started to shake, from shock or relief—maybe both.

"Ach, ye wee nuisance could ye kindly breathe a little quieter?" In his fevered state, Roderick sat up abruptly with a feeble attempt to stand, fearing the worst, looking around. "I have pesky scratch that is bothering me and could use a wee rest."

He kissed his large hand and placed it briefly on the top of my forehead, and crumbled back onto his makeshift bed. The old woman Kezia had moved behind me and placed her hand on my shoulder. She nudged me aside, holding a pewter bowl covered with symbols that felt familiar, which she had fetched from the back of the wagon. *The markings looked like those on the doors of the Abbey!* She slathered the balm from the dish on the lacerations on each of their wounds. The relief was instantaneous, marked by the heavy sighs and the calm sleep that ensued.

Kezia gestured towards a small night gown, and pointed at my own clothes with a look of disdain. No words were needed, and I was grateful to be rid of the clothes covered in filth. With the men asleep, I had the guaranteed privacy I needed to change into the clothes provided by the gypsy woman. She gathered up my dress, the skirts, the blouse and the boots and placed them in a burlap sack towards the side of the wagon. And then together we worked to remove the clothing from each of the wounded MacKenzie's, and replacing them with simple cloth shirts and trousers. I was spared any awkward moments with the men, as Kezia bid me to turn around while she managed the more intimate parts of the task set out for us. She was far stronger than her appearance indicated, and I was impressed at her ability to lift an entire limb of Roderick's with what appeared as ease. Their clothing joined mine outside the wagon, and I heard one of the men come around and remove it.

Sitting towards the end of the wagon, on a small mat of blankets, near Athdara and beside Roderick, I watched her carefully clean the wounds of my protectors, and with it some of the stench and filth from the tunnels, my exhaustion took over. I did not think it was possible for me to fall asleep, but the rocking of the carriage combined with the gentle crooning noises coming from Kezia, allowed me to drift into an exhausted sleep. I do not know how long I slept, but when I woke, I saw that everyone in the carriage was still asleep but no sign of Silvanus. Wanting to see the landscape to know where we were, I climbed through the canvas flap to the front of the carriage, and to my surprise, it was Silvanus himself leading our wagon. The sun was only just rising, and the beginnings of light were seen across the horizon.

"Look who we found along the way!" He gestured to his right, and to my delight, I saw our three horses. They had escaped the carnage at the Abbey.

"How did they find us?" I asked, thinking of how happy Kenneth would be.

"Well, they didna exactly find us," he said. "I sent a few o' my men to the Abbey to survey the aftermath and determine what danger may be coming our way. They found the horses grazing rather calmly by the meadow not far from the Abbey grounds. And, Athdara will be pleased to ken that we buried the bodies o' the nuns. Paid our respects, ye ken."

"Thank you Silvanus," I was moved to tears, when I thought about all those who had perished.

"Let's speak o' happier things, shall we?" He offered me a large terra cotta mug filled with a warm liquid I had never tasted. It was pleasant, comforting. "Take this drink for example. We take dandelion leaves, which grow wild everywhere, dry them out for a week or two by hanging them inside the wagons and grind them into a powder. Then we mix in some ginger, lemon, and honey all with hot water. And sometimes if we can get our hands on the precious spice…" He looked over at me and winked. "We add cinnamon."

"Well it tastes delicious." I sipped at the soothing warm drink, and having been curious about the connection from the moment I saw them embrace, I asked, "Silvanus, how did you come to know Athdara?"

"Oh that silly old fable? Well, we met many years ago, when we were both just barely thirteen." he said. "She was out harvesting in the convent orchard to the north, and I was a young gypsy trying to steal a few apples. The young Abbess-to-be, guessing my intentions, had seen me climb a tree and launched an apple straight at my head. I fell oot w' such force that I was knocked unconscious. The young lass, so worried she might ha' killed me, ran to see if her throw had indeed inflicted the damage she feared. When I awoke, I saw the most beautiful face I had ever or shall ever see again. From that moment, I made myself a promise to win her heart. She proved to be a hard catch, not because of her commitment to the church but because o' her fear that I would find out her true nature."

"So how did you find out that she could change her body into that of an animal?"

"The countryside had been plagued by the violence o' a rogue hellhound. Our people had tracked it to the moors. The men had decided to gather and hunt it before it could strike again. It had already killed five men over a few weeks. She begged me not to go out that night and asked me to stay safe inside the wagons. I told her I couldna do that, knowing it would put my whole tribe at risk. Asking me to trust her, she shared w' me ancient words in a language that sounds a wee bit like the Gaelic but subtle differences, which she then used to create a circle o' protection around the wagons. Ye see by then, I had already given my heart to her, and didna question where or how she knew those words would work. And despite the men's desire to hunt the vicious beast, they trusted me and allowed themselves and their families to be kept safe in the wagons. I waited nearly an hour, before my intuition, or maybe it was my curiosity, finally got too strong and I decided to venture oot onto the moors myself."

"But you were just a young man!" I interrupted. "Why did the men trust you?"

"Although I was a lad o' only seventeen years, I had already been given the role o' chief for some time. My family, the Chaucers, ha' held the seat of leadership for many generations, and my father, Gregori Chaucer, had been grooming me to become the next leader before he died that winter past."

He paused, took a deep breath. I sipped the comforting tonic from my mug, waiting for him to continue.

"Our caravan has crossed paths wi' hellhounds more times than I care to admit. For a few generations, we ha' shared stories and myths o' these creatures around our fires at night. I must ha' walked for nearly two miles, and I am no ashamed to admit I was more worried I might shite myself from fear, each step I remembered the horrific tales I heard as a child about these hellhounds. Almost ready to turn around, I heard the shuffling sounds. Walking towards the noise quickly and quietly, I chose a tree that would allow me to climb to a secure vantage point where I witnessed two animals wrestling along the ground. I had thought that perhaps the hellhound had crossed paths wi' a wild boar. Safe in the highest branches, I saw the beasts. One was a hellhound, the other was a snow-white creature unlike anything I had ever seen before. Not in all o' our stories or songs is there mention o' any living being like her."

He paused, the memory playing out vividly in his mind.

"I suppose my reaction was much the same." I added my own memories to the moment. "Only I had the benefit of watching the change take place so I understood. It would have been a very different story had I come across her in the wilds of a forest."

"Aye, then ye ken. Well, this creature, which was almost as large as the hellhound but resembled both a bear and a wolf, was winning. Despite a vicious wound along its upper back, bleeding from shoulder to shoulder, it was steady on all fours and had pinned the hellhound beneath a front claw. Wi' a ferocious bite, this magical creature had torn out the hound's throat, and the fight was over before I could reach the ground, mangled limbs were strewn across the damp grass. When I hopped down from the tree, the victor turned to face me and bared its blood-stained teeth. Unsure about its intentions, I thought about running, but I knew it woulda been pointless, so I pulled my dagger from my waistband, so I could at least go down fighting."

He paused.

"When, before my very eyes, the creature transformed into a young woman. And not just any woman, but the very one I had fallen in love with nearly four years prior. Stark naked, shivering, and covered in blood, she started to cry. Oh, how my heart cherished her in that moment."

Silvanus's face softened with a smile, and he let out a gentle sigh, the affection as strong now as it was then.

"I gave her my shirt and my cloak to cover her up and offered up my body for warmth. We huddled by a fire, built wi' wood and the remains o' the hellhound, so others couldna find it and trace it back to either the caravan or the Abbey. While I tended to her wounds, she told me o' her mission that night, o' the role she had been given by her brother—to protect the future, when a young woman o' unique birth would be hunted by those dark ones, the fallen angels. That would be you, lass." He winked at me. "I learned more about who the hellhounds were and what had brought them all into existence. It made me love her more, that her life should have such purpose. It explained a lot about her confidence and her courage. Yet, I also understood the burden o' responsibility she carried. After all, I too had been groomed to caretake my entire tribe. That night I bound myself to her forever, wi' a hand fasting ceremony which we held in front of my entire family.

"Silvanus, wasn't she living at the Abbey?"

"Ach aye, but we found ways to see each other, sometimes several days at a time, and other times only for a few short hours. But it was enough, it was always enough. We always ensured that the precious time we had together, was magical. I will die at that woman's side, a happy man."

As he shared more of their life journey with me, I felt envious. Here I was, nearly twenty years of age, and I felt I had barely lived when I thought of their story, or the lives of Kenneth and Roderick. And everyone knew my mother as a powerful angel, and I had yet to show any spark of her abilities. And then I started to think of Damian, and I felt my body temperature rise along with restless fidgeting, as I remembered his hands on my body and our kiss.

"If ye forgive my boldness, but I sense something is nagging yer thoughts—." Silvanus was more observant than I had expected. "Why don't ye go back into the wagon, and check on yer companions? Ask my mother how ye can help. Being o' service is a healthy way to keep thoughts from overwhelming ye."

For the next few days, we travelled slowly towards the north east coast, to confuse those who might come after us. On our first night we did not gather around a fire, for fear we were still within range of the hellhounds and the fallen one, Abbadon. I had been given a child's dress belonging to Silvanus's niece, as we discovered that I was too small for any of the women's clothing from the caravan. Roderick and Kenneth, still bare chested and healing, remained in our wagon, on strict orders that required little movement and much rest to allow their bodies to fully heal. Meanwhile, Athdara had been moved to another carriage and there was able to recover with the love and support of Silvanus. On the second night, and every night after, we gathered around a huge fire, sharing food and mead. Our wagon was pulled inside the circle of wagons, closest to the fire and we would open the back door and drop the steps down, so the brothers felt included. The gypsy men would bring out violins, guitars, pipes and small drums. The women would dance around the fire, so very different from the ones I was accustomed to seeing in London, in either the courts or the taverns—sultry, seductive, and very dominant, leaving every man hypnotized by their movements.

I did not join them at first. Claiming exhaustion as my excuse, but in truth I was struggling with my fears and doubts held me back. I was at war with my upbringing, and the new feelings which were awakening inside of me.

"Ach, go on ye wee minx, ye ken how much yer body wants to dance." Kenneth nudged me on the second night.

Yet, as much I longed for the freedom of the dance, even with his encouragement I felt too withdrawn. The sultry movements of the women reminded me of the heat I felt with Damian. Dresses of deep burgundies, emerald greens, royal purple and midnight blue trimmed with golds and silvers, twirled around the fire. Their long dark hair free, moving with their bodies while the glint from bracelets and necklaces created a magical light flashing in the dark of the night, like fire flies. It felt intimidating. There was no place for me to hide in the middle of the crowd. The laughter of the women, the friendly jeering of the men, all created conflicting emotions in my body. I wanted to join them, but it brought up all those unknown feelings that I had felt with Damian—desire, lust, passion and heat. So, I sat next to my protectors, in the child's dress I had been gifted, and watched…longingly but still feeling unsure of myself.

Until the night when Silvanus stood up with his violin. He played such a beautiful and haunting song that my feet moved of their own volition. Taking me away from the safety of the wagon, and before I could reconsider, I had leapt up with the women circling the fire. With each pluck from the strings, my arms lifted, and my heart soared. Soon, the other men joined their instruments with the wild and passionate sound. As the song sped up so did my dancing, and I began to pirouette around the fire. Moving with a different rhythm than the other women, completely out of sync, and yet completely in-sync with the movement of the flames. My eyes were half closed. Faster and faster, leaping with such joy, and feeling freedom.

The blaze of the fire, and the music brought memories of Damian's kiss—the heat I felt from his lips against mine. My breath came in shallow gasps, as my body tried to catch up with the quickening of my heart beat. I thought of this man—this angel. I thought of his eyes, his hands, his touch. I sensed movement very close behind me, unlike that of the women I could see in my peripheral, but I didn't pay attention. Dancing and my thoughts of the angel who inexplicably had a hold of my heart were all that I cared about in that moment. When the song abruptly came to an end, the flames erupted with volcanic proportion. Dazed, almost hypnotized, I stumbled towards the fire, the flames reaching out to me, as if they had a life of their own.

Everyone else had come to a standstill and watched with wide-eyed amazement. It was Silvanus, who had slowly walked up behind me, and who pulled me back from the flames, before they devoured me.

"Well, tiny fire dancer." He chuckled out loud. "It appears ye are yer mother's daughter after all."

I was bewildered. *Had I done that?*

CHAPTER 14

Our final destination was Eilean Donan, the place of my birth, along the west coast, but we continued a confusing path along the north east coast to confuse our enemies. We travelled at a slow but steady pace to allow my guardians to heal, and to give Silvanus's men time to scout the surrounding area before moving the caravan along. On more than one occasion one of them would spot hellhound tracks, and so we would have to reroute again, to avoid crossing paths with them.

And so our life with the gypsies unfolded. The brothers slept a lot the first few days, and were recovering at a healthy rate, for which I was very grateful. Their bodies were healing from the deep wounds and a few broken ribs which had drained them of their strength. Although neither of them was used to rest, so every day the two showed their frustration at being bedridden in various ways. Roderick, so used to organizing the household for father, made several attempts at helping the gypsies in a similar manner. However, after a few failed attempts, having witnessed how the gypsies had their own ways, which usually worked better than he had thought, he gave up. He kept his nose out of their business and allowed

Kezia, who had a fondness for the giant, to fuss over him extensively. Meanwhile Kenneth, kept trying to free himself of the wagon he was sequestered to so that he could take care for the horses. One evening we found him crumpled in a heap at the base of the steps of the wagon, leading from his place of rest, having fainted from the pain. He was unhappy and pouted like a child who did not get his way. Kezia found a solution; by moving the carriage next to where the horses were allowed to wander loose within a small enclosure when we would stop for the night. A small foal had found Kenneth and the bonding was instantaneous.

Meanwhile, Athdara limped around on her injured leg with Silvanus always at her side. She and Silvanus were free to enjoy the nights in the arms of the man she had loved for so long. During the day, they both spent a significant amount of time going over maps and other documents to which I was not privy. Every time I would approach them, the papers would be hastily covered.

Kezia's healing potions were key to their recovery, along with her knowledge of the old words. After the first day, she asked me to help her with grinding some herbs into a fine powder, and remarked in her broken english.

"My herbs good," she said. "Yer mother give me words. The words good. But Water Element best. Water to shape body. Water to heal fast."

News that my mother had been a part of Kezia's life astonished me but I no longer reacted with disbelief. So much of my life had changed that now even the abnormal seemed… well,…normal.

"Moireach, MacKenzie boys change shape at thirteen." Pointing at the two MacKenzie men. "They chose animal for life, but they can change if they want. Only Athdara cannot."

Finding out that the MacKenzie's had the power to choose any animal shape they liked was something I had not known, and that Athdara was stuck in that strange mythical form seemed almost…sad.

Then again, almost all of what I was learning these days was new. Colin MacKenzie, the youngest, was fifteen when I last saw him, after the boar attack. He had already stood over six feet tall. From memory alone, he was blonde with clear blue eyes and a lightness about him that the older two did not possess, and a rather cheeky smile. When my father had banished Nanny back to our lands in Scotland, her youngest son had returned with her. We had been childhood companions, but were often kept apart due to our sex and the roles we both had to play in society and in our households. I wondered what animal he had chosen.

In the mornings, I would help the other women with the daily chores. We were responsible for packing up each wagon to ready for the day's travel, preparing meals and washing clothes. Although I had run a household since I was very young, it was an entirely different thing to be doing the work physically, rather than delegate. One of the women enjoyed tasking me with the most menial duties, telling me that a high-born lady such as myself could never hope to complete them correctly. I was determined to prove her wrong. I burned my hands on the cauldron over the fire, blistered some of my fingers trying to pour oil over the pans, and cut the rest of my fingers while trying to prepare vegetables for the meals. But I was proud of my hands, they were proof that I was earning my keep and, for once, not relying on others to care or provide for me. It took a few days, but I was starting to feel like I was part of the tribe.

Having had some time to think of my odd predicament, I decided to speak with the leader of the gypsies.

"Silvanus?" I found him sitting under a nearby oak tree scribbling on some papers during our early midday rest. "Would you show me how to use a knife?"

"Ye mean for the cooking? Lass ye can ask any o' our women for that." He dismissed me, much like my father would.

"No, I mean to defend myself." I would not be swayed.

"Tiny Fire Dancer, why do ye wish to learn that?" He looked up and shuffling the papers out of sight. "Would ye not enjoy learning to sing or play the violin, or—."

"—No, I would not." I said, purposefully ignoring his wink. "I am tired of letting those I care about get hurt in order to protect me. It isn't right, nor fair. I know I am in need of protection, but I need to learn to do some of it myself!"

"Verra well," he paused, looking me up and down with discerning eyes. "We shall begin tomorrow, if ye still desire this. But, in truth, it would be far more effective, if ye truly want to learn to protect yerself and those ye love, to embrace the *fire*."

"Embrace the *fire?*" I walked closer to him, moved his papers, and peered down. "What do you mean, Silvanus? I don't understand."

"Think upon it. Yer heart will guide ye."

There was nothing else. I was left to wander about that day filled with thoughts of flames, burning, heat, and... Damian. However, the next day, Silvanus, true to his word, enlisted a few of his men to teach me how to defend myself with a dagger. I was clumsy and looked ridiculous, and felt absurdly incompetent. I had no idea how to hold onto the weapon and had little sense of how to control my body. Still, the men were gentle, yet they never missed an opportunity to mock or tease me, which gave me the sense that they were simply humouring their leader's request. *How was this teaching me anything?*

"Come wee one, show us how ye can prick us!" one of them taunted. "Before we prick you!"

Tears of indignation began to well up, followed by the kindling of frustration that arose from my belly. I turned to face my mocker and memories of the weeks past flooded my thoughts. My vision blurred, and my whole body felt intense heat. When I took a step forward, intending to strike back at my challenger, I was startled to find Silvanus standing before me, dagger in hand.

"Tiny Fire Dancer, ye wish to learn to use a weapon made by mortal hands when ye wield a weapon far greater than that o' even the Immortals." he said, lowering my knife. "We will teach ye, but ye must honour the *fire*."

He spoke not only directly to me, but also to his men.

"Silvanus, is the girl child willing to feel pain? And not just this silly game we've been playing at." A man named Matthias had stepped forward. "So she can truly ken what it feels like if a man attacks—"

"—I will take any physical punishment I need in order to learn the lessons."

Before Silvanus could acknowledge him, Matthias stepped forward, knife in hand, and grabbed me by my right shoulder. He spun me around so quick that I had no idea how I ended up pinned to his chest, knife at my throat, and one arm painfully twisted against my lower back. I kicked at his shins with my boot heel. *He winced but did not let go.* Next, I tried prying his arm from my throat with my free hand. *His grip only tightened.* I made another attempt to struggle free by wriggling my arms trying to shake him loose. *He twisted my pinned arm, wrenching it to an awkward, painful angle.* It occurred to me that my arm may break. *He forced my arm upwards and I heard a popping noise come from my shoulder.* I bit my own lip, refusing to cry. I was angry. Flashes of memories from this past week where I was helpless. I would not be a victim again. My hand was still latched onto the arm around my neck. I could feel the rough hairs on his skin.

With a cry of outrage and fury, I felt something inside of me—*fire.* Matthias yelped in pain. We were both so startled that he released his hold so suddenly that it dropped me painfully to my knees. My palm had seared his flesh. I rose to stand, examining my own hands in near disbelief.

Silvanus stepped in front of me, offering me his hand in a gentlemanly gesture to help me rise.

"We ha' known ye would come into our lives." He spoke quietly. All the men around us removed their hats, and bowed their heads towards me."Yer fire only proves what we ha' known all along. Ye are of yer mother's blood."

He looked at the injured man, and back at me.

"Matthias, go to my mother and ha' yer burn looked after. And Lady Moireach, yer arm will need tending to—if I'm not mistaken, I heard the familiar sound o' a shoulder popping out o' joint. Shall we get on wi' it?"

Already, my body had begun throbbing and the dull ache spreading down my arm. I suspected, the procedure would not be pleasant.

* * *

From then on, my training started in earnest. Outfitted in slim fitting trousers from one of the boys, and a snug blouse held in place by a leather vest, from one of the young girls in the caravan. It was only mildly amusing that all of the adult women's clothing were far too big for my frame. In the mornings, men took turns drilling me in the many techniques for defending myself against a human attack—using knives, daggers, swords and grappling styles used by circus wrestlers. Those lessons left my body bruised, and drained. My afternoons were spent with Kezia getting my battered body healed. It wasn't until my third day of lessons that the brothers found out and protested loudly. They awoke to my shouts of frustration, as I was again caught off guard during a grappling exercise. Thinking we were being attacked, both Roderick and Kenneth struggled out of their beds and hobbled towards my cries.

Matthias had been holding me up in the air, ready to drop my body towards the ground with the goal to pin me down. Showing more savvy than he expected, my squirming had loosened his grip. Resulting in my body landing a lot harder, and sooner, than he had intended. Out came the cry that drew the brothers to my rescue.

"What the bloody hell is going on here?" Roderick shouted as he hobbled towards us.

"Lady M, are ye alright?" Kenneth yelled from behind his brother.

"MacKenzie's…" Silvanus replied calmly. "We are showing Lady MacRae how to fight."

"No ye are nae!" Roderick continued to shout. "How is throwing her around like a rag doll helping her?"

"Roderick, Kenneth." I said, as I stood up and dusted off my trousers. "I'm alright. And I need this. I need to stop feeling like a hapless victim…to stop feeling like some useless pawn in a game I never signed up for."

"Brother, perhaps it's time we stop treating her like the wee lass she once was." Kenneth spoke quietly and looked poignantly at Roderick, placing his hand assuringly on his brother's shoulder. "And instead, like the grown and capable woman we know her to be?"

I didn't realize I was holding my breath, while Roderick pondered this new development in our journey.

"Aye, I suppose 'tis time," Roderick said with a mischievous look on his face. "So, are ye ready to learn more then?"

"I am more than ready!" My guardians would help train me, and I was grinning from ear to ear with gratitude and relief.

From that day on, the MacKenzie's joined in on my daily, unconventional education. And once their wounds healed enough that they could share their knowledge with me, Kenneth and Roderick took turns in showing me their skills—how to track animals, which plants would be safe to eat and which could be used for healing, and how to hide my own trail to avoid anyone who might be hunting me.

I relished all the lessons, recognizing that the knowledge these men, both gypsies and shape-shifters, were sharing with me would be valuable for months and years to come. I had not been able to summon the *fire* again since the day I had burned Matthias's arm. Every evening this weighed on me. As the gypsies would gather, dance, and drink around the fire, I was faced with both hope and frustration. I had no idea how to summon the flames—the *fire*.

"Lady…why can't ye just dance and ha' fun?" said, Niklas, Silvanus's seven year old nephew one evening.

I wanted to tell that child to respect his elders but I realized he had a point.

Joining the women that night, moving with the beat from the drums and sway from the violins, I stopped worrying. The *fire* would only come if I learned to surrender the outcome. And yet I would have to find a way to hold onto it, once I had it within my grasp. It would take over an hour of dancing, and losing myself to the music and the movement, before I was able to reach that precise point of surrender. Only then could I use the *fire* that had risen within me and influence the flames.

The success I felt was brief. As soon as I saw the flames move and grow as I had wished them, I lost that place of surrender.

On our sixth day, or maybe it was the seventh, in honesty I had lost track of the days we had been travelling, after having spent the day without pause and near exhaustion, I walked up to the communal fire pit. The skies were darkening with the sunset, and I had no patience to wait for anyone else. The stone circle was filled with branches, wood chips, and logs in preparation for the evening. Kindling just waiting for a spark to ignite it. I sat down on a blanket and found myself staring into the lifeless fire pit. I felt no resistance, just a desire for the fire to come alive and warm my cold and tired body.

A moment was all it took. I closed my eyes, turning my gaze inwards, and saw the *fire* inside of me. Opening my eyes, the kindling ignited so quickly, it startled not only myself but my two companions who had walked up behind me.

"Now, tiny fire dancer, ye truly are one of the Immortal Elements."

Silvanus was smiling, holding hands with Athdara, and they both sat down on a blanket across from me. Gathered around the fire, which I had ignited, that night with my guardians, and the gypsies who had become like family, I felt whole. I was not naive enough to think that our life could go on forever like this, after all, we were being chased. I was being hunted. But now, I was starting to grasp some understanding about the *fire* that lived within me. There was still so much to learn, but that night I felt more hope than frustration as I watched the flames dance.

Watching Silvanus and Athdara share a very intimate dance, I wondered if I would ever see Damian again. How my body reacted with warmth, whether it be anger, frustration, or the desire that Damian awoke, it was all too apparent that the *fire* had always been part of me. When I could barely keep my eyes open, I retreated to my wagon to take off my skirt and blouse from the day and changed into the roughly spun cotton night shift I had been given. Laying down on the bedding that Athdara had once occupied before moving into Silvanus's wagon, I pulled the blanket up to my chin and fell soundly asleep.

The dreams I had that night were almost a foreboding of events to come. Fire everywhere. Screams, blood and a noise I could not identify but associated with pain. Everything was so blurry and frightening that I was startled awake in the morning with everything quiet around me.

I put on a dress made from home-spun wool in a rich emerald green with a wide burgundy waistband to hold my dagger. I had inherited it from one of the young gypsy girls. We had to let the seams out at the bust area, but it allowed me some freedom of movement without the usual constraints of the corsets I wore in London. These days it seemed that there was nothing left of my old life, except the beautiful pendant, which I kept hidden within the confines of my stockings, not trusting the security of the pockets of the dresses or trousers. And it took all my willpower not to use it to call out to Damian, trusting he was protecting my father. I pulled my hair back into a simple, thick braid and laced the bottom with a short leather strap, before jumping down from the wagon to help the women who were preparing our morning meal of porridge, eggs, and fresh milk.

As I walked through the camp, something in the air didn't smell right but I couldn't put my finger on what was different. Perhaps it was just the strange dreams which had unsettled me. After breakfast, Kezia sent me to tighten the knots on several horses' reigns. The animals too showed signs of nervousness, barely eating their food and many had been pulling themselves loose throughout morning.

The line of horses were all that stood between me and edges of the trees which led to the forest, and I heard a rustle in the bushes just beyond the trees. That was when the pungent smell of sulphur hit me. *Hellhounds.* They had found us and had managed to stay downwind from the camp the entire time. Even though the horses had been nervous, there had been no way for the men, the animals, or the MacKenzie's to know they were near.

"HELLHOUNDS!"

I screamed out the alarm, and with a swift stroke of the blade at my waist, I cut the rope that tethered the horses' reigns to the rail along the trees. Each one of them galloped off to find their master, fighting horses, all trained well. I held onto the leads of the last horse, and swung myself up, racing across the field towards the wagon with the children. It had been agreed—only the night before—that I would stay with the young and the elderly.

Even though I was now comfortable with a blade, and had learned a measure of control of the *fire* within me, I still needed to be in a position of safety. The children and elderly were in the only wagon completely protected by the old words spoken by Athdara. It was easier to defend a single wagon than several scattered throughout the area. In anytime of attack, I was to ignite strategic fires to prevent a direct attack on the wagon. Fires that would slow down onslaught of beasts.

I was only a short distance away, and saw that most of the children had already climbed to safety inside the designated wagon, trusting the protection in place. With dozens of hellhounds behind me, it made it more challenging for me to go inwards to find the *fire*, but not impossible. Leaving patches of ground on fire scattered in my wake, I was preparing to release the *fire* around the outside of our wagon circle that would slow the onslaught of hellhounds.

"Moireach!" Kenneth bellowed in warning. "Watch out!"

All the beasts were focused on larger targets—the men on their horses and my beloved MacKenzie's. All but one. It was close enough that my nose burned from the stench. I looked over my shoulder. I was able to weave and zigzag my horse to dodge his grasp, but not the claws that sliced through the emerald wool and into the flesh of my back. The agony I felt drowned out the noise of the battle ensuing—and the sound coming from above.

It was too late when I looked up to see the blue shimmer of the wings belonging to Abbadon, and him leering at me from overheard. There was no time to draw my dagger from my waistband. The angel reached down and snatched me off the horse by my braid. Crying with agony, I thought my hair would tear completely off my scalp. With a quick yank, as if I were only a small sack of grain, he tossed my body higher and caught my right arm. My hair free, but now my shoulder pulled right out of the socket, which caused a pain so acute that my shriek echoed across the grounds.

I looked down, tears streaming from my eyes, to see dozens of hellhounds and men fighting them valiantly. The brothers had both shifted, but in vain because I could not be reached—too high in the sky.

I had to act, I had to do something. Abbadon still had my bicep in a vice grip, with no regards for my newly dislocated right shoulder. The pain made it all but impossible for me to tap into the power of *fire*. I tried to move my left hand along my body, to reach for my dagger, but the movement only triggered more pain. After a few attempts, which felt like an eternity, I was finally able to grasp the blade, but by then, Abbadon had already flown us miles from the camp. The blade, now in my hand, was my only hope of escape. I would not allow this fallen angel, this hunter, to bring me back to wherever he called home. *Focus, damn it!* Closing my eyes for just a brief moment, I found the *fire* inside and allowed it to erupt from my body through my hand and into the metal blade. Not enough to make it melt, but plenty to make it burn as I cut through the wrist of the hand that was holding onto me.

In hindsight, my moment of desperation to escape and was also one of stupidity. Abbadon shrieked in agony and let go of me. Plummeting to the earth—from at least forty feet above the ground, I brought both arms in close and tried to brace my body for the impact. The sky above me was clear, and the sun was shining. The ground below was a mystery. I expected death, *I have barely lived*, and thoughts of the pendant and Damian came too late.

My body collided with water, a murky bog, which pulled me under so quickly that drowning was imminent. I would be damned if I allowed the water to end my life, after having escaped Abbadon. Kicking my feet as hard as I could and reaching up with my good arm, I kept paddling until I finally broke the surface. I could hear the angel's screams fading into the distance. Even with the cold water all around, I felt the warmth of the fever beginning—so, the claws of the hellhounds had been poisoned again. I paddled towards the shore using my legs and the uninjured arm, with the weight of the water soaking through my dress threatening to pull me to my death.

I do not know how long it took, but when I reached the soft and muddy ground, I rolled to my side to look up at the sky and listened. I was covered in the foul-smelling mud of the bog, invisible from the skies—somewhat safe from hounds and angels. In time, I mustered the strength to pull myself to a wobbly standing position, my right arm useless and the searing pain down my back threatened to bring me again to my knees. Somewhere in my fevered state, I remembered the MacKenzie's telling me to always stay near water if I was lost. I would follow the small stream that seemed to be flowing northwards through the bog.

Hours had passed, and the warmth of the sun had dried the mud to my dress. It was well past the midday sun when the thirst hit me, and I stumbled to the banks of the stream. Using my one good hand to try and scoop water into my dry and cracked mouth, I sputtered at the salty substance. I groaned aloud when I realized this stream, running into these hills from the ocean, not to the ocean, would not quench my thirst. I floundered onward, keeping my eyes on the ground. It was all I could do not to fall or trip over the rocks, lumps of moss and fallen branches, which the forest and bog presented to me as their own gift of torture. I began to hallucinate that I was talking to Damian. I let him know that I was displeased with him, that he should never have left my side, that only he could protect me. I demanded to know why he had left me alone now. The pendant all but forgotten in my delusional state. Each step grew slower, and the tree branches and brambles tore small bits of cloth from dress. I had no energy to retrieve them, despite knowing that they would leave a trail that would lead the Hunter straight to me.

Sunset was darkening the sky with deep oranges and reds in contrast with the cerulean blue. The trees surrounding the stream had created a blanket of dark green which hid the nighttime skies from my view, and the unstable ground of the bog had transformed into more solid footing with an expanse of rocks, some covered in moss and heather. I could hear the sounds of a waterfall, and the smell of cedar filled the air, which gave a strange sense of comfort. Other noises filled my ears, those of animals I could not identify, but they all kept their distance as if knowing I did not belong there. The ground grew rougher and more uneven, the rocks deciding to make my life more difficult and every few steps resulted in a trip or stumble. It was only a mater of time before I fell, and I would not have the strength to stand again.

Not knowing how long I had been unconscious, I awoke in a grove of Ash, Oak and Hawthorne. In my feverish state, I reflected, amusingly, that Kenneth would have been proud of me for recognizing the trees. This place felt safe, almost sacred. Unable to stand or crawl on my knees, I used my one arm and squirmed along the mud to drag my body a few feet towards the small pond I saw. Every movement tore at the wound and brought new blood to the surface.

My skin felt cold as ice, yet the fever had me in such a frenzied state, that I wished to tear free the remains of the dress from my body and jump into the cool waters of the pond. Instead, I lay there with my thoughts, the last thoughts I would have before succumbing to the fever—the man...*the angel.* The one whom all my heart's desires reached for, illogical as it might seem.

The pendant!

With my last ounce of strength, I shimmied my hand down along my leg, trying to reach inside the stocking—the pendant. As I fainted, the last hope of Damian finding me, rolled useless from my weakened palms. I took a slow, ragged breath, a breath I was certain would be my last.

CHAPTER 15

My body stirred, and I woke up to the softness of furs on my bare skin. Disoriented and unsure of my surroundings, I tried to move, but my efforts were made impossible by someone pushing, albeit gently, down on both of my uncovered shoulders.

"Would you please not squirm about so much?"

That voice. Damian. My dark angel.

"Damian…" I said, my dry throat cracking my voice. "Where are the others?"

He slid a small cup under my chin and helped me sip its contents—cool, refreshing water.

"My sweet love, I am afraid you were the only one I have found."

He remained quiet, while my mind raced with thoughts, fears, and worries for my friends.

"Damian, where am I?" I whispered, still disoriented. "I mean, where are we?"

"My sweet little trouble maker," he sighed. "I have brought you to my home."

"Are we back in London?"

Fear was rising to the surface, causing me to shift and move about, and I was suddenly aware of the pain running through my body.

"No Moireach, I never lived in London. I only travelled there on occasion," he said. "This is my sanctuary. We are on the northern coast of Scotland. But you, my sweet love, must stay still. The wounds you suffered are still healing."

His words made me pause, as I had been wriggling about, trying glimpse my surroundings, even though the pain was making it a difficult. To my astonishment, I realized that all of my clothes had been removed and I was only covered by a soft, light-weight, fur the same shade of white that was underneath me.

"Er, Damian, why am I naked?"

"Because the laceration along your back is fairly extensive and putting any constricting clothing on was causing you even more pain. Are you cold?"

"No, I suppose I'm not." I replied, somewhat comforted by the reasons but altogether unnerved by what he had said about my injuries.

"We are near Stonehaven, close to the lands belonging to Clan Watson. It is very difficult to travel here by foot, because of the large ravines and cliffs. About a hundred years ago, I found an abandoned castle on top of one of the cliffs. I have built rooms beneath the ground, to keep away curious folk, each one with easy access to the ocean, but away from prying eyes. I can come and go as I please using the balconies facing the waters."

His deep voice had a soothing effect on my nerves, and I stopped moving. He still did not release his hold on my shoulders.

The white furs underneath were very soft and allowed me space to turn my head comfortable without rolling onto my back, and I vaguely heard him say they were from an animal far to the north, from another land, as I drifted back to sleep. For how long I slept, I shall never know. But I woke with agony coursing through my body. I had rolled over in my sleep and onto my back. It produced a shriek that startled Damian awake.

"Moireach," he pulled my shoulders forward gently, so that I could lie once again on my belly. "Here, is this better?"

"Christ that hurt! Yes, thank you." I moaned through the pain. "How did you find me?"

"Oh my sweet love that is a tale I don't even know I would believe had I not lived it."

"Tell me, please"

"Well since you insist, I shall, but I ask that you rest and do not interrupt me."

Nodding was the only movement that didn't seem to hurt.

"I had already started my journey towards the highlands, when I felt you call me through the pendant. I was more surprised than you can imagine to feel that you were so close to my own lands. Soaring above the ground, but as close to the ground as I dared, I searched for you. The current was strong and the water crashing up against the rocks created a heavy mist. making it rather challenging for me to see the ground clearly. Landing, I made my way along the turbulent river, flowing heavy with the remnants of a storm, with a growing sense of dread. Even that most pungent poison flowing in your veins could not hide your intoxicating fragrance, but it was that venom that pushed me to urgency. I hoped to find another torn piece of your dress that would tell me I was still on the right path. I walked on, mesmerized as the water curled and turned over itself. It was only when I looked up that I found myself among the ancient rocks on my own lands. There I was, on the side of the mountainous range that I am always careful to avoid. I have chosen these lands because the legends and stories kept most curious folk far away, myths that kept these lands secret and safe from outside influences. It's the kind of privacy that a stonewall could not afford."

He paused, and brought a mug of water to my lips.

"My search brought me to a waterfall, so I dove off the edge. Just as I prepared to unleash my wings, a strange noise distracted me, and I crashed into the water more clumsily than I had planned. When I scrambled up on the shore, I looked around to see what appeared to be an oasis. Clear and crisp blue waters fed by the falls, surrounded by a grove of ancient trees. Oak, Ash and even Hawthorne provided protection from the outside world. This place had power, and I felt caught in a vibration of age and timelessness. I had not known about this haven on my own lands for all these years. I found myself hesitant to take a step onward, but my hunger… my desire for you was growing stronger. Around the northern edge of the trees, I detected a faint scent that did not belong there. You had already been too long without food or water, and the poison running in your veins could kill a grown man within hours. I felt my throat tighten with the thought that I might find you too late. My home was not far, and my wings could bring us there within minutes. The night swept in quickly, and I found myself getting cold and worn out which felt odd. The moon cast a shimmer over the ground, I noticed that something caught the light, reflecting a liquid—blood."

"Mine?" I croaked.

"What did I ask? No interruptions!" he admonished me. "It was then, for the first time in centuries, that I knelt of my own volition and whispered a prayer, to my father, the one who cursed us to this earth. Asking him….pleading to him… that I would find you in time. I ran towards the scent, and almost tripped over myself when I saw you underneath an Ash tree, your body cushioned by soft moss and surrounded by the thick branches. Your flesh bruised and torn open in many places and covered in mud. It was the pendant, which was the beacon to find you. It had not been blood I had seen, but the light of the moon which had found the ruby amber. I knelt down to turn you over onto your back, but realized how badly you were injured beyond the poison flowing through your body."

So, what I had thought was just a scratch turned out to be far worse than I had thought. I remained quiet, and let him pause in his narrative. I could tell by his face that the rest of the story would hold a few more surprises.

"My sweet love, there is a broad, jagged gash from the left—starting near the base of your neck, down the shoulder and diagonally across your back to your right hip. I tried to pull away some of the dried mud that was caked to it, and you cried out. Had the hellhound gotten its claws any deeper, it might have separated your torso from the rest of your body. I slid my hands under you and slowly lifted you to my shoulders. You groaned from the pain. Carrying you towards the pool of clear water, to where I could safely fly upwards, clear from the trees, and take you to my castle. Something stopped me from being able to unleash my wings. It was as if an invisible force had clamped over all my extremities which would have allowed us to take to the skies and that is when I heard a strange voice say:

"Moireach is a child of the elements…Let our healing waters prepare her journey back to health. Trust us winged one, and we will help save your saviour."

"Was it a woman?"

"I could not tell. Since I was unable to take flight, I carried you into the water up to my knees, allowing your body to ease into the pool. I feared that you might cry out, but instead your whole body shuddered in relief. Water began to swirl around us, drawing the mud and blood from your clothes and body in a fashion far less harsh than my hands would have been. As your whole body was cleansed by the waters, I was finally able to see the extent of the slash across your body. The water stopped moving, and I knew it was time for us to leave. I flew slowly, using mostly the wind coming off the ocean to smooth our ascent. We arrived through the largest tower, facing the ocean, to my personal chambers where the fire in the hearth was roaring, yet I had not been home to light the wood myself. I laid you on the furs in front of the hearth. You cried out again. Once again, I attempted to roll you to one side, so that I could begin treating the wounds on your back. This time I realized that your shoulder had been dislocated. I had to act quickly, and as I moved your body, you woke. Even in your fever she recognized me. You tried to place a small hand on my cheek."

"I think I remember that moment…" my memory also reminded me of the pain that followed.

"I comforted you and told you we had to mend your shoulder. I removed my thick leather belt. I bid you to open your mouth and placed it between your teeth. Holding your small body as closely as I dared, I did not take my eyes from yours. Gripping your arm, just above the elbow, I stretched the arm far from my torso and realigned it with the shoulder. Next, I pushed the bone back into the socket. It made a sickening popping noise that was followed by your scream and a sudden burst of heat. It was as if someone had thrown brandy into the fire. You had fainted."

I was grateful that he did not have clear view to my face at that moment, knowing that the *fire* had been present… something I did not yet wish him to know.

"Carefully laying you back down on the furs beside the hearth, I was overwhelmed by thoughts. No other Hunter had ever let his soul-prey live. The need to kill them outgrows any desire for continued existence on this earth. But I could not bring myself to end you, and therefore myself. I watched you until you began to stir and your body started to twitch in pain. First, I prepared a cotton cloth and let it soak in the pot of boiling water I had over the fire, to prevent further contamination. I then cut the remaining material from your dress away to reveal your entire back, the skin shredded, revealing bone, blood discoloured by poison, what was certain to be an infection, gauging by the putrid, yellow-green puss oozing everywhere. This wound from the hellhound was worthy of nightmares, even among my kind. I gingerly washed the wounds. It was then that the urge—the instinct to end your life—became the strongest I had ever known. I had to take several steps away from you. Walking over to the window, I breathed in the ocean air to clear my head. Feeling steadier, I hastily returned to the task at hand."

He paused here, and brought his face lower so that he could look into my eyes. I was not afraid. Even knowing that I was his soul-prey. Instead, I felt desire, even amidst all the pain coursing through my body.

"Over the years, I have prepared several of these healing concoctions—for mortals and fallen brothers alike.

Adding the herbs that restore life, I placed the brew over the fire until it came to a boil. I plunged both of my hands into the blistering water next to the healing potion. For countless generations, my kind has known the secrets behind infections and other illness that could be prevented simply by purifying hands through boiling water. Soaking the cloth in the potion, I placed it over your back, letting the fluids seep into the skin and oozing wound. You started to writhe, then scream with your whole body violently shaking. But the odour of the poison had disappeared, and your blood smelled clean again—of your own fragrance, albeit weak, but noticeable. The large gash on your back, now clean, allowed me to see deep into the flesh, down to the bone. I had no idea how to close this human wound. My kind heals so much faster."

He stared off into the fire, before continuing.

"That is when I heard the voice again here, in my own home: *Moireach is a child of the elements. Let the fire heal.* I turned to the fire, as if it would magically tell me what to do next. The thought of burning you, causing more pain, almost brought me to my knees. Not once in my long years on this earth had I ever fretted so much about the care of another. Yet, in my hesitation, the fire altered in colour, changing from oranges and reds to blues and purples. Next, flames licked out of the fireplace into a spiral wave wrapping around you. The blue tips of the flame began to caress your back from the top of the left shoulder and slowly moved down across the body towards the right hip. Up and down the wound, five times, the flames went deeper into your body. When the fire retreated back to the hearth, the wound had closed, and the bones were no longer visible, but the skin was fragile. The scar would always be gruesome. You lay still, no longer moving, You had not cried out."

All I heard was love, genuine emotion in his voice.

"*Moireach is a child of the elements. We offer you air to clean the remaining toxins from her body and her heart.* Obediently, I carried you outside onto the balcony where the ocean roared beneath us. There I stood on the cold stones, holding you most carefully. Clouds from high above shifted, and one detached itself from the rest. It moved downward and wrapped itself around your unconscious body. Enveloped in the white softness of the cloud, I could barely see the outline of your body. The cloud lifted you from my arms, and I watched with amazement as it changed colours and pulled whatever poisons remained out of you and into itself. The cloud placed your body back in my care, and rose up to the sky, now tainted by tones of red and brown. Carrying you back inside, I laid your body face down into the warm furs that kept you nestled in some semblance of comfort. Sitting beside you, I stroked your hair, thinking it was over."

I knew by his tone, that his narrative was far from ending.

"*Moireach is a child of the elements. The earth must be allowed to complete her healing*. Well, there is where I wanted to draw a line. I did not want to leave your side. *You must return to the pool of waters and gather up the orange earth from beneath the surface. Do not let our daughter perish.* So it was. I leapt from the balcony and in quick haste found myself at the grove of trees. I looked down to the ground, and immediately saw that which I needed—the orange coloured earth. I had returned within moments, wet and damp earth in hand, with the specific instructions to smear it along the jagged skin on your back."

"Please." I asked. "Help me sit up."

Covering my naked body with the soft furs, he lifted my torso upright, and I looked around the room. The walls were nearly twelve-feet high, and the side that faced the ocean had a window overlooking the balcony. On the opposite side was a tall wooden door with a large iron lock. One wall had a huge fireplace and directly opposite was the bed. The stone walls were a dark grey and made of solid granite, like those from the renowned pits near Aberdeen. There were delicate figures carved alongside the fireplace—deer, trees, and small cherubs. *It was the same as the one from my dreams.* Pulling my legs around, so I could position myself into a seated position took what little strength I had. I felt dizzy. I reached my arms out towards Damian who caught me, as I fell forward into a faint.

When I awoke, I was laying face down on the same furs as before. and in my dazed state, I thought that somehow they reminded me of Athdara. Moving my head to the right, and then left, I saw him out of the corner of my eye standing at the edge of the fireplace. He was muttering to himself.

"Damian," I mumbled. "Where is my father?"

Through the fog of the pain, I had recalled that he was supposed to have watched over him while he was with Mr Cameron.

He brought over more water, and sat down, helping me sip the cooling liquid slowly and carefully.

"Your father and Mr. Cameron had indeed gone to Dover again." He gently stroked my hair, caressing, all of which had a very soothing affect on my nerves. "I followed them, from a distance. Every day your father seemed to act more strange than the previous day. One day in the marketplace, he started asking for his wife, your mother. It was as if he was expecting her to arrive at any moment. Then the next night, he was found wandering without a shirt or his shoes. His memory is being affected by something."

I sat quietly, listening, fearing for my father, and hesitant to mention my trepidation about the man I was supposed to marry, being my father's travel companion.

"And Moireach, every day, Mr Cameron gives your father tea that he has brewed himself. I tried getting a sample of it, but it was never left unattended. There is something quite off with that man. I cannot quite put my finger on it."

This gave me quite a start, and I pushed my hands onto the stone and was now able to sit up straight.

"And he reeks…" he said, scrunching his face as he recalled the stench I remembered all too well. "How can I say this in any other way, Moireach? He smells wrong?"

"I know what you mean! He *did* smell, and I don't know what I smelled, not only off-putting like rotting flesh and stale whisky, but something… sinister."

Hearing Damian speak words of distrust and concern over the type of man Mr. Cameron might be was a huge relief. If this angel too felt something amiss, I knew I was not going crazy. And it took only a moment to realize, we were alone… together. Through the torment of my body starting to heal, I still found myself inexplicably drawn to this man, this angel. His green eyes hovering over me, filled with concern. My heart was torn between action to find my companions and being blissfully alone with him. His body so close to mine, I could smell him, feel him…and truth be told, desire him.

"Will you tell me more about yourself, Damian?" I had to get him talking, otherwise I would betray my feelings. "About your past?"

"Where do I begin, my sweet love?" he sighed, adjusting his legs for comfort beside me. "My story begins many centuries before man discovered how to harness the power of fire."

We both looked over at the fire crackling in the hearth.

"Moireach, when my kind was first cast down on this planet by our father, we were all rebel warriors in a battle lost. We realized too late that our powers had been taken from us, and replaced by an infernal hunger that could not be satisfied. At first, I rejected my brother-in-arms' need for vengeance and tried to find contentment exploring the lands. For many years, I travelled alone, wanting nothing to do with my kind. Our Father had cursed us, and—."

He leaned back against the cushions and began to stare into the fire with a distant look, as his memories took him to another time and place.

"One day, when I came across another one such as I, somewhere in the plains of the lands you now call Africa. He was fighting with a mortal. I was mesmerized with the ferocity with which the battle raged. Both mortal and angel delivered fatal blows to each other. The mortal died quickly. I ran to my brother, expecting him to heal. Instead, I held him in my arms as his heart slowed down and his skin turned grey. His last words to me were of the discovery of his soul-prey, and he spoke of countless other warriors, angels as you call us, who had come across mortals that drew them with their scent. An angel's need and desire to kill this mortal, this soul-prey, overrides everything else."

He hesitated. His gaze could not meet mine.

"I…am…your…soul-prey?" I whispered.

With Athdara's help, I had already known this, but to hear it from him, was another matter entirely. It made it all too real. The pieces of the puzzle were falling together. I tried to wriggle some distance between our bodies.

"Please, my sweet love." he spoke quietly. "My heart could not bear the loss of you in my life. I cannot explain it. You are my release. Yet I do not have any hunger to end my life nor yours."

"You would not have saved me had you wanted my death." I spoke quietly, confidently, and yet still with hesitation. "That much I do know."

"Do not misunderstand Moireach, I am no saint, nor am I as virtuous as the angels that your bible has written about. My past has more bloodshed than I care to admit, and things I have done that I have regretted ever since. After I heard of soul-prey, I sought out my brother Samael, our leader. Once I found him, I shared what I had discovered, but he showed little interest, because his primary ambition has always been to find our sisters."

He stood up then, to walk towards the hearth, creating distance between our bodies and I felt a rush of embarrassment as I felt the loss of his warmth. A part of me wanted to tell him about my mother, her journal and what I had already learned. But, when I opened my mouth to speak, I hesitated. Heeding my intuition which told me to wait a little longer before I revealed what I knew.

"Who are your sisters?" I asked instead. "And why did he want to find them?"

Damian ran a hand through his untamed hair. I sensed his discomfort and reached out towards him, tentatively, gesturing for him to return to the furs, and by my side. Looking down, he let out a heavy sigh as he sank down next to me, and took my hand gently into his own.

"The one who created us had always said the sisters were the key to the gates, the only way to return to our home in the skies. Ever since we were cast down, Samael had been trying to capture them. He had discovered that they still possessed some of the powers that had been taken from us. There were eight sisters, four pairs of twins, and each set could influence one of the four elements. For years, they travelled across countries separately, never together. Something kept them apart, and it drove Samael to near madness because he felt they were plotting against him. Then, after decades of tracking them, one of Samael's mortal slaves stumbled upon them all together one night. The eldest of them, one of the Earth twins, had come across an Oracle. A mortal woman, born with no sight or the ability to hear and yet was able to speak with uncanny clarity. Somehow this woman possessed a connection to higher powers that no one could comprehend. Upon touching the hands of the Earth twin, this woman had a vision and told her that the Immortal Elements alone held the power to open the gates back to our kingdom, to our home. Thereby giving all of us a chance to return. For Samael, this confirmed everything—a way to get revenge on our father, and to reclaim our place in the sky."

It was during this part of his story, that Damian looked away, his eyes cast down. Reaching towards him, he pulled away, and I could not help but feel that he was trying to keep something from me.

"Samael found me in the Himalayan mountains on my own pilgrimage. He persuaded me to help him. My old bloodlust returned, standing side by side with my brother. Together we were ruthless in our pursuit of more power and strength. My sweet love, those years are filled with depravity and violence. I ask that you do not press me for more, I cannot bear for you to see me as I once was. Instead, let me share with you the night that you came into this world, many years after I left my brother's side."

"The night I was born?" I asked incredulously. "What does that have anything to do with—?"

"My sweet love, you are the daughter of one of the Fire Element twins." He paused there, and watched me carefully. To see how I would respond.

"You mean my mother is like you? An angel?" I feigned surprise, hoping he would not be able to see the small blush I felt creeping into my cheeks.

"Yes, you are my sweet love." he answered quietly. "It is only by chance that I heard stories of a mysterious woman who had been saved in a storm by one of the local gentry on the west coast of Scotland. The description of the woman made me think of her. They were expecting the birth of their first child—and I somehow knew it was Seraphina—."

"—My mother's name was Isabella?" My intuition prompted me to stay silent on what I already knew but saw no harm in expressing a little disbelief, so that I could learn more from him.

"It was only later that I found out that she chose that name when she met your father. You see, many of us travel under false names, we live so long it would become suspicious otherwise. I travelled to the lands of Clan MacRae, not knowing if I would find her, or simply a woman who looked like her. Yet, when I found myself at the borders to the south of Loch Shiel, my way was blocked by ancient words I had not heard nor spoken in eons. This only confirmed my suspicion that one of my sisters was indeed on those lands."

"So you were not able to cross into the lands because of words?" I asked, genuinely interested in what the words of protection meant to him.

"I spent days, trying to find a way to cross but the words create an invisible wall, which prevented me from taking another step forwards. And this was not the only thing that was out of the norm. There were a few times when I saw some highlanders across the way. In all my travels, I had never seen men of such immense size. Something about them made my skin tingle, and I sensed that there was more to them that meets the eye."

"You speak of the MacKenzie's?"

"Yes, I do. I kept travelling along the outskirts of the lands, hoping to find a crack in the protection. One morning, I found myself far up in the highland mountains overlooking the castle and the loch. I sensed a radiating vibration in the air, and with each passing moment it got stronger, emanating from Eilean Donan. Only then did I realize I was no longer the only fallen one to have made his way here. Dozens upon dozens of my brother-in-arms had gathered in the hills and mountainside around the castle. Violence, blood-thirst, and rage filled the air. The entire grounds were surrounded on all sides by those who would kill her and capture the child that was about to come into this world. We all felt the ripples of vibration as the labour started and felt the words of protection surrounding the castle crumble with the flashes of lightening bolts striking the walls. The assault began. None of my brothers were prepared for the counterattack from Clan MacKenzie. Even in their human form, they are formidable. When they transformed into their animal state, it shifted the battle in their favour. Shapeshifters had the ability to kill us—bring us to our mortal death."

"If a MacKenzie has the ability to kill your kind, what is the purpose of the soul-prey?"

Hearing about the sheer numbers of fallen ones who had come after my mother, I now understood why she had chosen the MacKenzie's to be her protectors and mine.

"Only the almighty Father can answer that, my sweet love, and I'm afraid he is not talking to us. I suspect it has to do with the eternal hunger we feel but since I've found you, I wonder if we haven't gotten it all wrong. Perhaps he created you, to offer us a normal life." He looked off into the distance, and shook his head as if he felt confusion. "There was a moment, during the heat of the battle, where every angel felt the powerful and painful vibration strike the air, and it brought every one of us out of the sky and crashing to the ground."

"What happened then?" I could not help voicing my thoughts, when he stood silent for minutes, his memory freezing him in a time past.

"My sweet love, understand that we came from above the mountain mists, beyond the reach of earth and clouds. We fought countless battles, surviving the blazing fire we descended covered in shrouds, and broke through the mist with thunder, crashing down rocky hills with lightning on the night of our arrival. The night you were born, was very much like that first night on earth for us."

Pulling the furs around me not only for warmth, I felt he was sharing more than he had originally intended.

"We walk among humans every day, as shadows of the past. Until the night where our world changed. Nigh on twenty years ago, with her death and your birth. Many came to claim her power, and dozens fell at the hands of the MacKenzie's who were protecting her…and you…with their very life. When I managed to make my way through the battlefield, I was able to climb the wall and found her bedroom. Her cold amber-green eyes, life had left her body frozen. The mortal woman holding a small bundle, too tiny to live, cold and unmoving. Every one of my kind, including me, felt it in the air. The fight was over. The prize, your mother, and you, lost—."

Tears streamed down his face, and he seemed as surprised as I was.

"Rest now my sweet love, and we shall speak more tomorrow."

He left me alone on the furs. After what he had shared, I had hoped he would lay beside me. For comfort, for warmth…my desire to be close to him was overwhelming. But, I was exhausted, and I fell asleep quickly and I dreamt vividly.

I found myself standing beside an unmarked grave alongside a church building. A tall and striking woman came out of the mist towards me. She had long, straight raven-red hair all the way down to her hips, interrupted by a white streak that began above her right brow. Taller than any woman I had ever met, except Athdara maybe, with long slender limbs and an ample chest and full hips, she was regal. Her dress was the colour of moss, in the high empire waisted design of ancient Rome*, held in place with a silver chain. A crescent moon talisman, dangled down past her hips, and in its centre was a trinity knot of old Celtic design. The tops of her wings reached nearly six inches above her head and the bottom nearly to the ground with feathers the same colour as her hair. She was barefoot. There was a white streak that ran along the right wing, along a jagged scar running down the length of it, very much like the white hair that cut through her raven-red locks. She walked towards me with a serene smile and reached out her hands. The voice I heard was feminine, strong* *and her accent was unlike I had ever heard before, most certainly not of Scottish origins. Yet her mouth never moved.*

"My beloved daughter of Fire, what I tell you now you must remember at all costs, even when you wake. Your father buried me among his clan, he did not know enough of my kind to understand, and he was grieving dearly. George MacKenzie came from his manor near the ocean, along with a few of his most trusted men, removed my body and replaced my grave stone. They wrapped my body in tartan woven with the old words of protection and took my body to a place my sisters and I call Avalon. There is only one person who could have taught them those words—my sister, my twin flame, Daphine—and my dear friend Gwenyver, must have aged at least ten years to cast them. Those words steal life in order to seal the longevity. My body protected from the dark ones, who would use it for their own nefarious purposes, it has been also been protected from decay. Now, you must wake and remember."

My eyes fluttered open suddenly, and I lay very still, allowing my breath to calm down. At first my desire to share this dream with Damian made me look about the room, searching for him. Then I paused, and I knew this was only shown to me. I would have to heal faster to reach Eilean Donan—and Gwenyver.

"My sweet love, I am loathe to leave you but I will fly across the moors today and search for your companions." Damian was not alongside me on the furs, but standing in the window frame blocking out the morning sun. "There is some food on the tray beside the furs. Please rest."

Damian turned towards the balcony, leaping into the sky and releasing his wings and left me alone. That day I slept so much I wondered if the water had been laced with a sleeping herb of some kind. And I dreamt.

My mother and I were standing together on higher ground, overlooking the same cemetery as before.

"My sisters and I realized from the start we would not be safe together, so we went our separate ways. My travels took me across the world, but after I had discovered the secrets of the dark one in Italy, I made my way to Scotland, hoping to find my sister or her daughter. I was caught unawares by a fallen brother, while wandering along a beach on the west coast. We fought, but he wounded me and I fell my knees. My skills

with the sword are not to be underestimated, and I prepared for my next strike. That is when a dozen beasts, bears, wolves and others I could not name, came upon us and claimed his life. Quickly. Brutally. And then to my surprise, they transformed into men, the largest of them introducing himself as George MacKenzie, descendent of my sister Merida…through her daughter, Dylynn. That is how my friendship with the shapeshifters began, and for a few years I travelled the outskirts of the lands, getting to know them. I was introduced to an extraordinary young woman who had been sheltered away in an Abbey near Orkney, and found myself taking on the role of mentor. And in the end, I feel love for her like I might a younger sister…or a daughter. Then came the day when we heard that more and more hellhounds were attacking the lands of Clan MacRae, and where the MacKenzeie's have always called home. I left, and made my way back with every intention of helping. I was attacked this time by a horde of the hellhounds. My wounds were many, and I feared I would not have the strength to heal but I found a way to mask the vibration of my presence, and called down a fire storm. That day was the day a young, fifteen year old man—John Alexander MacRae—accompanied by the MacKenzie's, found me."

When I roused from the second dream, writhing, Damian immediately rushed to my side. I had not known he had returned.

"Moireach, are you still in pain?"

I was never without pain during that time.

"Damian, how long have you been standing there?" I said, avoiding his question. "Did you find them? We need to go to Eilean Donan."

"My sweet love, I found the site of the attack and travelled in different directions hoping to catch their scent but to no avail. Can you manage without me a little while longer? I want to replenish our supplies."

"If you can, leave me some water in the jug close by?" I said, agreeing with his plans. "And some of the bread and cheese?"

Once he had left, I was determined to get my body moving so that I could regain my strength. I began a slow crawl across the fur I was laying on. I had only managed get a few feet from where I started, when the pain was so sharp it brought me into a dead faint, where my mother appeared once more in my dreams.

We stood on one of the high towers at Eilean Donan, overlooking the small island and village, and she told me of her beginnings with my father.

'I shared nine wonderful years with John. I introduced him to many within the shipping industry, to help build his empire. Avoiding my kind was one of the reasons we travelled around so much, but then John was called home to his ailing father. The shape shifters were all around, as family and as protectors. I taught them more of the ancient and magical old words for protection, the language of the skies. I had grown to love John, even though he only knew a small part of my origins. A sadness grew in my heart. John desired a child, to love and continue the family line. After nine years together, he had given up hope. Then one night, shortly after our return to Eilean Donan, after spending the day travelling around the countryside to visit some of the outlying villages, we found ourselves too far from man-made shelter. So we made a fire near a grove of old gnarled trees and by the light of a Blue Moon, under the open sky we made love. I woke up the next morning knowing that a life had started within me. When I told him, he was delirious with joy.

Nine months later, on a windy morning, when I was walking along the length of the balconies, the first contraction happened. I had experienced pain before, having been a warrior for most of my life. With the pain, came a deeper vibration, and it rippled out across the winds. I knew instantly that it was stronger than the field of protection I had created nine years ago on the shores of Loch Shiel. This would be felt by every one of my kind within the country. I could only hope it would not reach beyond the ocean.

I told the Clan MacKenzie, and George confirmed they too had felt it. He made the choice to call all the men to the castle to protect us. After spending nearly five days in labour, as if they sensed you would soon enter the world, my fallen brothers attacked. The chaos and the screams of fighting outside the walls was joined by the sound of thunder and lightening. One fighter broke through the line of those defending us and landed on the balcony.

I struggled to reach my sword while in the middle of the contractions. Barely able to walk, I made my way onto the balcony and fought. With the aid of George MacKenzie, who had broken through the lines and leaped up the walls, we defeated the fallen one and I collapsed onto the floor. I had been weakened by the days of agony, and had lost too much blood. On my hands and knees, with my last breath, I pushed you from my body into the waiting arms of Gwenyver. And with that last breath, every angel within range of the castle felt a shift in the air. Gwenyver had been taught some of the old words that would allow a body to mimic death without detection and spoke the words over your tiny body as you came into this world. All the angels believed that their fight was over. They believed we were both dead."

I woke up from the dream with tears in my eyes. The image of my bleeding and dying mother, with Nanny holding me, a newborn in her arms. My body ached. I still lay where I had fainted, only a few feet from where I had started on the furs. Not wanting to move again, fearing the pain, I closed my eyes to fall asleep again, and that is where Damian found me, after returning with fresh supplies, and he shook me awake.

"Don't you dare move without my permission…" He growled. "Or I'll open that wound again for you!"

He gently picked me up and brought me back in front of the warm fire.

"Now then, why don't you tell me what happened from the moment you arrived to the Abbey until I found you?" he asked, arranging the furs around my body.

I was only part-way into my story, telling him of our arrival at the Abbey where Athdara revealed herself—something made me hesitate. I paused. *Why did I not want to share everything with him?*

"Damian, would you mind fetching me more water?" I asked. "And I'm awfully hungry."

My heart was drawn to this man, to this angel who woke up such longings within me, this I knew. There was no proof of any insincerity, and he had saved my life. But his brother was Samael, the Dark One. He had confessed to a tainted past. *What kind of man…angel…was he now?*

He soothed me to sleep, stroking my hair lovingly by the warmth of the fire. Comforting. My heart was at war with my mind, as I wanted to give him everything I was.

CHAPTER 16

I awoke to loving hands caressing the length of my arms, fingers intertwining with mine. Mesmerizing green eyes gazing into my own, and a soft smile across his lips.

"Did you watch me sleep all night?" I murmured quietly.

"Yes." he murmured huskily. "What of it?"

This man, this angel, had held me throughout the night, making sure I didn't roll onto my back. His body offering mine warmth. My heart felt fit to burst with affection…with love.

"Would you help me sit up?"

Without saying a word, he supported me into a seated position, so that I could be fed nourishing broth and sip on warm tea. Damian was gentle and patient with my recovery. Meanwhile, I was seething at the rate at which my wounds were healing. Frustration was ever present, but there was something else. Every time Damian was near, a flush come over me and a warmth radiated from deep within my belly. Nothing in my life, nor my upbringing had prepared me for this feeling. With each touch, he lingered just bit longer than necessary. His eyes would find my gaze. Without words something was being shared in those moments. Time would stand still. I felt certain that he too was drawn to me. Like two stars circling each other.

Time lost its meaning but then a moment came that I was able to stand and manage a few steps at a time without feeling sharp, burning pain travel up and down my back. Wearing a simple linen shirt that Damian had given me, once my skin could bear the weight of it, oversized as it was, and a pair of woollen trousers, I found it much easier to maneuver around than had I been wearing a dress.

"My sweet love, my heart breaks to think of that scar on your body," Damian said, as he watched my efforts. "Every part of me wants to find a way to heal your beautiful skin."

"I am beyond the point of caring about my physical appearance, Damian." I spoke through gritted teeth as I walked slowly from one piece of furniture to the next, trying not to tumble. "I need to get strong enough to travel. What does it matter that my flesh is marred? We need to find the MacKenzie's or at the very least make our way to Eilean Donan."

As much as I wanted to stretch our precious time alone together, and ignore everything that had happened, I knew we could not remain here any longer than necessary. As I walked from one of the large armchairs to other, past the fireplace, I felt a surge of strength, of energy. I knew that my body was connected to the flames. *What if I kept close to the fire?* By the afternoon I had pushed my body beyond its limits and my legs buckled. Damian, who had been patiently watching me, leaped forward to catch me before the unforgiving stones underfoot stopped my fall. In his arms, looking up into those green eyes, I wanted to feel his lips on mine.

"Oh my sweet love, I daren't yet." he whispered. "You aren't even strong enough to stand on your own two feet."

I grabbed onto his strong forearms and pulled myself up so that I could reach his lips. Responding to my desire, he drew me in closer and our bodies found each other. Our kiss swept me up in a rippling wave of emotions—and *fire.* He could tell that even the most delicate touch on my back was still too much for me to bare, so he slid his hand down past my back to cup my buttocks. He lifted me from the ground, effortlessly, and I heard his wings release from their mysterious hidden place. With a deep groan from his throat, they spread.

His loss of control excited me, and I felt warmth in my body radiate outwards from the depths of my belly until the fire behind us surged, and pieces of wood exploded out from the flames and scattered in front of the hearth. The flames singed the tips of his outstretched wings, but he did not notice, nor did he stop his exploration. His lips left mine to trace a scorching line along my neck. The pain from my wound still throbbed, but the sensation now was too hot to ignore and overrode any pain my body still felt. All of my senses were on fire. He nibbled on my earlobe and maneuvered his tongue, warm and moist, along the outer edge of my ear, creating a quiver that travelled down my spine and would have made me crumble to the ground had I not been caught in his embrace.

He kissed my cheek and then the other, before fully pressing his lips to mine, once again. I parted my lips with a sigh of pure desire, still so innocent to all this. He took this naive invitation to flick his tongue between them. With a gasp, my mouth opened to welcome his taste. He sensed my lust and moaned as he drew me in closer yet, the heat of our bodies now melting into each other. Tenderly, he cradled the back of my head in his hand, looked into my eyes, and lowered me to sit on the soft bed of furs. He knelt down, and his strong arms flanked my waist, as he pressed kisses onto my forehead and down my neck. Caught up in the passion stirring between us, he tried to lay me down, having forgotten about my wound, but the pressure on my back brought the agonizing pain, so he lifted me to his lap.

"Ah, Damian." I straddled my legs around his hips. "My body feels like it's on fire."

I could barely get the words out before my mouth moaned with the lust awakening in my body. He brushed the hair from my neck and tasted the delicate skin along my collarbone. His throat thrummed softly with deep longing in response to my own sounds, and he grabbed the edges of the linen shirt, to lift above my head. My now exposed body was hot with desire. The *fire* stirring within me was becoming harder to control, and I knew that somehow it would need to release or otherwise consume me.

I threaded my fingers through his hair and tugged his head back to allow me to feel a small measure of control, as I leaned in to kiss him more deeply. We explored each other's taste and savoured the heat of our lips brushing against each other. He slid his fingers between the curls of my hair and pulled me away. As he drank in the sight of me, I too, became aware of my own body—my delicate neck, my supple shoulders, my small yet full breasts, and the curves that followed along my hips. He let out a deep sigh of pleasure before pulling his shirt over his head. He moved so fast, he became tangled in the sleeves, and we both laughed. My eyes beheld his body for the first time. There were deep black marks, tattoos, tangled up with silver scars, along his shoulders and over his heart that moved in perfect synchronicity with his muscles. I placed my hand over his chest and leaned closer, breathing him in. The fire leapt from its place in the hearth. Damian delighted in how eagerly I responded to his touch that he did not notice anything else. His kiss. My whole body was on fire with caresses.

His mouth traced lines from my collar bones and to my breasts already hard with desire. I arched upwards to welcome his suckling, and was left gasping when he pulled away after too short a time, only to travel further down past my belly button. Shifting his exploration to my right hip, my whole body tilted to meet him. Lazily, swirling his tongue across my lower belly, making his way to the left hip, my body arched to meet him, again. And then, he paused, gazing up into my eyes…seeking permission and finding nothing but desire in my own eyes. He leaned back down, and there. To the most intimate place of a woman, and there he worshipped me. Nothing in my wildest imagination could have prepared me for the intense pleasure his tongue created, and my hips started to respond of their own volition. Leaning back on my hands, not daring to lie down, I looked down at the man between my thighs, and I caught his gaze—filled with lust, longing…and something else. And I wanted him.

As I felt my body pleading, crying out, for something it had never experienced, he inched his way up between my thighs, pulled me gently back onto his lap…and slowly entered me with everything that made him male. The exquisite pain and pleasure I felt overcame any fear or trepidation I had. Our rhythm was slow, steady and yet it was filled with an ardent fervour that bound us together. With each thrust, I knew I was undone. With each breath, my body surrendered. Our gaze, locked together, just as our bodies were locked in this embrace. *Fire.*

To this day, I wonder what surprised Damian more—his losing control and finding his body surging forwards to his own release or being engulfed in flames as the whole room exploded with fire as my body rode the waves of pleasure into oblivion.

We both lay there, stunned and satiated, trying to make sense of what had happened. Our bodies unharmed, yet looking around the room, we saw that the fire had scorched everything. The walls were blackened with smoke, the glass windows had bubbled from the heat, and there were only ashes left from the wooden chairs and table, and the pieces of charred fur were scattered throughout the room.

"My sweet love," Damian looked at me with a glint of danger, and suspicion. "Why do I have the feeling that you have been keeping some secrets from me?"

"Oh…," I had the good sense to look down for only a moment, cheeks still flushed. I looked up at him then, our bodies still tangled together and me resting on his chest, hoping he would not press the issue further. My intention had been to look somewhat apologetic, but my stomach let out a rumble that broke the silence, and he let out such a great belly laugh that it shook both of us.

"Well, my sweet love, we shall talk more on this later, after we have fed you. Let's see if you left anything for me to cook." he chuckled, while he gently sat up and lifted me off his lap. His face turned away from mine, and I thought I saw a glance of agitation.

The rest of our evening was spent in quiet reflection, each of us with our own thoughts. Damian had brought some cheese, tomatoes and some bread from the kitchens, while I put a fresh nightshirt back on to keep out the cold that was starting to make its way through my body. I watched him walk over to one of the windows facing the hillside and pause.

"Damian, what is it?" I asked, knowing that something had caught his attention.

I stood up slowly, leaving the warmth of the hearth, and for the first time since the attack, I was able to walk across the room without support. Letting my hand rest on his arm, I waited for his reply, sensing some inner conflict.

"Why do you not trust me? You knew you had a connection to fire, but you didn't say anything during this entire time?" he voiced suddenly, his eyes filled with melancholy and disappointment.

"I don't know why Damian." I said truthfully, wrapping my arms around him from behind. "So much has happened in just a few short weeks. Finding out my guardians kept so many secrets for so many years. Discovering that angels exist, and that my mother was one of them? It's a miracle I don't doubt my own sanity, let alone struggling with trusting others."

"I suppose that's fair." he replied, still holding himself aloof from me, not reciprocating my affection. "After everything that I have shared with you, and what we just experienced together, can you still doubt me?"

So desperately did I want to say no, that I trusted him with all my heart. He would not turn towards me. He would not touch me.

"Damian, I—."

"—Your guardians are walking on the earth of my lands."

"Why, that is wonderful! How close are they? Are they hurt? When will they arrive?"

"They are a little over a day away." he gazed at me, intently, searching, for what I did not know.

"Do they know where to find me?"

Damian shook his head.

"There is a reason I chose this isolated castle, hidden away in these parts of the world."

I looked up at him, searching his eyes and his face. Damian knew how important it was for me that my companions found me and that we travel to Eilean Donan, but he was reluctant. *How could my body and heart belong to this angel, the man who had claimed me, while my mind was at war with everything?*

"They must be worried about me. Please, will you go to them?"

His eyes narrowed. A look of anger? Irritation? Without a word, he took a few steps towards the balcony and jumped off the edge, soaring above the waters under the night sky. His great wings lifted him above the seas, and he turned towards the hillside, leaving me alone in the great house he called a sanctuary.

Left alone, I walked the corridors and I found myself back in the main living quarters, in front of the large hearth. The sleeping chambers, smelled like the forest after a wild fire —a sweet, biting aroma that travelled the hallways. My body exhausted and spent, I fell asleep near the warmth of the fire, wrapped in furs.

I awoke tangled in the blanket of furs I had pulled up over myself. Standing gingerly, and feeling a sense of relief to find that my strength continued to grow. In my time here, I had only seen two of the rooms, his sleeping chambers and the main living room. Curiosity got the better of me, and I stepped outside the big room for the first time since arriving and searched some of the smaller chambers where I found a large trunk of heavier clothes, clearly belonging to a man. Rummaging through, I found some trousers, and long socks as well as some shirts that I could layer. I dressed myself for warmth, determined to explore the great house and try to discover more about this mysterious fallen angel. *How could one person awake such desire in me while a quiet mistrust was ever present?*

I found big wooden doors that opened into three separate hallways. Not knowing where any of them would lead, I hesitated. Closing my eyes, I held out my hand—there, wafting from the left was a slight draft. Opening the door, I found a dark hallway and with it came a strange odour. I wandered down the corridor only to find more doors on both sides, all of them locked, until I nearly tumbled down a staircase, unseen in the dark. Curiosity gave way to fear as a rancid stench reached my nose. At the base of the steps was a large cavern. I wanted to run back to the safety of the main living room, warm with fire and huddle under the security of the blankets and furs. I paused long enough to calm my nerves. As my eyes began to adjust to the dark, I saw in the centre of the cavern was a large cage, twelve-feet tall and just as wide with thick bars that no man could hope to ever breach. Remnants of straw and some other materials were strewn along its floor.

I walked up to the metal prison, the source of the horrible odour. The bars were cold and damp to the touch, too wide to wrap my hand around their width. In the far corner of the cage, I saw a carcass decomposing. Bones and dried sinews of muscles visible beneath the shreds of flesh. I nearly emptied my stomach but fought to keep my gorge at bay. Its taste was acid and bitter as I choked it back down.

Bringing the cloth of my sleeve to cover my nose and mouth, hoping to staunch the foul smell, I leaned closer. There. Wrapped around a large bear paw was a manacle. The light was just enough that I could see that the jagged bones had bite marks. Something had gnawed on the wrists. What stole the last of my courage was the crumpled, torn and bloody clothing alongside the body.

A… shapeshifter!

Stifling a scream, I sprinted up the stairs as fast as my weakened state would allow, grasping the railings for support, then down the hallway, and back to the safety of the large living room—back to the warmth of the fire in the hearth and under the layers of furs, shivering not from cold. *Could the angel, the man, that I had shared so much of myself with these last few days truly be capable of the horrors I just saw?*

Simmering in my own thoughts, despite the exhaustion my venture had caused, sleep would not come. He had made it clear that he had a sordid past, and that he had committed horrible acts of violence. His regret, his repentance had seemed genuine. As my mind tried to make sense of it all, my body…and my heart kept reminding me of what I had just experienced. The love. The desire. The affection. The *fire.* I sat in stillness, staring into the flames in the hearth.

"Daughter of Fire. Hear us."

The words startled me out of my daze, and I found myself drawn to the bodiless voice that came from the fire.

"Strength of mind will come through focus. Focus can be found in the fire. Breathe with the fire. Breath has fire. Fire will reveal the truth to you, every time."

Words like a riddle, and yet also clear with instruction. Trusting in the mystical was coming easier to me these days. *Breathe with the fire.* And so, I did. Slowly at first, emptying my mind of all thoughts but watching how the flames moved, unsure how I would match my breath with the rhythm of the fire. The flickering yellow, orange, and red hues created a swirling pattern rising up through the chimney of the hearth. A few moments passed, and I felt a shift in my energy and in the quality of my thoughts. The movements of the fire transfixed my gaze, and my body felt calm. A sense of peace came over me. My body eased into a trance, where I began to see images of the past. The fire was showing me the truth.

There were moments where I almost jumped into the flames to stop some calamity from happening, and I rebelled at the vision the fire revealed of Damian, not wanting to believe that he could ever have been such a cruel being. Standing alongside his brother, hunting and torturing men.

I asked to see more, and the fire shifted and showed me the life Damian had been living these last twenty years or so. Many acts of courage, love and compassion towards humanity, and a growing friendship with the MacKenzie's which had resulted in him wearing the medallion my mother had made. I watched him fight his fallen brothers outside the castle walls the night I was born. I saw his tears as he looked upon his dead sister, and her stillborn child…only I was not dead.

I opened my eyes and clung to the belief that he was a changed man, a repentant man who was helping me and who cared for me, as deeply as I cared for him. His careful attention to my wounds, helping me heal combined with the passionate, and devoted lovemaking all told me that Damian had a good heart, a soul worth of forgiveness and of trust. In the short time I had known him, I knew I had fallen in love with him. With all I was and would become, I knew my heart was his.

I fell asleep with thoughts of love—of Damian.

* * *

Waking to the sound of banging on the main doors the next day, I was greeted by Roderick, Kenneth and Athdara. They were nearly as surprised as I when I greeted them. And I was puzzled to see that Damian was not with them.

"Lady M, come here lass!" Roderick limped over to me and lifted me off the ground. "That bird-man made it sound as if you were on death's door!"

"Bloody hell, Roderick, put me down!" I cried out, his arms setting off screams of pain as the skin on my back rebelled against the pressure.

"I'm verra sorry lass, I didna mean to hurt ye." He swiftly dropped me and turned red in the face.

"Roderick," I pleaded. "There is a large gash along my back that is only just starting to heal. I beg you to not do that again."

"Aye, of course, Lass." he muttered. "And when did you start using such foul language?"

"Pain has an interesting way of bringing out colourful language, does it not?" I said, gesturing them inside.

"Ye ken it's a miracle that we even found this place," Kenneth spoke from his place behind his brother. "Given how few words of direction that bird-man gave us!'

"When we have a moment alone, my lady," Athdara stepped in front of the men. "I wish to see what's been done to help heal that wound."

I nodded and gestured them all to come inside to the foyer. Athdara was looking around at the sparse furnishing, the dark grey stones, and an old wooden bench just a few feet away. Once Roderick and Kenneth were inside, I closed the heavy wooden door and pulled the metal latch shut. I lead them to the living room where the warmth of the roaring fire greeted us. They looked tired and travel worn, but thank the heavens, unharmed. All of them looked around, somewhat astonished.

"Let me fetch some bread, and cheese from the pantry in the kitchen. I think we might also have some boiled eggs from yesterday, as well as some roasted pork." I started to walk towards the kitchens, still slow but now steady on my feet. "Please make yourself comfortable by the fire."

Athdara sank gratefully into the large cushioned chair next to the hearth. She smiled with contentment, as her body softened into pillows and furs. The brothers hunkered down on the large bench at a table opposite the fire, relieved to be off their feet, and leaned against the wool blankets draped against the back of the bench.

Upon my return, I placed the plates of bread, cheese and eggs onto the table while I arranged skewers of pig roast over the fire to cook.

While the brothers dug into their meal with a healthy appetite, Athdara kept looking around nervously, until finally, clearly agitated, she stood up and walked around the room. She began pressing her hand against the walls, at what seemed like random intervals. Roderick glanced up and slowed his eating. We all watched her circle the entire room.

"Lady M, there are absolutely no words of protection on these stones. No words of protection anywhere on this property." she uttered. "Without that assurance, you are open and vulnerable to the others. They will find you here."

"Of course, there are no words of protection on my own home!" Surprising us all with his sudden appearance, Damian glided in through the open balcony windows. As his feet landed, he folded his wings in behind him, and strode confidently through the room. "Remember, those words have a rather unpleasant affect on me as well."

He looked around at the MacKenzie's.

"Apologies for my late arrival, but I wanted to be sure that no one followed you three onto my lands."

Damian's presence brought the conflict I had been struggling with to the surface again, but I chose to ignore it by focusing on the food on my plate. During the meal, the brothers watched the angel very closely. They watched as he stood up to get more meat from one of the skewers on the fireplace. When as he leaned down to kiss the top of my head, and caressing my shoulder with his spare hand, which brought a slight blush to my cheeks, one of my guardian's broke the silence.

"Ahem, Lady M, I think it's best we discuss what's happened since ye were taken." Roderick said, and he gave Kenneth a rather baffled look.

"Aye, I saw ye riding across the meadow and heard ye holler out the warning." Kenneth spoke through a mouth full of food. "Did ye not hear me calling oot when I saw that cursed fallen one flying towards you? Right before that bloody bird-man took off with ye!"

"I did see you shout, but the hellhounds were so close, and I did not hear the angel above me until it was too late. He grabbed me by my braid and pulled me straight off the horse and into the air. In the chaos, I didn't even realize that a hellhound had managed to leaped towards me only moments before. Resulting in the large gash down along my back. Realizing he could not hold me by my hair for long, he tossed me around like doll to get a better grip, which dislocated my shoulder… right, Damian?"

All eyes turned to the angel who had just taken a rather large bite of the skewered meat and mumbled something unintelligible, while nodding in agreement.

"The pain made me dizzy, and I don't know how long we flew like that but I knew I had to do something. I managed to reach down with my free arm to grab the knife from my waist band, and thrust it up towards his wrist." I looked around at the MacKenzie's discreetly, silently wishing them to know that there was more to the story, but not yet feeling safe to allow Damian to learn of my ability to channel the *fire*. "Startling him into letting go, too late I realized that it would result in me plummeting towards the earth and likely my death. But I thought it would be a swifter end than whatever he had planned for me. Somehow, I survived the fall by landing in a thick swampy bog, absurd as that sounds."

Athdara leaned forward in her chair, listening attentively.

"My Lady, how did ye find yer way to Damian's castle?"

"I did not find him. He found me."

"Verra well then, bird-man…" Kenneth stood up and walked towards the hearth, eyeing more of the skewers. "Won't ye tell us what happened then."

"After watching over Lord MacRae in Dover for a few days, and discerning no immediate danger, I realized I needed more rest, to recover my strength after healing you Kenneth," he said, and I had to hold my tongue because he never had used those words when retelling me the events of how he came to be at his home. "Strangely enough, I also felt the call of my lands and over the centuries I have become very attuned when something or someone is out of place within my boundaries. From the moment that angel crossed the borders with Moireach in tow, I sensed the intruder and immediately left the castle to locate them—"

"—and how did ye ken where to look?" Kenneth asked.

"At first, I only had a vague sense of direction, but the closer I got the more I could smell Moireach—"

"—What the hell do ye mean by that?" Roderick was now up on his feet.

"Do you want to know the full story or not?" Damian retorted, standing up and turned to face my gigantic guardian.

The two, one man and one angel, exchanged challenging glares.

"Would you two cease this childish nonsense?" I blurted out, startling both of them with my volume. Damian returned to sit beside me.

"When I realized that the woods would cover any sign of her, I dropped out of the sky and searched on foot, and after some time, I found her." His voice stumbled, filling with emotion. "She was unconscious, covered in dried blood and mud…for a moment I thought I had lost her."

"And how did ye manage to bring her back to yer home?" Athdara asked, shifting in her seat to move some of the pillows around for comfort.

I felt Damian's body tense up, his hands tightened their grip on my shoulders.

"Not with any ease, I assure you that." he said. "Suffice it to say, that had I not been a *Bird-Man* I would not have been able to save her."

Just then, I recalled feeling the cool waters on my body, gentle flames soothing my skin, and wet earth being pressed into my wounds along my back. For the first time, I was able to remember that which Damian had said took place.

"But what allowed you to heal her, Damian?" Athdara was not allowing him to finish his story with that last sentence.

"I have had experience with the hellhounds over the years," he said, moving away from me and towards the hearth fire once more. "Is it not enough that she is recovering?"

"Aye, fair enough." Kenneth grumbled. "But that doesna explain why the two of ye look like a cat who's licking her cream. What—"

"—I think we best decide on what we need to do next." Athdara interrupted, and sending a knowing side glance my way.

I had plenty of time to think while Damian had been gone. The fire's revelation of the night before had placed an uneasiness in my mind, but not my heart, nor my body, and it was time to make some decisions of my own. No matter how much I wrestled internally with the confusion I felt.

"Provisions have already been packed." I said, standing up from the table, addressing the brothers. "We shall all remain here for one more night—to rest. And tomorrow, I will depart with the MacKenzie's to Eilean Donan.

I turned my awareness to the angel, my lover, and I almost wavered in my resolve.

"Damian, I am asking you to return to Dover and bring my father back to me, safely."

My companions all looked around at each other. Stunned.

"My sweet love, I will not leave you again." Damian took a step forward, placing his hands on my shoulders, pulling me closer, intimately. My body moved towards his and he embraced me, while carefully avoiding my back. We stood together, holding each other, as Roderick and Kenneth exchanged bewildered looks upon seeing him so affectionate towards me, and me reciprocating.

"Angel, the castle is well protected by the old words, which ha' been cast into every stone." Roderick rose from his seat to stand beside his brother. "And our younger brother, Colin, manages the lands and nothing enters the lands without us knowing. Once we arrive, we will send word to our father to send more o' our clansmen to protect the lands and Lady Moireach."

"After all that's happened, how can you ask me to trust you?" the Angel grumbled. "Do you truly think you can protect her? To show her what she is truly capable of? To let her grow her powers?"

Roderick stopped short at this. Looking to me, and back to the Angel, he realized that something had passed between us and Damian knew something of my powers.

"Damian, we can protect her at the castle. Our mother was Seraphina's companion for many years, and was taught many things which will now be taught to Moireach."

My angel did not like this answer, his face said it all. Taking a step forward, he looked like he was going to say something.

"—Bird-man," Kenneth interrupted. "I've been thinking about how we can make sure we are nae followed, to keep Moireach safe. Are there any remnants o' the dress Moireach wore when she escaped?"

"As a matter of fact…*Wolf*-man, there are," Damian said, taking a few steps towards him. "I have not had a chance to burn them."

"Fly across the highlands. Drop down at different places throughout the countryside and rub the cloth up against trees and leave bits behind. Anything to leave her scent behind, which will draw oot the hounds. Maybe even trick their master, ha' him thinking they are close to catching her."

"The last time I left Moireach in your care, you lost her," he hissed through gritted teeth. "She nearly died. Why should I leave her side now, just to sprinkle bits of her dress?"

"Because *I* am asking you."

I turned to him with a soft but steady voice, resolute. In his eyes, I saw his discontent and disappointment.

He left the room, only to return a few moments later with more furs, blankets, and cushions to prepare my guardians places to sleep near the hearth for the night. Kenneth had returned outside briefly to check on Samson, who had been sheltered in a small barn alongside the outside walls.

"And pray where Moireach sleeping?" Roderick asked, when Damian handed him a heavy fur.

"Wherever the bloody hell she pleases!"

He stormed out of the room. I looked at everyone settling into their warm furs and spaces for the night. Their boots were close to the fire to dry them out, and the jackets had been hung on the bench facing the fire. Athdara avoided my gaze, while Kenneth occupied himself tying his hair back into a loose braid.

My mind was at war yet again with the heart and my body. To stay with my companions, or to choose the arms of my lover, the fallen angel. The one whom my body ached for, desired more than anything I could rationally.

"Roderick," I leaned to kiss his cheek, and then turned to follow my beloved angel. "Please honour my choice tonight."

Laying on my side, wrapped in Damian's arm that night, sleep did not come easy. He refused to speak to me, yet the warmth of his touch and the fierceness with which he held me, said more than any words could have. There was no lovemaking that night, and when I tried to reach his lips with my own, he pulled away. Sulking. Leaving me to fall asleep with silent tears running down my cheeks.

When sleep did finally come, it brought no dreams, nor memories of my mother. Upon waking, I found myself alone. Damian had already left., without a word to me or anyone else. So, I joined the others in the main hall and prepared to depart for the west coast of Scotland with the remnants of supplies from the kitchens to sustain our journey.

There was only one horse among us, and it was decided that I ride behind Athdara to support my weakened body and still leave my healing back unencumbered by pressure. Kenneth and Roderick kept up by alternately jogging and walking alongside, senses on alert for possible attack. In hushed whispers, I shared with Athdara what had happened in the bedroom. She proved to be a discerning and knowledgable companion, experienced in the ways of love as I was not. She kept her own voice muted so that the brothers could not hear. It was a relief to share with another woman what I had experienced, and so relieved to know that it was possible to have a union between a man and woman that resulted in the type of euphoria I had felt. Her words of wisdom even helped me understand how the release I had experienced could have created such an explosion of *fire*.

The further we traveled from Damian's castle, and away from his presence, the more of a sense of loss I felt. My body desired him, craved his touch. Every breath, every moment, felt more empty than the last. I ached for my angel. In the social circles of London, other women my age had spoken of how horrible their experiences with their husbands had been. Unions such as mine were rare, according to Athdara.

My mind continued its battle with the rest of my being. His past was in direct contrast to the man he had shown me to be since the night I saw him at the tavern.

The pace of our journey was steady and quick. We intended to arrive at Eilean Donan in just under three days. All of us felt the rising sense of urgency to cross the Cairngorm mountains and press on into the highlands of my ancestors, and to do so before any hellhounds could realize that Damian had led them on a merry goose chase. Our brief rest periods allowed me time to continue my lessons, the manipulations and control with *fire*. The brothers would offer their thoughts on how to wield the element—target practice—where they would throw objects into the air that I was expected to hit. I grew more comfortable with the flames, and my aim was getting better by the day. Even Kenneth, the most skilled hunter, was impressed. And at night, I was exploring the visions which were to be seen in the *fire*.

When we were about half a day away from arriving at our destination, I had become strong enough to ride on my own. It was decided that Athdara would leave a trail behind us to cover our tracks. It was important that we confused any hellhounds who might have come across our scent.

We arrived just past suppertime, the courtyard empty, except for the stooped woman at the top of the stairs. *Nanny*! She was the only one there to herald our arrival. As we approached, she walked down to greet us, and I could see how much she had aged. With the distance between her and I less than twenty feet, I could see that all of her hair had turned stone grey, gathered in a long braid hanging over her right shoulder. She leaned on a beautifully carved wooden walking stick with three animals carved along its length. In rich mahogany, the bear at the bottom, in the middle a wolf and near the handle was an eagle.

Seeing Nanny again, gave me a small burst of energy, and I slid off the horse, eager to run into her arms. Roderick and Kenneth beat me to her. In moments, they had lifted her up off the ground, where she was caught in a hug between the two of them.

"*Ach*, ye big beasts," she yelled, smacking her walking stick along their sides. "Put yer mother back on the ground!"

They lowered her back down, somewhat sheepishly. For a moment, years were taken off her face by the joy she felt in seeing her eldest sons return to her once more. It had been seven years since she saw them both. She then turned her attention towards me. Her once rich brown eyes now a milky white, I felt a deep sorrow realizing she had lost most of her eyesight. Yet she still knew me.

"Moireach, daughter of my heart, ye ha' grown even more beautiful than yer mother."

I paused, not knowing if I should laugh or cry. Her hands came to rest on my shoulders as she leaned forward and rested her forehead against mine. Even though she was stooped with age, I still had to rise onto my tip toes to reach her.

"Although my dear, ye ha' certainly not grown any taller. Ye would think wi' a father who stands over six feet tall and a mother who could look him in the eye, ye might ha' at least grown taller than this shrunken old woman."

She smiled softly at me, and held my face between her hands, cramped with age, to look into my eyes. Even with her lack of sight, her eyes sparkled with laughter and mischief. Leaning closer, she took a deep breath through her nose.

"So, he has found ye."

Unsure if she spoke of the Hunter or of Damian, I felt myself blush.

"Dinna fasch yersel'!" she said dropping her hands from my face. "I kent he would one day. Though my hope was that ye would ha' been married wi' children before this day would come. That would ha' made it harder for him to find ye. Alas, there is nothing we can do to change that now. We will keep ye safe, as we always ha'."

And with that she swiftly turned around and walked back towards the house, gesturing for us to follow.

"Oh, and ye shall be sleeping in yer mother's old room!"

It was my first night in my ancestral home, and I looked out across the dark hills of the highlands to see a full moon cast a silver shimmer over Loch Duich, turning it into a mirror against the black sky. The stone walls my ancestors, Clan MacRae, built almost three hundred years ago, to guard the surrounding lands and watch over the Five Sisters of Kintail mountains ranges, had been protected by the old words. Eilean Donan was home to generations of my father's family, but he had taken me from these walls before my first birthday. Looking down off the balcony, I saw Roderick was standing below, sentry over the moors and highlands. Kenneth was talking to the horses outside the stables. I had expected to feel sadness and loss, knowing that this was the place where my mother had met her death the night I was born.

As I turned around to walk back inside the bedroom, I saw where the lightning had struck the walls. I could not help but wonder if these lands would also see my death. The threat of the Hunter now most prevalent in my thoughts. I ran my fingers over the carvings on the tall posts of the bed that nearly filled the entire room. Each corner post revealed a delicately carved woman with expansive wings, *angels*, holding a small sphere in protective hands. Their long hair flowed around the posts, their eyes held a soft and gentle gaze, while their bare feet nearly touched the ground. All four etched in place to stand watch over the one who would sleep in their midst. Even so, it was hard to see myself finding any sleep or comfort in this room.

I sat down at her dressing table and looked in her mirror, wondering how often she had sat at that very same place, brushing her hair, readying herself for bed. Next, I opened her closet and found a night gown that belonged to her. I had lost all of my clothing during the hunt in the highlands and arrived with only the make-shift riding clothes from Damian's castle. The soft linen fit comfortably, but when I looked down, material pooled around my feet, so I had to gather it in my hands to lift the gown high enough so I would not trip. There was no further doubt about the truth of the stories about her height, and it was comically obvious now that I did not take after her in that regard.

I crawled under the covers and lay awake thinking about everything. *How on earth could Nanny smell him on me?*

As always, Damian not far from my mind, and as I drifted to sleep, I wondered how long it would be before I was in his arms again.

CHAPTER 17

The next morning, I was startled out of a deep sleep by the sounds of a cock crowing outside. And I awoke with an odd feeling. *I was home.* During the night, there had been no dreams and…no pain. I tip-toed out of the bed, steeling myself for ice cold stone. To my surprise the floors were warm. Eager to wear something that had belonged to my mother, I stopped short of her closet when I saw that on top of the chest at the end of the bed someone had carefully laid out clothing for me. The dress, a dark moss green, was simple and still elegant enough to identify me as a lady of the house. The laces were in the front, which allowed me to dress myself without the help of a maid. There was no corset, the fabric around the torso being of sturdier material and held its shape. To my astonishment, it fit me perfectly!

Looking at myself in the mirror that morning, I did not want to have my hair like that of a lady of the house, but instead, that of a free woman. A simple long braid down my back. Plus, the careful act of braiding gave me more time to reflect on the past.

My father, John Alexander MacRae, could trace his roots back for generations in the western highlands as part of the Clan MacRae. He had left his ancestral home with me before I saw my first birthday, taking Nanny and her sons with him to London. Leaving Eilean Donan and its surrounding lands in the care of my father's trusted friend, Malcolm MacKenzie, brother-in-law to Nanny, who was to watch over the land and its people—as long as a MacRae held Eilean Donan a MacKenzie would be at their side. But on the day of my thirteenth birthday, father had sent Nanny from our home in London back to the highlands, along with her youngest son Colin, my childhood companion. She was the only woman I had known as mother, and she had loved me as if I were her own daughter. I remembered hearing them fight bitterly that night. Neither realized I was awake, sitting at the top of the stairs. She had threatened him.

"We have to tell her, whether you like it or not!" she had said. "It is her birthright and her mother, your wife wanted her to have a full life! This means knowing all parts of her!"

"Aye, I know full well what my wife wanted for our daughter, but she died, didn't she?" shouting back at her. "Leaving me alone, with only snippets of truth of the kind of woman she was!"

Father took the choice of telling me about my mother away from her. She was gone before sunrise.

I now appreciated what she had so desperately wanted me to know—the story of my past, of my mother, and of my heritage. Things my father still did not know.

I was lost in thought, until the smell of freshly baked bread and bacon wafted through my doors, and brought me back to the present. Wandering down the corridors, looking up at some paintings and tapestries, in awe of the history contained in these hallways. I had long ago learned to follow my nose when it came to wanting food. When I arrived in the large dining hall, I had hoped to see Athdara there, but she was not. She had only been behind us by half a day or so, and I wondered what had delayed her.

"Why, Moireach, whatever possessed you to wear your hair like that?" Nanny called from her place by the fire, next to the rows of dining tables, rocking on her well-worn rocking chair.

"How could she see my hair so clearly?"

"After all the travels, I fear anything but a braid seems too complicated." I replied, as I walked into the great room to sit by her on one of the benches. "It's simpler."

"Your beloved mother often wore her hair like that when she went out riding, or to patrol the grounds with my uncle Dougall." Nanny said. "No wonder your father has never found himself another woman to wed, with you as his constant reminder of the love he lost."

There was a great disturbance coming from the front of the hall and the heavy dining doors were thrown open. Nanny stood up faster than I thought possible, and immediately placed her hand on my arm. Two people covered in mud from head to toe, tumbled past the front foyer and into the dining hall. The white hair gleaming through some of the mud, identified Athdara, but she was wearing different clothing than when I last saw her. The enormous man next to her was of clearly Clan MacKenzie, although not quite the same size as Roderick or Kenneth. Both of them were doubled over, and for a moment, I feared one or both were injured.

Until I heard the man let out a rather womanly giggly snort.

"Colin? Is that you lad?" Nanny pointed at him with her cane. "I could ha' sworn the boy I gave birth to had better manners than to burst through a door covered in mud and dragging what appears to be a woman o' distinction along on one o' his wee adventures!"

Colin, the youngest and fairest of the McKenzie boys, and my childhood companion, stood taller than I had imagined. His brothers had always called him the runt of the litter, but he still towered over most men. Thoughts flashed back to when I had last set eyes on him. It was the wild boar hunt, back when he had only just started to grow into a man—gangly limbs and a cracking voice still evidence of his youth.

"Och ma, this is no woman o' distinction!" Colin rolled his eyes at Gwenyver, quieting his chuckles. "Please allow me to introduce Athdara, my aunt, yer sister-in-law?"

He started to bow but almost fell over, thanks to his unsuccessful attempt at trying to suppress a rousing fit of laughter again.

"Pleased to finally meet ye Gwenyver o' Clan MacKenzie," said Athdara, fighting off her own fit of laughter, only to lose that battle. Unable to contain herself, she fell to her knees.

By this point, two kitchen maids who had started to bring in the breakfast meal, were also giggling, and I, too, was no longer able to hold a sense of decorum about myself. I began to laugh, having no clue at what.

"No need to be so formal, dear sister," Nanny said, through stifled chuckles of her own. "Especially when ye are covered in mud from head to toe. But if either o' ye would kindly explain what has happened for ye both to arrive in such a state and why the bloody stars are we all laughing like wee babes—"

"—Well, Ma…" Colin said, trying to compose himself. "I was on patrol when I saw Silvanus and his caravan near the edge o' our borders near the bogs on the west side, ye ken, and it was clear one o' the wagons was in distress. I landed close by, and after some investigating, found that one o' the wheels had come loose, and the wagon was slowly sinking into the bog. A few o' the men had been trying to get underneath the wheel without success. Thanks to my older cousin's fondness for throwing me into the bog when I was but a lad, I kent verra well how to navigate the mud. Wanting to help, I shifted back into a man. Silvanus realized quickly that I would need something to wear if I was going to be o' any use, so he kindly offered me a pair o' his trousers—short and loose they were. I was just taking a closer look to see how best to determine to best course o' action, when someone jumped in ahead o' me."

Colin shot a mischievous glare at his aunt.

"Seems Athdara doesna ha' much experience wi' mud pits." he said, the laughter starting back up. "And she ended up sinking deeper into the mud than the wagon, and all the splashing around made it worse—and muddier. So, there I was having to pull a half a wagon out o' the mud and also my newly met Aunt who had gotten herself right stuck!"

"That's fine and dandy, but what is so funny about that?" Nanny said, raising her eyebrow at her youngest son.

"Once I got the wheel unstuck, using my bare toes to find the stones and wood always found beneath the murk, I was able to push the wagon high enough out o' the bog so that the men were able to pull it oot, but Athdara wasna able to move." Colin spoke through a mud smeared grin, "So, I grabbed her, best I could, and having found some better solid stone footing underneath, I figured the best way oot would be to jump straight up and shift. I've done something like that before wi' a farmer's coo, shifting mid-jump to get my wings, and it worked rather well. Problem is, I hadn't counted on the mud being quite so stubborn, nor did I realize how tall my aunt actually was, and her long legs being much further down into the bog than I thought. So, with a great big heave ho', I took the leap only to get us both oot half-way before the mud pulled us back in…wi' a giant farting sound!"

"And…?" Gwenyver gave her son a blank stare, as if saying his story was not that funny.

He all of a sudden looked down for a moment, shyness causing him pause.

"And the mud may ha' pulled me trousers off in the process."

My eyes were immediately drawn to where trousers should be.

"Dinna fasch yersel', I've got a pair o' trousers on Lady M," he said catching my glance and throwing back a smirk. "Albeit possibly a few sizes too small."

He then bowed rather formally, followed by the sound of seams splitting. It was now clear to all that those aforementioned trousers would be of use to no one.

"Colin, ye wee rascal, get yer muddy arse outside and clean yerself up." Nanny chuffed. "And Moireach, turn around and spare yerself the sight of my youngest making a fool o' himself."

Colin was heard giggle snorting all the way back down the hall and out towards the courtyard.

"Gwenyver, would ye kindly let me know where I may wash up?" Athdara bowed slightly, while clearly biting her cheek to prevent more chuckles from escaping.

"Athdara, I will say again, no need to bow to me. And aye, the room next to Moireach's, but I ask that ye join us in her quarters before ye clean up. There is an urgent matter I've been waiting to address until yer arrival."

Once in my room, Athdara stood near the closed door to avoid slathering mud all over the rug. Nanny closed the door.

"Now, my darling Moireach. Please, show us yer back."

I had not allowed my guardians to see the result of my attack after we left Damian. So far, I had taken care to avoid all talk of my experience in the moors and with Damian since I arrived, I was taken aback by this request, if only but for a moment. Standing in front of them, I felt no shame or embarrassment of my nakedness, but was very conscious of how the two women would react to the scars that would forever mar my flesh and be a reminder of the violent encounter. I did not want them to feel the horror I knew they would.

"Moireach," Nanny said, sitting down on the edge of the bed. "Please tell us what ye ken of yer healing, I sense it was not all due to this Damian's healing prowess."

Once the dress had fallen to my hips, she beckoned me closer, and placed her hands along the wound, her gentle touch traversing its length. And as she touched my still tender skin, I shared with her what Damian had told me and the fragments of memory I myself had of that time. By the time she had completed her inspection and listened to every word I spoke, she had begun to sob. Athdara who had stood at a distance did not need her hands to feel the agony of the wound, her eyes were enough. I sat on the edge of the bed, baring my scarred flesh, and in the telling of my story, I felt cleansed.

"—Oh darling daughter o' my heart, I would ha' spared ye this pain if I could and I would ha' taken it as my own if the fates had willed it so."

For a few moments, no words were spoken. As I began to dress, the memories of the elements which had aided in my recovery resurfaced. Both women looked at each other. Finally, Athdara shook her head.

"What have you two decided just now?" I said, breaking the silence, witnessing yet another classic MacKenzie exchange. "I am no longer a child to be kept in the dark."

"The elements ha' helped wi' the healing." Nanny said, "I've heard o' this happening only once before. When we first brought yer mother to our lands and she was near death. The elements spoke to me and instructed me how to heal the wounds she had suffered."

Somehow, hearing this news did not surprise me. I was no longer certain that anything would shock me anymore. Angels. Shapeshifters. Elemental Twins. Fire. Water…I felt numb.

"There is no more poison lingering in yer blood, but I'm afraid there is naught to be done about the scars." Nanny lowered her head. "Yer body will always bear the evidence o' your encounter wi' the hellhound."

"I am alive, I am healed, and I am whole." I said, sternly. "That is all that matters."

"Ye must tell us all that transpired wi' the winged one and leave not one detail out. It is plain on yer face, and his scent on yer body that ye ha' known each other… intimately."

"Gwenyver, may I ha' yer leave to wash up before dinner?" Athdara was clearly getting uncomfortable as the mud was drying and crusting over her clothes. "I've already heard this story from Moireach whilst travelling here."

"Of course dear, but join as us as soon as ye are able." Nanny replied. "You will find some of Seraphina's clothing laid out for you, I believe they should fit."

Once again, sharing what had taken place between Damian and me felt liberating. Gratifying. I also shared the mistrust my mind had towards him, and how I was in constant conflict, struggling with my desires and my thoughts.

"Aye, we ken the stories of the soul-prey well." Nanny spoke quietly. "I, I… never thought ye might become one o' them. How he was able to restrain himself from doing ye harm is a miracle, Moireach. We ha' never heard o' any o' the fallen ones letting their soul-prey live. I must think on this further. As for yer feelings and yer thoughts, I am afraid that only time will reveal the truth and help ye decide. It is often that our hearts are at war with our heads, but it is through life experiences and the choices we make that we can learn how to find the harmony between the two."

"I suppose you're right." I bowed my head with grief. "Nanny, the journal, was lost in the fire at the Abbey. I wish I had a chance to read more than the ten pages or so, to learn more."

"Oh my child, dinna worry. The knowledge is not lost. Her wisdom lives on. Dinna fear, dinna grieve."

As we turned down the right hallway, to return to the Dining Hall, Athdara joined us, having washed up and change into a clean pair of clothes. Sounds of men shouting and rowdy thumps were heard coming from the main hall below.

"Ach, what now—?" Gwenyver muttered with some flustering of her hands, as she walked faster towards the commotion.

I hurried down the large staircase ahead of the other two women, only to find the youngest MacKenzie, now all washed up, trying to lift Roderick over his broad shoulders. Kenneth was standing by, goading them both on in this show of strength.

"Come on lad, Roderick could manage to lift us both!"

"Why Kenneth, I don't think that's a feat you have managed yet, have you?" I challenged him with a smile. "Lifting Roderick over *your* shoulders?"

Colin turned around rather abruptly at the sound of my voice. Barely holding his eldest brother up overhead, his hair damp and his face flushed from scrubbing the mud clean. He had short blonde hair, most unusual for man. And I could have sworn he had *blue* eyes, and I definitely remembered a rounder face. Standing before me was a man with eyes the colour of the fairy pools we had seen on our journey—a shimmering blue-green, gazing at me with such intensity that I could not turn away.

When he opened his mouth to speak—words I will never know—because at that very moment his oldest brother came crashing down with a surprised yelp. Tumbling down in a heap of limbs, I heard some fairly foul-mouthed words from Roderick.

"Bloody hell, piss on the dark one and lick it off the arse, Colin!"

"Dinna dare to utter such foul language in this home, Roderick!" Nanny had arrived, and admonished her eldest. And with a single look, the kind that only a mother could give, the boys hustled to right themselves.

"Shall we sit for breakfast?" she looked to Athdara, who nodded in agreement. Both women were determined to keep a sense of decorum.

Gathered at the dining table, my eyes kept wandering towards Colin throughout most of the meal. Realizing I had lost much of our childhood memories, I tried to recollect what he had looked like back then. There was something about him now that I couldn't put my finger on, and every time he looked my way, I couldn't help but smile. Yet, my body did not respond with the heat and desire it did with Damian, my angel, my lover.

"Colin, I think ye should guide Moireach around the castle." Nanny must have been watching our strange exchange. "Make sure she doesna get lost and show her all the little nooks and crannies where she can hide. Heavens forbid it should ever come to that."

And so, I spent the rest of the morning and part of the early afternoon, following Colin around, through each room, up and down each staircase, and down each hallway. The number of hidden passageways was staggering.

"Want to ken a wee secret on how not to get lost?" he called over his shoulder while navigating yet another corridor, lined with tapestries, swords and portraits.

"Yes, of course I would."

"Each direction of the castle has it's own colour theme—just look at the tapestries, carpets and flags. North is blue, East is Red, South is Green and West is yellow…although I think my mother plans to change that soon. It's quite ghastly to be honest."

So, it was as easy as that. All I had to do was remember which direction was which colour and I would be able to use that to help navigate to where I wanted to be.

When we reached the top of the south tower, the stairway became very narrow, and Colin had to turn sideways to see that his shoulders didn't get stuck. I had been so absorbed in his voice, in a brogue thicker than his brothers' that sometimes had me asking him to repeat himself, that I didn't notice when he stopped at a narrow part of the stairs. I bumped into his side, with such force that I nearly knocked myself back down the steps. Colin reached out to catch me just in time.

I noticed, for the first time, his scent. Fresh, clean, and very much like the earth after a rainfall.

"Watch yersel'…Canna ha' ye falling down the stairs while wi' me, can I?"

He looked down at me with those compelling eyes of his. Strange, how in that moment I felt a spark of warmth inside of me, yet it felt nothing like what I had experienced with Damian. An instant later, I felt his arm reach behind me as he tore a burning tapestry from the staircase wall.

"By the stars, my brothers were nae lying when they said ye were wee fire starter!"

"I'm sorry. I didn't realize. I—" I mumbled.

Embarrassed, I watched him stomp the smouldering wool, until we both saw the sizeable hole I had burnt through the very centre. My lack of control over this power would be the death of me. Or worse, the death of someone I cared about.

"Listen lass, if ye only kent what I went through as I learned to shift, ye would not—."

"—What did you go through?" I blurted. "Because I haven't heard of any MacKenzie's who sets things on fire?"

"Fine, if ye want to ken, I was so eager to join my brothers that every day I would hide in the barn, behind the London manor, trying to shift. Even though my body wasna old enough for the change, I thought I had figured out the logistics o' it. So, wouldn't ye ken it? Mother found me one day, trying to force the shift, and to her surprise I had managed to shift every part of my body that I could see."

"What's so bad about that?" I asked, still annoyed with my own antics. "It's not like you start fires everywhere!"

"Ach, get yer heed out of yer arse Moireach." he said, rolling his eyes. "I'll not treat ye like some high brow lady who needs coddling. Ye deserve better than that."

He chuckled.

"Now, think again, what did I just say?"

"You said you had managed to shift every part of your body that you could see?"

I wondered where he was going with this.

"Aye, exactly. Ha' ye ever tried to look at yer own arse?"

He began his free-spirited, snorting laughter again.

"My ma found me that day shifted into a wee lion cub. I had all the parts right, but there I was with my tail sticking right out o' me bare human arse!"

"Oh my heavens, what did she do." I burst out laughing.

"Oh I canna tell ye that!" He grinned at me, with a ridiculous sheepish smirk. "Unless ye swear to keep it a secret?"

"Of course I will!"

He leaned in closer, conspiratorially, and whispered.

"She pissed hersel' wi' laughter!"

"You must be joking?" I asked, incredulously.

When we finally returned to the main floor, Roderick and Kenneth recruited Colin to renew words of protection around the castle. Nanny had said that the power of three would give the words extra potency. Meanwhile, I was too exhausted to do anything but sleep until dinner. My wounds, although healed were still affecting my body. By the time one of the maids had been sent to fetch me for dinner, everyone had gathered around the table and were enjoying the wonderful meal of roasted venison and vegetables that the kitchen had prepared.

I sat down next to Nanny, feeling comforted by her presence. As I ate, Colin stole glances my way. He was so different from Damian. Everything about this young man was light, gentle, and…joyful.

"Roderick, tomorrow I wish to ride with you on patrol." I said between bites. "I want to see the lands, meet the people and maybe find an opportunity to practice."

"Aye, lass, I think that's a verra good idea." he replied, through bites of his food. "Be sure to rise early."

On a full belly, I excused myself to my room for the night. I sat in my mother's night gown on the edge of her bed, lost in my thoughts, when Gwenyver knocked on my door.

"Come in!"

"Moireach, before I retire I wanted to tell ye what yer mother shared wi' me." Sitting down on the chair, just next to the door. "A word o' warning—she said the dark one, the Hunter o' whom she wrote about in her journal, would only be the foot soldier for another."

"So, this Hunter is only the first of many?" I gasped.

"Aye, he is a fallen one. A dark, and evil one ya can be sure o' that." Shifting uncomfortably in her seat, she moved her walking cane into her right hand, steadying herself to stand. "But somehow he has not the one we need to fear the most."

Standing up, leaving the comfort of the bed, I walked towards her.

"I've had a vision, darling daughter o' my heart. This Hunter is but one o' a handful o' commanders, those who are loyal to the one who started their rebellion many eons ago. The Dark One—Samael. The oldest, strongest, and most cunning o' their kind. I pray that ye find her sisters, and perhaps even the Lady o' Water. And that together ye will find a way to not only protect yerself but to save yer world.

CHAPTER 18

As soon as I woke, the memories of my dreams faded but I remembered the crescent moon talisman, the same one I had seen my mother wear in my dreams. Only this time, it was on a necklace, on a woman not much taller than me with jet black hair, slicked back away from her face. The piercing ice blue eyes in direct contrast to her dark hair. Startled out of my slumber, I stumbled out of bed and saw the sunrise had only just begun. Someone had left a cool basin of water for me so that I could wash. By the light of the fire still flickering from hearth, I searched for something to wear in the closet but everything was far too big. Just when I was about to give up, I noticed something tucked behind the clothes, I saw a wooden box adorned with the carving of a crescent moon, so like as the talisman on my mother's belt—from my dreams. I pulled out the box and opened it.

Inside I found a tunic made of dark brown leather suede, the seams nearly invisible, and when I put it on, the sleeves extended past my wrists with a small opening where I could slide my thumb through. Instead of tying up at the front, like most blouses, there was an excess of material on each side that when wrapped around the waist could be tied in a knot at the front. The shirt was clearly made for a woman, and the suede was thick and sturdy enough to offer protection from the elements, my body felt the chill of the morning ease as soon as I gathered the final knot above my hips. Even more astonishing was that it fit me nearly perfectly.

There were also pants in the box, made of the same brown leather, with no seams in sight, which laced up the front. Although I was unaccustomed to wearing pants, I tried this pair on, which fit as perfectly as the shirt. I walked around my bedroom, testing this new outfit for comfort and functionality for today's riding excursion. It became clear that these garments did not belong to my mother. The pants were only an inch or two too long for me instead of the nearly eight extra inches of length that her night dress had.

As I sat down to braid my hair, I wondered where these clothes came from. *Who did they belong to?* My thoughts were disrupted by a commotion I heard outside my window. I jumped up to see what was happening. Roderick was about to leave for patrol—without me.

With a huff of annoyance, I tugged on the riding boots, which I had found tucked away behind the box, over the leather pants and discovered yet again that they were a perfect fit for me. Nearly falling on my arse, I raced down the stairs, and grabbed a butter roll from the top of the oven on my way out the back kitchen door.

"Moireach, return this instance!"

I heard Nanny yell after me, but there was no way I was going to be left behind that day. I was determined to continue my practice with the *fire*, and I could not do that behind these castle walls. Samson was not saddled yet, but I took the risk of jumping onto him bareback with only the reigns to help me control him. Leaving the castle walls, I pushed my horse and myself to the limits, by spurring him on to greater speeds. I was grateful for the pants, which did not allow any of the chafing I would have normally felt on my inner thighs. When I finally caught sight of Roderick and the beast of a horse he was riding, he had already turned to face me.

"Lady M, ye may be wearing leathers belonging to my clan ancestress," he said, accompanied by one of his low rumbling belly laughs. "But I can still smell ye underneath it all"

"This belonged to Dylynn?" Somehow, I had imagined her to be a rather large woman, perhaps tall like my own mother, especially seeing big most of her descendants were.

"Aye lass, that outfit has been in our family for many generations. Always keeping it safe and ready for its owner to return, should she choose." He slowed the pace of his horse and turned towards me. "My mother thought it would fit ye, and I can see that ye are almost as big as her!"

"Why did you not wait for me?"

"I warned ye to rise early. Ye made it clear ye wanted to come on patrol, and I was curious to see if ye wanted it badly enough."

For the next hour, we trekked with our horses in silence. I watched the giant carefully, trying to understand what one actually does on a patrol, and he occasionally glanced over when he sensed my eyes on him.

"Going on patrol means many things Lady M." he said, breaking the silence. "First, we always stay on our side o' the land. Here the old words offer the most protection. See the stone fence over there? It surrounds the vast lands, belonging to yer family. Each stone has been gifted wi' words o' power. We ensure that nothing is obstructing the flow o' the water in the creek that traverses both sides o' the stones."

He slid off his horse and helped me down from Samson.

"Sometimes, ye might want to get closer to the ground. Look for signs o' disturbed earth or stone."

Walking alongside the low stone wall, leading our horses in amicable but watchful silence, I felt gratitude towards my guardian—for teaching me now, for protecting me all my life, and for loving me as a sister. I was nearly lost in my thoughts, when I found upturned earth and some signs of disturbed stones and called him over immediately.

"Oh, aye, this is verra suspicious." He chuckled deeply in the back of his throat. "But I wouldna disturb that hole if I were you. Not unless you want to piss off a mother fox who is just trying to protect her newborns."

As we walked, I realized that I had been so self-centred for much of my life that I never once had shown an interest in the lives of the MacKenzie who had watched over me.

"Roderick, what was it like having to take care of me?" I ventured. "Keeping this whole other world secret from me, and living away from your family?"

He paused in his stride, for only a moment, deciding something.

"Moireach, first o' all, ye need to ken that I chose this life. As honour-bound as we MacKenzie's are, we always ha' a choice." Looking down at me, his eyes crinkled with affection. "And lass, ye were an easy choice."

"What about living in London, leaving your family here?"

"Well, for thirteen years I had my ma, and both my brothers nearby, so it never felt like I was away from my family. But if I'm honest, returning home means more to me than I had realized. Although I would ha' preferred under different circumstances. It's been nigh seven years, when I brought my mother and wee Colin back here, but a part o' my heart has always been here."

"Because you grew up here?" I asked.

"Actually, my childhood was spent at the MacKenzie Manor, only later in my early teenage years did I come to live here at Eilean Donan." He sighed.

Reaching my hand over to his, I gave it a little squeeze, encouraging him to tell me more.

"Ye see, there is a woman here whom my heart belongs to. She and I first met when I was but a young lad, and she only a snot nosed bairn, but then when I came back seven years ago, I saw her again and she was all grown up." He started to blush. "My life is sworn to yers, by choice, and I have no regrets but my heart belongs to her in ways I canna explain."

"Is she a fair and delicate maiden that will always need your protection?" I gently chided him, somehow not able to shake the image of him always being a protector.

"No, lass, as a matter o' fact, her head reaches my shoulders, her dark hair reaches all the way down to her ample bottom, and oh by the stars, the rest o' her curves…large enough for a man o' my proportions." He blurted out, before he realized that he was speaking aloud and promptly blushed a deeper shade of red. "Her name is Liza, the housekeeper's daughter and lives on her own on a farm not too far from the castle. She is nearly fifteen years younger but I dinna care. I visited her the night we arrived, and she remembered me with much fondness. She is not yet betrothed or promised to another, and by the heavens, she would be a braw lass to ha' at my side."

I didn't think it possible, but he blushed more.

"Lady M, I havena asked her to marry me yet." He shrugged his shoulders, and walked a few steps forward. "I wanted to get yer blessing first."

"My blessing? Why would you want that?" I was a bit stunned.

"Moireach, I swore on oath on the day ye were born to always be by yer side, to protect ye wi' my very life if needed." he stammered. "It's only now, that I realize how much I want to ha' children o' my own, to have a woman at my side whom I can share my life wi'. I would verra much like yer blessing, my Lady."

It took a moment to realize that his request would mean that he would no longer be part of my life, he would not return to London if we ever survived this Hunt, and I would be without his daily encouragement and support—and protection.

"Roderick MacKenzie, I not only give my whole hearted blessing for you to ask for Liza's hand in marriage, but I release you from the oath you took nearly twenty years ago." I was sincere in my reply. "I cannot say I shall not miss you dearly, but now is the time for your happiness. It is time for me to figure out a few things on my own."

"Oh Lady M, ye've made me verra happy. I would gladly ha' ten children wi' her, if our age allows for such a miracle and if we ha' a girl, we shall name her after ye." He had skipped a few steps, from sheer joy, and his large stride put him several feet ahead of me.

"Roderick, I wish I had known sooner what your family was doing." Running up behind him, I yanked on his arm to force him to turn around. Rising up onto my tip toes, I reached up as high as my arms allowed and hugged him like I had never before. "For so many years, I was ignorant to so much of the world."

"Ye should never feel guilty about who ye are!" he said, leaning down to kiss the top of my head.

"But you didn't choose *this* family, you didn't choose to sacrifice your life for mine, your happiness for mine."

"Moireach, that's where ye are wrong. It's not just because we are honour bound, but because from the moment ye were born…" His eyes were far away. "Well, ye were a wee miracle. When I held ye for the first time—after mother determined that I wouldna accidentally crush ye—I looked down into those golden amber eyes o' yers. I placed my finger carefully on yer chest just to give ye a wee tickle. Ye grabbed it and pulled it to yer face and rubbed yer cheek and starting cooing softly. My heart melted. And I kent I would be yer guardian for as long as I was capable."

Strolling side by side, we shared a comfortable silence again for a while, until the horses pulled on their leads, shying at a large tree that had fallen across the low stonewall, breaking the line of the border. It looked as if it had been cut down by lighting. The stones were scattered loosely around the battered tree. The only thing to do was to remove the tree from the stone wall and set about repairing the fence.

"Do you want me to fetch the cutting tools from the castle?" I asked.

"Lass, ye forget ye are travelling wi' a MacKenzie!"

In one leap, Roderick was over the wall and had stretched his arms to the limits around the tree's trunk. Looking around, I realized we were on the far borders of the lands, and we had not seen a village or a person in quite some time. The words of protection might have been compromised, and immediately I sensed that something was not quite right. As he began to muster all his strength to lift the tree, I saw that the tree had no roots! This tree had not just fallen over in a storm!

"Roderick, you're on the wrong side of the stone wall!" I called out. "Leave the tree."

"Lady M, I—."

Just then five hellhounds came bounding towards us, having crept alongside the creek on the other side, staying downwind where neither the horses nor the MacKenzie had been able to detect their approach.

He turned too late.

"Get on yer damn horse—" Roderick was hardly able to shout at me through his shifting into the powerful bear. "—and ride back!"

The hellhounds did not slow their attack, and Roderick was forced to fight them through the shift. He looked over his shoulder and roared at me. There was no translation needed. His guttural animal sounds wanted me on my horse and out of danger. He moved his body in front of the small gap the tree had left in the stone wall to stop them from reaching me.

One hound leaped into the air, jaws wide and ready to kill, only to be grabbed around the neck by Roderick's strong claws. Within seconds, its neck was broken and throat torn open. The beast lay on the ground, unmoving. Roderick had told me to flee, but I was tired of running. I wanted to help him. I wanted to kill those hellhounds who had hurt me, who had hurt him, and killed countless others. Obeying his orders started my feet moving towards my horse, but I rebelled. I hesitated, body frozen in time, while my mind was spinning as I tried to figure out what I should do.

Two more hounds surged towards Roderick, one from each side, and sunk their vicious fangs into his arms. Their teeth dug deep into his flesh, and as they swung from his arms their weight buried them further into my guardian, tearing muscle. Roderick roared with ferocity and torment. It was clear that the lacerations went to the bone, and would be agonizing.

He used his legs to brace himself, swung both his arms forward and smashed the monster's heads together so ferociously that the skulls cracked open and all matter of flesh seeped from between his claws.

As the last of the hounds closed in, Roderick now fully transformed into a bear, walked determinedly towards the stone wall where I stood. He braced himself, and for a moment I thought he would beat off the two remaining hounds, and we would take the horses back to the castles and have an ale by the fire tonight telling the others of this victory.

My heart sank when I saw an imposing figure looming above him. Looking up I saw the fallen one, who dropped out of the sky and with it, more hounds bounding towards us from the hillside.

Abbadon, the damned blue-winged angel who had plucked me from my horse, and nearly caused my death, now landed close enough behind the bear, my guardian, and wrapped his arms around the thick-furred neck. The hounds came to the aid of their master, attacking the legs and arms. Desperately attempting to swing his weight around, Roderick tried to shake the angel loose, but his legs buckled from underneath the weight of the hounds. The poisoned claws already weakening him. Abbadon pulled the bear's head back to expose his throat, and I feared he would cut it before my very eyes. Instead, what happened next was far worse.

"You are going to be my most prized hellhound!" he cackled maniacally, as he pulled a large flask from his coat pocket.

In one swift move, he opened the bear's jaws and poured the contents down the bear's throat. Roderick started to shake violently and began to shift back into his human form. The hellhounds had released him, creating a circle around my guardian and the angel who stood over him triumphantly. There was no escape. There was no question. This was the evil concoction that turned good MacKenzie men into vicious hellhounds. Roderick fell to his knees, shaking and gagging on the vile mixture making its way down his throat and into his body. He looked across the stone fence. Our eyes locked. His jaw tightened and he clenched his fists, pushing them into the earth.

"Moireach MacRae!" Roderick gasped. "Dinna hold back!"

I had only a moment to process what he had said. The hounds and the angel had not bothered with my presence, thinking I presented no threat, like the last time. My body had been building up heat. Burning rage. *Fire.* I watched Roderick struggle back to his feet and launch himself at the angel. His arms locked in a death grip and his whole body focused on that one purpose. Yet even as he was determined to hold the angel, his body started to change. His fingers lengthened into lizards claws, the hair on his head fell out in clumps with each movement, as he kept fighting. Releasing an excruciating scream, his mouth open, I saw his teeth lengthen, cutting his lips and cheeks in the process. He was becoming a hellhound before my very eyes.

He was changing too fast!

The outrage I felt at seeing my guardian succumb to the poison, watching him fight with his very last human breath. Perhaps the poisoned claws had made him more susceptible. My rage screamed that this was not right, that Roderick was supposed to marry Liza, to have children and live happily ever after like in the storybooks of my youth. My despair, watching helplessly as his body started to mutate, grew into hatred. I knew what I had to do.

Fire was part of me, and I was part of it. Throughout all of my training, brief as it was, I had focused on control. I had tried to shape it, move it, and bend it to my will. No longer. Time stood still. I no longer needed an open flame to unleash my fury. The sound of my scream was drowned out by the noise of the fire exploding in all directions from my body. Abbadon was stunned into stillness. The hellhounds were frozen with fear. Roderick never loosened his grip.

The *fire* that left my body, was my twin in all ways except one—it had wings. It was a Fire Angel, manifested by my powers, and it moved rapidly towards Abbadon and Roderick. I watched the fallen angel try to put my protector in front of him as a shield. Roderick only gripped harder. His hands, now the claws of a hellhound, tearing into the flesh of the wings. At the last second, Roderick managed to move the weight to the left, throwing Abbadon off balance, forcing them both to the ground and directly in the path of the raging fire. The brunt of it hitting the angel, but also the one man who had protected me all his life. The flames engulfed them both.

I asked the *fire*—nay, I pleaded—for it to wrap itself around Abbadon. At first it seemed like the embrace of lovers, but within seconds the flames grew and turned from rich reds and oranges into deep purples and hues of dark blue. I watched his body burn, the wings starting to curl up as the feathers turned into burned scrap metal. The screams became louder. That of the angel and those of Roderick—whose body was still trying to transform into a hellhound through the pain of the flames. The weight of metal wings brought Abbadon to the ground. His flesh was melting, and the skin on his face poured down his neck to reveal a skull of black bones. The remaining beasts turned and ran while in my grief, I threw *fire* to engulf them, burning every single last one of them.

By the time the angel had stopped moving, I got to my feet and stepped over his crumpled heap of ash, bones and metal to find Roderick's body. Somehow, somewhere, he had found the strength to shift back to his human form. His face nearly unmarked, but the rest of his body was deeply burned. My heart was breaking into a million pieces, tearing me apart from the inside out, and my tears began to flow. I barely registered his laboured breathing which meant he still had some life in him yet.

"Moireach…thank ye." he whispered weakly.

"Roderick," Wailing uncontrollably in my grief. "—I'm so sorry. Please—don't leave me. Forgive me, I—."

"Lass, there is nothing to forgive. Ye saved me from a fate worse than death."

Tears and sobs threatened to rip my body apart, as I cradled his head in my lap. He took a slow, strained breath.

"Tell Liza I ha' always loved her."

I knew when he was gone then, I could feel it in the air, and all I could do was sit there with tears streaming down my face, while the embers of Abbadon and the hellhounds burned around me.

* * *

I do not know how much time passed while I sat holding Roderick's lifeless body. Despair had taken a hold of my own, and my heart felt fractured, broken beyond repair. I shook with grief.

Dearest child of the Elements, take him home.

I heard the whisper on the wind. Dazed, for but a moment, I got up and walked over to Roderick's horse. Struggling with the saddle, I pulled the riding blanket down. Barely able to see through the tears streaming down my face, I fought to roll the body of my guardian onto the saddle blanket. I would use the reigns of the horse as a harness—to pull the body. However, when I turned around to fix the reigns, his horse had run off. *Bloody hell!*

Even if it took me an eternity, I would bring Roderick home. Samson allowed me to tie his reigns to two corners of the blankets. He put his head down, followed my lead, and we walked slowly, pulling the make-shift stretcher. Once safely on our side of the stone wall, I took a moment to place the old words of protection over the gap. Fresh tears sprang from my eyes, as I realized he had only just taught them to me the day before. I would not leave without securing the land, and thereby protecting Roderick's body. His death would not be in vain.

Samson, though a strong horse, moved tediously given the weight and size of the body we were pulling. My makeshift harness and stretcher also made the journey cumbersome. After a few strides, the knots would come undone and I would have to scramble to tie them back together. With every heave, I feared my body would break from the strain, but it was nothing to the pain I felt in my heart. My tears would not end. Dragging his body across the lands in the direction of the castle, one stride at a time, one heave at a time, I had no concept of time. At some point, I had become oblivious to the fatigue that was setting into my body. All my energy was focused on bringing him home. I had lost track of time and most of my senses.

Step one foot in front of the other. Guide the horse. Pull blanket. Repeat.

I had walked, and pulled and cried for might have been minutes, hours or days, when I heard the sound of wings flapping overhead. I shrieked with anger without looking up. *Another angel.* I do not know where I got the strength, but I blindly released a fire bolt into the sky. Alas, the creature above managed to avoid being hit, hearing the wings flap away. As long as it didn't come back, I no longer cared. Roderick was coming home.

Not long after, a pair of large bare feet blocked my path, and I looked up to see Colin standing before me. He was wearing nothing but a pair of leather shorts, and in my stupor I vaguely noticed they were made of a similar material as the pants I wore.

"Moireach, please stop." I must have looked confused. "Let me help ye, lass."

He, too, had tears in his eyes as he looked down at the burned body of his brother.

"Colin, the hellhounds…." I collapsed into hysterics. "And Abbadon… Roderick would have….I'm so sorry—"

My words came with no rhyme or reason. I couldn't even string two sentences in a cohesive order, and this frustrated me into a fresh burst of tears.

"Shhh, Moireach, it's alright." Colin said, as he took me into his arms to hold me tight. "I dinna ken what ye are trying to say, but I'm here now. Ye dinna ha' to do this alone."

I tried to push him away. *How could he even bear to touch me? I had just murdered his brother?*

"Don't touch me!" I shrieked. "I killed him! I will bring him back!"

Finally finding words, I was ruthless. There was no punishment harsh enough for what I had done. Colin was in my way, and I was not going to stop.

"Listen ye wee banshee, he's my brother." He pulled me by my shoulders, forcing me to stand still. "Hold still but a moment and I will discern the truth for myself."

Kneeling in front of me, he placed his thumbs over my eyes, closing them gently. We stayed still together like that for a few moments. I felt my own thoughts pulled back to the beginning, back to the moment when Roderick and I found the felled tree. I saw everything all over again. At first, I remained steadfast on my feet, but as I watched Roderick look at me while flames reached Abbadon, and then him, and saw myself hold him while he died in my arms, my knees buckled and I fell to the ground. My eyes still closed, I heard Colin sob as he took me into his arms.

"Oh lass, I canna imagine the pain ye are feeling." He was the one now sobbing. "But I ha' seen what ye ha seen, and ye are no murderer."

"How can anyone not blame me for the death of Roderick?" Screaming at him, throwing myself at his chest, beating my small fists against him. "I killed him."

The reality of what had happened was settling in. I felt nauseous. I wailed and started to struggle in his arms again.

"Listen lass, Kenneth should be here shortly wi' the carriage. When I saw ye below, I kent we would need help—"

"—What? How were you flying overhead?" I interrupted.

"Aye, lass, when you and Roderick didna come home for lunch, I sensed something was amiss, and then Ma sent me out straight away saying you needed me."

"So, it was *you* I heard?" I brought my hand to my mouth. "I sent a fire bolt at you, I almost killed you, too!"

"Moireach, my life wasna in danger from yer fireball, given that ye didna even look up." Colin pulled me in closer, and gently stroked the crown of my head, uttering soft hushing sounds, much like I had seen Kenneth do with the young foals when they were anxious. "Although I must say I am verra impressed ye didna need an actual fire around to control it. I didna ken ye could do that."

I was so disoriented.

"I'm afraid even I am nae strong enough to pull my dear brother across these hills, even wi' Samson's help." he said as he looked at where my journey had started. "I am still shocked at how far ye managed."

True to his words, Kenneth arrived not long after with two horses leading the hay wagon from the barn. It took both of their muscle to lift their brother onto the back. When I refused to move, Kenneth picked me up unceremoniously, and dumped me next to his seat at the front of the wagon.

"Kenneth, I will fly back to check the gap in the wall and mend any repairs." the youngest MacKenzie called to his brother, "I will meet ye at the castle."

Colin took a few running steps before leaping into the air and transforming into a man-sized eagle. He flew towards the stone wall, while Kenneth and I rode on in silence. My tears would not stop, and Kenneth was unsure of what to say to comfort me. So, instead, he stayed quiet. Respecting that I needed this space.

We arrived home near sundown. Gwenyver was standing at the gates, leaning on it for support, watching for us. Kenneth ran towards his mother, fell to his knees at her feet, and cried as I have never seen a grown man cry before. Athdara came running through the gates shortly afterwards, dropping her basket of vegetables and herbs along the way.

"Boy, get off the ground," she said, unlatching her son to take unsteady steps towards the wagon. "Do ye think Roderick would approve o' such childish behaviour?"

Her grief was clearly visible as she staggered against the wagon, and then placed her hand on Roderick's burned chest.

"Athdara, please take Moireach up to her rooms, and the rest of ye…well, ye ken what we ha' to do. I expect yer father will be here sooner than we had thought. Let's prepare for the vigil."

I don't remember being led into my room. My exhausted body forced sleep on me, but I woke up in the middle of the night, not knowing how many minutes or hours had passed. Hearing the wind tugging at my window, I stumbled numbly out of the bed to secure the latch, when I saw Nanny sitting in the chair by the door.

"Moireach MacRae," she said. "After I had given birth to all three o' my boys, I was told by an oracle, that I would live to see all o' them become fathers. I canna imagine what is being done to throw the fates off their normal course."

Then she stood up slowly, almost painfully, and left the room.

I refused to leave the bed, replaying what had happened over and over in my mind. I could not even take pleasure in the fact that I had destroyed Abbadon. The pain I felt for killing Roderick clouded all logic. I refused all food and drink, and would not let anyone kindle a fire in my room nor open the curtains to let any light in. My shivers developed into a fever and my thoughts turned bleak. I had no desire to go on. I felt empty and yet filled with pain, anguish and sorrow. On the third day, my bedroom door was slammed open, startling me out of my stupor.

Into my bedroom walked a man of such size that he could only have been Lord George MacKenzie. The castle was not built for the likes of him, and he did not duck his head down in time, and smacked his forehead quite soundly off the door frame.

"Bloody hell!" he grunted, while rubbing the very spot with his hand, and seeing me for the first time. "I canna tell ye how often that's happened."

In my stupor, I couldn't even find the humour in that moment. He was dressed in an oversize fur coat, with a high collar that wrapped around most of his head. The sound of his boot heels told me that he had just arrived from riding a horse, and his hunting kilt showed me that he was a MacKenzie. A broadsword that must have been longer than I was tall, hung off his belt, and as he turned towards me it whacked off the side of the door.

"So, ye are *her* daughter?" He sat on the edge of my bed, and it let out such a loud creak that I feared it would break. "Ye are the reason why my eldest son Roderick now lies on the funeral pyre below waiting to be united wi' our ancestors. The reason I hadna seen my wife for nearly thirteen years, and the reason my two oldest sons had to stay in London, *aye*?"

His accusation only reaffirmed my belief of guilt and shame, and I started crying again. The misery had made its way to my bones, and the grief made them feel like lead. The shame I felt when I remembered how good it felt to release the fire angel, the power that coursed through my whole body. Only to watch my guardian die in my arms.

"Why are ye crying like a wee bairn missing its mother's teat?"

"Lord MacKenzie," I said, sitting up in bed, strengthened by the singular thought which had festered in my mind. "I humbly ask you to end my life so that your son Roderick can be avenged."

He laughed. Loudly. I pulled away in confusion. It was the only repeating thought since the day Roderick had fallen beneath my flames.

"My Gwenyver didna tell me ye were also daft!"

"Lord MacKenzie," I pleaded. "I am afraid of the darkness growing inside of me, and I want to ensure that I never hurt anyone again."

"For that ye are going to ha' to find yersel' another village idiot, because I am nae here to get revenge." he said, chuckling. "I am here to thank ye for saving my son."

"But…" My voice shook saying the words out loud again. "—I was the one who killed him."

"Moireach, I ken firsthand what those dark devils will do when they catch a MacKenzie. Ye spared my son a lifetime of agony, pain, and destruction—a lifetime o' slavery. He didna ha' to follow in his grandsire's footsteps." He leaned in to wrap his big arms around me. "I dinna think I coulda survived my son's transformation into one o' those hellhounds."

"Sir…" I sniffled. "I wanted to save him"

"Aye lass, I ken. The earth has a way o' speaking to me. I ken the truth of what transpired. If there was any doubt, Colin wi' his special seeing sight that only comes once in every generation, also told me what happened. Roderick had been force-fed that vile concoction, and he was changing too fast. I wish we kent why—was it the poison from the hellhounds that weakened him or ha' they found a way to make the toxic potion stronger. Anyways, it was clear there was no hope o' saving his life. The Angel and the hounds were going to win. Yet somehow ye managed to burn that blue devil into a pile o' melted rubble? For that alone, I would welcome ye into my arms. Now I insist ye join my wife and my sons, as we celebrate Roderick's life together."

Looking up into his eyes, I noticed for the first time that they were exactly like Roderick's. The dark mahogany brown, kind and compassionate, fringed with thick black lashes.

"Now, would ye kindly honour my son, and change into some proper attire?" He encouraged me as he rose from the bed, pausing just before reaching the doorframe, this time ducking. "Not this time."

My tears had gone, and I felt numb, but I would do as Lord MacKenzie had requested. I got up, washed, chose a dress from the closet without taking note of colour or style except to see that it fit, plaited my hair into a reverent braid down my back tied with a black velvet ribbon. Walking downstairs to join the immense crowd gathered in the courtyard around the pyre, I saw Lord and Lady MacKenzie, reunited after years of separation. The affection they showed towards each other was plain to everyone, and many smiled in their direction, seeing a love that survived many trials and separations.

"As we gather here today, to celebrate the life o' my son and help him find his way to our ancestors, I canna help but be grateful that so many o' ye ha' joined us." Lord MacKenzie spoke loudly over the crowd. "I still remember the day he was born, and my beloved wife Gwenyver bade me to hold the wee bundle in my arms. I was scairt to death I would break the damn thing! My own son! That feeling didna last long as by the time he was five years old, he already reached well past my waist!"

"Roderick was sworn to Lady Moireach," Gwenyver now spoke, struggling for volume. "But not just because of our family oath to the Elementals, but because she captured his heart as a wee bairn. How else can ye explain a young man at that age volunteering to change her nappies?"

I had never heard this story. It brought fresh tears to my face, only this time of love, not grief.

"Our son was a true MacKenzie, and honoured all the old ways." Lord MacKenzie's voice was loud and clear across the courtyard. "When he was tasked to the vital role of watching over Lady Moireach, he didna hesitate. Until the very end, he was true to himself. A warrior, a man and a son. His life held meaning. He will always be remembered, from now until the end of times. May he find our ancestors in the sky and join them to watch over us."

Different people, cousins, uncles and aunts, all came to stand by the pyre, to speak about their love for Roderick and share a story or two. In the midst of the procession, we heard a carriage come along the bridge. No arrivals had been announced. The Clan MacKenzie responded like seasoned soldiers. Within moments, the men had moved into a formation protecting the women and children within their circle. George stood in front of his wife, and Kenneth and Athdara both stood at my sides, hands to their daggers on their belts while Colin took up the rear.

I felt him. I sensed him. How, I did not know, but I knew that inside the carriage was Damian, and my heart rejoiced through the pain I still felt in my heart. As soon as the carriage stopped just inside the gates, I stepped forward but was blocked by Kenneth.

"Ach Moireach, wise up!" he growled. "Wait until we can see who is inside!"

Duncan and Connor were both sitting at the front, jumping down to open the carriage doors. The first man to step outside was my father, looking dazed and very confused. He nearly fell had it not been for the man behind him with quiet and sure footing, who caught him under his arms, stopping him from falling. He lifted his gaze to the crowd, and seeing his face brought a quiver along my spine and I felt my skin grow warm. I watched as he placed his hand on my father's shoulder to help guide him through the crowd. John

MacRae was a much changed man. Always so strong and self-assured, yet he now walked as if he had only learned how a few days ago, muttering to himself with each step.

Damian walked my father over to George.

"George, you have not aged since last we saw each other, but I daresay I think that you have put some girth!"

"Well, ye, blonde rascal, ye still ha' that medallion that my Gwen gave ye?" George laughed. "And my girth is none o' yer business!"

"I'm afraid I am returning your friend John in poorer condition than when you saw him last, and for that I must apologize." He bowed deeply with respect. "…And my timing could have been better, I see?"

Looking around, Damian saw the Pyre, the crowd, and finally laid eyes on me standing behind Kenneth.

"Well, let's have a look at my old friend John, shall we?"

Lord MacKenzie walked over and looked my father directly in the eye. He spoke to him so quietly no one could hear the words. A few times, it seemed as if father was getting very agitated, but George kept his hands on both shoulders to keep him steady. Damian took several paces back, visibly uncomfortable. My body felt warm again, not feverish like the last few days, but it reminded me how much my body inexplicably responded to his presence, even with the cloud of pain and grief hovering over me.

"Damian, bring Moireach to me and keep Kenneth close by."

George barked the order so abruptly that everyone was startled. Within an instant Kenneth had placed his hand on my lower back and was gently guiding me toward my father, and Damian. He did not leave my side.

"George, what is wrong with my father?" I whispered.

"Lady MacRae, yer father has been poisoned, daily I might add. By my estimate, for nearly two years. Slowly at first, but perhaps the dosages ha' been increased recently to make him even more susceptible to the suggestion o' the one doing the poisoning. I ha' seen this only once before, when I was still a young lad. I witnessed firsthand what a draught of dark angel blood can do to mortal man. It does not change them into hellhounds like us. Instead, it affects the mind."

It took a few minutes for me to comprehend.

"Yer mother taught us some words, to determine if my suspicion was correct. And I'm afraid there is no question as to what has happened to John—."

"—that means Mr Cameron." I could not find the connection, but knew that somehow it existed.

"Well, John, my dear friend." George turned to my father. "The next few days are nae going to be verra pleasant. But I promise ye we will make things right. Ye will find yer way back to us. Kenneth, take him back inside and then join us."

"Let me help." Damian leaned towards his old friend. "My blood can provide the anti-dote if you will allow. And to guarantee my sincerity, you can be the one to use the words that would weaken me."

There was a moment of pause, as the large man took this into consideration.

"Thank ye, Damian, but what we really need is the blood o' the strongest MacKenzie's. Myself, my remaining sons and my brother will provide the necessary ingredients which my beloved will make to help free John from this poison."

Athdara had found her way to the front of the crowd to find out what was happening. "Do ye think that my blood would also be strong enough?"

"My fair sister, I am verra pleased to see ye among yer family at last." he reached out to embrace her. "And aye, ye are surely one o' the strongest o' us. Thank you."

"Father," Colin, who had been in the shadows all this time, spoke now. "Should we wait until after we have completed the celebration for Roderick?"

"My dear boy, I'm afraid this canna wait any longer, every moment we delay we risk losing the John we know forever. I will be damned if I allow those filthy winged demons to win one more battle!"

All of us, the immediate family members, returned inside heading towards the kitchens. Safely within the walls, I watched Nanny use a sharp blade to draw the blood from the forearms of her children, her sister-in-law, and finally her husband. To create a potion in the cauldron on the fire that she brought to a boil three times, all the while whispering the old words taught to her by my mother. Lastly, she added wine to make it more palatable and gave the concoction to my father, who by this point was almost unconscious and completely incoherent.

"Moireach, what you are seeing now is not the effects of the poison but the lack of them in his body." Damian whispered to me, standing at the doorway. "He is experiencing extreme withdrawal symptoms."

My father refused the cup from Gwenyver once again, so she turned to me to administer the antidote. It took several tries before he recognized me, but he drank the entire cup and promptly fell asleep.

"John, let's take ye to yer room to rest." Lord MacKenzie carried my father to his rooms. "I shall meet the rest o' ye outside shortly."

Outside, the men and women had waited patiently, understanding that my father's return heralded a pause in the evening's events. By the time we returned outside for Roderick's funeral, the night had arrived and the skies were dark. Stars gleamed and the moon shone brightly, and the time had come. Lord MacKenzie and Gwenyver, held hands while Kenneth and Colin stood just behind them. Together they put the torch to the pyre and the twins, Connor and Duncan completed the circle. I stood wrapped in the warm arms of Damian, watching the body of the man who had protected me since birth turn into dust and float into the skies. The blaze brought back the gruesome memories of the day that my *fire* had killed him. I held onto Damian tightly, watching, until the flames dimmed and the wind turned cold. Just as I was about to go back inside, Damian leaned down to whisper in my ear.

"Moireach, do you know that unnaturally tall woman standing near the gates? The one who seems to be holding in sobs of grief."

I looked up, and my breath caught in my throat. There could not be so many women in these parts with that height, that build, and that length of hair. I broke free of Damian's arms and ran over to her, tears welling up in my eyes.

"Are you Liza?" I barely managed to get out over the noise of the crowd.

"Lady MacRae? She curtsied, bewildered. "Er, aye, my name is Liza."

"Why are you standing back here?" I grabbed her wrist and started to pull her towards the stairs, where both George and Gwenyver were watching over the pyre. "I am sure his parents will want to speak with you!"

But she pulled back, resisting me, and Roderick had been right about her size…and her strength.

"Oh, please Lady, I wouldna ken what to say to such highborn folk."

"Well, I am not going to let you just stand here. Now move those long legs and come with me!" I was not going to take no for an answer, and she followed me, grudgingly, to where the MacKenzie's were still standing.

"Gwenyver, may I present Liza!" I blurted out rather loudly, unsure of what else to say.

The stillness that fell across the crowd was only broken by the crackling of the coals from the pyre. Gwenyver and George both walked toward the trembling woman, and to her surprise put their arms around her.

"My dear lass, our son Roderick came home the night before he died and told us he intended to make ye his wife," Nanny said. "That he had reunited wi' the love o' his life and wanted to remain here and ha' children. Ye are most welcome into our family—always."

Nanny's soothing words helped Liza to feel more at ease, but it was what she said next that had her trembling again.

"My dearest, you and your child, our grandchild, will always be a part of this family."

She placed her hands on Liza belly and smiled.

CHAPTER 19

The celebration of life for Roderick MacKenzie continued well into the night. The kitchens were working into the late hours, making sure anyone who needed nourishment would not go wanting. Some went to bed, others stayed up into the early hours of the morning. Normally, there would have been hangovers a plenty, but Lord MacKenzie had ordered double the guards and requested that everyone remain sober. We all knew—Mr Cameron was not far, the hellhounds were still hunting me, and we did not know who their master was—an attack was imminent.

Before Damian had returned with my father, I had greatly feared that the enemy would find my father and hold him hostage in exchange for my surrender. Now with my father safe with us at Eilean Donan, protected by both the old words and a huge gathering of the Clan MacKenzie, I had hopes that our enemies would not dare to broach the castle. Damian, however, was in constant pain from the protection of the old words. Even with the medallion for support, being inside the castle walls was more than uncomfortable. He had chosen to sleep just beyond the castle walls in one of the carriage houses, where the potency of the words were not as strong.

The morning after, as I was leaving my bedroom, to join others for breakfast, I ran headlong into the youngest MacKenzie.

"Do ye always run without looking first?" Colin quipped.

"Well, do you always stand in front of a door waiting for ladies to come out and crash into your massive chest?"

Something about him made me feel light, and dangerously happy, even. It was so different than how I felt with Damian. After what I had done to Roderick, I felt I had no right to those feelings—for either Colin or Damian. He placed his hand deliberately on my shoulder, and my body responded in a way that confused me. His touch felt cool, but comforting. *I do not deserve to feel this way.*

"Lady Moireach, I saw—through yer own eyes— what happened that day wi' Roderick," he said. "My family has what they call a seer in every generation. It appears I'm the oddity wi' that gift, which in truth I see as a curse. I thought a seer would see the future and be able do something about what he saw. Not a helpless bystander to what has already happened in the past!"

He kicked his foot against the wall in frustration, and I couldn't help but understand his feelings of helplessness.

I leaned into him, a clumsy attempt at an embrace, intending to show him…*what exactly?* But he froze when I put my arms around his waist. *He is disgusted with what I have done.* I was the wrong person to console him. I abruptly let go, mumbled an apology, and scurried off to the dining hall too fast to hear his remark.

Entering the great room, I found my father sharing a table with my companions. He looked tired, but I could see that his eyes held a little of the light I remembered. And then, to my amazement, he spoke.

"Moireach, thank the heavens you are alright!" I rushed to him, and we embraced each other, awkwardly and somewhat formally, as we had not held each other since I had turned thirteen. "George has told me everything! Your mother, her wounds when I found her, angels and the origins of the MacKenzie's. In truth, I am horrified at all that has taken place and beg your forgiveness for my actions as of late. And now, the loss of Roderick—."

He was filled with anguish, and looked upon me with such pleading in his yes, hoping that I might forgive him.

It is I that should be begging your forgiveness for having taken your life-long friend Roderick from this world, I thought. My father saw dark thoughts cloud my face just as George entered the room, with Silvanus right behind him. Athdara leaped out of her seat and rushed towards him. He took her into his arms, and they exchanged such a kiss of passion it made the whole room blush. Not just me for once.

"Gather round everyone, we must make ready." I wasn't sure I would ever get used to George's booming voice. "We have news."

We cleared space around the table and made way for Silvanus and a few of his men to join us. Gwenyver sat next to her husband, Athdara sat next to her beloved, and my father stayed close to the warmth of the fire. I sat on the bench along the long table. The men in the group led the discussion right away, and that is when I noticed that Damian was not present. I was just about mention that fact, when he lurched through the doors, wobbling on his feet, as if he were drunk.

"George, I must insist that you at least release the words from this room…" He grunted, in discomfort. "…so that I may sit here without having my skin on fire."

"Bloody devils, how did ye even get through the front door?" Lord MacKenzie boomed. "Not even the medallion is that powerful!"

"To be honest, I don't have the faintest notion," Damian groaned through gritted teeth. "I wanted to see Moireach, and when I saw the arrival of Silvanus I knew there would be a meeting—at which I should be present."

He stood in glaringly obvious discomfort, pain even. George had not been informed of the nature of mine and Damian's relationship, that much was clear as he looked to his wife. When the angel leaned towards me to kiss my cheek and I felt the warmth of the blush rise into my cheeks, his scrutinous eyes missed nothing.

"Gwenyver, please release this room."

She stepped towards the door and walked around the edge of the room whispering words too quiet for us to hear. Colin and Kenneth stood near the large fireplace keeping a watch over the proceedings, and moments later Damian released an audible sigh, and sat next to me on the bench. It had been Colin who looked more perturbed than Kenneth when Damian had chosen his particular seat.

"Our caravan has been travelling towards Eilean Donan since the attack, by routes we normally wouldna take." Silvanus leaned back in his seat, resuming where he had left off. "The hope was to cause confusion for anyone that may be following us. Along the way, we came across a carriage alongside the road. One o' the wheels had caught between some rough stones and broken in half."

Damian put his arm around me, drawing me in close. As always, the presence of his body stirred desire in mine, the longing and the ache for his intimate touch. Now was not the time, and my body began a silent war with my mind. His actions drew looks from everyone around us, including my father.

"It didna take long to discover that the man in the carriage was none other than William Cameron himself, on his way to Eilean Donan to find Lord John MacRae. We offered to fix his wheel in exchange for payment, and all the while feeding him drink to help loosen his tongue."

"You sneaky devil..." Damian muttered.

"Sadly, the man didna offer much information, except that he was in the shipping industry and riding out to meet wi' his business partner and soon to be father-in-law, who was very ill. He had four men wi' him, all o' whom seemed to be mute. Not a one o' us could get any o' them to talk, not even the women."

"He made no mention of Moireach?" John asked, with trepidation.

"Her name was not mentioned once. He has simply been following rumours that Lord MacRae has returned to his family lands. He made several comments about John's health, and it is clear he assumes you are still under his control. He played very loving towards his bride to be."

Damian's whole body tensed up and his grip tightened around my shoulders.

"That man will not get close enough to claim her as bride before I take his head." he growled through gritted teeth.

The whole room startled at the vehemence of Damian's voice, and Gwenyver rested her hands on Lord MacKenzie's arm to stop him from standing up. My father, still weakened and tired, did stand up and walked towards the table and sat down beside me. He took my hand in his, and gestured for Silvanus to continue.

"While he was distracted by the men fixing the wheel, Mother suggested we set a trap. So, I told him Mr. Cameron that we too had heard rumours o' the laird returning to his home. To allow his ailing daughter to see her ancestral home before she left this world."

"That's bloody brilliant, Silvanus." George stood up with his large tankard filled with ale and took a huge gulp. "He will now ha' a sense o' urgency! Oh, and ye should know that we believe Mr Cameron may have connections to a fallen one, perhaps a servant to one, doing his bidding. He has been poisoning Lord MacRae for over a year wi' a potion o' angel's blood."

"That would explain a great deal." Silvanus sat back against his chair, letting out his breath in a big exhale, as we all started to puzzle pieces of this mystery together.

So, we set about our plans. It was agreed that men of the MacKenzie Clan, would hide on the closest farmstead, ready to converge on the castle or stop any incoming hellhounds. The gypsies were to stay out of sight, their primary objective to help support the farmers in the event that any of the fight came to them. Silvanus insisted on staying within the castle, refusing to leave Athdara again. Colin, with his keen eye sight, was posted at the top of the north tower where he would have full view in all directions. Kenneth's role would be by my father's side, as Mr. Cameron was used to seeing them together, and it would raise no alarms to see them again like that. I was to remain inside, with Gwenyver, all under the ruse of an illness that prevented me from leaving my rooms within the castle. And just inside the main doors, George would stand out of sight, but close enough to serve as protection for Gwenyver and me.

Damian remained very quiet. The challenge of his presence, which was made difficult by the words of protection, was only partially resolved. To create a role for him in the ensuing fight, Gwenyver would walk the grounds and put releases on only small section scattered quite randomly, including the gates. No one wanted to risk the entire walls, but his help might be needed against any hellhounds. It was agreed that Damian would remain hidden along the south wall.

"Damian, tell me, what do you make o' this Mr Cameron?" George looked over at him intently. "How has he fed John the concoction—?"

"—In truth, I'm not sure." Damian said, with hesitation. "I can only speculate that he is working for one of my brothers."

"Never mind then, back to the business at hand." George said. "When his carriage arrives, we want to get him all the way into the courtyard, near the bottom o' the steps. Connor, Duncan—ye will flank from behind the carriage. John, my friend, ye will be the bait."

"Father, you are not well enough for this!" I stood up to make my point. "You can barely stand, and it is plain as day that your mind is still foggy from withdrawal of that horrible poison!"

But looking around I realized, much to my chagrin, that standing made me no taller than the shoulders of the large men around the table.

"Moireach, that is precisely why I need to be the one." He placed a reassuring hand on my shoulder, encouraging me to sit back down. "He will see weakness, and be lulled into a false sense of security."

The meeting was adjourned without further fuss. Damian and I walked back into the courtyard, and took me into his arms, lifting me up into the skies as he flew us across the walls. We landed just beyond the gates in a small stretch of grass, and sat down under a tree. We held hands, and I was reminded of how much heat was generated between us. Yet, the inner conflict of my mind still lingered.

"My sweet love, how have you fared? I've thought about you every breath since we parted ways."

He pulled me into his arms. And for a moment, I felt safe and secure. In those breaths, all thoughts of William and the coming danger were forgotten. He stroked the top of my head bringing shivers down my spine. As his fingers slid down my back, my body responded of its own volition and moved closer to him. The desire grew quickly, the ache in my body to feel him inside of me was in conflict with my thoughts, my mind and I felt so overwhelmed. Pulling away from his embrace, from his kiss took more strength than it should have.

"So much has happened since that night I first saw you." I began to cry. "I don't even know who I am anymore, I —"

"There is nothing to fear, I am with you now, and I will see to it that we leave this place safe and unharmed."

"I've only just returned home to where it all began." I looked at him through tears, and for a moment his face turned dark. "How can I think of leaving already?"

"Whoever is hunting you will not stop and will keep sending more hellhounds and other Hunters after you until he has you." Damian murmured, his voice still heavy with lust but also filled with concern. "How many more of your loved ones will have to perish? By staying here, you put them all at risk."

There was truth in his words. The loss of Roderick was still painful for me, and my body shook from the grief as the memories flooded back.

"My sweet love," he said, holding me close. "What has brought such sadness? Is it Roderick? George told me that he died defending you from Abbadon."

"Damian, he died because of me. If it hadn't been for —"

"—you cannot blame yourself for his death, Moireach. There is nothing you could have done once Abbadon fed the poison to Roderick." He rested his chin on the top of my head. "Frankly, I am surprised that Roderick even had the strength to turn on the angel and kill him in the last few moments before he turned."

I stopped shaking. *George had not told Damian who had actually killed Roderick.* He had kept my role in Roderick's death a secret. Damian left me no time to process this.

"I would love nothing more than to take you into my arms and fly away from here." He lifted my chin up. "To show you the world, and to teach you more about your powers."

He leaned in to kiss me. The warmth in my body, overcame my grief, and our embrace stirred a dangerous fire in me. I struggled with the conflict taking place in my body. I was spared a decision, because at that moment, we were interrupted by someone clearing their throat rather loudly.

"I beg yer pardon," Colin said, coming up from behind us.

Damian and I quickly leaned away from each other.

"I'm sorry to disturb ye....uh...two—" Colin stuttered, somewhat embarrassed by having caught us in a moment of passion. "—but Mr Cameron will be arriving within the hour, and Moireach needs to get inside to safety. Now."

Damian gripped my arm tighter, stopping me from taking a step towards him. Colin, in turn stepped forward. They exchanged looks of hatred, after which the young MacKenzie spun on his heel like a soldier dismissed from duty, and stormed back down the stairs towards the castle. Damian glared after him.

"Damian? What has come over you?"

"My sweet love, you are mine, always, and forever. I do not like the way that young pup was looking at you."

The vehemence in his voice startled me. There was no further opportunity to think on what had just taken place, as he wrapped his arms around me and launched himself into the air.

Leaving me to ascend the stairs alone, as he flew back to his post outside the walls, no sooner had I reached the safety of the front hallway, finding Nanny already waiting for me, when William Cameron's carriage arrived through the gates and was heading towards the courtyard. The time had come to spring our trap.

Walking down the stone stairs, away from the safety of the front door, my father used a cane to assist him. Kenneth only a few feet behind him, playing is part in the charade. My vantage point from the front foyer window did not allow me clear sight towards the courtyard. Still I was able to see the carriage doors open and heard a voice call out.

"John, my friend, is that you?"

William stepped out of the carriage slowly, followed out by three other men. The voices were muffled, so I had to pay careful attention to try and catch every word.

"How fare you?"

My father continued down the last few steps, bringing him far too close to William. The fourth man stepped down from the front of the carriage, and joined the others standing behind Mr. Cameron.

"I've seen better days, William." his voice shook with genuine weakness. "My body has been shutting down day by day and my head feels fit to burst at any moment. Would you have any of your tea with you? I remember it gave me much comfort."

"Of course John," Williams stepped forward. "I have more of the tea here with me. But what is this I hear of my betrothed being unwell?"

He now stood directly in front of my father.

"I'm afraid the truth must be known, William. She was gravely injured during a mysterious attack on Denny Abbey." When a lie is based on truth, it is easier for others to believe.

Mr Cameron leaned in towards my father, and smelled him, much in the same way that Damian would smell me. This set tingles of fear crawling across my skin. He pulled back so quickly it was as if he was stung by a bee, then he sneered. *Could it be?*

"Oh John, I thought we were friends?" he sneered, while gesturing towards his men. "You are full of lies… and full of blood that isn't yours! I demand you bring Moireach out here at once."

The man we knew as William Cameron tore his jacket off and unleashed a pair of black wings. *How had Damian not recognized one of his brothers?* William began tearing at his face with his bare hands, discarding scraps of bloody flesh to the ground, until his true face was revealed, along with a deep scar along the base of his neck. *He*—the angel whom my mother had injured. *He*—whom she had called the Hunter. *He* was standing in the courtyard of my family's home. *And we had let him through the gates by releasing the words of protection for Damian!* This changed everything. My father was in immediate danger. I sensed movement by the front door at the same time as Gwenyver called out desperately.

"NO!"

George had burst through the door, out of his hiding place, his massive size and incredible strength demonstrated in his long strides as he confronted this unexpected threat. Yet, even with those great steps, he did not reach my father in time. The angel grabbed my father by the throat, lifted him off the ground, and flung him aside like a rag doll. My father hit the ground and did not move.

I screamed.

"Ah, so Moireach is just inside those doors?" William hissed at George. "And you, MacKenzie, you think you can stop me?"

Kenneth ran to my father, while George continued his advance, ready to do battle. The villainous angel took a step back, pursed his lips together and made a horrible shrilling noise. The eery vibration travelled down my spine. It was a sound that brought everyone's hands to their ears, and would travel beyond the range of mortal ears. Gwenyver put her hands on my shoulders, stopping me from running to my father's aid. She kept me safe behind the walls, her grip tight as

I struggled in vain and watched the scene unfold in the courtyard.

Just then, the four men began to writhe and twist and tear at their clothes. Within moments, they had completely mutated into hellhounds and were launching an assault. George, who was so taken aback by their rapid change had no time to transform himself. Kenneth leaped forward, along with two of the cousins from their flank position, in front of his father, all in their animal form, and began the counterattack. The snarling of beasts, the sound of ripping flesh, and the howls of pain could be heard across the courtyard.

Athdara and Silvanus were still inside with Gwenyver and me, when we heard a large thud come from behind us from the inner courtyard just beyond the kitchens. Silvanus and Athdara both charged to the back for fear it was an ambush, but it was Colin barreling through the heavy kitchen doors.

"Bloody hell—" he panted, out of breath. "—that awful sound that damned winged one made… he has called other hellhounds. I counted nearly twenty o' them, maybe more, coming from all directions."

"The protection barriers should hold them back and away from the fight," Athdara said.

"I'm afraid not." Colin said. "It's like they have sniffed oot the small gaps that Ma created for Damian to pass through. I just watched them break through. They are coming."

"I can try to mend them from here, but it will be difficult." Gwenyver started shivering, from fear or shock, I did not know.

"What about my men?" Silvanus asked. "Are they in pursuit? Fighting?"

"Aye, they are trying, along wi' my brothers-in-arms, but I fear there are too many of them. And they are fast. They will reach the castle soon."

"If we can kill William, will the beasts continue to attack?" I asked.

"I believe that the hellhounds willna stop until they are all dead." Athdara answered first. "But… if we can kill that damned winged one, they will surely lose their focus and be easier to take down."

"Colin, make yer way back up to the tower," Silvanus ordered. "Make sure we know which direction the next attack will come from, and how close our men are to catching up to them. In the meantime, Athdara, ye have always been the love of my life and my heart is yers to command in all things but this."

Silvanus pulled away from her and took hurried steps towards the front door. Athdara watched her lover join the fight, and I knew it would not be long before she too would become part of the raging battle below. We took our place by the window once more, our attention returning to the courtyard. George had finally been able to transform. Two of the hellhounds had escaped past the reach of Kenneth and the cousins, and were ferociously attacking him, but he was still intent on reaching William. Silvanus was close on his heels and truth be told was performing admirably with his gypsy sword, slashing at the legs of the enemy and lithely dancing out of the way to avoid their counter attacks. I looked away from the battle to find Nanny slumped into her chair.

"Nanny, are you alright?"

"My child, whatever has given those tortured brethren the ability to find the small gaps I created, and through their sheer mass force more barriers down, is also slowly draining me," she said, looking up at me, a sheen of sweat appearing on her skin which was slowly paling. "I fear that the power o' the words will soon be lost completely. The entire castle will be open to attack when the words are gone."

I began to wonder why Damian had not left his place of hiding yet to aid his friend George, when Colin came rushing from the kitchens. An onslaught of hellhounds, led by a beast even more enormous than George, had breached the outer gates.

"Ma, our men werena able to intercept all the hellhound, but are not far behind."

There were now more hellhounds in the courtyard than MacKenzie's. Colin ran through the front door and leapt into the air, shifting into an enormous eagle. His wings carried him above the battle, and he began a series of ambush attacks. First, he grabbed a hellhound off the ground and flung it savagely against the castle walls, breaking its neck in the process. Then he veered over, at an impossibly steep angle, towards another hellhound and snatched it off one of his transformed clansmen. Throwing it against the castle wall to break its neck. Kenneth had been pinned down by two of the beasts when the eagle careened down and clasped large claws around one of the hellhounds' haunches—just as the jaws would have closed on Kenneth's throat. He, too, was flung at the wall.

I saw George and Silvanus fighting side by side, trying to get closer to William while being thwarted by the onslaught of hellhounds. One vicious claw caught Silvanus on his leg, causing him to holler from the pain and collapsed to his knees. Without hesitation, Athdara bolted forward, remaining human and drawing her sword from its scabbard. She reached Silvanus's side quickly and together they acted as a shield for George, who was still intent on reaching the black-winged angel. If we stood any chance at stopping the rest of the hellhounds, William had to be stopped and Lord MacKenzie was our best chance.

Gwenyver and I could no longer stay behind the window, too much of the fight was taking place out of our sight. I helped her walk towards the front door. We watched in horror as William leapt into the air, just as the gigantic hellhound launched himself underneath, forward and caught George by surprise. The two beasts—hellhound and shifter—tumbled across the bloodied cobblestones and engaged in fierce and brutal battle. The beast pinned George to the ground, who let out a pain-filled howl, as his arm and shoulder were torn by the beasts fangs. Gwenyver, hands covering her face, began to weep.

Athdara rushed to the aid of her brother, just as the hound's ferocious teeth came baring down on George's thick neck. The blood was slick on the cobble stones, and she slipped, slid, and collided with her brother to find herself on her back and face to face with the beast above. Her arms reached up, catching its thick fur underneath the jaw, preventing it from reaching either herself or George with its fangs. Then, it pulled back, preparing for another attack. It hesitated. It stared intently at Athdara, standing up on its haunches, towering over everyone. Then it yowled in pain, with no visible wounds. Starting with the head, the fur started shedding, and fall from the body, as the beast changed shape—into that of a mortal man.

"Da'?" George croaked.

He too had shifted back into his human form, despite the pain of the inflicted wound along his shoulder and arm. The former hellhound stumbled to his knees. Looking around dazed, he focused on Athdara.

"Ye are my daughter." The now transformed hellhound, revealing himself to be Hector MacKenzie, their father. Now white-haired, and aged beyond his years. "Ye have yer mother's eyes, and I would ken them anywhere. Her kindness was ne'er forgotten."

Then he began to weep and placed his hand on George's chest.

"Oh, my dear son, what have I done?" His words were unsure, having not spoken in many years.

Athdara helped George into a more comfortable position, the wound from his shoulder now seeping into the ground.

"You miserable, useless and pathetic beast!" William landed just behind Hector, his expansive wings casting shadows across Hector. "How dare you betray your master? Kill them both now!"

Hector's body was marked by scars over scars, telling a tale of the tortured life he had been living. He looked at both of his children and spoke words I could not hear. Then, he turned dutifully towards his master.

"I hae killed hundreds o' men, and many o' my own kin for ye. I will nae kill my own children!"

Hector leapt forward and attacked his former master, but without the strength of a hellhound, he was at a disadvantage. William quickly overpowered him, the human form being weak in comparison to the beast. I watched in complete terror, as the angel forced the aged man to his knees, tore the head from the body, blood spewing everywhere, and with disdain, threw it off to the side. He then turned to face the man's wounded children—Athdara and George. Stalking towards them with malevolence in his eyes, ready to claim their lives as he had just done their father's. Athdara was desperately trying to get to her feet, and George was pulling her behind him, ever the protective brother.

Mr Cameron, the angel, took a few more steps but paused. Looking up, he watched mouth agape, as Damian landed right in front of him.

"Barachiel?" The black-winged angel spat at Damian's face. "*You* defend these wretched beings?"

"Kushiel," he sauntered at a leisurely pace, it was disturbing. "I should have sensed your clumsy hand in this ridiculous farce."

"You betray your own brother in this?" the man I had known as William Cameron, uttered in disbelief.

"You have made a complete mess of this entire affair." Damian spoke with a steady, calm voice. Taking one step at a time, bringing him closer to the monster. *Why wasn't he attacking?*

"Samael has gotten soft and too lenient these last millennia! She was there, all along, for the taking!"

Without a word, Damian took one more step forward, and tore into the dark angel's chest, and ripping out his heart, leaving Kushiel, the man I had known as William Cameron, crumbling to his knees. Watching the demise of the man, this monster who had wrecked such havoc in my life was liberating and very gratifying. Pulling away from Gwenyver, I was determined to run into the arms of my saviour—my lover.

All around, the hellhounds stumbled mid-motion, giving all the MacKenzie's the advantage and a chance to launch a renewed attack. I had just made it to the steps, and watched Damian walk towards George and Athdara, and what I thought was their aid.

But mid-stride, he pulled two long feather blades from behind his back. Athdara jumped to her feet to shield George, but was shoved aside by Silvanus rushing to her aid. Damian's blade slid clean through his chest and exited through his back.

"My love—" Silvanus whispered through blood soaked lips.

He was dead before he hit the ground. Athdara screamed her loss. She then hurdled through the air, shifting into her full animal form, as she charged Damian who caught her by her throat and squeezed. Within moments, she, too, was discarded, throwing her limp body carelessly to the side.

Gwenyver had reached my side, and too, stood frozen with shock. Witnessing Damian's betrayal, seeing her family and our friends at the mercy of his wrath.

Colin and Kenneth came out of nowhere and attacked the angel, that had once been called friend, from each side. Damian was thrown off balance, and the three tumbled to the ground into a confusing heap of bodies. I heard the sounds of roaring and ripping flesh as claws and feather knives inflicted damage. I could feel the *fire* inside of me, begging to be let out, all the while my heart and body pleading with my mind that I was having a nightmare. *This cannot be happening!* I watched until Kenneth rose from the pile, blood pouring from an open wound—his flesh cut deep from belly to thigh by one of Damian's deadly blades. As he toppled to the ground, his blood covered the cobble stones, and I stepped out of my place of hiding. Nanny's hand on my shoulder did not deter my stride. Damian brushed himself off and walked over the bodies. It was then that I noticed Colin, a beautiful eagle, lying unconscious, maybe dead. The angel looked around and saw me standing at the doorway.

"Come my sweet love, it's time to leave," he called to me over dead bodies laying at his feet. "I've had enough of these distractions. You are mine, always and forever."

Tears streamed down my face. No sound escaped my lips. It was as if I had no control over my body, I took the first step down the stairs that would lead to him.

"Don't worry my sweet love, Moireach." He reached his hands out to me as he advanced. "My brother, Samael, and I will help you find your powers and use them! You need us. We alone can teach you what it means to have such gifts. You will be the most powerful of them all, and I will be at your side, always and forever."

I took another step forward. And another. *I would not let anyone else die because of me!*

"Damian, promise me that no one else will be harmed if I will leave with you."

Ever since the battle had begun, the *fire* within me had been steadily growing. My body felt the power but it also ached with desire for Damian. My soul had learned how to surrender, but my mind was at war, always the mind fighting. I continued to walk purposefully towards my lover, to my Damian.

"Moireach, you have my word of honour." he said, only a few paces from me. "I will not harm any more of your loved ones."

Our hands met and intertwined. I gathered my arms around his waist and allowed his arms to pull me in closer. I found myself once again in his embrace. Enveloped in his scent, my lips turning upwards to meet his passionate kiss. His gaze found mine, as he secured his grasp, and his wings started to move. He leapt into the sky, with me as his prize and I with the knowledge that no one else would be harmed. They would be safe.

"You are mine, now and forever." he moaned into my ear, as we took flight.

He was wrong.

I unleashed hell. All the fury and rage that had been boiling inside of me from the moment my father ordered me to marry Mr Cameron. All the frustrating of feeling helpless. The indignation, the bitterness and the resentment. All of it…I let it out.

Damian screamed.

We were locked in a fiery embrace above the courtyard. The *fire* would not release him from my arms, nor would I let go…not until his flesh melted away, his wings dripped pools of hot metal to the stones below us, and his shrieks came to an end.

My lover was no more, always and forever.

With his death, came my fall, as I knew it would. The last time I fell to the earth, I had not realized the consequences of my actions. This time, I did. Samael would have no reason to continue his savage search for me or the attacks on those that I loved. Without hesitation, I chose to bring an end to the Hunt. And…

…I surrendered.

EPILOGUE

It had been nearly a month since that fateful day.

After I had destroyed the one I had fallen in love with, and surrendered my life.

I had been saved by the youngest MacKenzie, who despite his injuries had surged into the air just in time to catch me before I crashed into the stones of the courtyard.

Standing on the shores of Loch Duich, I could not help but wonder if I would look upon these waters again.

My father had regained enough strength to travel and was planning to return to London with intentions of taking up the ministry and retiring from the shipping business. Lord MacKenzie and Gwenyver were heading home to the far north-western highlands, while Malcolm MacKenzie would stay at Eilean Donan to care for the lands and continue to teach the next generation of shapeshifters.

Every MacKenzie would know the truth—that Kushiel's death would not bring an end to the hunt. He was not the puppet-master, only a dark angel who was only one of many commanders. Samael was behind the plot, and all the plots, the one who had started the rebellion in their time countless generations ago. Damian, his brother, had played the role of *friend* for many years—creating false trust and hope. He had fooled many.

Inside the carriage that had brought Mr Cameron through our castle gates, we had found a notebook, written in his hand. It bore ill tidings—of a new poison discovered that could weaken the MacKenzie's, of a stronger potion to create hellhounds, and finally how an Angel could wear a human disguise without discovery even from his own kind. It all incited fear. Except for the last page

There we learned that I was not the first born of the children of the Elemental Angels. I was the third. The Lady of Water, who had been born nearly seven-hundred years before me, was the second. To our astonishment, we discovered that one of the earth elemental twins had given birth to a daughter, the Lady of Earth, born during the reign of Marcus Aurelius Antoninus Augustus.

Today, we prepared to depart the lands of my ancestors, the lands of the Scots, and travel south, across oceans, and land towards Greece, the last place known to be home to Dylynn, the Lady of Water. Kenneth had recovered from his life-threatening wounds, and would continue to honour his oath and remain by my side, as my protector and now…my friend and teacher. Athdara had chosen to come with us, in the hopes of finding a sense of purpose from the loss of her beloved Silvanus.

"Moireach, are you ready?"

Without turning around, I had sensed Colin behind me. His comforting presence would also be a part of this journey. I smiled to myself. Although I do not know what the future holds, I do know that my life will be of my own creation, my own choice.

I am no longer afraid of my power.

I am the Lady of Fire.

ABOUT THE AUTHOR

Melanie Frome has always been a dreamer, a weaver of stories and a lover of books. In May 2013, something magical happened - she dreamt of Moireach, and every night she would go to sleep, the dream would pick up where it left off the prior morning. After dreaming for nearly two months, she knew she had to bring the story to life.

For the last decade Melanie has devoted her life to rewriting her story to become the hero of her own life - through rediscovering movement as medicine, evolving her mindset, and igniting her true authentic self.

A champion for self-love. A seeker of the unconventional. A revolutionary for the raw beauty of authenticity. A conjuror of passion and imagination. A warrior for joy and laughter.

She now leads others on their own soul-journey by offering movement medicine, life-guidance, and through her written words and motivational speaking.

...She still dreams.

www.melaniefrome.com
@melaniefrome

Made in the USA
Middletown, DE
17 January 2020

83087275R00182